Transitions

Journeys Across Time,
to a New Place,
and of the Heart

**REDWOOD WRITERS
2024 ANTHOLOGY**

**JANICE ROWLEY
EDITOR IN CHIEF**

Transitions
2024 Redwood Writers Anthology
Janice Rowley, Editor in Chief
Copyright © 2024 Redwood Writers
All Rights Reserved.

Library of Congress Control Number: 2024918060
ISBN: 979-8-9853503-8-8

Cover art and design: Crissi Langwell
Interior design: Mara Lynn Johnstone

First printing 2024

Redwood Writers Press
P.O. Box 4687
Santa Rosa, CA 95401
redwoodwriters.org

Table of Contents

FOREWORD
Janice Rowley, Editor in Chief

If I waited for perfection... I would never write a word.
—Margaret Atwood

The Redwood Writers motto is *writers helping writers*. To me, this means every member is a writer, and every member has the opportunity to learn and the obligation to teach. Redwood Writers provides the environment and the vehicles by which we stretch toward our highest potential.

For some authors, this will be the first time they are published. All of these stories are the culmination of years of learning and honing the craft.

Improvement—learning—is our goal, not perfection. It is the journey we celebrate with *Transitions*.

Improvement comes when other writers judge our work and provide evaluation and comment to further educate. Improvement comes when we work one-on-one with other writers and editors forming a two-way street; after all, next year the roles may be reversed.

A personal story: I remember how dismayed I was when my editor for "The Stick House" in the 2016 *Untold Stories* wanted me to reduce the "plethora" of ellipses. But, I earnestly explained, without the ellipses the reader would not understand how to read the story. After offering to withdraw the story, then reconsidering the editing advice, I agreed. Of course, the story was better once I got out of my own way. Learning to work with an editor is part of the craft of writing.

Since that time, my work has appeared in many anthologies, including *Transitions* and four poetry anthologies. I place a high value on those lessons from the judges, the editors, and the other writers. I still have a lot to learn.

ACKNOWLEDGEMENTS
Janice Rowley, Editor in Chief

It is July 2024 as I sit with fingers on keyboard to thank the Redwood Writers' family members who helped make *Transitions* possible.

Thank you, Judges, Editors, and Proofreaders. Thank you, Crissi Langwell, who took an idea in my head and turned it into a beautiful cover. Thank you to each person who submitted their writing to the scrutiny of so many of us. Every submission held promise.

Some judges were performing this much-appreciated task for the first time. By their twentieth piece, no doubt there were questions about why they had accepted my invitation. This time next year, the experience will have settled in their minds and hearts and they will recognize how much they learned and also taught.

And the editors. Oh, what a job they have done. Improvement is clear, with each story in this anthology, from the version initially submitted. There were a few hard-fought battles, but always give and take.

A few judges were also editors whose stories were judged and edited by others. Some of us are impatient to learn it all, practice it all, teach it all. I am indebted to each of these courageous members.

Did I mention that this is a team of volunteers? This is a team of volunteers!

Transitions

Journeys Across Time,
to a New Place,
and of the Heart

Grace
Stephen Abbott

My teammates and I were waiting in the bus shaded by the ancient sycamores for the trip to the league track and field championship. We looked down the aisle through the windshield for our only missing teammate, Joe. Our team couldn't win without him. Then, in a trot, he rounded the corner of the field house, wearing his blue university blazer, white shirt, university tie, and his travel bag in hand.

Joe differed from the vast majority of students on campus. He was Black, his hair close cropped and naturally curly, a little older than the rest of us, more mature, an army veteran with a Purple Heart, married with a young son. He wasn't the star of the team, but the best competitor, entering several events and guaranteed to garner a few critical points.

We had not seen Joe the previous day, the last practice of the year, just a pro-forma session for last-minute matters, if there were any. Earlier in the day, there had been a frog-strangling rain, lightning, and thunder. The track became an oval lake, the infield an island of green, the team members like shipwrecked survivors. We jogged on the grass, stretched, joked, and yawned. I had almost skipped this practice because of the downpour and gone to a part-time job where Joe and I both worked. The coach counted heads and asked if anyone had seen Joe. I said I thought Joe had skipped practice because of the rain, probably gone to work, and I would tell him if there were any changes. There were none, just the standard get a good night's rest, eat a light breakfast, and be on the bus at nine.

The next morning, as Joe approached the bus, the coach left his front-row seat, stepped off the bus, and asked Joe, "Young man, where do you think you are going?"

"To the track meet."

"No, you're not. You're off the team. You cut practice yesterday and today left us waiting past nine. Turn in your stuff Monday, all of it." He stepped back onto the bus, closed the door, told the driver to leave, and left Joe standing by himself, his hands raised, palms upturned questioningly, no clenched fists or muttering. I and my teammates were stunned by the coach's treatment of Joe. We exchanged glances, but none of us said anything.

A similar incident had occurred the previous year. A three-sport recruited athlete named Charlie had turned out to be worthless. He had been benched in football, basketball, and came to track practice when it suited him. He put the shot and threw the discus without the advantage of conditioning or practice. He was flunking out of school and had violated most of the coach's rules, but had the nerve to show up for the league meet. The coach stopped Charlie from entering the bus, closed the door, then asked the team members if they wanted Charlie to go. He reminded us that Charlie had not been a good team member, but still might place in an event which would give us points toward the championship. A vote was taken. Charlie went to the meet, didn't score a point, then disappeared from campus forever.

The difference between the two years and two athletes was that Charlie was white. Joe was not. We teammates were conscious of the physical dissimilarity between the two, but either were unconscious of the social inequality of their skin colors or cowered behind our own prejudices. Still, at the time, I knew there was something wrong, and it continued to gnaw on me for years until I knew I had to acknowledge what had happened and try to make whatever amends I could. So I planned a return to the university, a reunion of teammates, and to make peace with Joe and my conscience.

Fifty years had passed since I stood on this spot. The decaying and crumbling mortar between the red bricks of the athletic field house had been repointed. The wooden sign TEAM BUSSES ONLY had been replaced with a blue-and-white porcelain one. The crushed rock parking area below the sign had been paved with asphalt. The dirt path leading down a steep hill from the field house to the track was now terraced with concrete steps. The gray cinder track and runways for high jump, broad jump, and pole vault had been surfaced with a royal blue synthetic. Instead of sawdust landing pits, huge red pillow-like cushions softened the fall of high jumpers and pole vaulters.

But fifty years had not changed everything. There is a type of wound over which scar tissue forms, but the wound never heals. Wounds of the psyche are like this and never disappear. A career, marriage, hobbies, earthquakes, floods, gardening, surgeries, or deaths of loved ones may occupy some moments of consciousness, but an act of moral cowardice may fester in one's conscience for days, months, years, then slowly surface and make one cringe as if stabbed with an ice pick.

During Joe's six-year army stint, the campus had seen many changes, some looking forward and some toward the past. Corporate donations had built more gothic-style buildings quarried from ancient limestone seabeds to give the appearance of a medieval cloister of privilege, a museum of social castes, hierarchies of legacies, fraternities, and sororities. A modern precast concrete hall which housed the municipal symphony and music school, a library designed by an eminent Japanese architect, an observatory, and carillon tower all pointed to a future unlinked to the past. There was an underlying feeling that to become a different university, it had to look like a different university. But the growth rings of ancient sycamores throughout campus were silent historians of the continuing moral deficiencies of the university.

While the school's founder had been a Civil War abolitionist, his state was only the breadth of the Ohio River from slavery. When the war ended, both abject poverty and heavy industrialization persuaded many from the former Confederacy to seek their fortunes north of the river. Life for people of color was just a shade or two different from the South. Until the *Brown vs. Board of Education* Supreme Court decision, there were few concessions to civil rights. Poll taxes, segregated schools, parks, restaurants, movie theaters, and public transportation were all blemished with the stain of racial discrimination, and the university was not without a smudge.

In the 1930s, the university board of directors established a student admission quota, which limited dark-skinned students to ten per class. After the Supreme Court decision, the board of directors thought it prudent to end this official policy. As a student in the late 1950s, I never knew the policy had existed, but I was conscious of a noticeable absence of students of color. However, this never rose to a level of concern. I and my Black neighbors did not play in the same sandbox, swing and slide on the same playground equipment, escape the summer heat in a park swimming pool, play pitch and catch on the same baseball diamond, sing hymns in the same church, dress in the uniforms of Boy Scouts, or ride together on city busses. I was socially immunized to a plague surrounding me.

A half century had passed and now I, who had never revisited the school, had come back for a reunion with my old teammates, to walk the school grounds, to look down the runways, to pause at the bus loading sign, to be reminded of what I had witnessed without protest. The sycamores had not changed, but I had. When I had seen the Freedom Riders in the South, listened to Martin Luther King, Jr., watched the Voting Rights Act signed, and observed the incremental steps taken to eliminate Jim Crow, I was reminded cerebrally and viscerally of my moral weakness as a youth and adult. None of the wrongs of the past could ever be made right with an apology, but if there was ever to be an attempt, this was the time. Two score and ten years had passed. This was my last chance.

I had mailed invitations to the surviving members of the team to join me for lunch at the oldest delicatessen in a town, a place where all of us were now welcome, but where Joe would not have been served years ago. When Joe had been a freshman in 1952 and the team traveled out of town, Joe often had to eat in the kitchen while his teammates enjoyed the dining room. There were times after track meets when the boys wanted to celebrate with a beer but had to go from bar to bar to find one that would serve Joe. Times had changed. Memories were intact.

We arrived individually, some having not seen each other for a half century. Could that be Bill, Jerry, Jack, Roy? As they entered, I made some incorrect guesses, but when Joe arrived, there was no mistaking him. There was an affection among us, empathy for the ravages time had inflicted on us, some imaginary pretense that time had not passed, that we still had the virility of twenty-somethings. And as parting neared, our hearts grew fonder.

The pastrami, corned-, and peppered-beef sandwiches on rye with German mustard tasted as good to seventy-year-olds as they had to twenty-year-olds, though the second half of the sandwiches remained mostly untouched. The stealing of a hundred-pound bag of raw popcorn which provided snacks for the men's dorm for an entire winter, peeking into the women's dressing room through cracks in the mortar of a brick wall, placing a dead cockroach into someone's jock strap … these were all funnier now than they had been years before.

We exchanged phone numbers, mailing addresses, and, yes, email addresses. The time for some of us to never see each other again approached. I had delayed my real reason for wanting to gather the teammates one more time. I had not wanted to float a gray cloud over the reunion at its beginning, but the time to part had come. I asked my aged teammates for their indulgence for one last story.

I said that I had lived my entire adulthood with many things on my conscience, and this was an opportunity to rid myself of one of them. I grasped one of Joe's hands and retold the story of my cowardice on the bus, when a blatant act of racial discrimination to a friend occurred before my eyes and I did nothing to protest. I choked a bit, then faced Joe and asked for his forgiveness. Joe smiled and said, "Really? I don't even remember that." Having the grace to pretend what had happened on that particular day long ago and many other days of his life had never happened at all.

A Perfect Game
Mary Adler

I tapped a Marlboro out of the box, lit it, inhaled, and felt that satisfying hitch as the smoke passed through my throat on its way to my lungs. A robin checked the pan usually filled with water for the wildlife, and flew away, disappointed. It was March, nearly the end of a rainy season that hadn't lived up to its name. The summer would be even drier.

I rinsed the dust from the pan and filled it. Before I'd finished stubbing out my cigarette, the robin returned to splash and scatter glistening drops on the dry grass. It flew to a branch to fluff and dry, and I topped off the pan. My cell phone rang. I looked at the caller ID. Not someone I wanted to talk to, especially now. On my way back to the grave, I turned the ringer off. *Ghosting someone in the cemetery. Perfect.*

"That took a while, Michael." Debra slid the re-snipped flower stems into the water.

"The bird pan was dry."

"Uh huh." She gave me the look she usually reserved for our children when she thought there was more to the story. She placed the flowers beneath the enamel photograph of Leonard, her father, and mine in more than just marriage. I spread the picnic blanket on the grass and uncapped the Pliny the Younger ale I'd waited in a seemingly endless line for. Leonard's favorite. We toasted the man we loved and drank the ale while eating chili and cornbread, a tradition he'd established on Pliny the Younger release day.

"Will we ever stop missing him?" The muscles in Deb's clenched jaw rippled as she tried to keep from crying. Her dark eyes glistened, and she turned away.

I sheltered her in my arms, her back pressed against my chest, and swallowed hard. "I don't see how we could."

"My mother used to half-tease me that you married me because of my dad."

"You mean she didn't know it was because of her baking?" I kissed the top of Deb's head, comforted by the scent of vanilla.

She elbowed me in the stomach.

I grunted. "I fell for you in the sixth grade, you hooligan. Before I really knew Leonard."

She sighed. "We were Amy's age. So young. Imagine her falling in love now and marrying the guy one day."

I ran through the cast of male sixth graders I'd met and hoped one of them wouldn't become my future son-in-law, then said, "Your dad showed me how to be a father. I wanted to be just like him when I grew up."

"And you are, except your chili lacks a certain *je ne sais quoi*."

"I think you mean it lacks a touch of *Sriracha*."

We sat for a bit, then she stirred. "I have a brief to write."

"Yep. I have papers to grade."

She anointed the grave with the last drops of the ale, and we said goodbye to Leonard. For the moment.

A blue jay hopped along behind us as our feet crunched on the gravel. Debra put the bottles in the recycling bin, then cast the rest of our corn bread on the ground for him.

* * *

When I opened our front door, the dogs greeted us with whines and eddied around us as we shuffled our way into the kitchen. Amy sat at the table with folded arms and a look she'd inherited from Debra. Eight-year-old Lennie wasn't too old to run to his mom and hug her.

"A man came." Amy's accusing tone made me flinch. "Said he was your brother, Daddy. Our Uncle Carl."

I caught the look Debra shot me. Chickens coming home to roost. There'd never been a good time to tell the children about my father's second family. I'd hoped I'd never have to.

"Why wouldn't he call your cell?" Debra asked me.

I winced and mouthed "Sorry." I'd turned off all thoughts of Carl when I turned off the ringer.

She cast me the original of Amy's smoldering look. "We'll talk about this later."

Amy said, "We told him through the video doorbell we only had one uncle and we couldn't open the door, but he said we had two more uncles. And a grandfather!"

Lennie said, "I told him if we had another grandfather, someone would've introduced us by now. He laughed at me." My son seemed to hold me responsible for my half-brother's rudeness.

"He said this was from your father and slid it under the door." Amy handed me an envelope.

I read the contents, half listening to Debra tell them about Sam and why we didn't see him or his other sons. She glanced over when I swore under my breath.

* * *

The kids pestered me with questions while I started dinner. I did my best to answer them until Debra rescued me by sending them to set the table, but my reprieve was short-lived.

"Well?" she asked.

I reached into the refrigerator for the risotto cakes.

She took them from me. "Spill."

"Later. Okay?"

She must have heard something in my voice because she nodded, her eyes soft with kindness.

* * *

After the kids were in bed, she poured herself a glass of wine and brought me a beer. I grabbed her shawl off the peg.

"This will be better on the deck." Code for I needed a cigarette. She never nagged about my smoking as long as I did it outside and never around the kids.

She licked her finger and held it up. I wondered why she bothered. She never could tell which way the wind would blow the smoke. Besides, the air was albatross still.

I lit a cigarette and inhaled deeply. "If we were sailing, we'd be 'a painted ship upon a painted ocean.' Dead in the water."

"You're going to be dead in the water if you don't tell me what was in Sam's envelope." She wrapped herself in the shawl and curled up in an Adirondack chair.

"Sam wants to see me. He's in Kaiser. Oncology."

8

We sat for a while as the sky darkened, and a mockingbird ran through its repertoire.

"What are you going to do?" she asked.

"I'm tired, so I'll skip all the reasons to say *no*: abusing us, abandoning us when my mom was sick, starting a new family, and forgetting Mom and I existed."

"So much for skipping the reasons you shouldn't go." Debra's smile, loving and tinged with wry humor, knocked me out. "Any reason you should?"

I shrugged.

"Aren't you curious about what he wants, Mike?" She yawned, then covered her mouth. "Maybe he wants to say he's sorry. Maybe spend time with you if he's that sick."

"Maybe he wants to meet his grandchildren before he dies."

"I'm not sure how I feel about that." Her completely emotionless lawyer's voice told me she knew exactly how she felt.

"Don't worry. I wouldn't promise him anything without talking to you first."

She shivered and wrapped the shawl tighter. "Let's go up."

"You go. I'll be there as soon as I finish this." I held up my cigarette.

* * *

The next day, I found a space at Kaiser without circling the lot three times. Probably Debra's parking karma. She'd insisted on coming with me, even though she had no intention of seeing Sam. She told me to find her in the lobby when I was ready to leave. I sent her on ahead, then sat on a wall to gather myself, watching visitors with plants and balloons disappear into the buildings like figures on an assembly line. I tapped the box in my shirt pocket. Reassured, I joined the parade.

When the hospital doors slid apart, a gust of cool air escaped, followed by a new mom in a wheelchair with an overnight bag and vase of flowers on her lap. A beaming man cradled a newborn and assured the mother he knew how to put the baby in the baby seat.

In the elevator, I remembered holding Amy for the first time. The power of the love, the fierce desire to protect her, knowing I would give my life for her. Debra's father had grasped my shoulder and said, "You'll be a great dad." I never told Leonard how that sustained me when memories of my own father filled me with doubt.

My tennis shoes squeaked on the vinyl floor when I exited the elevator. Not one of the nurses or doctors looked up from their computers. I felt invisible as I walked by the desk to Sam's room hoping none of his second family, his "real" family, would be there.

He lay in the bed, his back to the door. A monitor beeped rhythmically. A baseball game flickering on the wall-hung TV reminded me of Little League and Debra's dad cheering when the batter swung, missed my final pitch, and our team won three to zero. I'd thrown a no-hitter. Leonard ruffled my hair and said, "Well done!"

When I told Sam about the game the next morning, he shrugged and said, "Big deal. No hits or runs, but you let the other team get on base. How? Walks? Wild pitches?" His waving hand erased my accomplishment. "Let me know when you pitch a *perfect* game."

My excitement had fizzled out like the cigarette he dropped in the dregs of his coffee.

So, what was I doing in his hospital room now?

Sam rolled over to face the door. He looked vulnerable, snared in a confusion of tubing and wires. A plastic vein carried fluid from an IV bag to the port in his bruised hand. A tube dark with liquid snaked from beneath the bedcovers to a waste bag. Another tube emerged from a gauze bandage on his neck and tethered him to the oxygen supply.

He had a hole in his throat.

He scowled and waved me to the bed while he scribbled on a Magic Slate. He thrust it at me.

Get a good look?

I pointed to his throat. "Is that permanent?"

The geniuses don't know, he scrawled, the writing ghostly beneath the cover film.

How could he survive without talking? Telling jokes, stories, lies. Bellowing at the television, flirting with waitresses. Bullying his other sons. No slate was magic enough to contain all the words he flung at the world.

I asked, "What do you need?"

He wrote: *Jim Beam,* then gestured at the IV pole and pantomimed hanging the bottle there.

"I'm afraid not."

Scritch, scritch, scritch.

Always goody two-shoes

I read the sneer in the words and took a deep breath. "You wanted to see me?"

He shook his head at me disapproving, no … disappointed. Maybe both. His blue eyes, once as clear and deep as mine, were gray. Some unkind impulse made me wish my mother could have seen him laid low, but I knew she wouldn't have enjoyed his misery. I didn't.

He picked up the slate, scribbled, and showed me.

I forgive you

I waited for him to write more. Had he made a mistake? Did he mean to ask *me* to forgive *him*?

He stared at me.

Oh. He expected me to be grateful.

Fury surged through me, and words I'd wanted to scream at him all my life filled my mind, but the damn tube in his throat muted me.

I couldn't kick him while he was down.

The anger passed, leaving resignation in its wake. I felt the same compassion for him as I would for a stranger. Perhaps less.

He shook the slate at me and looked surprised when I took it from him. I wrote,

Thank you for forgiving me. I forgave you long ago and held it for him to read.

He yanked it from my hand, almost ripping the film when he erased my words. He wrote,

What?

"We're even, Sam. I hope everything goes well," I pointed at his throat, "and I wish you a long, talkative life when you're through this."

He made a rough sound in his throat. A laugh? A cough?

Sadness washed over me.

His face turned red, and he scrawled, *I don't need your pity*. He lifted the film and the words disappeared.

* * *

In the lobby, Debra searched my face. "How was he?"

"He has throat cancer. They've operated and left a hole in his throat. They're not sure he'll be able to talk again."

"That must be killing him. Mister Life-of-the-Party." She slipped her arm through mine.

"He looked frail. And scared, but he's trying to tough it out."

"What did he want, Mike?"

"To tell me he forgave me."

A group of nurses flowed around us when Debra stopped short. "No. How could he? For what?"

"Does it matter?"

"Of course it does." She looked ready to march to the elevator and give him a piece of her mind.

"No, it doesn't." I took her hand and moved toward the door again. "It hurt to see him diminished and in pain, and I don't even love him. Imagine if I did. How heartbreaking it would be to see someone you loved suffering like that."

She stopped again to watch my face. "Do you wish you hadn't come?"

"Absolutely not. I'll always be grateful for what I learned from Sam today."

"What?"

"I never want to be in a hospital bed looking like him. And I never want you or Amy and Lennie hurting for me, fearing for me because of something I did to myself. Something I could have protected you from."

The glass doors slid open, and we stepped out into a sprinkling of raindrops. We turned our faces to the sky, the way we'd done when we were kids. As the drops fell faster, I fished the box of Marlboros out of my pocket and tossed it in the trash.

Sea Change
Joseph Affolter

I grew up in the 1970s, living on Lower Great Highway, which is the last of the Avenues in the San Francisco Sunset District, just before the actual Great Highway and Ocean Beach. As early as I could remember, my dad would go across the highway and down to the beach to surf fish. This was something he almost always did alone, rarely even letting my uncle John come with him, but never my brother Patrick or me.

Dad used to take Patrick fishing on Lake Merced. I was allowed to go sometimes, but honestly, I didn't like it. I liked to practice casting, to see how far I could get the hook and sinker out into the lake, but I didn't like the idea of actually catching anything. I stopped asking to come when I was ten or twelve. Sometimes, rarely, Patrick and Dad would go down the coast to Pacifica to fish from the pier there, but I never went on those trips.

Dad used to get up early in the morning before sunrise. Sunrise is an odd thing along Ocean Beach. I think people are used to movies, where the sun rises out of the ocean and lights up the sea and the beach before anything else. But that's an East Coast thing. For us in San Francisco, the sun rises behind us, over the East Bay hills. Looking to the west at sunrise, with the light behind us, the sky, and the ocean both get darker and darker as you look further out to sea, until they eventually meet at the horizon, with the night and the sea having no line between them.

Dad's two ancient fishing rods hung from hooks above his workbench in the basement. One was a solid seven-foot rod, and the other had two pieces and was over ten feet long when put together. Some surfcasters use rods much longer than this, but Dad didn't like to get too extreme. As with his 'good' tools, Patrick and I were forbidden to touch Dad's fishing poles. We did touch them, of course, when Dad wasn't home, imagining ourselves fishing for great white sharks or whales.

Since our bedroom was in the basement, Dad had to walk past us to get his gear, so Patrick and I usually knew when he was going fishing. We'd hear him gathering up his things through the thin walls of our room. Usually, we'd just roll over and sleep a little longer. But a few times,

Patrick and I got up quietly and followed Dad across the highway, keeping a safe distance, to watch him.

Most of the surf fishers would cast out their line from on shore, and then slot their fishing rod into a rod holder that they would drive into the sand. They would bring a folding chair and sit next to their pole, drinking coffee or beer. But my dad always waded into the water and stood with his pole in hand, waiting for a bite. He had a rod holder, but he rarely used it.

Dad wore chest-high waders and would go into the surf up to his knees. The way he cast was different than how he'd do it at Lake Merced. He'd hold the rod with both hands, like holding a flagpole, and when he cast, he'd use his whole body, slowly winding up, almost like a baseball pitcher. He'd start by twisting backwards, getting the pole and his hook way out behind him, and then make a huge sweeping arc, around and out, straight in front of him. It wasn't a fast snap from the wrist, like at the lake. The pole would bend almost double, as if it were about to break. Then it would spring the other way, and the hook and bait would fly out at least two or three hundred feet into the surf. The whole process seemed to happen in slow motion and had power and grace to it.

Ocean Beach was not really a great place to surf fish. Mostly, Dad caught surfperch, which tasted pretty nasty. Sometimes he got a striped bass. He said he once caught a shark, but he threw it back to grow up. Then there was this one time he brought home a small octopus. Mom had no idea what to do with it, and from then on, if Dad caught anything like that, he'd either let it go or turn it into bait.

I thought about all these memories the evening after I had to call the ambulance.

It was early spring, 2001, not long after my 34th birthday. Dad and I were the only ones living at the house. This was three years after Mom had passed away and I had moved back home to look after Dad.

It started when I came out of my bedroom that morning. It felt colder than normal, even for the basement. When I came to the foyer, I saw someone had left the front door open. I went upstairs and found the house was empty. Dad should have been in the living room or kitchen, but I checked every room and didn't find him. I went out the front door and looked up and down the block. Nobody was on the street at all. Dad was not the type to go for a walk. His car was still in the garage—he'd given up driving a year before. I double-checked the calendar in the kitchen to make sure he had no appointments or treatments that day. At that point, Dad had type 2 diabetes and some other issues with his heart and kidneys.

I took another look out our front window, checking the still empty street, but I happened to glance up toward the highway. Someone was up there, crossing to the beach. It was a man, but the figure seemed too small to be my dad.

Regardless, I ran down the stairs, across the street, and up the ice plant-covered hill to the highway. Traffic was still light because of the early hour. Between the cars, I crossed over to the beach side, and I saw a man alone near the surf. He stood statuelike, facing the ocean. Small though he seemed, it was definitely my father.

"Dad!" I called out. He didn't turn. "Patrick Lynch!" I shouted, trying his real name, but no response.

He was wearing his trousers and pajama shirt. This was what Dad used to do if he had to get up in the middle of the night for some emergency. When I reached him, I was panting from running on the deep sand. He didn't acknowledge me. The waves were reaching our feet with two or three inches of water. I had on my work shoes; he was just wearing his worn-out slippers. He didn't seem to notice the cold water soaking his feet.

I took his shoulder and he finally turned, but looked at me with no recognition. His mouth was hanging open in a way it never did. He turned back towards the waves and stepped forward. "No!" I yelled, as if yelling would make him know me. I took him by the shoulders and steered him away from the water. Thankfully, I had my cellphone with me, and I called 911.

It seemed like an hour for the paramedics to arrive. They couldn't get any information from Dad—he wasn't speaking. I answered what I could. They believed he was having some sort of episode stemming from his diabetes. The paramedics had to carry Dad off the beach on a gurney. It was hard going over the sand dunes. My mind went to stories Dad had told us as kids, of him carrying wounded soldiers off a beach in France during the war.

During the ambulance ride to the hospital with Dad on an IV, I saw his senses slowly returning. By the time we reached the emergency room, he had some idea of where he was and what was happening.

I stayed at the hospital most of the day. Dad had suffered something akin to dementia, from extremely low blood sugar. The doctor told me he most likely would have passed out in the water if I hadn't found him. From the hospital, I called Patrick, and we talked through all that was happening. He said he'd call the rest of the family.

Around 5:00 or 6:00 p.m., the doctor kindly but aggressively told me to go home. There was nothing for me to do there—Dad was sleeping. I went home and called my boss to take off work for the rest of the week. The house was impossibly silent. Even after I turned on the TV, the feeling of vacancy was heavy. I took a beer from the fridge, but just carried it around the house unopened.

Without a plan, I found myself down the stairs, outside, to the highway, and across to the beach. Unlike in the morning, there was traffic now. The Great Highway has stoplights and crosswalks every few blocks, but I just dashed across when there was a break in traffic. I went down the beach about halfway to the surf, plopped down in the sand, and finally opened the beer. I thought for a long time, mainly about the times Patrick and I had followed Dad to watch him surf fish.

The setting sun had changed from bright yellow to a golden orange. As the sun dropped lower, it lit the clouds from beneath with the same orange glow that was now painting the waves. I watched a set of waves wash in and pull back, even as the next set was rolling in over them. The sounds I was hearing didn't quite match the waves I was watching. There were more waves breaking and rolling than I could see. But the different rhythms all meshed in the overall rush in and out of the water.

There's an expression I've heard before: "sea change." Mostly I've heard it at work, to describe sweeping changes to some segment of industry. It's meant as a metaphor for how an industry can change in direction and force the way tides and swells on the ocean can change without warning or control. That day marked a sea change for my dad and myself, and how we lived together. Our roles had changed and reversed, like the direction of the tide, with the power of sudden and unexpected waves. It was only early spring, but the night air chilled me like winter.

16

Promises
Kristine Rae Anderson

From Marla, I learned to bite my fingernails down to the bleeding cuticles, learned to say "sorry" for everything from a burned dinner to the rain, learned to ache in an empty room. She taught me to maneuver around questions by putting my idle hands to work.

Sometimes, my brother and sister slipped and called me "Mom." Susie was five when our parents divorced and our mother, Marla, went to work. Jason was six, and I was eleven. This was three-quarters of the way into the twentieth century, when suburban jobs took workers to multi-story office buildings surrounded by parking lots. Marla was over thirty and, I learned later, hadn't worked since she'd earned pocket money as a carhop in high school. Folks described Marla as quick and bubbly, and I guess because of that, she soon landed a sales position. She moved us into a three-bedroom apartment. Susie and I shared a room. Jason had a small bedroom to himself.

Often, Marla said she had to work late and would come home after I'd already tucked Susie and Jason into bed. "Thanks for everything you do, Emily," she'd say when she got home, her black pumps clipping on the kitchen linoleum, starched blouse loosened a bit, curly hair escaping its bobby pins. She still smelled faintly of Charlie perfume, citrus, jasmine, and rose.

* * *

Even today, those memories catch in my throat.

This morning, light from a streetlamp filters through half-closed wooden blinds. It's not yet dawn.

I turn to see Alan lying on his side next to me, a thin white sheet covering him. He faces away, the contour of his body a slope and curve. It's early, but I think of quietly slipping out of bed, going to the kitchen and sitting alone, two hands around a ceramic mug full to the brim with steaming coffee.

"Emily?" His voice is quiet, sleepy.

"Shh," I whisper. His breathing softens to regular beats. I envy his dreams.

In two weeks, we're supposed to be married. Flowers are ordered, dresses sized, priest and church reserved. Our lives will intertwine from then as surely as our arms in sleep wrap around one another, as surely as the sheet now clings to Alan's warm form.

Again last night, we talked. Alan wants a family, he says. He envisions playing kickball with daughters and sons, teaching them to ride a bicycle, hook bait onto a fishing line.

He won't be satisfied with my response.

"We don't have to decide right now," he said.

I have children in my life. I teach third grade. I don't want children at home and children at work.

Alan knows but can't understand. "You love children," he said. "Your students are crazy about you. Your brother and sister adore you."

Aren't the two of us enough?

* * *

Marla taught me how to apply Band-Aids to soothe Susie's skinned knees, to absorb blood from Jason's deep cuts. She taught me to tell phone callers, "My parents are busy and can't come to the phone," and say, "Can I take a message?" I learned that the market on the corner had good bananas and apples, but the market downtown had cheaper milk. Marla taught me how a mom should take care of a family.

One time, when Susie was six and sick with a loud, deep cough, I stayed home from school with her. That afternoon, her cough became so bad that I had to take her into the small bathroom and run the shower water as hot as it would get so she could breathe in the steam. My heart pounded and the humid air closed in around me. I hugged Susie as she struggled for great swallows of air. Once her coughing subsided and, exhausted, she leaned her head against my chest, I stroked her hair and hummed "Rock-a-Bye Baby." She was asleep in bed by the time I heard Marla's keys jingle in the front door lock a couple of hours later. When I told Marla, her face flushed. She mumbled an apology and looked away.

When I was a freshman at North Chester High, I stopped calling Marla "Mom."

In high school, Dana Stratt was the closest I had to a friend. The other kids said she was slow and fat. We shared the distinction of being outsiders. She was a freshman when I was a sophomore. She came to the apartment once. "Where's your mom?" she asked.

"Who knows?" I said. "Working, I guess. She's never around."

I was seventeen when Marla received a promotion. We moved to a nicer neighborhood. Suddenly, Marla had regular hours. She was home by five thirty in the afternoon. Soon, she began cooking dinner for us, attempting homemade casseroles and fried chicken. I could hear her humming from the kitchen, "Everything's Coming Up Roses." Marla never let on whether it bothered her when Susie pushed casserole noodles around on her plate, asking for "Emily's Hamburger Helper," and Jason wondered if he could have a TV dinner instead.

The new apartment complex was large, with lots of buildings surrounded by trees, big lawns and a brightly colored playground. By then, even Susie had outgrown a playground like that. Jason spent hours playing baseball after school, and Susie preferred sleepovers at her girlfriends' houses.

I felt dropped into another person's life, like my clothes were hanging in someone else's closet. Sunday afternoons, I stayed in my room and worked on algebra or history assignments. I could hear Marla running the vacuum cleaner in the hallway and living room, a job I used to do. When Marla stopped for a phone call, as she usually would, I'd put down my books, find the Hoover still plugged in, and finish what she'd started, making sure to catch the dust bunnies she missed. Out of habit one day as I walked home from school, I took the long way by the market to buy milk. When I got home, I discovered that Marla had taken care of that already. There it was in the refrigerator, an unopened carton, waiting to be of use.

Evenings at the kitchen table after dinner, Susie and Jason having gone off to watch TV, Marla wanted to talk with me, to chatter on and on about people at work. After a polite minute, I'd excuse myself, saying I had homework.

Then I got a job at the ice cream shop downtown. I worked as many hours as they'd give me after school and on weekends. Marla said she was proud of me and gave me her old car, the one she'd driven since she and my dad had split up. I think she wanted an excuse to buy a brand-new model.

One spring afternoon when I wasn't working, Jason and I went for a drive. We did that sometimes, just got in my car to drive somewhere, rolling down the windows and pretending we could get away. That day, I drove to the mountains for a view of the scattered yellows and reds and purples of wildflowers all over the new green hillsides. But on our way up the winding, two-lane road, the sky melted into dark clouds, then exploded in flashes of light. Jason was old enough to pretend he wasn't thrilled or afraid.

"What do you want to be when you grow up?" I asked him. Growing up was on my mind those days.

"I want to be Daddy," he said. The childish word "Daddy" hung in the air.

I flinched. In our family, we never mentioned him. Yet there must have been an unspoken understanding among us siblings that this man, whose life we did not know, who lived somewhere without us, must be happy.

* * *

Leaving Alan in bed, I tiptoe out of the room, turning the handle of the door to close it silently behind me. In the kitchen, I set up the Mr. Coffee. It's the season of cold mornings, and I pull my robe tighter, waiting for coffee to warm me from inside. No cream, no sugar, just coffee. I like the honesty of its bitterness.

* * *

College was my escape. It was there I learned to drink coffee to get through long nights in the dorm, typing papers until 4:00 a.m. or studying for tests. Some nights I read textbooks until dawn, a pen in my hand to ready questions for class the next day and to think about anything that wasn't my life.

One night during freshman year, just before midnight, Marla called. It was a particularly chilly night in the dorm, the heat turned down, and I was sitting next to a drafty window reading by a small book light.

Marla was getting married again, and wasn't I thrilled?

It was nice, I said. I was happy if she was happy. It's what I figured she wanted me to say.

"He says I can quit my job, have friends over to our new house for bridge in the afternoon if I want to." She paused, then added, "I'm going to stay home now with Jason and Susie."

But, I wanted to say, *Jason and Susie are teenagers now. They don't need you the way they did before. The way I did.*

Instead, I mumbled into the phone, "Sure, that's nice."

I shivered as a deep, cold sadness settled in my stomach.

* * *

Daylight outside the kitchen blooms into a clear morning. I fill my coffee cup and carry it back to the bedroom.

Alan moans and turns his head toward me, but doesn't open his eyes. "Come to bed," he whispers.

I walk over to the bed and sit on the edge. Alan's hand reaches over and touches mine. My skin feels the pull to lie next to him.

"Sleep," I say softly. The word sounds like a lullaby. Or a prayer.

He exhales one soothing note and rolls away.

I sip coffee and look on him, this man with whom I've vowed to share a future.

People don't equally field the weight of promises. I know. My mother, young, suddenly alone and burdened with children, without direction. She didn't have a choice.

But I do.

Word Thieves
Judy Baker

No one knows the precise moment when the words began to fade from the books. The librarians don't know. The scribes don't know. The printers don't know. Even the books don't know.

At first, people blamed their eyesight for the dimming ink and fading words. Who could have suspected the true cause or the depth of the damage to the knowledge of Scriptoria?

* * *

Marcella Quill, the town's head librarian, scrunches her forehead. Something catches her attention.

"Must be time for new spectacles," Marcella mumbles after a dark spot niggles at the edge of her vision. "Probably a floater or too little sleep."

Determined to complete her nightly rounds of tidying up the library shelves, she returns to her task. The wisp appears again in the corner of her eye. Blinking furiously to clear her sight as she bustles into the stacks, she sees nothing out of place, until she discovers several dozen open books, their pages blank. The words have vanished.

Marcella is known as a meticulous and attentive guardian of Scriptoria's vast collection of books. Her broad shoulders may be slightly rounded from years spent immersed in books. She is steadfast, deeply knowledgeable, and respected by the community.

She can feel the pressure of blood thumping as her chest squeezes the air from her lungs. The telepathic connection between the sisterhood of librarians reverberates in each of their heads as they discover more books with fading text across the library system.

Murmurs and whispers coat the wooden floors of the library, swirling, as fine as pollen, settling into corners, layer upon layer, adding weight to the particles of fine dust and forgotten memories, growing into a cacophony of distress, blaring into an auditory rash.

In the days to come, the library stands emptied of patrons, a place of dread. The librarians hold out longest, until they too are forced to flee the insidious noise and mysterious blank pages. Seeking refuge from the persistent chatter and disappearing stories, the librarians retreat to pay homage to the trees in the sacred grove of Scriptoria.

Instead of a pristine sanctuary nestled in the hollow of Lexicon Valley, the librarians feel disoriented by the changes in Verbum Grove. They stumble and grab their heads, attempting to stop, or at least dampen, the piercing sound emanating from the grove and worming into their ears.

At twilight, an eerie glow shimmers in the grove. Words are barely visible on the surface of leaves. Crackles and sparks replace the weird humming.

"The air is thick with the scent of old parchment and fresh pine. The leaves rustle in a language all their own, like ancient songs carried on the wind," Dr. Orion Savatini whispers in wonder.

Dr. Savatini, a distinguished Scriptorian scholar, has always been intrigued by the Sacred Grove and the mystical properties it seems to possess.

He has noticed subtle changes in the grove over the years—glimpses of words on leaves, unusual growth patterns in the trees, and a faint, almost imperceptible hum in the air when he is nearby. These observations have led him to hypothesize that the grove has a deeper connection to the written word than previously understood.

Fascination with the interplay between nature and language is the life work of Dr. Savatini. He has immersed himself in studying ancient manuscripts that most of Scriptoria's scholars overlooked or dismissed as myths. These texts describe a time when the words of the community were directly linked to the natural world, suggesting a cyclical flow of knowledge between the books and the grove.

Through his experiments, Dr. Savatini discovered the unique alchemical properties of trees in the Sacred Grove. Combining rare herbs found only in Scriptoria with sap from the resident trees produces a substance that can absorb and transfer written words. His discovery indicates that the migration of words might be part of a natural process facilitated by the trees.

The librarians, town scholars, and scientists like Dr. Savatini come to observe the grove. As foliage matures, complete sentences appear and phrases twine around the trunks of trees. Sometimes, all the lines of a poem or the full page of a book are inscribed upon a single leaf.

But there aren't enough trees in the grove to hold Scriptoria's words and wisdom. If they can't reverse or halt the fading words and migration, will the fading words be lost forever?

And only some trees thrive as they become tattooed with words. A mysterious blight shrivels the leaves and infests the bark with a sludge that suffocates the infected trees. Even trees with symbols of magical protection wither. It is a race against the coming of winter when the trees will shed their leaves.

***

Even as the trees dwindle in number, Calista's skin glistens with words. Since childhood, Calista Lexi could absorb words into her skin. Words appear as intricate tattoos that shift and change with the addition of new texts. Words are drawn to her, finding sanctuary in her skin. She can feel the words inscribe themselves.

When asked, Calista says, "It feels like a feathery electrical tingle of pleasure along my nerves. I feel a soft kiss as the words bond with my skin."

Calista becomes a living archive, preserving the stories and knowledge that would otherwise be lost. Calista doubts she can hold all the words necessary to ensure that Scriptoria's rich history and literature are not erased forever. She doesn't even know how she came to possess this rare ability. When found orphaned, Calista's tiny hands clutched a gold locket engraved with the initials SL.

Even Marcella Quinn, the town's head librarian who raised Calista, doesn't know all of Calista's secrets.

"I keep having dreams of a majestic woman in ancient Scriptorian robes. She feels so familiar. And there is a man cloaked in shadows, wielding strange powers. Air sparks around his hands and head. He makes lightning dance. The two seem connected somehow, but I can't figure out how," Calista confides to Marcella.

Calista's powerful connection to the words allows her to communicate with the Sacred Grove. She can read and understand the words on the leaves in a way no one else can, bridging the gap between the written texts and the natural world.

All of Scriptoria hopes Calista's unique skills are the key to unlocking the mystery of the migrating words.

The land of Scriptoria is a realm where words hold immense power and reverence. Nestled in a lush valley surrounded by rolling hills, Scriptoria is an idyll where the natural world and written language lived in harmony, until now.

The heart of Scriptoria is the Sacred Grove, a mystical forest filled with ancient trees. Each tree in the grove is unique, with bark etched in intricate patterns resembling flowing script, and leaves that glow faintly in the twilight, each inscribed with a myriad of words and phrases. The air within the grove hums with an almost imperceptible murmur, the song of countless stories and knowledge shared among the leaves.

When Calista, an entity with a deep connection to words, touches the bark, she can feel the emotions of the trees, which provide insights or convey messages through a sense of shared feeling.

"Each word is a fragment of a story, a piece of someone's heart. It's a blessing and a burden. Sometimes, the weight of all these words feels overwhelming, but they're a part of me, and I must honor them," Calista gently exhales in a soft voice edged with fatigue.

Dr. Savatini has theorized that the trees in the Sacred Grove have a symbiotic relationship with the words. His experiments revealed the words provide the trees with nourishment, and in return, the trees preserve and protect the words. This knowledge is crucial because it suggests that the fading words are not lost but are safeguarded in a different form.

Dr. Orion Savatini's unique insights are vital for understanding the phenomenon of fading words. His research suggests the Sacred Grove is not merely a passive repository, but an active participant in the cycle of knowledge preservation.

"Standing here, you can feel the history of our people. It's as if the very essence of Scriptoria is woven into the fabric of this grove. It's humbling and invigorating, knowing we are a part of something so grand."

As the situation grows more dire, Calista and Dr. Savatini are drawn to the grove, compelled by the energy emanating from the trees. Together, as they study the trees, Dr. Savatini asks, "How do you know these symbols, Calista? They're from an ancient Obfuscari text no one here has seen before."

Before she can answer, the locket slips from her pocket. As he picks it up, Dr. Savatini's face splits into a wide grin.

He recognizes the locket. It belonged to his classmate at university, Sophia Linden. She ran away when she fell in love with a member of the Obfuscari and was disowned by her parents. No one in Scriptoria, except Dr. Savatini, knows the name of Sophia's love. The truth is embedded in the skin of his chest.

The golden perfection of Dr. Savatini's chest is irregularly puckered over his heart, a nasty souvenir of his encounter with Lexian Mordant, the leader of the Obfuscari, a rival group jealous of Scriptoria's knowledge.

The Obfuscari have discovered the fading words phenomenon and aim to exploit this by capturing the trees' alchemical properties for their dark purposes, further endangering the grove and its secrets.

As he gazes at Calista, Dr. Savatini realizes he must spill the tea about Sophia and Lexian. By bringing this skeleton out of the closet, he hopes the clans can unite and share their knowledge and resources instead of competing against each other in fear and hatred. After all, Calista is proof the Scriptorians and Obfuscari can create miracles together.

* * *

Dr. Savatini brokers a meeting between Lexian and Calista. When the time comes, and Lexian is introduced to his daughter, Calista, the gasps and grins that ripple throughout the crowd crescendo into applause and whoops of joy.

Calista thought she would have to defeat the leader of the Obfuscari, Lexian Mordant.

Father and daughter are in shock. When Calista can breathe again, her deep understanding of words and empathy wins Lexian's heart.

Reminded of the love of his life while he gazes at Calista, Sophia, like the words and books, is part of a shared history.

With Lexian, Dr. Savatini, and Calista collaborating, they can help the Scriptorians and Obfuscari develop new methods to harness the symbiotic relationship found in nature and each other. Their joint wisdom will ensure their stories and history remain intact. Moreover, the knowledge of the alchemical properties of the trees might offer solutions for restoring the words to the books or finding new ways to integrate the words within the community, perhaps even enhancing the role of individuals like Calista Lexi.

The slight quaver in Dr. Savatini's voice is unmistakable as he proclaims, "Calista, the grove's response and your abilities—everything points to a deeper truth. You carry the legacy of both the Scriptorians and the Obfuscari. You are the key to our future."

"All the signs were there—the dreams, the grove's whispers. I see it now. I am both Scriptorian and Obfuscari. This is my destiny, and I will honor it," Calista declares, as tears spill from her eyes.

Calista, Marcella, and the librarians will perform a cleansing ritual to restore the words to the pages of the books.

Tonight, father and daughter join hands and hearts. With glistening tattoos, and words living on their skin, they are librarians, and their words never fade.

The Christmas Boy
Susan Church-Downer

He had laughed off her fears, admonitions and hurt feelings, as always. When he called her on Christmas morning from Ensenada, he told her he loved her and was "having a blast." It was two days later when Norma received word of her son's death, twenty-two kilometers south of the turnoff to Bahia de Los Angeles. He had died on Christmas, only hours after their last call, missing a sharp curve in the road, his red convertible sailing off a small cliff.

His boyhood friends, Eddie and Robert, had been following in Robert's car but had stopped in time. When they came to see her, awkward and grief-stricken, she asked if he had been drunk or smoking marijuana. Had he taken any pills?

"Oh no! We just had a few beers at the hotel in Catavina and then decided to push on to Guerrero Negro."

Eddie had stayed at the scene while Robert went for help. At first, he told her Joe had died instantly. Norma had known both boys since they were kids and knew when they were lying. Pressed, Eddie admitted Joe had lived for about twenty minutes after the crash. "Although," he said, "maybe it was just two or three."

"What else didn't you tell me?"

"That's it."

"What did he say?"

Eddie reluctantly gave it up. "Mostly, uh, just, 'oh no, oh no.'"

When she tried to repeat the conversation to her husband, Greg, she couldn't bring herself to give voice to their son's last words. She carried that burden alone, unable to get them out of her head. The windshield wipers, the dishwasher, even the refrigerator took them up, "oh no oh no oh no." Watching TV at night, she'd hear Joe moaning in her ear, "oh no oh no." That her son had died in pain and despair, without her to comfort him, was more than she felt she could bear.

Her husband grieved differently. They had clung to each other when they first got the news, but Greg's tears seemed to dry shortly after the funeral. He had never been one to show much emotion, and up to this point, they had been alike in that way. But losing her boy had cut through her normal reserve, and her husband's attempts at comfort just infuriated her. She resented his bland assurances that time would ease their loss and his defensiveness when she tried to wrest from him some emotion that would match hers.

Nobody knew what to say; she had gone behind a wall of grief her friends could only imagine and could not penetrate. Some suggested she see a doctor about her depression. "What's a doctor going to do," she barked, "bring my Joey back?" Another had offered that "God will never give you more than you can handle." She had gritted her teeth to keep from screaming out that there was no God. If there were a God, her boy would not have died in the desert! Sometimes she couldn't help herself and would let loose a barrage of heresy that made her peers uncomfortable. Their murmured platitudes ("Norma, you must move on, you must get on with your life. Joe would want you to.") failed to comfort. How could they know what he would want? By the end of the first year, most of her friends stopped calling, and she never called them.

Her sister-in-law, Bette, tried to commiserate by talking about her miscarriage. Norma felt the rage well up in her, threatening to take over her entire being. When she could hold it down no longer, she screamed at Bette, "Shut up about your damn fetus! This was my real child, my son!"

Not long after that, Greg left. He was anxious to begin life anew with a cheerful and adoring woman he had met shortly after their son's death. Greg waited until three weeks after the second Christmas, and Norma realized later he had only hung in through December out of duty. He needn't have bothered. Joey had been their only shared joy, and with his absence, they had nothing left but a dull civility.

In most ways, it was easier with Greg gone. She didn't have to worry about him worrying about her or tolerate his invasive attentions. She had wanted to scream him away when he touched her or tried to cheer her up, to retreat to the dark comfort of her grief, alone. When he left, she could finally move from the margins to the very center of it.

Greg left Norma with the house, her car, the furniture, and an adequate income. He had always been the one to handle the finances, and Norma seemed uninterested in the details, so they agreed to have their friend and banker, Evan McDonough, manage her affairs. He was a kind man, one of the few who hadn't offended her with clumsy condolences. He had simply said, "I can't imagine how you feel, but I wish I could help."

"No one can, Evan. I'm lost."

"I'm so sorry. I'm in your corner, Norma, whenever you need me."

* * *

She continued to take care of her house, her health, and her hygiene, knowing there had been some talk of committing her, particularly after the Bette incident. She made these activities fill most of her days, maintaining a solitary, marginally bearable existence. And then, shortly after Halloween, the Christmas decorations appeared.

She hadn't expected to see them so early, but there they were, the same tired gold streamers and the dingy candy canes on the streetlights. At first, she could ignore them by avoiding the downtown area, but as November rolled on, it seemed as though the entire city and the air waves were conspiring to drag her into the season, taunting her with Christmas music, announcements of sales, and the tingling of the Salvation Army bells, which sounded an insistent, incessant chorus, "oh no, oh no, oh no."

She avoided going out, kept the TV off, and had groceries delivered. She read a lot, planning to read every book she had collected over the years, finding that a manual on cross country skiing, which she had never attempted, was as interesting as anything else—particularly the section on avalanches. On her better days, she listened to music and was mildly amused to discover that rap, which she disliked but which had been Joey's favorite, was the only musical form which never echoed her son's dying refrain.

A call from Evan the week before Christmas interrupted her solitude.

"We need to go over your year-end financials and strategy for next year. Why don't we meet halfway for coffee at Klugman's on Tuesday? It won't take long."

"I hate going downtown. If it won't take long, can't you just tell me?"

"There are a couple of papers for you to sign."

"Can you just come here, then?"

"I'm sorry, Norma, I can't be away from the office that long. It's that time of year. Everybody's suddenly remembered to do their tax planning. Klugman's isn't that far. Ten a.m. then?"

"Sure. Okay."

What an annoyance even Evan was turning out to be! She sensed he was under the delusion that getting out would be good for her.

The outing seemed anything but good as she waited tensely for him to arrive. Trapped among Christmas shoppers, bags piled awkwardly at their feet, she was irritated by them and everything about them—the bells dangling from their earlobes, their elfin hats, their expressions of stress, of elation. Suddenly, she heard her own thoughts vocalized at the next table.

"I hate Christmas!" exclaimed a girl about Joey's age to her friend. "Next year, I'm gonna get in the car, drive down to Baja, and party from Thanksgiving to Mardi Gras."

"That would be so awesome," agreed her friend.

If any conversation followed, Norma didn't hear it. The girl's sentiment had drawn her in, but "Baja" pierced her heart. How could anyone go there for fun? Silly girl! Joey had, and Joey had died—without her. As that familiar regret welled up, a possibility she had never considered hit her like a thunderbolt. She could go to that place! Maybe she would feel his spirit—it certainly wasn't at the cemetery. Yes. She needed to see the last place he had last been alive, to feel it, to curse it. Maybe she could just lie down there and die, if there were a God.

Evan tried to talk her out of it, but having known her since high school, he didn't struggle to change her mind. Instead, he offered to accompany her, but she just looked at him as though he were insane. Finally, he insisted she call him every day so he would know she was okay. She agreed, but they both knew she wouldn't.

* * *

She prepared minimally for the trip by buying a Spanish-English dictionary and researching visa and car insurance requirements. She refused to feel anything about the task ahead, focusing instead on the mechanics of packing, driving, border crossing, eating, and sleeping. Her singular focus was aided by the monotony of the landscape—flat desert and cacti, with an occasional settlement. On Christmas Eve, she arrived at the hotel in Catavina, where Joey had had his last beer. It was surprisingly elegant, but nearly empty. She couldn't avoid the Christmas decorations in the lobby, but at least there weren't any in her room.

The next morning, she set out and had no trouble finding the spot, exactly 11 kilometers—6.8 miles—south of the sign, as reported. There was the curve, the cliff, and a winding footpath leading downward. A warning sign marked the fatal curve: "*Curva Peligrosa.*" Had it always been there, she wondered, or had they put it up after the fact, too late? As she made her way to the desert floor, she noted the tall cacti that had probably watched her son die and saw what looked like two figures in the distance.

Before she could make them out, she had reached the bottom, where she encountered an incongruously placed, weathered table supporting a rough wooden box which lay on its side, topped by a jar filled with wilting flowers. Looking inside, she saw three monochrome drawings on the panels. The artist had not been particularly skilled, but the images were clear. The first was of a car sailing off the cliff, the second showed a boy—her Joey!—lying next to the overturned car. The third panel showed him being lifted toward the clouds and an outstretched hand. The jar partially covered some lettering and, when she moved it, she read the words "*El Chico de Navidad.*" The Christmas Boy.

Whatever she had expected, this was not it, and the shock burst open the container she had built for her deepest grief. Dropping to her knees as the pain spasmed through her body, she screamed and beat her fists on the hard sand, leaving traces of her own blood where her son's had been. As she gulped for breath, wave after wave of sobs wracked her body until she had no more, only long shrieks that rasped as they passed from her womb to the warm desert air. Panting as she lay on the sand, she moaned through her chest, wailing and whimpering until, exhausted, she felt an unfamiliar peace and a need to rest.

When she opened her eyes, Norma first noted the particles of sand —not one color but a myriad of reds, whites, blacks, and browns. Rising slowly to her feet, she admired the graceful shape of a cirio cactus. The sky was bright, the air clean and warm. She took a deep breath, and it felt like the first she had taken in years. Then, on the periphery, she saw the two figures she had noticed earlier approaching. Had they been there the whole time? Had they seen everything? She was pleasantly surprised to find she didn't care.

A young man carrying a jar with fresh flowers was accompanied by an older, pregnant woman. The woman knew. "*Su hijo?*" she asked kindly. Norma nodded. "Joey."

The young man spoke English and gently introduced himself as Javier, and the woman as his mother, Inez. Walking home that night, he had witnessed the accident. He had created the box, he told her, inspired by a vision of Joey's spirit, shimmering with a golden light, rising from his body to meet God. They visited the site often to bring flowers and sometimes to pray, knowing the Christmas boy's family lived far away.

Norma felt the tears come again, but this time flickers of gratitude tempered her grief. She could barely get the word out. "*Gracias.*"

"*De nada,*" responded Inez, her lined, brown face glistening with her own remembered sorrows. Javier replaced the old flowers with the ones they had brought. Inez crossed herself, and the three stood in silence, savoring the slight, sweet breeze.

When it was time to leave, Norma asked if they needed a ride and Inez smiled for the first time. Javier explained that there was no road, pointing into the desert. "Our house is over there." As she gazed in that direction, no house in sight, she found the subtle grays, beiges, and greens of the landscape serenely beautiful, and the dignity of the tall columnar cardon cacti made them suitable guardians of this place.

* * *

Back at the hotel, over a lunch of papaya and fish, she had a long conversation with the waiter. "Baja is beautiful," he told her, "especially Baja Sur. I was born in Santa Rosalia. It's a beautiful little town on the Sea of Cortez. And La Paz! La Paz is a grand old city with a *malecón*, a promenade along the beach. They have a big Mardi Gras there. It's not like your crazy one in *Los Estados Unidos*. It's families and celebration, dancing, parades, and feasting!"

After lunch, she called Evan.

"I just wanted you to know I'm okay. It feels good to be here, and I'm staying in Mexico for a while. How about you? How have you been, Evan?"

"Oh, I've been okay. Busy, of course. Working today. Not much of a Christmas… I'm so glad to hear from you, Norma. I was worried! Let me know where you are. Maybe I'll come see you. It's too cold and rainy here." He chuckled, but she sensed he would welcome an opening.

"Thank you, Evan. You're a good friend. I'll keep in touch."

This time, she meant it. She didn't want company just yet, but thought it might do him good to get away from the bank. In the meantime, she would head south and east toward La Paz. It would be best to settle in before Mardi Gras.

Why the Very Best?
Patrice Deems

I've seen you on
my mind patio
surfing, clouds, wakes
Jimi Hendrix guitar in hand
Then
hanging Cheshire-style from tree limbs

Oh, to keep … to keep … to keep
to not forget

After her final conversation with her younger brother, Rusty, the poetry started coming. Anne keeps his energy by her right ear, and a tablet always within reach.

* * *

On May 16, 2020, Anne and her partner Gary leave home on the morning of her youngest brother, Rusty's fifty-eighth birthday. The night before, another brother, Dillon, had orchestrated a family Zoom call.

"He wants to see you all, Covid be damned. Mary said we all can come and stay at their house." Dillon's voice broke as he continued, "I don't think he has much time left."

Anne had already packed a suitcase—one advantage of being a worst-scenario type. Their wheels hardly touch Highway 5 asphalt, and they arrive at Rusty's Altadena house in a record six hours. Anne doesn't take the time to remove her suitcase from the car. She rushes inside.

Rusty sits propped up by pillows on a couch in his living room, set against a long Victorian front window. Dillon had warned them in the call, "Don't be surprised by Rusty's appearance … he doesn't look like himself … I hardly recognized him."

Anne hasn't seen her brother since Thanksgiving. The handsome, warm-complexioned, robust man is now a skeletal pinkish ash-gray, weighing maybe eighty pounds. Once vibrant green eyes—now chalky orbs—sweep around slowly, eyeballing the couple as they approach.

"I love my birthday presents," he force-whispers. His wingspan opens wide, following a big smile. He gasps with the effort of speech. Raspy sounds gurgle from deep in his chest.

The room is half full of people wearing Covid masks, mostly Anne's immediate family. Dillon, a doctor, manages the balance of visits. The brothers have a shorthand between them: A look, a hand signal, and people are shooed out of the room.

What could possibly suffice for the most important conversation she would have with one of her favorite people in the world? As her turn to visit approaches, Anne feels strangely shy with the impending gravity, the finality. She *cannot* hold anything back.

"So, this is *it* now, my love?" She forces an opening line and sits close on the facing chair.

"It went south fast. Dr. Freeman suggested I think of quality of life at this point." He pauses, wheezes, then continues. "Mary wasn't even allowed in the hospital room. Actually, I feel empowered."

"To be able to be home?"

"To be here with Mary and the kids … not staring down … four hospital walls, alone … a sea of masks … I think I have maybe two days."

He says that with such stoic certainty. She is a bit taken aback. *Now is the time, now is the time* announces a loudspeaker in her brain.

"Rusty, I've always wanted to apologize for … remember when you jumped off that bridge? You were twelve, in my care. I was stoned on acid … you could've died. I…"

He leans back, forcefully gathers a handful of air in his palm, defying his weakened mass, and swats her statement forward, out of his ballpark, leaving her with no uncertainty that a confession is neither wanted nor needed. Anne grasps the hands he holds folded in his lap, with both of hers. They each gaze lovingly into the window of the other's soul. Silently. What powerful innocence, to look into the face of death.

* * *

Death Watch

That first day, Rusty's wife Mary has generously given Anne and her siblings the honor of the first alone time with their brother. No gifts for his fifty-eighth birthday, the present is theirs: his best and last conscious presence. Verity and love devour the time as they each have their private audience with him.

Twenty-four hours later, when Rusty's in-laws and close friends scuttle through the house, Rusty is already bed-bound in a hospital twin in the center of the living room. It is outfitted with a button on the back attached to an IV going into his arm. Rusty opted out of the usual morphine. Now Anne regrets he is *not* comatose as she watches his face flag in a succession of expressions, pain that Dillon tirelessly attempts to numb by pushing the button.

Anne feels possessive, desires to monopolize these authentic moments. She is exhausted for Rusty, empathetic of his pain. She hurts just watching. The parade of company saunters around, squandering his essence as he labors to breathe. Despite his degrading condition, Anne guesses Rusty still feels the need to be magnanimous and accept all company. *Like a helpless host.* She has to contain the resentment that arises when some sit nearby, chattering noisily about shopping and various mundanities. Anne wants to protect Rusty's privacy, help accommodate his final meditation in this life. She has a sense that he is uncomfortable, wants less commotion as he shifts his legs from side to side and pulls at his underwear.

"He has some bed sores," Dillon informs her. "I'll talk to his doctor." Then he hand-motions Anne, her sisters, Teri and Mo, and two nieces to watch. Cupping his hands, he gently thumps Rusty's upper thorax. "If I am not here, this is how you would pat. Gently palpitate here, so he can expel the buildup in his lungs." He discreetly turns his head away from Rusty and whispers, "He and I decided that lung drowning would not be a good way to go."

People continue to show up and beg in. She would have hated the lack of tranquility; her inner cynic sees those friends and family like that biblical feast of Cana—everyone hungry for some last morsel. Of Rusty.

The circle of humanity around the hospital bed numbers twenty or so late that afternoon. Rusty sits up suddenly and gags. Teri bolts up from her seat to his back and pats him as Dillon had shown. A few minutes into her effort, Rusty, who can't physically swallow, and hasn't had water for almost a week, spits up the foam that fills his lungs into a Kleenex, as those gathered hold their collective breath.

Rusty dramatically lifts his chin, and his eyes scan a rapt audience. Then he winks and hoarsely breathes out, "Like my latest party trick?"

The room explodes into hysterics. None of them would ever forget the dying witticism that commandeered that sorrowful airspace—that perfectly timed moment. Nothing competes with comedy in a tragedy.

Dillon hadn't had uninterrupted sleep since he arrived in Altadena five days before. He helicopters over Rusty, ceaselessly trying to intuit and manage his pain. He walks around in a daze, coffee in hand. The rest of the household drag about like zombies.

Finally, the decision is made to call hospice. Anne remembers Rusty had thought he would already be gone; his body has other ideas. *Death is not always kind / it applies the brakes for some reason / to torture you for what gain?*

Anne, Teri, and Mo decide to give Dillon some nighttime relief. Hospice is stingy with the Fentanyl and won't up the basal rate. They decide to tag-team Rusty's meds at night: three-hour shifts with fifteen-minute med-delivery intervals to add additional pain meds. Anne takes the 4:00–7:00 a.m. shift. Setting her cellphone to go off every fifteen minutes, she nestles it in her robe pocket and scrunches herself side-body on a loveseat in a room near the sickbed as another relative is on the couch. She attempts to steal a few nods before its floating chime sounds.

At four thirty, Anne shuffles out to her task the second time on her shift. Rusty's presence startles her. He sits upright, silhouetted by the nightlight, his happy round-eyed face exuberant. He looks to her like a wide-eyed boy excited to see someone. Is she witness to a metaphysical experience? Has he traveled to a former or future point in time? The vibe is almost his casual self.

"Well, hello there lovey," Anne coos, feeling like the *chosen one*. "What are you doing so awake at this hour?" She kisses his forehead, and helps him settle back, goes around to the button on the back of the bed and pushes. Two beeps confirm the med delivery. She sits and holds his hand, watching the calm come over his mouth and roll down muscles in his cheeks. Oh, that face, more skeletal by the moment.

* * *

The oppression of the smoke and sludge-toned skies of September's fires lifts as the sun smiles out of a cool blue sky this morning. It's been so long. So easy to forget the positivity of beauty as we labor within fear and conflict, Anne thinks. That color is uplifting, like a giggle, freeing, peace-giving.

The card shuffling universe continues to deal crazy hands these days, makes Anne wonder how much of life is random. She doesn't think these rampant fires are simply a hiccup; she believes it is global warming. But, was Rusty's departure a terribly timed accident, a fatal sidecar riding alongside the pandemic, or just his time? She curses the forces that took him when so many malicious people are allowed to live.

Part of her daily mourning routine since his death involves staring at the "favorites" album in her cell phone photo library. She scrolls through the pictures that are a Rusty-themed gallery, indulging sentimental nostalgia.

Today she pauses at one taken on the Duffy boat that Friday in July when they scattered his ashes in Newport Bay. The focal point of the photo is a cluster of rose petals, floating specks of yellow, pink and red, gathered to make a journey. The water is creamy and viscous, and a blue as deep as an infinite sapphire desert, textured with nubile sand-nipples. Her gaze fixes onto an imperceptible zigzag in the gentle waves rolling toward the horizon. A pair of pink petals at the top of the zigzag closes in on the vanishing point, the seam between water and sky. In the foreground, one lone floppy, yellow one straggles behind.

The convoy of petals lassoes a reminiscence, a comment Rusty made ten years before, preceding a multiple household trip. Her family had purchased a week-long rental on the ocean in San Diego. The night before their scheduled arrival, they had a group conference call to plan last minute itinerary and timing.

"Hey, what if we all caravan tomorrow?" Teri offers excitedly.

A collective silence filled a few seconds.

"I can't think of anything worse," Rusty screeched in the comic falsetto of a ventriloquist dummy sensing imprisonment.

Anne had exhaled in grateful agreement, hard-pressed to express how impatient she would have felt in such confinement on a long L.A. freeway trek. Fearful of hurting her sister's feelings that night, she had muted her own.

That type of honesty was Rusty's "brand." He owned himself, knew who he was, said his truth kindly, without schadenfreude or malice. He often iced it with a dollop of humor.

Honesty and Truth seem to be a lost art these days. *Why do the very best / die first / does the universe need their energy elsewhere?*

* * *

"Samsara" means to flow, the continuing cycle of birth and death. Buddhists say there is no difference between life and death, that it is all a continuum. Ha, tell that to Mary, the widow.

Anne gives herself permission to take in the beautiful aqua sky. She still wears the hollow malaise of the previous four months. Dispirited and drained by the shadow, the sorrow of experiencing Rusty's last days.

Her cellphone, in vibrate mode, jitterbugs on the windowsill. Anne answers immediately, seeing Mary's name.

"Did you hear RBG died? Oh god what's gonna happen next!"

"Hi sweetie, yeah, just heard. I'm feeling despondent, too," Anne responds.

"I miss him so much." Mary's voice is cut up with emotion.

"I do too, honey."

"You know, don't you, that Rusty was the one who planned everything, not me? I'm totally lost."

"Mary, call me anytime. I'm here, forever. I got you."

* * *

Rusty was a ringmaster. Anne and her siblings and his friends had giddily followed their pied-piper on all his brilliantly planned excursions.

Can't trail you this time, my bro. The gates are locked, the theme park closed.

At once a warmth pulses inside Anne's head, travels down through her body. It is sensate bliss, the gift of his joyful energy communing within her. *The best guy ever.* She grabs her pencil and tilts her head.

You'll always be
a part of me
apart from me.

Photo Synthesis
Mike Dwyer

All set for Saturday Group then groceries after, Ray stops and nods to his car's windshield before getting in. A regular ritual these days.

On a hollowed out, way-late-for-work Tuesday morning ten months prior, a young man's face had smiled at Ray from an 8x10 photo tucked behind the driver's side wiper. An ad, Ray thought. Not at all in the mood, he removed it, made to tear it. But he stopped. It was a face, a smile, that made Ray keep looking and start feeling. Calmer. Safer. Hopeful, even.

Rippling forth below that face and smile was sinewed brawn. Neck, shoulders, arms, chest—all concrete slabs. Surprised, Ray turned over the photo to see what the huge human was selling. It was a note to Ray: *Last night I walked by and heard yelling. I went closer and saw you inside, grabbing a frightened woman. You stooped and put your face right to hers, then screamed at her till she cried. You threw a bottle and it smashed, then you punched a hole in the wall and your fist just missed her face. And in an upstairs window, a little girl, scared as hell, stood with both hands over her ears.*

In smaller letters to squeeze everything in, it continued: *"I try to see the good in people, or the potential for it. Right now, I won't call the cops or give you a beating. I WILL do more night walks past your window, and I'd better not see or hear anything like last night. You need to change, so start NOW. For that woman and little girl, and for yourself, do it. I'll be watching."*

The note now sits on Ray's nightstand next to the bed he gratefully still shares with Gwen, his wife. He often reads it at night, when the urge to use is strongest and relapse looms. It is a vital portal to Ray's last fury, a transport to his front yard that awful night. It whisks him there and then, to stand with the stranger and witness the mayhem inside.

They see Ray, brutish and hateful, hurling raw abuse at Gwen. He wields his size and force, his substance-fueled noise, his thrown bottles and wall punches, to rain fear upon her and Amy. Like the stranger beside him, Ray wants the abuser gone. Stop him, protect them. Ray didn't see the terror when he brought it, but the note enables him to see it all. This *seeing* is a gift he must not waste.

As he did that morning at the car and throughout his sixty-day rehab, Ray regularly goes through the note's portal, views the terrible scene, then re-emerges, shaken. He then turns over the note to see the giant man, whose wide-open smile sends Ray a surge of strength and purpose. Around his house and neighborhood, especially at night, Ray keeps an eye out for the giant. He hopes to give him his deepest thanks, and a hug that a cinder block body might feel. If the man refuses the hug and berates or even pummels Ray, that would be fine.

* * *

As Ray backs out, Agnes is at his home's side door. They wave to each other, then Agnes enters smiling. She lives four doors down and has been Gwen's confidant almost since they moved in two years ago. She is a weekend morning regular at their kitchen table. Amy, five, gets a kick out of seventy-something Agnes, who is kind, droll, and generous with her winks and grins despite the constant soft shadow of heartbreak enshrouding her.

Gwen and Agnes drink tea and eat pastries while they talk about Amy, Gwen's garden, and pesky rabbits in that garden. They discuss Gwen's PTSD therapy, her work-at-home career, and Ray's still-new job. They speak of today's Ray, who works his steps, speaks at meetings, confers with his sponsor, and intently makes amends. This healthier Ray who gives Gwen and Amy his honest love and, so far—yes, so far—his steadfast commitment to rebuilding the wreckage. Gwen is sure that Ray now takes nothing for granted. For her, that sureness is a fortress of hope.

Agnes is the only person privy to the worst of it: Ray's benders and tantrums, his threats to hurt Gwen and himself. She heard each detail of that final rampage when Gwen called her after Ray passed out. Gwen was sure his next punch wouldn't miss, but once again asked Agnes not to call the police. "Next time, I'll do it myself. Really." Agnes nodded her assent, but silently vowed to head off another *next time*. To try, at least.

Agnes thanks Gwen for the snack, tracks down Amy in the playroom for a hug, and walks back home. She goes to a drawer in the living room's credenza and takes out some photos of Andy, then kisses her fingers and touches them to each one.

With Gwen and Ray, Agnes is the visitor, not the visited. Their single time in her home was almost two years ago when Agnes told them about her son, Andy. His sunlit, open-door smile, his ever-flowing kindnesses to all he knew and many he didn't. His once mighty body, a sight to see, weakened and shrunken by lymphoma. Taken from her fifteen years ago, Andy was the age Gwen and Ray are now.

They learned much about Andy, but luckily for Agnes, they were in the kitchen and didn't ask to see photos of him. Those photos were in the living room, taking pride of place atop the credenza. Since the morning that she put the photo on Ray's car, she has tucked those pictures of Andy in a drawer, in case Ray might one day be in her living room. He doesn't know the truth.

Ray's wife does know. Seven months back, Gwen asked Agnes point blank if she was the note's author, and if the photo was of Andy. Agnes came clean, telling Gwen she wrote it just the way Andy would have.

Ray still hasn't connected the massive build of his note-writer, or the note-writer's singular smile, to what Agnes once said about her son. Gwen and Agnes hope it stays that way.

Gwen is loath to risk any change to Ray's recovery process, of which the note and photo are key parts, or to his relationship with the stranger from whom he draws precious extra willpower. Let Ray keep his hope to one day meet and thank that stranger.

So, Ray still thinks the man in the photo lives and breathes and at nighttime patrols their street. Agnes deems that a fine thing. She sees her son in some real way doing just that. Her Andy still shines his radiant, encouraging smile upon folks who, like her and Ray, need it.

A Better Place
Arleen Eagling

One March afternoon in downtown San Francisco, seven members of a tech support team went for lunch, all buddy-buddy. Their contract programmer, Darren Adams, wasn't with them. He was in his cubicle with their manager, packing his personal belongings into a gym bag. Darren said a final goodbye to the rickety old South of Market building and the nearby high-rise construction that pounded and shook the ground every day.

He knew he had screwed up, and they were entitled to cut him loose over two missed production support calls the night before. They had reached his backup to help with a severe processing problem. In five years of contracting at three different companies, Darren had gotten zero complaints. This time, sleep-deprived, he flat-out hadn't heard his pager at 3:00 a.m.

He did deserve more appreciation for being brilliant than he ever got from that second-rate data services facility. The universal Y2K coding frenzy had ended the year before, and now he had new skills to offer. He would get a haircut, put on his suit and tie, and begin another round of interviews. He could shine his own bright light, his flair for solving technical issues beyond mere program logic. At age twenty-seven, he had plenty of time to start fresh, somewhere quiet, maybe in a suburban office park with open space and trees. Not in chaotic downtown San Francisco.

Darren rode the bus out Geary Boulevard into the foggy avenues and their rows of stucco buildings squeezed together. He focused on his second challenge: another place to live. In his head he created a chart of related concerns—weather, open space, noise, greenery—and rated locations he knew in each category.

Currently, he rented a room from a nurse named Cheryl. She had a small, ground floor two-bedroom apartment far from downtown. There'd been no "meet cute" or romance involved. He had found her room-to-rent flyer posted at a laundromat. She actually looked okay, had black hair like his and skin as pale as vanilla pudding. They both were rather thin. He liked how smart she was, but not that she was seven years older or four inches taller than him.

Darren normally traveled through life with few constraints beyond a job. Now, he didn't have to work for that fumbling company anymore, but another issue remained: a cat named Matthew.

Cheryl didn't understand the problem. She'd lived with pets most of her life. Five months ago, out of the blue, she'd brought home a four-year-old, part-Siamese rescue cat. He was supposed to be Darren's pet.

"For companionship," she said. "Evenings while I'm on shift and you're home. You'll like how smart he is."

"Look, Cheryl," Darren said, "I do some of my best work late, when I'm alone at home. I don't need distractions from a cat. Or any new responsibilities."

His logic didn't work on her. She was his landlady and she supported that four-legged aggravation, no matter what.

"Not to worry," she said in her gentle nurse's voice. "I have enough time and patience for you both. I'll make it easy on you. You can just enjoy his company and relax. He'll sleep nights in my room."

Okay, except that, if she worked an overnight shift, the cat's restless scratching at the furniture and howling and waking him too early made him crazy. Cheryl might be the kindest person Darren had ever roomed with, but he had to find someplace better. He made a plan and, once he did the deed, he did not expect to see her or the cat again.

Cheryl was currently in Mendocino for her sister Sheila's wedding, and would be there for another three days. Darren was not willing to wait around for her return, but he couldn't merely leave Matthew alone with some food, either. Neighbors freely pounded on the walls when the cat wailed his misery. It had happened every night since Cheryl left and they were going nuts next door. That morning, they'd complained in writing, both to him and the building manager.

Well, what if Cheryl's soon-to-be-ex-housemate took *his cat* up to her parents' loving arms in Mendocino? There must be lots of bugs and mice for Matthew to eat up there, like those he caught in a vacant lot when he slipped outside. Mendocino would be very convenient, with redwood trees to shred into slivers and a vast, environmentally correct cat box in the woods.

Darren had to be careful, though. He couldn't simply call Cheryl to explain his situation. Much better if he just showed up with the cat. From what she'd said about her family, they wouldn't be able to resist Matthew if she decided not to keep him. By then, Darren would be on his way, cat free. Next stop, a motel for much-needed sleep. Then, a visit to his father in Sacramento—possibly for quite a while, if any good jobs were available—despite how flat and boring the scenery was to him.

Darren quickly walked the last two blocks to their building. Cheryl had left the Sunday before, handing him her parents' contact info and a copy of the wedding invitation. She'd be helping with the preparations all week. Darren packed his belongings into two duffel bags and jammed them behind the back seats of his Mini Cooper. He grabbed Cheryl's box of Clif Bars to avoid stopping for a burger during the three-hour drive. Assuming it would spoil before her return, he filled his old thermos with milk. She had once teased him for drinking milk at dinner, like a kid. While his mother was still alive, she'd insisted he have milk with dinner. He still did. Rather than explain, he'd simply told Cheryl that milk made him feel healthy. Didn't nurses know about those things, anyway?

* * *

Later that afternoon, driving along the freeway helped Darren to unwind. However, that changed after he headed west from Cloverdale on the state highway. At times he had to slow down for one hairpin turn after another, causing a rumbling lurch when the ABS brakes kicked in. Shrill protests emerged from the cat carrier behind him. Matthew did not appreciate being jolted. If Cheryl were there, she'd say something to calm him down. Darren didn't.

He did glance over his shoulder a few times. A large sack with cat food and a couple of cat toys cushioned the laptop behind his seat. The carrier stayed wedged behind the passenger seat, rattling wherever the road was rough, his rolled-up down jacket stuffed against its door to hold it closed. He didn't have to look to know the cat was glowering at him.

Around sunset, a gusty rainstorm arrived from Oregon. Drenching rain and steeper slopes came all at once. Darren clenched the steering wheel tighter. He considered taking deep, yoga-inspired breaths, a hopelessly Cheryl thing to try. But no. He'd always scoffed when she recommended one of her calming routines. He reacted the same way to her sentimental side. She'd practically cried to see Matthew so frightened during the neighborhood fireworks for Chinese New Year.

Darren had been an only child. He imagined having Cheryl as a housemate must be like having a bossy big sister. She'd badgered him into getting health insurance when he admitted having none, insisted he buy a jacket for his first San Francisco summer, always left him reminders to get more cat food. Soon he could say goodbye to such annoyances. He would rather live alone.

The rain continued and lightning flashed up ahead. He saw a tree crash onto the road ahead, but swerved too late. The car slid sideways, over the shoulder, plunging down a good thirty feet into dense underbrush. Branches scraped the car as it careened between boulders in the mud. Finally, one front wheel sank into soggy debris near a fast-moving stream. The car listed to one side, the driver's door up in the air.

Stunned, Darren cautiously wiped blood from his forehead. Sharp pain shot along his right leg. He turned slowly to look behind him. The carrier was not where it belonged. It must have slammed against the shattered side window, which was mostly gone. The carrier was empty.

"Matthew? Where are you?" His voice sounded weak to him.

No response. He faced forward and clutched the steering wheel, leaning his head on his arms. Rain pounded hard on the car roof, then with more muted sounds, and finally with no sound at all as he blacked out.

It was still dark when he came to. The rain had stopped. His head and right shin throbbed every time he moved. The chaos behind him remained: no Matthew. Darren could only just reach his jacket and pulled it by a sleeve to cover himself. He couldn't stop shivering. A dank smell from mud and soggy leaves outside the car made him nauseous, though the car was dry inside. He heard only the rushing stream nearby.

He struggled to concentrate. Could he climb out of the car? No chance. What if he bled to death in that out-of-the-way ravine? What if a concussion had permanently damaged his thinking? He'd never had serious injuries before, never been adventurous enough for sports. He played quiet games, did puzzles. He never had tried to be brave or tough. Could he now?

He had to.

He took the deepest breath he could manage, let it out, then shouted as loud as he could.

"Get a grip, Darren Adams! You are not over with yet! Think straight, damn you!"

He tried to focus on what animals in danger would do. They'd go all out, smacking and gouging and hurtling themselves at whatever threatened them. Like Matthew with his toys. Cats are ferocious when their instincts kick in. If only he could borrow courage like that from Matthew.

That animal could survive on his own. Darren remembered when the cat had left a dead mouse at their back door and Cheryl said he'd brought them a gift. Matthew would catch moths and crickets, any small creatures with legs or wings, and happily eat them. He might be out there in the bushes, stalking breakfast already.

But what if Matthew couldn't climb or leap or capture anything? There was blood near the side window where he must have gotten out. What if he couldn't defend himself from bigger, wilder animals? They'd have instincts and appetites, too. Or what if another downpour started? The car could slide into that stream! Darren felt light-headed. His mind couldn't process all the dire possibilities, so much dread.

Darren shook his head. He always wanted to feel in control. He needed it too much; he could admit that now. At first, Matthew had shown a softer side, acting friendly towards him, but Darren had pushed him away. Today, the cat had been a pawn in a game Darren had not mastered. He'd put Matthew in a desperate situation—a car wreck out in the woods at night—presuming that only his own problems were important.

What could Matthew possibly do if a coyote or mountain lion found him out there? If he couldn't run, would he hiss and growl or shriek his piercing yowl? Attack?

Darren wanted to cry. Matthew didn't deserve any of this.

He shouted through the broken window. "Matts! Where are you? Come back! I'll keep you safe! I won't leave you here!" His voice wavered. "Matthew? Please, come back!"

Nothing. No cries, no movement in the shadows.

Darren found his thermos on the floor. He opened it and took three cautious swallows of the milk. Then he carefully poured some into the cup for Matthew.

With that, he felt as though his heart had somehow opened for the first time. Maybe, after Matthew came back, he would want to stay. Would he rest, purring on his lap? That would be so reassuring, so comforting. Like they were friends.

There was nothing else he could do but hope.

* * *

Soon after sunrise, workmen arrived to clear the fallen tree and discovered the wrecked car. The driver was conscious, though his hair was matted with blood. A cat lay curled on the man's lap with a bandana wrapped around its foreleg. They shared a scruffy down jacket draped over them.

One of the men radioed dispatch to contact Highway Patrol to get an ambulance, then Animal Control to handle the cat. He told the EMTs who arrived, "Except for all the blood, those two in the car almost looked cozy."

His partner stared at the slope where the car had slid down and stopped just above a swollen stream.

"They had really good luck going for them. That was one mean storm. Water getting inside their car would've been a disaster."

Two hours later, Darren called Cheryl's family from a clinic in Mendocino. Her brother, Shawn, persuaded her not to leave the wedding rehearsal since he could go. When he arrived, Darren's leg was in a cast, his scalp wound sutured, and all of his paperwork was done.

Shawn maneuvered the wheelchair outside and sat on a conveniently placed bench. Darren admitted he couldn't see returning to San Francisco. Beyond the damage to his car, much of his technical gear was smashed and he had no job back there.

"There's little chance I'll have a quick recovery," he said. "I may move back to Sacramento with my father, though that would be awkward. I keep telling him how independent I am."

Shawn said, "You're welcome to stay with us here. The animal hospital isn't far away." He pointed at Darren's leg. "The same for any doctors you'll need."

"Thank you, Shawn. You are so like your big sister." He smiled. "But … could we possibly go see Matthew today? They told me he got stitches."

"Sure thing. And next week, I can help you look into some tech jobs here, if you want."

Darren sighed and took a long look at the forested hills nearby. "I would love to stay someplace like this, away from the city. I could finally learn to ease up a little."

* * *

Confined in the wreckage of his car, Darren had become aware that something he'd longed for was already there for him. He hadn't believed he could show strength unless he had firm control of a situation. Yet here, Matthew had trust in him or he wouldn't have come back. Darren had calmed his frightened companion, and Matthew had comforted his lonely friend.

He had learned much more than that. There was a richer way to live than being trapped inside his own needs and weaknesses. Darren had found a better place, and he wanted to stay.

A Short Sweet Life
Alethea Eason

Legends say Merpeople lure humans to Neptune's depths, but none of us come this way unwillingly. There is always a desire for death, or for passion, or to become part of a myth. Merpeople are the ghosts of the sea. Once we transform, we long to be part of both worlds.

We swim beneath the shadows of whales, eat abalone straight from the shell, and go to the ancient theater to watch the original versions of legends. We will live in robust health until the sun goes supernova. But the memories of our terrestrial lives never fade. We long for air and sun, the gray fog on our faces, the sensation of sunlight on skin, the soft texture of a rose, a good Merlot, having toes again.

But the bonds with people we once loved hold the most power.

The day I met my first mermaid, I was stupid and went out snorkeling alone after a fight with my wife.

I don't think the mermaid noticed me until I'd swum beyond the rocky outcrop that lay a hundred yards from the beach. The sun in her hair sparked like electricity, a phosphorus red, and was long, like you'd expect a mermaid's hair to be. Her tail was red, more bronze than her hair, but the scales that laced over the skin sparkled with aquamarine iridescence. She slipped through the sunlit waves. Indigo sparks flashed, followed by deep purple ones, then a violet afterglow.

My eyes strayed from breast to her tail and back again.

I guess that puts me in Neptune's passion category.

"Welcome," the mermaid said when she surfaced again. "My name is Marie. I'm so glad you made it out this far."

A large wave broke, sooner than it should have. I looked back to shore and realized I was in trouble. The sky was still clear, but farther out the water was lifting again. My heart stopped when I realized the crest would break right in front of me. I held my breath for three long seconds as the wave crashed down.

When the water retreated to Neptune, Marie seemed unperturbed as she watched my body thrash. When I finally was still, just floating there, she flicked her tail. My wetsuit dissolved and I found my legs encased in twenty pounds of blubber and scale.

Marie had to know I wasn't going to be some hunky merman specimen, but I don't think it mattered to her. Still, I was uneasy. I had lost the prescription mask I needed for my nearsightedness, but my anxiety faded when I realized I could see just fine. And my naked body with its new jade green tail was comfortable in the frigid Pacific water. Once I stopped fighting the shape of my new body, relief washed over me. The only thing that clouded the moment was the grief of knowing I left my wife Emily alone. Back on land.

Marie whisked the water with her tail flirtatiously. I let myself drift. I've worn a ponytail since my early twenties, and she swooped past my head and freed my hair. I wondered if the mermaid magic would make me younger. But alas, my receding hairline was still there. I was destined to be fifty-two for eternity.

The sunlight shone through the first few feet of water. I looked down to where a cluster of pink sea anemones swayed on a small hill of submerged rock. Their silky arms snatched at the mitochondria that floated by them.

Marie swam so close I felt her body tickle my back. Then she was in front of me, holding my waist. "Why do you think of her?"

Telepathy, of course, the next evolution after cell phones. Merpeople were a little ahead of their landlubbing cousins.

"Her? You mean my wife, Emily? That's private."

She wrapped her arms around my neck and pressed closer. I felt myself stir. I couldn't help but be curious about what was going on beneath my waist. I withdrew to discover I had a pouch, much like a codpiece of old. She didn't have one.

"Your thoughts are so much on the surface anyone could read them," Marie told me. "You'll have to dig down with your mind, learn to ink out your thoughts if you're going to have any privacy."

Well, there was nothing private about what poked against my codpiece. She slowly oozed down my body. I sucked in water and began to choke. She looked up.

"Breathe through your gills," she commanded, sounding agitated.

I let go and forgot about everything.

Even my wife.

I might have been dead, but what did it matter? At that moment, I felt more alive than ever."

I didn't know at the time Marie had a reputation. She greeted many men who were entranced by her and swam too far into the Pacific. There were tales I heard later about how she had a knack for knowing when someone was going to be swept overboard. She could gauge the rough waves that assaulted the native fishing boats, could sense sailors who got drunk enough to fall from schooners or from the occasional yacht.

I'd come from an empty shell of a marriage to this exquisitely sensual new existence. The failure wasn't my wife's fault. We both had demanding jobs. By the time we came home at night, we were exhausted and collapsed into bed. And there were twenty-seven years of marriage behind us. I married young, at twenty-five. For the first time since we exchanged vows, I now had an opportunity to make my own life.

Marie took me to her chamber in Dea Oceanus, the mermaid city ten miles off the Bodega headland.

She was my everything at first—an anchor to my strange new existence, the cloud of anesthesia that numbed me to the terrestrial world I left behind. I believe she would have been happy to live in polyamorous harmony if given the opportunity. But when she heard that her main squeeze had returned from the water of his youth off the coast of Barcelona, Marie showed she was indeed a mermaid who changed with the tides.

"You couldn't stay with me forever, anyway," she consoled me as she took off a strand of pearls and put them over my head. "You can pay for a year's lodging with these. There's an inn a few towers from here. A perfect hiding place. I can visit you there."

She tried to kiss me, but I pulled away. "I don't know anything about him," I grumbled.

"Juan? He's a poet."

I grew cold sober. "And I'm an electrical engineer. What does that have to do with anything?"

Marie's bottom lip extended into a pout. Emily would brood rain clouds when she was mad, but she never acted coy. I suddenly missed how my wife's silence kept me company. How she'd suddenly break out of the darkness and flash a smile that brought spring to me even in January.

"I'll find my own way," I insisted as I swam out Marie's door.

I kept the pearls. I exchanged half of them for a modest apartment near the city portal. Before I took up residence, I had to pass through a fleshy membrane that cleansed parasites from anyone entering the city from the greater sea. When I went through the border between the two worlds, I felt like I was being massaged by two pieces of liver. Once I was on the other side, the Pacific Ocean found its voice. It sang to me. Music enveloped me like the breath of the sea, rolling waves and rain, crystal chimes and Celtic harps.

The pearls Marie gave me wouldn't last forever. I became acquainted with a portal guard at a sushi bar and learned that the city would appreciate my earthly skills as an engineer to keep Dea Oceanus hidden from the terrestrial world.

As the city grew over the century, its presence needed to be masked. As you might imagine, only a handful of mathematicians, physicists, and engineers with the vision and skills to do this type of work had crossed over the mer-vail. I was a hack compared to most of them, but I could work on the power array that amplified the protective frequency. I worked alongside a crew of bio-engineered octopi. I enjoyed the work and their company.

One night, after having a few beers made from bladderwrack and a sweet kombu fermented with phytoplankton, a knock on my door startled me. I opened it to find Philippe, Marie's octopus butler, standing on his two modified legs. He held a letter out in a free hand. Yes, he was an octopus, but he had tiny little hands.

"Mademoiselle Marie requests that you read this."

The next day at work, I couldn't hide my thoughts of what Marie and I could do together if we met again. That whole telepathy thing.

George, one of the big minds of the operation, a jovial merman with ebony skin and bronze cauda, caught me mid-thought. "Hey, get your head out of your tail."

I blushed, feeling like a boy who just entered puberty.

He looked angry, but then a wide smile broke across his face. "You've been entertaining the crew all morning." He lowered his voice and tapped the side of his head. "Imagine steel walls. Have you started to receive thoughts yet?"

I shook my head.

"You will. We all leak our secrets from time to time. Just ignore it. After a while, it'll become background noise. Which is good because we'd all be insane." He smiled again. "That Marie, she's merciless. Your girl, she's wicked, man. She greeted Harry the same way she did you. I'd steer clear of him until he calms down."

Then he leaned in and told me everything he knew about Marie.

Before we got back to work, he put a big hand on my shoulder. "Every one of us has been tempted to look to shore. The ones who are most haunted will even leave. When you hit that wall and want to go home so bad you can taste that steak on the grill, you come talk to me. You don't want to ever go back. You're likely to get stuck. Then the clock starts to tick."

And so I lived my life as a geeky merman. George was right. The murmuring of the thoughts did leak into my head from time to time. I let them spiral through me like a cloud of silvery sardines.

I don't get poetry myself, but Juan Nicolas Montañez Diaz turned out to be a rockstar in Dea Oceanus. One day, I was having a lovely swim through the water gardens. The water level there was always low so citizens could breathe air as they perched on little raised islands. Palm trees with enormous fronds shielded me from the artificial sun that beamed from the highest building in the distance. A double rainbow arched across everything.

I heard Juan the poet's voice first and turned into a crowded canal. He sat on what looked like a throne on a raised platform. Marie sat at his feet. She clutched her pearls like a rosary and had such an adoring look on her face, my stomach turned.

Was she praying or just entranced by the melody of his voice? I wondered.

My face grew red as I remembered how Marie initiated me into becoming a merman.

Suddenly, Juan stopped reciting. His voice in my head sounded as weary as I felt the day I drowned. "You are just one of many," he sighed.

Marie heard him too. She glanced up, saw me, and swam away as he began to recite his poetry again.

After that day, I yearned for my old life. The desire to feel Emily reach for my hand, to see Emily's lips curl into a half-smile, made me weep. Early one morning I decided I'd had enough. Despite George's warning, I swam out of the city gates and made my way home.

After all, death was just a metaphor, wasn't it? In the mythic, anything is possible. Even being reborn to the life I abandoned. I swam to the east, to the California shoreline I knew so well.

The outcrop where I first saw Marie called to me like a beacon. As soon as I reached the other side, where the sand met the breaking waves, a circle of fire seared my torso. My tail was ripped from me, and I was in my wetsuit again. I sighed in relief. I was glad I didn't come back naked and have to explain that to the Bodega Bay police. I stumbled out of the water and found my pickup parked where I'd left it. The keys were still there, hidden inside a magnetic case on the undercarriage. According to the clock in the truck, only a few hours had passed. It was still early afternoon. Traffic was light as I headed home, which was a good thing. The trip between worlds left me disoriented, like I'd smoked an entire joint.

I walked inside our house. Its normalcy, the sweet mundaneness of my easy chair, my stereo with the stack of LPs I hadn't put away for months, the sight of Emily's sandals upside down beneath the coffee table, all of it made me quiver.

Emily came out of the bedroom, her white robe wrapped around her.

I gasped.

"You look so beautiful."

My wife scowled at me. "I was worried sick about you. I was about to call the sheriff. Don't you ever go out there again alone!"

Ah, yes. That was what our fight was about. My being a thoughtless idiot.

"I'm sorry, Emily. You were right. I did have a scare out there."

She let her robe fall open.

She nodded, but then her face became a question. "I went to the beach and watched you for a while today. I saw a woman out there with you."

I opened my mouth but stood there like a fish trying to gulp air.

"A moment later, she was gone. I don't think you saw her."

I inhaled, but I felt a ghostly mertail instead of two feet.

"I think I saw a mermaid, Greg." Emily looked at me, her lovely brown eyes wet and glistening. "That's crazy, right?"

I pulled her to me. "No, I saw her too. She wanted to seduce me and join her forever in the sea."

"Well, she should have known better. You'd never leave me."

The next morning, I called the office and took all the vacation days owed to me. I convinced Emily to do the same. My wife and I have been reborn. But it's been a year, and the doctor just called. He says the tests I recently took show something has happened to my blood. When I pressed him, he told me I'm dying.

I ended the call and set down my phone.

My blood is too full of the sea. I'm dying. Dying to return to my Marie.

Gold Country Hillside
June Gillam

Gracie stood at the kitchen sink, staring out her window. Lumps of quartz poked up through patches of dry grass on the hillside. The earth looked dead this morning and now it covered up her two darlings. Special rocks marked their resting place. For all she knew, animal bones from over the centuries kept them company. There could even be some unlucky prospectors from when the Forty-Niners pickaxed all over these hills, afire with gold rush fever, ripping up the Mother Lode.

She began washing the dishes by hand for the soothing feel of the hot soapy water and because she had little else to occupy her time. She studied the view out the window and frowned. Was she imagining things? Were those sinkholes on her hillside? A year or so back, a guest had said he sensed their house sat in a vortex. "Your place could get folded up into the earth," he'd pronounced. "Any slight shift in the Maidu Fault, and boom, you're gone." The man was a new acquaintance, a tall, thin coin collector who shopped at Don's store in Placerville. Don always invited the important buyers back to the house; he said it made them feel special. The man's remarks had slipped Gracie's mind until this morning.

Don had died a few weeks ago, his massive energy depleted, his health ground down by the press of business. It wasn't easy making a living buying and selling precious metals. She had looked the other way at some of his practices; everyone had a streak of gold fever in them, after all.

When he realized how sick he was, he made her promise to scatter his ashes on the hillside. He said he wanted to give back to the earth and be near their stillborn daughter, Rachel. Before the cremation, the attendant had handed Gracie a small velvet pouch. "His gold ring," the attendant said in a low tone. At her puzzled look, he continued, "The metal." She nodded, and the next day she got the never-worn gold infant bracelet out of her jewelry box. She slipped it into the small pouch containing Don's wedding ring, hung it from a silk cord and wore it around her neck.

She'd secreted herself in the house ever since she sprinkled Don's remains on the hillside over the place where Rachel lay. The gravel-like ashes, particles of bone, had slipped quickly below the dry grass and vanished into the scarred earth. After that, a lassitude embraced Gracie's every waking hour.

Today, standing at the kitchen sink, she barely felt the hot water sluicing the mound of dirty dishes that seemed to have grown in the sink of their own accord. She squinted at the brown hillside and the new potholes. A dozen green shoots had poked their way up through the dead grass. The spade-shaped leaf tips looked to be in a spiral, a sort of maze etched on the earth. A memory of that tall coin collector and his "vortex" sprang to her mind. She shook the suds from her fingers, ran to her office and typed "vortex" into her computer.

> vor·tex | ˈvôrˌteks | noun (plural **vortexes** or **vortices** | -təˌsēz |) a mass of whirling fluid or air, especially a whirlpool or whirlwind: *we were caught in a vortex of water* | *figurative : a swirling vortex of emotions.*

Was that spiral of green shoots on the dry hillside some kind of sign? She shook her head. No. She gazed out her front window at the Sierra Nevada in the distance, naked of snow. Lying low between the mountains and her custom-built home, a gated community sprawled across the depleted earth of the gold rush days.

Gracie went back to the kitchen. Looking at the hillside was giving her the creeps. The earth had swallowed up Don's ashes. Now he was down there with their baby girl, and she was up here all alone.

She lowered the window shades. She had to get herself out of the house. Go see how Riley was doing running the store. She wasn't ready to let Don's hard work vanish without a trace. People cared about their collections of precious metals and coins. Silver. Gold. Gifts of the Magi. She should preserve Don's legacy.

In town, she parked her white Mercedes in the narrow lot. Two men in dark suits were getting out of a black sedan next to her car. A tingle ran through her veins. She decided to visit the drugstore first. Get a milkshake at the old-fashioned fountain Harry Jr. prided himself on keeping.

While the teenaged soda jerk fastened a stainless-steel mixing cup into the blender, Gracie went to the back office. Harry was bent over his computer, as usual. "What's up, Harry?"

"Gracie!" The slim young man stood and hugged her. "Just keeping current with my former colleagues. Good to see you in town. Been worried about you out on that hillside all alone."

"I'm keeping busy," she lied.

"You ever want to come stay with Dad and me, just come on down. We've got that little cottage out in the yard, you know. You helped us with Mom, and we'll never forget it."

Gracie flushed. "How sweet of you."

"Dad says it's only right we should help you out now." He took her elbow and gestured toward the counter. "Looks like your shake's ready." He peered with squinted eyes. "I'm guessing you ordered peanut butter?"

Gracie laughed and nodded as she walked alongside Harry Jr., toward the counter.

"Especially since all this talk…" he said as she stepped up to the swivel chair and reached out for her milkshake.

"What talk?" She took a sip of her shake and licked her lips.

"Probably means nothing, but rumors are that the Maidu Fault has been active. Just talk, you know."

Gracie set her tall, thick glass on the counter and stared at Harry.

"A couple of my old buddies at the casino think you'll be able to tell earthquakes are coming by the lights. Mother earth shining over what she wants to take back."

Gracie's jaw dropped.

"But most guys in the seismic department don't give those native superstitions the time of day. I kinda miss working there, but got to keep this place going and care for my dad. Don't you worry, I think you're safe up on your hill."

Gracie rubbed the velvet pouch hanging from the black silk cord around her neck. "I've already turned over my most precious ones to the earth."

* * *

She walked half a block and entered Nuggets R Us, dismayed to see no one in the front of the shop. Her heels clicked loud on the old plank floor as she went to the back. In the office, she found the two men in black suits she'd seen in the parking lot. They stood in front of Riley, seated at Don's old desk.

"Customers complaining about delayed or unfulfilled orders," the short blond man told Riley.

Riley stood. "This is the owner's widow, Gracie Voss." He nodded to the men who maintained their erect postures while whipping out their badges.

"Secret Service, ma'am," said the plump man with the salt and pepper hair.

Gracie leaned against Don's tall black iron safe to keep from trembling. "Secret Service? We have nothing to do with the President."

"It's our job to investigate financial crimes. If coins are not delivered within twenty-eight days of receiving payment, it's our job to start asking questions, ma'am."

"Well, nothing is amiss here, is it, Riley?" She thumbed the velvet pouch around her neck and held it steady against her heart. "Everything's in good order, I'm sure."

The blond man nodded. "Have you been involved in the business, ma'am?"

"She's never worked in the back here," Riley said, wiping his forehead with a blue paisley handkerchief. "I've been running the store since Mr. Voss took ill."

The Secret Service agent turned to Riley. "Have you accepted payments for orders you knew could not be fulfilled?"

Riley sat down on his wooden swivel chair. "This kind of work puts a lot of pressure on a man. There's been a downturn in the coin business, you likely never heard tell of. Mr. Voss, he ended up taking it hard. I suspect you men might simply be looking at a miscommunication situation." Riley wiped his mouth with his handkerchief.

The blond agent asked, "Mind if we look through your paperwork?"

"I most certainly do," said Gracie, suddenly riveted with a steely resolve. "I know you must need a search warrant or something like that."

Just then, a voice called from the front of the store. "Hallo! Anyone here?"

Gracie left the back office and was stunned to recognize the tall, thin man who'd been to her house last year. "Yes," she said. "I'm here. What can I do for you?"

"You mean what did you do *to* me? You and that scumbag of a husband of yours. Overpricing rare coins and going back on return guarantees!"

Gracie's mouth flew open. With a shaking hand, she clutched at the velvet pouch. "I'm sure there must be some reasonable explanation."

"I was inspired to invest in precious metals after hearing Don tout them in the event of a 'world financial collapse,'" he said. "I looked at coins as insurance. Better than my savings." He glared at Gracie. "And I paid handsomely! But I never got my coins."

He marched to the back room. "Been keeping track of you Secret Service boys. Glad to see my complaints on victimizing investors finally produced some action." He whirled around to tower over Gracie.

"Your greedy husband skipped out of this life before he could get the payback he deserved, years in the pen for defrauding clients. I'm not doing this just for myself," he said, giving her a stern look, "but for the New York police captain, a 9/11 responder. He lost his retirement savings, began abusing prescription drugs, and now he's dead."

Gracie stood in shocked silence as the man continued his tirade. "A retired Air Force veteran from Kentucky never received his $10,000 order of American Eagle silver coins, although he paid the price. It's not fair Don didn't have to pay any price." He shook his finger in Gracie's face, drained of color. "And you haven't had to either!"

She whirled around, a cape of guilt falling on her shoulders, and ran out to her car.

* * *

She sat clutching the steering wheel, breathing fast and hard. No wonder Don had been so sick. His heart gave out. He had been about to get caught. What should she do? How much money would it bring to sell the store? Enough to make things right for those people? She drove halfway back up the hill before she saw spinning balls of light rising from the ground and hovering in the air.

The car radio blared the news. It was a 4.9 earthquake. Not major. The announcer warned the public to be ready for aftershocks. Gracie parked at the end of their street. Her house was shaking, tiles falling off the roof. She sat paralyzed, fascinated. Then she felt an odd compulsion to get out of the car.

The air had turned hot under a dark sky. There was a wild wind blowing. A crack in the street emitted smoke as it widened into a yawning maw. Ashes flew through the air, blinding her. She knew what to do. Clutching the small velvet bag holding her gold, Gracie stumbled forward. Chunks of quartz shot into the sky, leaving holes in the hillside. Her heart was in her throat. Her blood surged in her veins. She felt herself spinning in a dance with unseen forces. Relieved, she stepped onto the slope of the hill, into the hungry mouth of the Mother Lode, ready to pay the price.

Eviction
Joan Goodreau

Anna lay on her hospital bed and watched the gray walls and curtains of the hospital room turn into a fog. The doctor said she had to have this operation. That thing that lived inside her had to go. But what if the doctor was wrong?

A squat figure covered in greasy gray hair sat on a chair beside her bed, clutching a limp bouquet of dandelions. He plucked a chocolate from her candy box on the bedside table. "Ah ha. Having second thoughts, are you? I knew it. You still have time to change your mind before that needle guy comes in."

"Do you have to follow me everywhere? Stop eating my chocolates!" said Anna. She squirmed away from him on her mattress. "I don't want you around. You're an ugly lump that somehow wound up in my breast."

Lump reached out to take her hand.

Anna grabbed her hand away. "You're an unwelcome guest that's overstayed his welcome. We've got to end this relationship right now. We're splitting up."

"Honey bunny, don't do anything rash. Just calm down."

"Lump, I'm going in for this serious operation, and you tell me to calm down."

"You don't have to agree to this icky surgery. Trust me, no one knows you the way I know you and your heart. After all, I do live right over your heart."

Lump moved closer to her, but Anna pushed him away. "Look my crazy lodger, if I don't take you out, you're going to live over my heart and everywhere else in my body. I'm not going to let that happen."

"Don't be so dramatic. Stop and breathe. Breathe in. Breathe out. Deep cleansing breaths."

Anna yawned and closed her eyes. Lump gently nudged her. "You've listened to the wrong people. There's still time to stop this operation. Think about our future together."

Anna opened her eyes. "That's the whole point. My future is all you and no me. I never invited you. You just snuck in one day."

Lump bent over her and said, "You can't blame me. I was just cruising your blood stream and hit what I thought was a cloud formation, soft like cotton."

"I never thought of my breast as a cloud formation."

Lump held her hand and said, "That's because you're looking at 'em from the outside. I've got the inside perspective. They're soft and comfy, like pillows."

"Lump, that's gross. I never even knew what you looked like until I got a good look at that x-ray."

"They took my bad side. I've had better mug shots."

Anna took a mirror from her bed-side table and told him, "Just look at yourself. You are one ugly, ugly lump."

Lump held the mirror close to his face, smiled, and waved at himself. "I've got those rugged he-man looks. Check it out. What's not to love?"

She held up her hands to block him from her view. "You're getting bigger and stronger. You've got to go. But I still wish the doctor hadn't rushed me into all this."

He sat on the bed, squinched his face and whispered, "You're scared, aren't you? What if you go to sleep and don't wake up? What if that scalpel slips? Oops."

She put her fingers in her ears. "I'm not listening to you. They told me I don't have a choice about this surgery. I have to go through with it."

Lump patted her shoulder and said, "Trust me, you always have a choice. You don't have to be butchered. There're all kinds of healing. There's ionic foot detox," he said and tickled her foot. "Or you could connect with your energy field and your harmonic beats." He clapped his hands near her pale face. "Or we could come together and integrate our expression of emotional fragility. More New Age, less bloody."

Anna shook her head and told him, "I don't need your fake remedies."

"There's always ionized water. We could drink that for a few months. Wait and see if it does us any good."

"Us? There is no us."

Lump danced a few cha-cha steps. "See what a fun guy I am?"

"Why can't you leave me alone?"

"We're meant to be together. It's fate, Kismet."

"Shush. I can't think straight with you around."

Just as Anna said those words, the anesthesiologist rushed in. "I'm sorry you can't think straight. The surgery is running a little behind schedule, so I wanted to reassure you we hadn't forgotten you."

"I still can't decide if I want this operation or not," Anna said.

The doctor smiled and said, "Time is running out. Your pre-op shot should come soon."

Lump squeezed between the anesthesiologist and Anna singing, "I've grown accustomed to your breast…"

"Stop. I want you out," said Anna.

"Okay. Okay. You don't have to get hostile," the anesthesiologist said, as he jumped away from her bedside and ran out of the room.

Lump plucked the wilted dandelion blossoms from her bouquet. "You're no fun anymore like you used to be."

"I'm not supposed to be fun. I'm supposed to be sick."

"Well, don't blame it on me."

"Of course I blame you. You're my disease."

"I've been called quite a few things in my life, but never a disease."

"Lump, you're a parasite, a leech."

"Anna, that's not so bad. We have a symbiotic relationship."

"You wear me out." She rolled away from the hairy lump. "I'm going to get some rest."

Lump paced the room. "I wish there was a TV in this room. There's a big cage fight on Channel 7 right now," he whined. "It's too bad we can't watch it together."

Anna closed her eyes to block her imaginary sight of two greased muscle men beating on each other. Lump walked around the bed and peered through the smeared glass of her small window. "There's a big, beautiful world out there. And it's all waiting for us."

Anna thought about the parking lot outside her window and saw nothing waiting for them. Lump said, "All we have to do is walk out together now and leave this dingy room behind." He heard Anna's soft snoring sounds. "I know you're just pretending to sleep. All right. Even if I can't watch my fight, at least I can have a cool one. Get me a beer, will you?"

"I must be dreaming. You sound like my ex. Where do you think you are? This is a surgery center, not a bar. Do you see a neon martini glass flashing on and off? And who do you think you are?"

"Someone who will always be true to you, honey bunny. There's never been anyone else."

"Really?"

"Well, except for that little lymph node I hooked up with."

"You're like my ex, just hairier."

"But it didn't mean anything. I'll never leave you, Babe."

"That's what I'm afraid of." She rolled out of bed. No more rest now. She had to make her decision.

Lump tried to put his arms around her, but she pushed him away. "You'll never leave, so I must evict you. I'm having this surgery, and I'm kicking you out."

Lump fell backwards, leered, and said, "If I ever went away, I'd leave a big old dirty scar. Then how will you look in your bikini?" He blew her a hiss.

Anna pictured her bathing suit with a skirt down to her knees and laughed. Lump asked how she'd look in a negligee for that special guy. But Anna said, "Don't even go there. I wear a jogging suit to bed, as you well know. You can't scare me with your scars."

"I don't want to scare you. I just want a little understanding." Lump sidled over to her.

"I don't want to understand you," Anna said and stomped on his webbed foot.

"Ow. It wasn't easy growing up. No one listened to me or understood me. No one wanted me around. And now you're rejecting me too," he sobbed.

"I don't want to understand you. You are inside me and you don't belong, like an alien from outer space."

"An alien like E.T.?"

"No, not a cuddly alien. You're going down." Anna poked him on his hairy chest, and Lump fell backwards. He tried to get up but was too weak.

"I don't feel so good. I feel…"

"Weak," Anna whispered into his pointy ears. "You're getting weaker and weaker."

Lump said in a whiny voice, "I don't want to die and end up in a specimen jar! I hope you're happy now. All you wanted to do this whole time was dump the lump, dump the lump, dump the…"

His body deflated into a shapeless blob. "Hasta la vista," she said and looked out her window. Lump was right about one thing. There was a big, beautiful world out there, and after this operation, she was going to get out and explore it. "I want to enjoy my new health with my children and grandkids. Maybe I'll take a cruise, learn French cooking, and start to write in my journal again."

The anesthetist peeked around the door to see if Anna was in a better mood. She smiled at him as he walked into the room and stepped over what looked like a furry, deflated inner tube. He picked it up and threw it in the Hazardous Waste container. "We're ready to go. What are you doing out of bed?"

"Looking at my new life."

Leaving Neverland
Pamela Heck

Marriages that end usually die slowly—like a lingering illness. At first, just a minor pain. "It's nothing," you tell yourself. The pain gets worse, but you put off going to the doctor, because you don't want to know. When you can't stand it anymore, you reach out for a diagnosis. Cancer. Everywhere. End of marriage.

I married Peter Pan. Ironically, his name was Peter, and he never grew up—not really. But when faced with a handsome, 6'3" man on a vintage, British racing green BMW, I wasn't thinking about what kind of husband this guy would make in the future. I was totally in the moment. He was hotter than the motorcycle engine revving for my attention.

Pausing the engine, he gave me "the look." I'd already been looking. The horned Viking helmet he sported made for an easy conversation opener.

"Nice helmet."

"Nice legs."

"Nice bike."

"Hop on. Take you for a spin?"

I froze like a deer in his headlight, torn between fear and desire. We hadn't even been introduced and motorcycles scare the hell out of me. Not that I intended to divulge that fact. Just how daring was I?

He dismounted and held out his hand.

I took it. "Amy," I said.

"Amy, it's a beautiful day for a walk in Golden Gate Park, but an even better one for a ride on a BMW. Name's Peter. I moved from Boston to San Francisco on this bike and never had an accident. I'll be careful. Promise."

I nodded. Peter smiled, straddled the bike, and motioned for me to hop on. When he kick-started the engine, I wound my arms around him and held on like my life depended on it. Maybe it did. He smelled like fresh air and aftershave. Our journey had begun.

Weaving through traffic on the Golden Gate Bridge terrified me, but the view from the top of the Marin Headlands made it all worthwhile.

"Baghdad by the Bay, my lady."

Magic. A dream. A romance novel come to life.

I would like to tell you I practiced restraint, that I wanted to make sure Peter respected me before giving in to my carnal longings. But I can't. Returning to the city, we gorged on Chinese food at Yet Wah, and ended the adventure at my place. I broke my no-sex-on-the-first-date rule. Full speed ahead.

Two months later, I gave up my apartment and moved into Peter's roomy flat on Pierce Street. Peter had boasted on one of our earlier dates that he loved to cook and enjoyed cleaning house. He neglected to tell me that, while he enjoyed cooking, washing up afterwards wasn't really his thing. As for cleaning—when I realized I'd be spending time at Peter's apartment, I showed up with a toilet bowl brush and gave the porcelain throne a much-needed cleaning. Nobody's perfect, right?

One might think that Peter and I would be in no hurry to trade our happy, living-in-sin life for one of wedded bliss. However, there were complications. When informed of our new living situation, my mother called in tears—numerous times—with the same message, "You're going to hell."

As for Peter's parents, a sudden longing for a California vacation overtook them. Mike and Sylvia booked a non-stop from Boston to San Francisco and spent a week with Peter and me. Their motive was transparent. They were checking out the floozie cohabitating with their precious son. The pressure was on.

I slept in a bit in the mornings so Peter could spend some alone time with his parents. They pumped him for information. As God fearing Catholics, they did not approve of our living situation. Were we serious? What were his intentions?

On day one, Peter told his parents we had made no plans for the future.

On day two, Peter told his parents, "It's serious."

On day three, Peter told his parents, "I'm in love with her."

On day four, he told them, "We're getting married." They found out before I did.

Peter and I decided against a diamond engagement ring in favor of two simple gold bands. We didn't need no stinking diamond and, frankly, we couldn't afford one. At the time, Peter managed a motorcycle shop, and I taught English and art at a private school in the city. We didn't have much money, but we had enough to spend weekends traveling around the Bay Area on Peter's BMW or my VW bug. On Saturday mornings, Peter played soccer. The rest of the weekend belonged to us. We explored Gold Country, visited a yoga farm, attended concerts at the Fillmore and Stern Grove. We went all in on the Renaissance Fair. Peter dressed as the Lord High Executioner and I as his wench. We should have charged for all the photo ops people demanded.

Peter and I chased each other around the apartment with toy guns that shot foam arrows, gave each other massages on the kitchen table and made love on a waterbed that felt like sex at sea. I asked myself, "If nothing changes. If Peter never changes. Will this be enough?" And I answered—"Yes! Definitely, yes."

We got married at city hall—a small ceremony but beautiful, nevertheless. My mother came and so did Peter's parents. We reserved the space for Saturday afternoon. Peters insisted we coordinate the wedding with his soccer schedule. His teammate, David, was the best man and Linda, my closest friend, the maid of honor. Most of the soccer guys came. Having celebrated their team's win earlier in the day, they were all drunk, including the best man. Peter seemed OK. His parents were disappointed that we didn't have a Catholic wedding. No priest, just a Justice of the Peace. When Linda preceded me down the aisle, one of the guys shouted, "You look beautiful, baby!" My mother looked pained. She would have liked a big church wedding. But the photos taken of Peter and me posed on City Hall's ornate staircase were stunning.

We held the reception at a friend's restaurant, after which Peter and I got a hotel room for the night. We couldn't leave for our honeymoon because my mother's flight home didn't leave for two more days. I'm still not sure why and, fearing waterworks, didn't have the nerve to ask. Peter and I dutifully entertained her, got her to her flight, and finally embarked on our honeymoon. We stayed at The Fools Rush Inn in Mendocino. Ironic.

Peter and I were the fun couple. Everyone wanted to hang out with us. Peter quit his job managing the motorcycle shop and got a job as a claims adjuster with AAA. His specialty? Motorcycle accidents. I left the private school and got a public-school job at twice the salary. We were on our way.

So, we bought a house. It seemed like the next step. The Victorian cottage needed a kitchen and bathroom update, but it was cute and affordable. At least, I thought we could afford it until I caught Peter altering his W2 form.

"Peter, what are you doing?"

"I'm just making a few adjustments to make sure we qualify for the loan."

"Are you crazy? You can't do that. What if you get caught? It's illegal."

"Relax, Amy, you worry too much. Everyone wants this deal to go through. No one is going to look too closely at my W2."

They didn't. We owned a home. Real estate was booming. Peter quit his job and became a realtor. He promised he would make us rich, but it was a financial roller coaster—feast or famine. Too often, his "sure deals" fell apart at the last moment. Peter impressed his potential clients with custom, monogrammed shirts. I hesitated to buy a sale blouse at Macy's.

We still ran around the house now and then, shooting each other with foam arrows. We still spent weekends exploring the Bay Area. However, the waterbed wasn't getting the same workout, and I was increasingly the brunt of Peter's "jokes"—little zingers that stung. If I appeared wounded, if I defended myself, I just "couldn't take a joke." He was in rare form at my school's staff Christmas party. I don't remember the punchline, but the "joke" opened with, "My wife is so lazy she…" It opened the door for a complete monolog at my expense. At school the following Monday, the guidance counselor ran up to me, threw his arms around me, and said, "I hate when he talks that way to you." People noticed. I felt humiliated.

* * *

Interest rates rose and the real estate market took a dive. We lived on my teacher's salary. I went to school every morning. My depressed husband stayed in bed. Since we couldn't afford our house, we sold it, packed up our belongings and moved to Sonoma County. I got a teaching job in Santa Rosa and Peter, for the second time, became a claims adjuster. We rented a house in the country and planted a garden.

Peter joined another soccer league. We made new friends, had a new lease on life. Things seemed good. So why wasn't I happier? The carefree life I'd envisioned for the two of us had vanished. I'd been married for five years and spent a lot of that time worried about money (or lack of), worried about Peter's job prospects (or lack of) and was exhausted from teaching and taking care of a house. I wasn't getting much help from Peter on the home front.

"Peter, can we come up with a plan for chores? It doesn't seem fair for me to be doing all the cleaning and cooking."

"You're right, babe. Why don't you make a schedule, and we'll sit down and go over it."

So, I did. It was Peter's job to do the dishes and take out the trash. I'd cook and vacuum. We'd both pick up after ourselves. Peter looked at the plan and agreed, but the garbage smelled, and the dishes piled up in the sink. Was he trying to wait me out, thinking I'd give in and wash the damn dishes?

"Peter, how can you justify letting the dishes pile up like that?"

"I can't," he said, smiled and left.

What can you say to that?

* * *

Every year, on the Fourth of July, our friends Don and Marion had a blow-out party. When we walked through the door, someone winked and said, "Try the brownies." They were delicious. Several hours later, after the food and fireworks, those brownies really kicked in. For the first time in months, I felt amorous.

Returning home, Peter asked, "Is it safe?"

"Sure!" I replied.

It wasn't. Six weeks later, the test confirmed my suspicions—pregnant. It wasn't planned, but I was excited. Still, it would require planning. The baby was due in March. I'd take a maternity leave at the end of February and return to work the following September. I'd have to find childcare. We'd have to manage on one salary for a while. The doctor's office called with big news, "It's a boy." We signed up for Lamaze classes and argued over names. I wanted to name the baby Ethan. Peter wanted Brett.

I went to school every day. Peter worked from home. Shortly after the baby news, Peter announced he was drowning in paperwork and headquarters had authorized the hiring of a part-time secretary. We knew Rhoda slightly through mutual friends. She had recently lost her job at a bank. Perfect timing. Or was it?

Peter and I bought a crib and set up the baby's room. Finding me surrounded by baby paraphernalia, Peter demanded to know, "Whatever happened to the spontaneity in our marriage?"

Onesies, diapers, a changing table—so many necessities. The list seemed endless. And we still hadn't settled on a name. Then, one day, I arrived home to a beaming Peter. "You win," he said. "It's Ethan." I didn't know it then, but Peter capitulated because of a guilty conscience.

Ethan arrived two weeks early. It was a home birth. I'd already scheduled a visit that morning with the midwife to check out the birthing room. Nan arrived just as the contractions started. Peter announced he needed to pick up some supplies for us at Safeway. He was gone for hours and arrived just in time to see Ethan make his appearance. The little guy didn't even cry. I swear, when they handed him to me, he wore a little smile.

Three weeks later, I carried Ethan into Peter's office to relay something cute he did and found Peter and Rhoda in an embrace. I walked out, erased it, pretended I never saw what I saw. I had a baby. This couldn't be happening.

My denial was short-lived. Peter announced that he and Rhoda loved each other. I learned his trip to Safeway on birthing day had involved an amorous stop at Rhoda's. The end. He moved in with Rhoda, leaving me to figure out the logistics of caring for an infant as a single mother on maternity leave with no savings. How I managed is a long story. The important thing to know is that I did manage thanks to a kindly neighbor who took us in rent free for months, and a best friend who gave me the down payment on a house. Amazing, but true. Another friend fell in love with my smiling Ethan and broke the no-babies-rule at her home daycare. Miracles sometime do happen in modern times.

Peter lost his job several months after our split. Rhoda kicked him out. He couch-surfed with friends for months. Eventually, he found a new job and an apartment and became an active co-parent. Ethan is in high school and thriving.

* * *

As a child, I loved the story of Peter Pan. Like Wendy, I flew away with my Peter without a second thought. I chose Neverland and fairy dust. I should have read the story more carefully. Peter Pan didn't want a partner in adventure, he wanted a mother. In the end, the story isn't about Peter at all—it's about Wendy and growing up.

Being a single parent is less exhausting than living with Peter. When he left, I finally found myself—strong, resilient, capable, and FUN. I came to realize that freedom is more important to me than commitment. Commitment involves too many expectations and compromises. I never remarried. I doubt I ever will.

Perspectives from a Barstool
John Heide

He sat a few stools away from me at the bar, looking like someone to avoid. His disarrayed gray hair, overdue for a trim, spilled over the collar of a heavy coat he hadn't bothered to take off, despite the warm interior. I gauged him to have about fifteen years on me, with a handsome face that hadn't felt the scrape of a razor in over a week. He stared into his glass and seemed not to notice the comings and goings of patrons.

My inner voice told me to ignore him, but I was alone with too much time on my hands. There was something else going on here that I couldn't quite figure out. I kept glancing his way. I motioned to the bartender and leaned close to his ear to be heard over the jukebox. "What's the story with that guy?" My thumb flicked to the side.

The bartender raised his eyebrows and shrugged. "I don't know his whole story. You're not a cop, are you? He's never been in any trouble with the law that I know of."

"No," I said. "I'm just curious."

"I hear he wrote some books. Some people in town thought he was a big deal when he first moved here. Taught at the university for a while. Then I heard he got fired, and now he comes in here regularly. Pleasant enough, but doesn't talk with anybody."

I nodded. "Will you tell him I'll buy him a round?"

"He's not going to like that."

"Try it. I'll take my chances." The "something" kept nagging at me. I watched the bartender lean over the counter and speak to the man, who immediately turned and glared at me. He shook his head "no." I raised my hands in a gesture of surrender and made my face as friendly as I imagined it could be. Deciding to push my luck, I rose from my stool and approached him.

Inspiration struck at that moment. "I read your book," I blurted out when I was still ten feet from him.

His narrowed eyes showed a spark of interest, and his hand swiped across his mouth. "Oh, yeah? Which one?" he challenged.

"You know, it was a while back," I said, my mind racing with excuses. "That particular one eludes my memory right now."

What was I doing, anyway? Why was I so fascinated by this guy?

"You're full of shit," he muttered, keeping his head down and turning away.

I sighed. "Yup. That would be correct. But my drink offer still stands. I'd just like to talk to you."

"I'm not gay," he said, over his shoulder.

"I'm not, either," I said. He turned back to me, and we nodded as heterosexual men do after clarifying such things.

"Nothing wrong with it, you understand," he offered. "I have gay friends. I just didn't want you to be disappointed at some point."

"Of course."

"So why do you want to talk to me?"

"No real reason. I'm by myself and passing through. Sometimes I write about travels and people I meet. Whad'da ya say?" I waited for what seemed like a long minute.

"Not much of a story here," he said, scrutinizing my countenance. He glanced at his empty glass. "I drink whiskey."

I gave a thumbs up to the bartender and settled onto the stool beside the man. "Sorry to lead with bullshit, but it just popped out. I'm the curious sort." I stopped to gauge his reaction. None. "Everybody has a past. Don't know why, but you seem interesting," I added, with a hint of hopefulness in my voice.

"Interesting?" He spat. "I'll tell you something interesting." He paused, holding the whiskey inches from his mouth. "I entered this world out of a vagina and have spent the whole of my entire adult life trying to get back into one."

"Oh," I said. Not knowing where this surprise thread was leading, I turned to my own drink and kept quiet.

"They're better than us, you know. Men are so fucking stupid. And I'm right there out front, bearing the droopy testosterone-drenched flag." He blew out a long breath. "I know it's hard to believe, but underneath this debonair and sophisticated exterior beats the heart of a true, intelligent idiot."

"What do you mean by that?"

"I'm barely smart enough, or maybe I just pay more attention than most due to my profession, but I recognize that women have something we don't."

"What would that be?"

He chuckled. "Ha. Well, that's the thing, isn't it? No one has ever pinpointed exactly what it is, not even women. I, along with you and all men, certainly don't have a clue. The question chases an ever-morphing answer." He took a sip of whiskey. "Tell me this. How is it they can manifest peace amid strife, chaos, and war? Why can women create life, protect and nurture it in extreme circumstances while men consistently do their best to minimize their worth and meanwhile destroy everything around them?"

Like schoolboys reminded of their place in the pecking order, we remained silent. I took a sip.

"And they also manage to twist a man's mind into pretzels with ease, seemingly whenever the hell they want to," he added. Images of two past wives rose from my memories, along with my complicated girlfriend sitting back home right now. I very much hope to see her again. Maybe I will. Maybe not.

I noted the throbbing vein in his temple and changed course. "You mentioned your profession. And the books. What did you teach and write about?"

"Nothing you'd give a shit about. I taught social psychology and wrote a couple of boring treatises that only a handful of even more boring people read. Big fucking deal."

I nodded in sympathy, as my own writings have had little in the way of success or following. "Okay. Sounds like you had a life, maybe not so exciting, but a real career and everything. Now you're drinking whiskey with a stranger. What happened?"

He chuffed. "That will take another drink."

I ordered two more. After downing a half shot, he slammed his palm down on the counter. "Remember what I said about getting back into that holy grail of femininity?" He waited until I nodded in acknowledgement.

"Well?" he demanded. "You're not a stupid man. Use your imagination!"

"That's not fair," I said. "I can conjure up all kinds of deeds, some of them larger than others."

"Damn, don't even go there," he warned. "Everyone knew it was consensual, but she was a beautiful twenty-two-year-old student, and professors are supposed to be above all temptation. Big no-no. Her constant attention seduced and blindsided me. She seemed enthralled by my majestic maleness." He flourished a hand in an upward regal gesture.

He raised his gaze to the ceiling and shook his head. "History teaches that even intelligent idiots such as yours truly predictably get their hearts broken. I was compromising not only myself, but evidently, the entirety of higher learning. By the time I realized this, I had hopelessly fallen for her, but like a moth to flame, I went after it again and again. I finally chose to do the right thing, what needed to be done, and broke it off. On that wine-enhanced fateful last night, I so wanted to go there one more time, but instead, did the noble deed, told her it was over. I'll never forget the look on her face." He shook his head, gave a bitter laugh.

"Turns out, all she needed from me was a B or better grade in order to graduate. Sweet as honey, but her bulb was on the dim side, if you know what I mean, and having a tough go of it in school. Her papers and test scores were appalling by any standard, but I managed to grade this sexy, but academically challenged siren, with a barely deserved D, so she wouldn't fail the class. My magnanimous gesture was not greeted well."

"I can imagine," I said, shifting in my seat and trying to erase a few images of the siren from my mind.

"I underestimated her acumen when it came to calculated feelings. Three days later, the chancellor called me into her office and read me the email she had received from the young lady's attorney. Young people are very proficient with screenshots of their text messages, be forewarned. It didn't take long after that. The college settled out of court for a tidy sum, and I was out of a job. Not much more to say."

"In some big lesson learned kind of way, was it worth it?" I asked, expecting a complete supplication and apology to humanity.

"Of course it was!" He smiled and drained his glass. "I'm old enough to be thankful for it all. In the end, she taught me a lot about myself. It's all good. I can't blame her and bear no ill feelings. She used venerable female wiles and superior street smarts. I actually don't blame myself, either. We were using each other to get something. I wanted that elusive and wonderful feminine adoration that can masquerade as love. What she was after became more and more obvious once I blew it all up. We're all human animals and have sex and survival at a base level in our brains. Some, more than others, but our instincts are the same as they were in ancient times, now buried beneath our modern lifestyles."

"Yeah, I suppose. So, no regrets?"

"Only about a thousand." He snorted. "Give or take."

I leaned forward, my now blurry vision focused on my acquaintance. "C'mon, I want to hear a sample. I've got a few of my own."

He gazed at the ceiling for a moment. "The short snippets of conversation where I wish I would have said something different. The sideways glance from an interesting stranger that I could have pursued. You know, ships passing-in-the-night kind of moments. The turned-down invitation to go to Costa Rica with some friends. My inability to open up to my first true love. So many little things."

He stopped and stared straight ahead. "And not earlier realizing how bored I was in academia."

After a moment, he spun around and drilled me with his gaze. "Here's the thing about the past. It doesn't exist. You know what I mean? Now I look at my situation like the road under my feet. I could sit down, but I choose not to. I'm free to walk on and shed some baggage along the way."

"Yeah, I guess we've all got some baggage," I said.

"Well, my brand centered on needing others to love me. It feels like I chased that one my whole life. There was just a big ol' hole in me." He could speak no further. This world-weary wise man's eyes misted. We allowed a blessed silence.

After a few minutes, I broke in. "There's a ton of sadness in that tale. I'm thinking you should have better times than sitting in this place getting drunk and talking to a stranger."

"Yeah, that looks sad on the surface, but for the first time in my life, I'm okay with being alone. I like my whiskey, and once in a while I talk to nosy strangers." He shot a brief smirk in my direction.

"What's next for you?"

His eyebrows arched higher over eyes that showed a glimmer. "They say time heals. Well, I finally had a lot of that every day. So, I did a lot of thinking. I stretched my legs and brain in a different direction." His chin jutted out. "I finished a long-procrastinated novel, and much to my surprise, a publisher recently accepted it. It should be out pretty soon."

"Fantastic! Congratulations," I gushed with liquor-laden sincerity and, I had to admit, some envy. Images of my own rejected manuscripts flashed through my mind. "What's it about?"

He shrugged a bit sheepishly. "A murder mystery. The protagonist is a female detective. She's awesome and figures it all out."

"Of course," I murmur.

Excited chatter coming from the entrance disrupted our mutual whisky-fueled contemplation as two high-heeled women swept into the bar. They gave a cursory glance in our direction and sauntered over to a nearby table where a lot of hair flipping took place.

I nudged my new friend. He spun and glared at me. "We're not going there," he warned in a determined tone.

"We shall not! Or rather, we shall hold out as long as we can." I smiled and signaled for one more round. "I feel like this brief conversation has given me some real perspective. I admire the way you've bounced back and made changes in your life." I glanced over my shoulder at the women. "Perhaps someday I will also find a new path. But for now, the truth of it is, I'm still a moth."

The Locket
Lenore Hirsch

Eleanor walked briskly through the crisp spring air. She used to clock her times as she jogged in this park surrounded by vineyards. Now she enjoyed a slower pace. It was enough to feel her heart rate rise and to breathe rhythmically while her feet, hips, and arms moved of their own accord.

Lots of folks listened to music or books while they exercised or played podcasts. Eleanor would rather hear the birds and rustling of leaves. It was usually a meditative hour. Today, however, was different.

She couldn't get out of her head the unkind words spoken to her last night by that annoying Betty Stein. They had both been in the book group for years. Each of the twelve gals had a month assigned to pick the book they would all read. It seemed fair. The book Eleanor picked for this month was a lighthearted romance. Not a bodice ripper—those were ridiculous—but a sweet story about a woman left by her husband who finds love with someone new.

Most of the women enjoyed Eleanor's book, even if it was an "easy read." But Betty tore into it, and Eleanor fell into *her* for suggesting it. "I didn't feel it was worth my time," Betty said. "It's pretty lightweight. I'd rather read a book with depth."

The previous month, Betty had selected a novel set during the Holocaust. She introduced it, saying, "This book makes me feel more connected to my Jewish roots in Eastern Europe." Eleanor tried to read the book. It had too many scenes of cruelty and death. She put it away half-read and kept quiet during the group's discussion. The brutal Holocaust imagery made her shudder. *It's over. Why do I have to keep reading about it?* The group's next book would be a relief—contemporary fiction. If it included murder and mayhem, at least it would be on a smaller scale and not from real life.

Eleanor paused her walk and took a deep breath, relishing the sweet scent of blossoms on nearby trees. As she leaned forward for a long, satisfying exhale, something sparkled in the grass a few feet in front of her. Bending forward, closer inspection revealed a gold, heart-shaped locket on a slim, broken chain. An inlay of mother-of-pearl decorated one side. Engraved on the back were the faint initials, D H. Inserting her thumbnail, Eleanor popped open the locket to reveal a black-and-white photograph of a man and woman. Old-fashioned curls framed the woman's face. Lace adorned her throat. The man sported a long mustache, a stiff collar, and a fancy cravat. An old wedding portrait?

Eleanor saw nobody else on the trail whom she might ask about the locket. Such a shame. The gold heart must be a personal keepsake as well as an item of monetary value. She slipped the necklace into her pocket and zipped it up.

Back at home, Eleanor was eager to start the new novel for the book club. It turned out to be a detective tale about a female cop who interviewed people of interest, not at the police station, but at her favorite coffee shop. Finding her inquiry low key, the witnesses relaxed and let information fly that, under pressure, they might not have remembered. The murder at the beginning of the book was thankfully depicted without graphic details, and each chapter ended with a clue that made Eleanor want to keep reading.

Several days later, preparing to walk, Eleanor grabbed her jacket, felt something in the pocket, and remembered the locket. She took it out and rubbed her thumb over the smooth surface once again, turned it over to examine the engraving, and opened it to gaze at the photo. *Someone is surely sad to have lost this,* she thought. Leaving the locket on her desk, she went out for a walk, wondering, *how might I look for the owner?*

Later that day, Eleanor sat at her computer and opened the link to her NextDoor social media platform. Never having posted before, she laughed at the messages that received the most attention. "Can you identify this critter in my yard?" Or a dim photo of someone taken with one of those doorbell devices: "Do you know this person sneaking around my house?"

She found the place for a new entry and wrote: "Did you lose a piece of jewelry at Alston Park? Found near the entrance on March tenth, mid-morning."

Eleanor knew she shouldn't give details about the locket. That would only invite someone greedy to claim it. She listed her email and phone number and pushed send. She checked every day, but besides a few people thanking her for being honest, there were no leads. Until this response appeared: "There was a cross country meet that day. Perhaps someone from a visiting school lost the item you found? You might check with the high school."

This was turning into a detective story of its own. How many high schools were involved in the meet? She started by calling her local school and leaving a message.

Keeping the locket on her desk, she examined it again and again. To whom did it belong? Somebody's parents? Grandparents? She hoped the owner had another picture, as it looked like they weren't getting this one back. She was close to putting the locket in a drawer and forgetting it, when she received a phone message from a coach at the high school, "Thanks for calling. We've asked our students, and nobody has responded. If you want to contact the other schools, they're Patterson High and Adams High. Good luck."

Eleanor knew the nearby schools from the sports page. Was this worth more of her time? Well, to one young woman it could be. She called the two schools. Both secretaries promised to pass the message on to staff involved in the meet. Eleanor waited.

She had almost finished reading the new book. The clever and funny female detective followed the clues and taught a few things to the senior men on the force. Even when the clues didn't pan out, the detective didn't give up. Eleanor knew the sleuth would solve the case in the end. That's the pleasure of detective stories. She wondered if it had enough "depth" for Betty.

After a few days, Eleanor received a call from Patterson. Their students weren't missing anything. "One chance left," she said out loud. She returned from a walk to find this message from Adams High: "Thanks so much for being a good neighbor. Our student Vanessa Hilburn lost a family heirloom that day, and she's hoping that's what you found." The coach left Vanessa's cell phone number.

Eleanor's heartbeat quickened as she planned what to do next. She waited until early evening, hoping Vanessa would be available, and dialed the number.

"Is this Vanessa Hilburn?"

"Yes."

"Hi, my name is Eleanor and I'm calling about the lost jewelry. Can you describe it to me?"

Vanessa gushed, "Thanks so much, you have no idea how worried I've been." Her voice quavered as she accurately described the gold and pearl locket and the photo—"My great-grandparents."

"I'm so excited," said Eleanor. "I was afraid I wouldn't find the owner. Shall I drop it by your house?"

"I haven't told my dad I lost it, and I'd rather not. Could we meet somewhere?"

Eleanor suggested they rendezvous at a local coffee shop on Saturday morning. Coffee shop, why not? Maybe she'd find out more about this mysterious wedding photo and its current owner. Vanessa sounded like a nice girl, but who knew about teenagers these days? She could be covered with tattoos and have a nose ring. *No matter,* thought Eleanor. It was only important she give the locket back. And maybe find out its story.

Saturday morning, Eleanor dressed in slacks and a blouse instead of her usual athletic gear and packed the locket in a mesh gift bag. She arrived early at the coffeehouse and wondered, *How will I recognize Vanessa? I should have asked for her description or offered to wear a red scarf.*

But the shop was not busy, and Eleanor thought it must be Vanessa when a young woman entered and immediately scanned the room. Eleanor raised her eyebrows in a silent question and held up the mesh bag. Vanessa's face broke into a grin, and she joined Eleanor at her table. The girl was tall and lean, with long brown hair hanging in her face. No visible tattoos or piercings. Eleanor invited the girl to sit down, handed over the locket, and got up to get them each a latte.

When she returned, Vanessa had taken the locket out of the bag and was caressing it in her hand. She opened it to examine the photo and said, "This is so special to me. I was worried after the meet when I couldn't find it. My dad would kill me if he knew I lost it. Thanks so much."

"Do you always wear it when you're running?" asked Eleanor.

"It's kind of like my good luck charm," answered Vanessa. "I should put it on a heavier chain, so I won't lose it again."

"I'd love to know more about it," said Eleanor.

"Why?" the girl asked. "It's a family thing."

"Well, that picture looks like maybe an old wedding photo. I'm just curious."

"Yes, it's my great-grandparents. My grandfather had it with him when—" She paused and gazed at the older woman. Eleanor could see the wheels turning in the girl's head. Did she want to share this story?

"It's OK," Eleanor said, "if you'd rather not tell me."

Vanessa frowned, then continued, "It's a long story, but I guess it's the least I can do to thank you. My grandfather was born in Poland just before the Holocaust. When he was six years old, the Nazis raided his town and took all the Jews to a concentration camp."

"Oh," gasped Eleanor. "I'm so sorry. How did he survive?"

Vanessa continued, "His parents feared it might happen, so a few days before the raid, they handed Grandpa to a nanny and sent them to her family's farm far away. He never saw his parents again. He used to tell me about the nightmares he had as a child and how lonely he was without his parents. He gave me this a few years ago, before he passed. He called me his special *Bubbeleh*. That's Yiddish."

Eleanor felt heat rise to her face. She tried to imagine sending a child away. She couldn't. "And the photo?"

"His mother ripped this piece out of her wedding photo and placed it in the locket before sending him away. She buttoned it into his little pocket and made him promise to treasure it always. Of course, he didn't know what was going to happen."

Eleanor took a sip of her coffee and sat back in her seat. She thought of her children, now grown and independent. She remembered the sleepless nights when they were ill, the time John broke his leg playing football, the night that Lauren missed her curfew and Eleanor was convinced something terrible had happened. All the worry that comes from love. What would it be like to send your child away? And how could you face your own likely death at the hands of hate-filled strangers? She gazed at Vanessa, feeling her eyes moisten.

"That's a lot to take in, Vanessa. How did your grandfather end up here?"

"The nanny's family fled Poland and took Grandpa with them, pretending he was one of their own. He didn't have papers, but they managed somehow. Before the war was over, they were in Cleveland. That's where he grew up. He met Grandma at college, and they moved to California when they graduated."

"And are you—do you practice Judaism?"

"Sometimes. Dad was raised Jewish. My mom grew up Christian, so we celebrate all the holidays. You know, Christmas and Hanukkah." Vanessa chuckled. "The locket is all that's left of my grandpa's early life. It's kind of his only legacy."

"Well, he has you," said Eleanor. "That's a legacy too. And his story, which you can tell. I've never known anyone with connections to the Holocaust. Your grandfather was a lucky man, if you can call it luck to be taken away from your parents."

"I know," said Vanessa. "Dad says I'll be passing the locket on to my own children someday, so they'll know their heritage. You know, 'Never forget.'"

Eleanor drove home in a happy daze. Her heart bruised but full. She finished the detective story and ruminated over how murder in books and films can be entertaining. *Only because it isn't real,* she thought. She vowed to revisit the Holocaust book she'd left in the box of discards in her garage. Meeting Vanessa made these events seem personal and more approachable. She wondered if Betty Stein would be willing to share her family's story. And she knew when she interacted with Betty the next time, it would be with new eyes.

After the Bite
Mara Lynn Johnstone

Getting bitten by a zombie shouldn't have been a relief, but I was so tired. All the panic and the scrambling for safety, the paranoia that someone may have been infected without saying anything, the aggravating frustration that *this is so stupid; this shouldn't be happening*—it wears on the soul. So when I got too close to a zombie when I was pulling someone else to safety and lost a painful chunk of my arm, all I could do was yell about it.

Everyone saw, of course. Not that I would have hidden it from them —I'm not that kind of jackass—but it was embarrassing. Rookie mistakes get you killed. Or zombified, which is basically the same thing. All the science labs in the world hadn't been able to manufacture a cure for something that turned out to be more of a good, old-fashioned curse. And they were mostly overrun by now anyway.

I didn't object when the group locked me in a side room while they decided what to do with me. I didn't really know this gaggle of survivors that well. They could have easily shoved me outside to join the shambling hordes. Nice of them not to. Those hordes will rip you apart if you're not rotten enough.

I settled in as best I could on the folding chair among the boxes of junk. I bandaged my arm with Kleenex and tape, then waited. The bandage was just practical, so blood would stop dripping on my pants. I might as well be comfortable in my final moments.

I shifted on my chair. These final moments sure were boring. It had to be close to an hour by now.

I called through the door, "Hey, anybody got a magazine or something? There's nothing to do in here."

I hoped they would shove something under the door, but instead, they burst into frenzied conversation. I sighed. Maybe there was something to read in the boxes. Pretty sure all I would find were office supplies. The place smelled like glue and printer ink. I was rotating the nearest box in search of labels when a voice sounded at the door.

"Are you still okay?" asked whatshisface the tall guy. Jared.

"Yeah, so far," I said. "Not gonna lunge at you if you open the door. Promise."

"*How* are you still okay?" he asked.

"Uh, what?" was my witty response.

"You should have turned by now. I've seen it happen. Are you sure it bit you?"

"Of course I'm sure!" I held up my arm, even though I knew he couldn't see it. The Kleenex was red all the way through. "You saw the bite! It hurts!"

"Is it turning green at all?"

"Ugh, fine. I guess I need a new bandage anyway. I'll look." I picked at the edge of the tape to get a solid hold on it. "I didn't plan on having to rip tape off my arm hair shortly before death. You're cruel, you know."

More whispering. No direct answers.

I pulled off the tape, which was exactly as painful as I'd expected. "Ow! Fartknocker!"

"What? Is it decaying?"

"No, you turdweasel, I just bikini waxed my wounded arm!" The Kleenex had even stuck a bit, making everything worse. I was bleeding on my pants again. I grabbed more Kleenex and pressed it into place. "Nothing green. Just very red and getting everywhere."

Jared paused. "How are you still healthy?" he asked again.

"I don't know!" I said in exasperation. "I'm trying to come to terms with my impending death here. You don't have to get my hopes up by asking about how long it's taking."

More voices talked quietly. Then the older lady spoke up. "Answer truthfully," she said. "Are you a vampire?"

"WHAT?" I burst out. "Are you kidding me? Vampires don't exist!"

"Neither did zombies until now," she said. "Answer the question."

"No, I'm not a freakin' vampire!"

Other people sounded like they were giving her suggestions. "Are you a lich? Or a ghoul?"

"What the hell, no! Why would you even ask that?"

She kept her cool. "The writing on that tomb said that the dead would devour the living. The zombies don't attack each other. *To the best of your knowledge*, are you, or have you ever been, a member of the undead?"

"No! Well…" I had to pause at that.

They noticed my hesitation.

"Well, *what?*" the woman demanded.

This was stupid. "My heart stopped once? When I fell through the ice on a lake? That really shouldn't count, but the paramedics *did* think I was dead for a few minutes." I swallowed, looking at my arm. "Do you think that counts?"

"Jared, open the door," the woman said.

It opened with a click. Wide-eyed faces gawked at me. I stayed in my chair, probably looking just as shocked. Maybe more, because of the blood loss.

"Let me see it," the older lady said, stepping forward.

I showed her. It wasn't bleeding as much, but there was still no sign of green.

She didn't say anything.

I started to hope. "Am I really not gonna die?"

"It appears," she drawled, "That by the rules of magic, you already have. Congratulations on the loophole. I think you'll be okay."

I didn't think I had any emotions left, but there they were, spilling out of my tear ducts. "Really?"

"We'll keep an eye on you to make sure that curse doesn't decide to change its terms," she said. "But you look healthy to me."

I burst into the most embarrassing blubbering, completely missing whatever she said next. Pretty sure it was something about antiseptic, since somebody else brought in the medical kit that they hadn't bothered with earlier.

The antiseptic stung like a jellyfish with a grudge, but I kept my complaining down to a few unhinged syllables. Then I got a real bandage. It felt amazing.

I realized the conversation had gone on without me and taken an interesting turn. The group was brainstorming safe ways to stop and restart a heart for zombie-proofing purposes. Well, safe-ish. There wasn't much ice around, but apparently there was a hospital nearby that *might* still be intact.

I realized something. "I can go scout!" I exclaimed. "The zombies won't bother me, right? I mean, that one only bit me because I stuck my arm in its mouth. D'you think they'll leave me alone?"

Jared blew out a breath. "If you want to test it, we'll watch."

"Thanks," I said flatly.

Everyone agreed it was worth a try and started grabbing weapons. A few minutes later, we were outside again. We crept down a side street between a mountain of garbage and walls smeared with blood. I led the way with the rest of the team behind as backup. I had a broom handle and a lot of doubts.

We reached the corner where all the moans were coming from. I gripped my stick tighter and inched forward while the others kept their distance.

Yup, those were zombies. A bunch of them, stumbling along the road like drunk commuters, moaning faintly and smelling like roadkill. None of them looked at me.

None looked even when I stepped farther out, then farther, then climbed on top of a brown station wagon. The metal creaked and dented under my feet. No interest from the zombies.

Just because I'd always wanted to—and if a zombiepocalypse isn't the time, then when is?—I swung the broom handle with both hands and shattered the windscreen. Sparkles of glass burst outward.

"Hey zombies!" I shouted. "What do you think? Huh?"

A few turned lazily at the noise, but none moved toward me.

They did seem to get a whiff of the tasty people around the corner, though. A handful started shuffling in that direction.

"Hey guys, incoming!" I yelled. "I'll check out the hospital and report back!"

"Got it!" Jared shouted.

Footsteps stampeded back toward the safe house, with most of the people wishing me luck.

"You too!" I called after them. They'd need it more.

I stood tall atop the car, broomstick on my shoulder like the most heroic of action movie stars. Zombies bumbled around, ignoring me.

With a laugh, I jumped down and raced off toward the hospital.

I'd never felt so alive.

The List of Reasons
Rebecca Olivia Jones

Callie's heart slams against her ribs. Her ex-husband informs her he fell asleep and didn't take their daughter to her soccer game. She knows he'd been guzzling beers. Callie tells him she will come get her. They argue. It's his weekend with their daughter. Callie acquiesces. She hangs up the phone and yells a flurry of cuss words. Callie's rage is with him and with herself. She married an alcoholic. She wants to pick up her daughter but fears a shouting match. Her face is taut; she wants to scream.

She needs to talk to someone. She thinks she needs help to manage her stress. Callie searches the internet for the nearest support group for divorced people, or women, or anger management. She is intrigued by a group starting in fifteen minutes, at a church in town. It's called a *Self-Compassion Workshop*. She wonders, what is that?

As she drives to the workshop, Callie yawns to unclench her jaw. She finds a parking spot a couple of blocks from the meeting location, attempts to parallel park three times before managing it, and runs to the church. Calming herself, she enters the church social hall, finds an empty chair in the circle of serious faces, and sits on the metal folding chair.

"Hello. My name is Lauren. There are a few new faces today. Welcome, I'm glad you're here. All of us carry burdens from our past; anger at others, and anger at ourselves. We will practice techniques of new ways to think. We will learn positive self-talk. We will learn to forgive ourselves. We will learn to love ourselves. Sound good?"

People squirm in their seats or shut their eyes as if to hide.

"I invite you to share with us how you are doing today. This will help you reclaim yourselves without fear for tomorrow. Who would like to begin?"

Callie listens to three people's stories. She sits with a stone in her gut. Then, she raises her hand. With eyes down, she clears her throat and stutters her first name. She came to this meeting because of her bad choices—in romance, in marriage, with credit card abuse, her use of wine to numb her bruised heart, hating herself. With white noise filling her ears, Callie looks around. The group is waiting patiently to listen to her.

"Umm, uh," Callie's mouth is dry. She sucks on her cheeks to create some saliva and runs through all the bullshit in her mind to find where to start.

"When I turned thirteen, Daddy stopped holding my hand or kissing my cheek. Around that time, he started drinking. He'd come home from teaching high school, fix a highball, by seven thirty he'd pass out."

Callie notices several heads nodding.

"Then, he fell in love with the woman who directed Band. He'd stay late after school. Mom spent more time in her art studio and attending book clubs. There was no divorce. We lived in silence. I was on my own. I needed attention. And started messing around with boys."

Callie shakes her head, loosening her messy bun, grinding her teeth.

"I just … I just don't want to feel anything. I want my life to be different." Callie swallows.

Lauren prompts, "Different in what way?"

"I don't know. It's like I wear a vest of shame. It's heavy." The woman next to Callie sighs. "I just want to say I'm sorry. I'm sorry to my daughter, I'm sorry to my mother and to my brother. I'm sorry I married my ex … and I'm sorry to me." The woman sniffs.

"I'm like a bird who can't fly, just stuck in a hole in the ground." Callie slumps as tears drip to her chin. The woman passes her the tissue box.

Lauren's voice is a mellow alto. "Why do you think your dad pulled away from you?"

"I don't know … I heard from an older cousin his mother had been raped at age sixteen." Callie shrugs. "Maybe he didn't trust himself."

"Oh, an inherited scar. How did his behavior make you feel?"

"Well, I felt confused. I guess I felt abandoned." The woman next to her touches Callie's arm.

"Thank you, Callie."

Callie's chest softens and her scalp tingles. It is a relief to share her story. Callie closes her eyes and thinks, "Dear God, how can I be stronger?"

Four others share stories of parental neglect, losing a job, an ugly divorce, and abuse. They are all broken and childlike, as vulnerable as rescue dogs held in cages. Callie no longer feels alone.

Lauren continues the meeting. "This is not how we want to live. Let's climb the mountain. Let's grow wings and fly." Lauren holds up a book entitled *Self-Compassion*. "I encourage you to purchase this book by Kristin Neff. She gives you assignments for reflection and exercises to practice. She helps you find the words to change. For example, if you say, 'I am so stupid. I'm incompetent. It's my fault we lost that client.' What could you say instead?"

The group sits there. No one looks as if they can find other words.

"What about, 'I tried my best. These things happen. Next time I will do better.' Please say it out loud." Lauren gestures like a conductor. The group mumbles with embarrassment. Callie sits still, listening.

"It will get easier the more you say it. What could you say instead of, 'I married an asshole, what was I thinking?'"

The woman next to Callie speaks up, "I was young when I married. It seemed like the right thing at the time."

"Good, thank you. That is how to forgive yourself. That is self-compassion." Lauren pauses. "Let's finish with a brief meditation: close your eyes; place one hand on your heart and the other on your belly. Take a couple of deep breaths. Think about a self-affirming statement you want to carry out of this meeting. This will be the first step to becoming who you want to be."

The quiet expands into the room for a few minutes, then Lauren says, "Thank you for showing up for yourself today. See you next week."

People stand and move toward the kitchen. The air smells of cheap black coffee. The breeze outside the door feels like a waft of hope.

Callie strolls out the door holding a Styrofoam cup filled with coffee and powdered milk and sits on a cement bench under a small magnolia tree. A man about her age sits down near her and smiles gently. Callie returns his smile. She notices his kind hazel eyes and crinkling burnished skin.

"I'm Daniel. Thank you for telling your story today." He sips and swallows. He releases his breath. "My Dad poured cement. He would start the day of a pour irritated. It's all about timing. Cement dries fast and if it's not right the first time, it's a huge do-over."

There is a pause. Callie says, "Well, he must have worked a lot. There's a lot of cement in the world."

They chuckle. "Yeah, he'd come home, drop into his lounger with a bottle of whiskey and no shot glass. Drink himself into oblivion."

"Oh, jeez, yeah. I'm sorry."

"No need to be sorry. It wasn't anyone's fault but his own."

Daniel looks at her sideways. "You say you're sorry a lot."

Callie takes out the scrunchy from her bun and scratches her head. She forces a laugh. "Well, there's a long list of reasons."

Daniel waits for her to say more. When she doesn't, he lightens up, "Hey, you want to go for a walk?"

"Oh, OK. Sure. Where do you like to walk?"

Daniel stands up, takes her cold coffee, and tosses their cups into the trash.

"If we take a car, there's an easy trail about a mile up this road with spectacular views. I used to take my kids up there. Do you want to drive? Or we could take my Jeep."

Callie considers for a moment. She feels safe around Daniel. He's open and honest and she wants to reflect his trust.

"You know where the trail is, so you drive. Plus, I doubt if my old Subaru wagon could make it up the hill."

The road winds through ravines shadowed with groves of redwoods, and around sun-filled knolls thick with oaks and bays. Homes of every vintage look like treehouses tucked into the woods. The road narrows and gets steeper. The Jeep revs up in first gear until they arrive at a gate marking an access fire road. It is overgrown with hanging oak branches and scotch broom.

Daniel pulls hard on the parking brake. They step out onto loose dirt and climb the last hundred feet. The views are breathtaking. Below, traffic hustles and the dense development of towns that line The San Francisco Bay look like Legoland. Above stands the solid peak of the quiet giant Mount Tamalpais.

"Let's take the road that descends into the ravine."

Callie hears birds call and squirrels squabble in the trees. A lizard scrambles under a rock. A cool breeze reminds her of the elevation as the sun warms her back. Callie breathes in the earth, and her mind stills for the first time in months.

Daniel sticks his hands in his pockets. They walk kicking rocks and viewing the surroundings. Callie marvels at the complex beauty of nature —trees, wild animals, floating clouds. She appreciates the silence of being present with no expectations.

Daniel points overhead at a hawk riding the airstream along the tree line. It twists its head right and left, scanning the earth for lunch.

Callie says, "I wish I could fly. When I was about five years old, my mother sat me in front of the TV to watch *Peter Pan*. To my eyes, Peter really flew! I was in awe and cried." She pauses to sense that moment. "Mom asked me why I was crying. I said, 'I want to fly.'"

Daniel doesn't say anything for a while. "There are a lot of ways to fly."

"What do you mean?"

"I think flying doesn't have to be literal, like a bird flies. It can be a feeling of freedom, whether dancing, painting, loud music, or an accomplishment."

"Oh? Give me an example."

Daniel lifts his chin to the sky. "I went fly-fishing in Montana during college. I couldn't, for the life of me, cast a line without getting it tangled. I spent the day standing in the river, untying knots. Very frustrating. I loved being in the river—the solitude, the sound, the green smell. But damn, I wanted to release the line like Brad Pitt in *A River Runs Through It*, you know?"

"Yes, I remember that scene."

"By the late afternoon I was cold and tired, but I thought, I've got to try it one more time before calling it a wasted day."

Daniel stops to act out his story. "So, I set my feet wide apart, release my shoulders, lift my right arm, pull out some line with my left hand, tilt the rod back, flick it forward and release the line. It arcs high in the air and, in slow motion, the fly descends and alights in a swirling pool behind a fallen tree trunk. It was so beautiful. I stayed still and held my breath. I wanted that moment to last." They continue strolling.

Callie waits, then asks, "So, did you catch a fish?"

"No. But I didn't care. I didn't really want to bother the fish. I wanted; I don't know."

"You wanted to fly. I get it."

"Have you experienced a moment like that?"

Callie blows out her cheeks. "It's hard to remember ever feeling that free."

They walk and kick loose rocks.

She cocks her head in thought and says, "I remember holding a scratchy rope, swinging over a lake, and letting go at the right time to jump through the air into the cold water."

"Me, too! Summers, at Lake Tahoe."

"Or, when I took my daughter, she was about four, to the water park." Callie's eyes gleam. "I sat with her little body between my knees, drenched and giggling. We slipped down the giant slide and splashed into the catch pool at full speed. It was like riding a magic carpet."

Callie suddenly stops. She looks at Daniel.

"Thank you. I didn't realize how many times I have felt like I was flying. It was thrilling. It was exhilarating. Thank you for helping me remember."

"Sure. Joy is everywhere. Tell me more."

"Um … Well, have you ever listened to a grand opera that makes you weep? The lush sound of a full orchestra, the emotional pull of singers' soaring high notes?"

"I usually find that at Yoshi's Jazz Club," Daniel says.

Callie is on a roll. "Oh, and what about the time my mother took me to view an exhibition of paintings by Howard Hodgkin? I experienced a release in my arms and shoulders by his style of painting beyond the canvas. He brushed all over his frames. It was like he couldn't contain the colors he saw in his mind."

"See, he was flying with his paintbrush!"

"Oh, yes, Daniel, I have flown many times! Damn, I tend to wallow in self-pity and regrets. How do you handle it?"

"Like this. Take a walk. Make a new friend. Spend time with my kids. And practice self-compassion."

Callie says, "Life is hard. I guess I should feel compassion for my dad. He did the best he could."

"That's good. But start with compassion for yourself." Daniel picks up a stone and throws it long over the ravine. "And don't be such a drama queen," he teases.

She laughs at the phrase and laughs harder at herself, big gulping guffaws. Daniel joins her. Callie can't stop laughing. The stone in her gut splits open. They approach a downslope in the road and take off running with flailing arms, scattering gravel and screaming like children as their hearts take flight.

The Last Dive
Denise Kalm

Phil Hawkins dumped the air from his buoyancy vest and began his ocean descent. The serene landscape of the Palancar Reef clashed with the rushing water noises in his ears; he always expected the underwater world to be as quiet as it looked. A 150-pound grouper drifted by, focused on a distant objective—a meal, perhaps, or a place to sleep.

Phil checked his gauges as he slipped slowly down the wall: sixty … seventy … eighty feet. Finning slowly, he held back until he was at the rear of the dive group. When the divemaster led them into the first of many 'swim-thru' caves, Phil saw his chance to escape the watchful divemaster's eye. With the two-hundred-foot visibility, it was hard to swim away from the herd, but in the tunnels, swimming single-file, falling off the radar would be a snap. Leveling off, he took a final look at the aquamarine parrotfish and dazzling queen triggerfish, so much a part of his love for Cozumel.

A four-foot-long, green moray eel poked its head out of its crevice home, surprising Phil by slipping its entire body free, flowing around him in a sinuous dance. The wise old eyes warned him to keep his distance. It bared its sharp teeth at him; an empty threat, as Phil knew from experience.

Phil swam into a school of jacks, their silver bodies glinting in the filtered sunlight. He marveled at how they maintained a tight formation, varying their course only slightly to pass alongside him. He came to a giant basket sponge, smiling at the memory of what his camera would make of the dusty color. Red vanishes at depth, he remembered.

On his birthday, Phil convinced himself that he had beaten the genetic odds by getting to the age of forty with no symptoms. He would not die the way his forty-two-year-old father had, jerking and twisting uncontrollably, while his mind deteriorated. He felt he'd just know if he had come up on the wrong side of the coin flip and, most of the time, didn't live in fear. *Nothing I can do anyway.* But last month, scientists had finally found a way to test for the gene for Huntington's chorea. Phil only made the appointment after his mother begged.

"What's the point of a test?" Phil had challenged his doctor, reminding him of his wife-less, childless status. "You can't cure it; you don't even have a viable treatment."

"Some people like to make plans," Dr. Lewis had said. "Or travel more, quit work ... Just do things differently."

Phil couldn't imagine what he would change. He had the best job possible—writing vitriolic prose for a bi-weekly syndicated column, biting humor on any subject of his choosing. "The Hawk," as he was known, was feared on Capitol Hill and loved by his readers. He reveled in his reputation, earned over years of slaving at small papers writing about bingo games and town council meetings.

His low-maintenance condo was comfortable, his BMW Z-3 took him where he wanted to go, and when he got there, he had good friends to party with after a long day at work. No wife, but he felt sure that he would find the right woman when he was ready. Sometimes, he regretted leaving Gail, but his job required that he move where the work dictated. Gail never understood, but having had that relationship, Phil knew what he wanted. Just not yet. Phil felt blessed—he couldn't see anything he would want to change right now.

He had taken the test. *I have control from knowing the truth,* he thought. Fear had never stopped him before, not from trying to scale the Matterhorn, not from trying out skydiving when none of his friends would join him.

One night, after reading the book, *Final Exit,* as background for an article, Phil realized the need to have a plan worked out, a way to forestall years of suffering, whether it was due to a stroke, cancer, or ... He didn't name the disease he feared. Loath to look into the future, he decided he would only need the option if he carried the gene. *And there was no chance he would lose this genetic chess game.*

After leaving the vial of blood, irrevocably committed to knowing, Phil began to panic. Fifty-fifty odds; you either have the gene or you don't. A blasted coin flip. Suddenly, the odds seemed much worse than they had. The nurse handed him some literature as he left, mentioning how important it was for him to come back to receive the results in person.

Phil called the office instead, and while the nurse searched for his file, he thumbed through a pile of mail. With shaking hands, he attempted a careless perusal of ads and bills, unable to convince himself that whatever the outcome, it didn't matter. As sure as he had been of his health only minutes before, now he felt a fog settling into his brain, much as he imagined it darkening his father's thoughts.

"Mr. Hawkins," the nurse said. "Dr. Lewis is most insistent that you come in to discuss the results. We can't reveal lab results by phone."

She didn't have to continue. Phil knew from her voice, dripping with concern.

"Your voice gave away the results. Discuss what?" he said, cutting her off. "How bad it will be? I already know; I lived a lifetime of it with my dad."

"Dr. Lewis said that the test could easily be wrong. It's very sensitive. He always likes to repeat it in the case of positive results. Please come in. The doctor will want to talk with you."

Phil grunted. "They took enough blood for six tests. I'm sure the technicians ran it several times. And there's nothing Dr. Lewis could tell me I don't already know. Forget it!"

He slammed the phone down, and then shuddered, remembering his frail, trembling father at thirty-five; he always thought of him as an old man. The healthy, mind-whole man he must have been had begun to disappear before Phil really knew him. Personality changes came first, and as Phil aged in years, he watched his father age in weeks and months. He knew what it would be like, every degradation, every loss.

Always sure of his health, Phil found that his unconscious mind had prepared for the worst. Inspired by his personal crisis, he dashed off a few columns on the lack of research done on orphan diseases. *Orphans? One in twenty thousand people is hardly an orphan.*

He took a short leave of absence from work and left a note with his lawyer. *Always careful to tie up loose ends, aren't you?* he chided himself. *Got to milk even this situation with one last article.* He wondered who would pick up his last paycheck and why he even cared.

He bought a one-way ticket to Cozumel, but left his underwater camera at home. Even with no one to leave it to, it gave him a sharp, visceral twinge to think of the camera being lost with him. Phil even rented dive gear—let them take the cost of it out of his estate. He tried to convince several boat captains to let him take a boat out by himself, but found Cozumel's history of dive accidents had made everyone cautious.

Grumbling at the inconvenience, Phil signed up for a dive with the largest and least organized operation he could find.

Grouped with twenty inexperienced divers, Phil smiled at the divemaster's obvious relief when he checked Phil's dive rating and log. "You've dived Cozumel before—that's great," he said.

He checked his air gauge—2700 psi—plenty of time for a short tour of the caves and swim-throughs on Santa Rosa, his favorite dive site. Last rites before he did what he had come here to do. As the last of the group followed the dive leader into a cave, Phil began his descent, selecting a different swim-thru to explore. Impatience overcame him as he waited for the last fin-tip to disappear into the cave. He couldn't afford to let a slow diver see what he planned.

What am I waiting for? Let's get this done.

Descending to 120 feet, he allowed nitrogen narcosis to intoxicate him, enjoying the buzz. The tug of the deep grew stronger as pressure enveloped him in its watery glove. Narcosis would bury the pain of the oxygen headache the deeper waters would induce. The abyss below him stretched for at least two thousand feet—much too deep for compressed air. Too deep for life.

Phil let the water pull him down, breathing slowly, conserving air … why? *Habit,* he thought, while he could still form a coherent thought. A barracuda bared his teeth at him, then vanished.

A fifteen-foot tiger shark swam toward him, appearing suddenly out of the gin-clear water. Phil held his breath and his position, hoping not to attract its attention. Out of the corner of his eye, he saw the fluttering of a dying jack, the focus of the shark's attention.

The tiger gulped down the fish, his slanting, dangerous teeth only inches from Phil's face. He imagined he could hear the grumbling of the shark's stomach and see the naked hunger in the obsidian eye. *The jack had only been an appetizer.*

Lazily, the shark circled him, tightening his orbit with each pass. The rough skin abraded Phil's arm, blood seeping out from the scrapes. Images of shark videos played out in his mind. A large, hinged jaw snapping down on the bloody hunk of meat. His body.

"I don't want to die this way," he shrieked through his regulator. Not the peaceful slipping-away of a narcosis coma, before his air ran out. Not the dive he planned. Tearing, rendering teeth, painfully ripping away his life.

"Go for it," he told the shark, meeting its unblinking eye. "Make it quick." He scrunched his eyes closed.

Phil felt the razor teeth on his chest and his back and he panicked. He drove his fist into the shark's cloaked eye and kept punching. He felt the teeth release, a sensation almost as painful as the first bite. The shark vanished. His chest stung and greenish-brown beads floated from the puncture points. *It really happened*, he thought, *and I survived*. Phil took a long, deep breath and sighed audibly. Water leaked into his mask as he smiled.

The regulator indicated how little air he had left. *Decision time*, he told himself. *Down or up—what will it be?* Never superstitious, he relived the relief experienced when the shark let him go. In that moment, he had wanted to live. Did he still, knowing what was left of his life? *Yes*.

A memory flashed into his mind. On his deathbed, his father had told his family he had no regrets. He had smiled and then reminded them of the good times. *If he can do it, so can I.*

Wasting no time pondering the shark's disappearance, he began an emergency ascent to fifteen feet, fighting the urge to take great, gulping gasps of air. *I survived*, he shouted in his mind. *And I'm going to keep going. When did I ever walk away from my fears?*

Years of training overrode his desire for the surface. Using the last of his air, he decompressed for five minutes. Blood surged through his veins, as if the nitrogen had super-charged it, banishing his despair. At fifteen feet, he couldn't be suffering from nitrogen narcosis, but the relief he felt was palpable.

Phil surfaced to the roar of the boat engine. Before he could manually inflate his vest, or attempt a surface swim, hands reached down to help him up the ladder and divest him of his gear.

"What happened to you?" the divemaster asked, frowning at him. "You left the group."

Phil shrugged. "I got lost. I don't know … got narked."

The divemaster nodded. "Stay closer to the group next time or you can't dive with us."

"What in hell happened to your chest?" the captain exclaimed.

"Must have brushed against some coral," Phil said.

"Get some vinegar on it and be more careful. What were you doing going off like that? You could have died out there."

"I know," Phil said. "A shark saved my life." The last words were whispered; no one heard him nor saw the tears he blinked away.

* * *

Phil relished the familiarity of his condo, the lumpy sofa he had long planned to replace, the torn Persian carpet more valuable as a memory than a collector's item. He patted the ash-filled fireplace, remembering winter evenings in front of it, nursing a glass of oaky cabernet. He scratched lightly at the scabs on his chest, remembering.

"A cat. This place needs a cat," he declared. "A basic mutt of a cat, not a purebred." He wanted to commit to something, to someone. He liked the aloofness and independence of his friends' cats. You had to earn a cat's love. It felt like a first step to something more for him, something he hadn't known he wanted.

As he started to leave for the SPCA, he noted the red indicator light on his answering machine. Five messages. *Everyone knew I was out of town.* Phil shrugged. He had a lot of thinking to do before he was ready to talk to anyone. Finally, he pushed the button. *I don't have to return the calls yet.*

"Mr. Hawkins?" The female voice was shrill and panicky. "Please pick up. It's urgent. I'm calling from Dr. Lewis' office."

Phil froze.

"The test results were wrong. I repeat. The lab got your sample mixed up with another patient's. Dr. Lewis wants you to know how sorry he is about this. Please call us as soon as you get in."

In shock, he played the message back several times. *I escaped*, he thought. *No, I had already escaped when I decided to live.* He wished he had a picture of the shark. Smiling, Phil erased the message and headed out to pick out his cat.

Beautiful Again
Anne Keck

"Mom, you can't be serious." I was about to say more, but stopped myself before I said something I'd regret.

She looked up at me from her clinic bed, her dyed blond hair perfectly coifed. "Of course I'm serious. I wouldn't joke about a thing like this. What do you think I am, senile?"

I ignored her rhetorical question. "But it's a really big step. Lots of possible unintended consequences. So many unknowns…"

She gave an exasperated huff. "Elaina, you know I've wanted to do this for a long time. I deserve it. I'd like you to support me, even if you wouldn't make the same choice."

Her point was valid. We were so different, her day to my night, my pessimism to her optimism, her extravagance to my frugalness—flip sides of a coin. She yearned to be young again; I just never thought she'd jettison her body to do it. And the procedure would drain her small lifetime of savings. I reached for her hand and squeezed it. "All right, Mom. I'm here for you."

She relaxed and leaned back into her pillows. "I knew you'd see reason. It's because you love me." She pushed a button on her bed. A nurse opened the door and said in a condescending tone, "Doctor Monroe will be here soon."

Yeah, right, that's what they always say. But as I was pulling out my phone, a woman breezed into the room.

"Hello, Grace. Are you ready for the big day?" The doctor was white-coated and carried a tablet in front of her like a shield.

"Yes, Doctor. I can't wait." Mom gestured toward me. "This is my daughter, Elaina. She's willing to listen to you with both ears open." She emphasized the last few words, looking at me with her signature glare. It still worked. I'd behave. Sort of.

Dr. Monroe tilted her head at me. "Hello, Elaina. It's nice to finally meet you. Do you understand the procedure your mother has chosen?"

I looked at Mom, my resolve to stop the process melting like wax in the sun. But my smarmy side remained irrepressible. "Yes. I understand you're going to kill my mother and take her consciousness or soul or whatever you want to call it, and download it into a robot. Into a piece of machinery. Have I got that right?"

Mom tsked and Dr. Monroe gave me the type of patient smile usually reserved for toddlers. "Mostly, yes. Her memories and personality, likes and dislikes, the very essence of who she is, will be placed inside a cybernetic organism. Part robot, part body grown from your mother's own cells and DNA, it will be an anatomical match for her. Once she enters that body, she will be free from the pain and other inconveniences of her current state."

I looked at Mom. Her hopeful expression drove the smarmy right out of me. "But doesn't that mean she won't feel anything at all? Won't she lose body sensations like touch and taste?"

Dr. Monroe shook her head. "No—the neurological receptors connected to the system's brain will allow her to experience all the five major sensations. Our clients also usually achieve heightened positive emotions, most notably elation, at being inside bodies that can perform physical tasks better than they ever could before."

Mom gripped my hand. "See, Elaina? I'll be younger and stronger and beautiful once again."

"Oh, Mom. You're beautiful now."

She gave me a placating smile, but we both knew the truth. She had a lithe and athletic body, but lately it had spurned her like an unfaithful lover. I'd watched as she gradually became unable to do the things she loved, then lost the ability to take care of basic needs. The tables had turned and I was now her caretaker, supporting her physically, emotionally, and monetarily. She didn't like being an invalid. She wasn't good at it.

I turned to the doctor. "If Mom went through with this, how soon would it happen?"

"She's scheduled for tomorrow morning."

Mom didn't flinch when I gripped her hand even tighter to stop the room from lurching and glared at her. "Tomorrow morning?"

"Yes, Elaina. I can't take another minute in this body. I'm ready for a new one."

There was no use arguing when she made her intractable decision-made-and-you-can't-change-my-mind face. "I understand, Mom." I needed to get out of here before I lost it. "See you tomorrow before the procedure." I leaned over, kissed her soft cheek, and fled the room while the two of them were still talking.

I caught the e-train, got home, shucked off my clothes, crawled into bed, and pulled the covers over my head. I wasn't processing this very well, but it was happening tomorrow, so I'd better just swallow the bitter pill.

* * *

When I arrived at the clinic the next morning, Mom's bed was empty. I tracked down a nurse and asked, "Where's my mother?" I didn't hear her response because I spotted Dr. Monroe and a woman walking down the hallway straight toward me.

The woman looked exactly like our old family photos of Mom when she was in her mid- twenties. Tall and graceful, her blonde hair curling around her shoulders, she wore a yellow sundress and walked with a lift in her step like she was on Cloud Nine.

My emotions tumbled in a dryer set on high. Was this still my mom? I wasn't sure who this young woman was. But what could I do? I held out my arms to her. "Mom! You look amazing." The woman stopped abruptly and stared at me with raised eyebrows.

"You've confused me with someone else. I'm not your mother." Her voice was younger and higher, but definitely my mother's.

Dr. Monroe stepped in between us, took my arm, and said to her, "Grace, please wait here." She steered me into an empty waiting room and shut the door.

I was fuming. "What the hell is going on? Why didn't my mother recognize me?"

The doctor was shaking her head. "I thought you'd understood. When we placed her into a younger body, we gave her only the memories appropriate for her age, so she has her memories up to age twenty-five. Giving her the memories of an older woman would contravene her appearance and negatively affect her psyche and the assimilation process. She has no memory of you because, in her mind, she was never pregnant and you were never born."

An acidic copper tang flooded my mouth as the doctor continued. "And it's very important you refrain from telling her you're her daughter. Doing so could cause her mental processes to go into meltdown and trigger a full system crash. She would then be lost forever."

This was fucking unbelievable. "Then what am I supposed to do? Never see my mother ever again? Ignore the fact she exists?"

"Well, that *would* be best for her. You could always approach her as a family friend, but you must be careful what you say to prevent corrupting her sense of self." The doctor looked at her watch. "I must go."

As she turned, I grabbed her arm. "Wait—did you tell Mom this ahead of time? Did she know she'd lose sixty years' worth of memories? That she'd lose all memory of me?"

The doctor jerked back as if I'd struck her. "Of course we told her! We talked about it at length and she signed all the papers. She chose the age of her new body and the scope of her memories. I'm sorry you're unhappy, Elaina, but you're not my client." She pulled away from me, opened the door, and left the room.

I stepped out into the bleach-smelling corridor and watched the doctor escort my mother down the hallway. They turned a corner and were gone.

My mother was gone.

She had chosen to be beautiful again over me. To relive her youth, she had decided to forget me. After all we were to each other. After all I'd done for her. She'd discarded me like an out-of-fashion pair of pumps. My gut twisted with the impact of rejection.

What did she plan on doing now? She wasn't going back to my apartment because she wouldn't even remember it. Where would she go? How would she live? The hell if I wouldn't find out. I jolted into action and ran down the corridor after her.

The doctor was holding open the door of an auto-cab and she was climbing inside. I jumped into the auto-cab behind hers and ordered the AI driver to follow it. Mom's cab traveled only a few miles before stopping in front of a glass-walled skyscraper. She exited the cab, went up to the front door, and opened it using a code on her bright blue phone. After waiting a bit, I got out of the cab and followed her.

"Paradise Suites" blazed across an arch over the building entrance. Ironic under the circumstances. Peeking inside, I couldn't see my mother, but I could see a map showing several buildings, swimming pools, sports courts, a few restaurants. An entire luxury community. A uniformed man squinted at me for a moment, then opened the door and asked officiously, "May I help you?"

"Hi. Yes. I'm looking for Grace Gander." Shit, that's her married name, and she didn't marry Dad until her late twenties. "I mean, Grace Kaiden. I just saw her arrive."

"Who may I say is calling on her?"

"I'm—" Should I give him my real name? Best not. Who would Mom want to see instead of me? "I'm her sister, Liz." She'd died years ago, but Mom probably wouldn't know that. The guard lifted one eyebrow in suspicion, but pulled a device out of this pocket, punched in some numbers, and said into it, "This is Nick at the front door. I have your sister, Liz, asking to see you."

Mom's voice replied, "Oh—what a surprise! Please let her up to unit 1123."

I stepped inside and walked through the hallway across granite floors, repro Grecian statues staring at me from alcoves. Definitely posh. *Monied*. As the elevator rose, a story began taking shape in my mind.

That blue phone she used to unlock the entrance—that was new, because her phone was red. She must have bought the blue one and downloaded all the information she would need when she got her new body and old memories.

That means my mother must have owned this place for years. I'd always thought she should've had more assets than the pittance I managed for her. She'd apparently had a lot more. She'd bought this place and hired someone to care for it until she made ready her escape. And she'd kept all of it hidden from me.

She'd lied to me, used me, and then ditched me. A tidal wave of comprehension blurred my vision, my body shaking with righteous rage.

I was a dupe.

But I didn't have to remain one.

I was my mother's sole beneficiary, meaning I would get everything she owned when she was certified as dead. Including the body she now inhabited. It was a piece of property, pure and simple.

It could all be mine sooner rather than later.

I could abandon my old frumpy body in exchange for my mother's new one. I could take over my mother's beautiful body and designer life.

The door opened before I could knock on it. Behind Mom, I could see a richly-appointed home in the cream and gold colors she'd always loved.

"Hey—you're not Liz. Who are you? Oh—you're the woman from the clinic! I'm calling security." I grabbed her wrist before her fingers reached the intercom.

"Not so fast, Mom. We have some things to talk about." I slipped inside and closed the door behind me.

"You're delusional. You need help. Let me call someone." She tried to back away from me, but I held her wrist in a firm grip.

"I'm not the one who needs help. You are. You've lost your memories, but I'm here to help you regain them."

"My memories are just fine." But her blue eyes looked confused.

"No, Mom. You've lost *sixty years'* worth of memories. You're not twenty-five or however old you think you are. You are eighty-five years old. Your real body, it's *dead*. Only part of your memories were downloaded into this semi-robotic thing." I held up her arm. She didn't resist. "This body, it's not your own. You dumped your real body to get into this facsimile. You're just a bunch of neural networks downloaded to an AI inside this construct."

Something was happening to Mom's face. Her face muscles were slackening.

"That's right. You're starting to understand, aren't you? You married Dad, Kevin Gander, and you had me. We were a family. He died five years ago, then you came to live with me."

Mom's mouth formed an "O" that was unnaturally round. Her body went rigid and her eyes rolled back in their sockets.

This was what the doctor had warned against. Mom was going into a full system crash. She'd soon be lost. Her essence or spirit or whatever it was they'd managed to get into this piece of fleshed-out hardware, would disappear. Like a wisp in the wind.

Crap. What was I doing? I wasn't my mother, a heartless betrayer. I was mad—I mean really mad at how she'd belittled me and our relationship—but I couldn't do this. I couldn't kick her out of this body and take it over. She'd be gone for good. It was akin to murder, and I was no murderer.

I'd loved Mom. Okay, I still loved her, even if she had quit motherhood.

I had to stop her breakdown. What had the doctor said? Pretend to be a family friend?

"Grace—listen to me. Look at me." I used my commanding school-teacher voice, shaking her. Her eyes rolled forward to meet mine.

"I'm your friend and I want what's best for you. This is your body now. You should keep this body, stay in it."

"But you said—"

"Never mind what I said." Her eyes were becoming more focused. "I was confused, but I'm all right now." That sounded lame, even to my ears.

But it worked. Mom got control of herself and gave me her signature glare. "I think you should leave now." She was her normal self again, full of hauteur.

I'd always lived in my mother's shadow, a member of the cult who worshipped her. As it turns out, I was the better person. I was the hero of this story. Well, maybe not the hero, but at least not the villain.

"Yes, I think it's time I left." I opened the door. "Goodbye, Grace."

She closed the door on me just as I heard her say, "Goodbye, Elaina."

The Piano Shawl
Joanna Kraus

The first time Evelyn saw double, she was puzzled.

When she couldn't climb stairs, she was concerned.

When she couldn't comb her long, auburn hair, she panicked.

When she couldn't swallow part of her sixteenth birthday cake, she was horrified.

The fears wrapped her body in a terrifying embrace she couldn't escape.

Yet now, scarcely three years later, she waited to make her first entrance as a model in a benefit fashion show. She perspired. Her hands felt clammy. Her heart raced.

She peeked through the curtain of an improvised dressing area.

Shocked, she realized the runway stretched halfway across a large hall. It ended in a T-shaped platform where steps led down to the guests. She had three entrances. After each one, she had to switch into a different outfit supplied by A La Mode, an upscale clothing boutique. In the hall, spring daffodils decorated the dining tables. The audience cheerfully chatted over tea and scones while a pianist played a medley of Broadway show tunes.

This is supposed to be fun, she told herself. *It's for a good cause.*

Maybe that's why Dr. Ross, the neurologist, had shown her the notice requesting volunteers for the show. It sounded like light-hearted fun. Something she'd never done before.

Plus, it was to raise funds for the hospital.

Dr. Ross had tapped her finger on the sentence: "No experience necessary." She had looked at Evelyn, who was half out of her chair, grabbing her purse from the floor.

"You're in remission. You're doing well. Time to take a peek at the world again."

Dr. Ross had smiled. "And you can still get your ten-minute walks in."

So Evelyn had agreed to be in the fashion show.

Now she was convinced it was a mistake. She should be home reading a book.

The dresser came over to adjust the collar on her travel pantsuit. *As if I'll ever travel again*, she thought.

"Remember to smile," the dresser said. "And listen for your cue."

Breathe. Inhale, exhale. Breathe.

Patiently, her cousin had shown her how to walk and turn, but when the pianist played her entrance cue, she froze. All she wanted to do was flee and go hide in her own room.

She remembered vividly when the yet unknown disease took hold. That was when her world collapsed. Blurred double vision was only the start. In rapid progression, she couldn't comb her hair, write her name, or even feed herself. Her arms refused to lift the spoon to her mouth, even after her father piled books on the table to make the distance shorter.

She remembered the morning when she lay on the bed struggling to put her legs into pull-on denim jeans.

Pull-on for who, she thought furiously. *For whom*, she corrected herself, as if it mattered anymore.

Her gait became a drunken lurch and climbing the eight steps to their home felt as daunting as ascending Mt. Everest.

As she endured countless neurological tests, she foresaw the rest of her life as a dependent, disgruntled invalid. What kind of life would she have? Could she have a career or even a job? Who would ever hire her? Would all her friends disappear? Would she be alone for the rest of her life?

Some close friends, unable to cope with her initial transformation, did disappear. It made her feel unwanted, discarded, as if she were a dying ember in a barbecue pit, once glowing, now extinguished. A few strangers offered help, but her pride wouldn't let her accept.

The worst test of all was when they tested her muscle function. Unprepared, Evelyn was led into a dark room for an EMG. A technician strapped her into a huge, brown leather chair that had countless wires running from it. Then he poked needles into her body as electric shocks increased in intensity. It reminded her of a jail execution she'd seen once in a movie.

"Stop," Evelyn screamed. "Stop!"

"Almost finished," the technician said as he calmly continued his assigned job. "Be through in a minute."

Evelyn wondered if he meant the test. Or her?

Later, when the results came back, the doctors concluded she had an extremely rare autoimmune neuromuscular disorder. So rare that there were only roughly three hundred and twenty cases in a million people. Called Myasthenia Gravis, the disorder prevented nerve impulses from reaching the muscles in her case.

No one could explain why the disorder struck.

She found out it wasn't contagious. It wasn't hereditary. It wasn't fatal, and so far, medical science had not found a cure.

But it was treatable.

In despair, she asked, "Will I get better?"

"In time," the doctor answered, "with proper medication."

Her heart beat faster. "How much time?" Her eyes filled with tears.

The doctor handed her a tissue and gently said, "It's called the snowflake disease. Evelyn, every patient is different; no two are alike. You will improve, but you may have flare-ups. Remember, wherever you go, it's imperative you have the ability and energy to return."

Evelyn did not like the idea of some bodily malfunction in charge of her, something she couldn't see, or say, or even spell.

Losing control of her body was like losing her best friend.

Over several years, with the care of excellent doctors, strong medication, a supportive family, and the obligatory rest, she showed improvement.

"Last night I cut my toenails," she gleefully informed Dr. Ross.

"I'll put that in your file." Dr. Ross grinned.

They both knew that any small success was significant.

Evelyn focused on what she could do instead of what she couldn't. If she could no longer walk three miles, she'd manage a shorter walk.

She edited her activities, eliminating situations that caused undue stress. She allowed extra time. No longer tried to accomplish five events in a day. Not even three. Often, only one. And sometimes she put a large "R" on her calendar, reminding her to rest.

They can fly rockets to the moon, Evelyn thought, *but they can't figure out why this happened to me. Is it because it's so rare they don't want to bother? Am I supposed to sit in a wheelchair for the next half century? Does it mean I can never do all the things I planned: drama camp counselor, pickleball team, hiking in Hawaii, finding someone special who'd make me smile, even laugh? I want to laugh. I don't want to be just a spectator of life. I want to live again.*

Now Evelyn waited in the wings. What if she had a relapse? What if she embarrassed everyone? Yes, she was in remission, but what if …

The pianist repeated her entrance cue. There was no more time to fret.

* * *

By her third change of attire, swathed in a creamy piano shawl over a long, black, slit skirt, she felt more at ease. The backstage dresser suddenly added a flower to her hair.

"You look glamorous. Look in the mirror, Evelyn."

And when she did, a poised, elegant woman stared back.

At the curtain call, she felt victorious. Only a few years prior, she couldn't have walked that ramp, descended those stairs, or even, with help, made the quick outfit changes.

Maybe I have to accept what I can't change. I can't let it defeat me. Maybe I've had my own small miracle.

She flung the long, gauzy shawl around her shoulders. Her smile was triumphant as she glided past tables filled with yellow daffodils, a harbinger of her own spring.

It was time to appreciate every day and to welcome the unexpected flashes of delight.

Amelia's Magic Traveling Bookshop
Crissi Langwell

The second hand clicks on my mother's old clock, counting down the seconds to when I would say goodbye to "Amelia's Book Lounge," named after me when I was only three years old. My mom had had such grand visions for her bookshop. But five years after her passing, I've managed to run this place into the ground.

Now here I am, in the final five minutes of business, and not one person has come in to buy a book. Not even a good old fashioned "Everything Must Go" sign could bring me new readers.

"Brrr?" my Maine Coon cat chirps beside me on the counter.

"You're right, Pajamas. It's quitting time."

I stroke her fur, then move around the counter to turn the sign to "Closed" and let it remain that way forever. Tomorrow I'll pack up the store. But tonight, I'll enjoy a whole bottle of wine and a carton of ice cream while I search Craigslist for my next job.

Just as I'm about to reach the door, however, it opens with a jingle of bells, followed by a breathless man.

"Are you still open?" He's about my father's age, from what I can tell, his peppery hair clinging to his sweaty brow like he ran the whole way here.

"Of course! Can I help you find anything?" I vow to remain open as long as he wants. He can search the shelves all night.

"A bathroom."

I lose my customer service smile and point toward the room in the back. He makes haste, leaving me with Pajamas, wishing I'd turned the sign five minutes earlier.

I look out the window while I wait, noting the Volkswagen bus sitting against the curb, a "For Sale" sign in the window. It's red and white, just like a model one I had as a kid. I used to push that car around, pretending I was traveling the countryside with no home to call my own.

The guy returns from the bathroom looking a whole lot more relaxed.

"Sorry about that. The air conditioner quit about an hour ago and it's hot as blazes. And my bladder…" He waves his hand. "Sorry, TMI." He shoots me an apologetic smile, then pushes through the door. I watch as he leaves, my breath quickening when I see him unlock the front door of the VW bus.

"Sir!" I burst outside and jog to him. He turns, a secret in his smile.

"The bus," I say. "It's for sale?"

I don't know why I'm asking. I have nothing left.

"It is. Do you want to take a look?" He leans close. "Careful, it's magic," he teases.

"I don't doubt it. How much is it?" He could say five dollars, and I couldn't pay him.

"Well, I haven't decided yet," he admits. "But for the right person, I'd work something out."

I'm a goner when he opens the sliding door.

"It has bookshelves?" I exclaim, my eyes raking over shelves of books with latching doors. It's as if this bus was made for me! I can't help fantasizing about owning my own traveling bookshop, spreading joy through books all across the country.

He peers in, almost as if he's surprised. But then he grins.

"It sure does. Why don't you take it for a spin?"

I have no business feeding this fantasy. Still, I nod my head, eyes wide, and he places the keys in my hand. I look at them, in awe of even holding them. I want this bookmobile so bad. It's going to break my heart to tell him I can't afford it.

But when I look up, there's no one there. I look to the right, to the left. Back in the shop. Then I search the bus.

Pajamas hops in with a chirp, then finds her place in the passenger seat. Next to her is my purse, which I don't remember retrieving. Behind her are shelves filled with books.

The man is gone, and everything about this van feels like it was meant for me.

What if I just … went?

I sit in the driver's seat. Turning the key in the ignition, I'm met by a blast of cold air from the air conditioner.

"His AC works just fine," I tell Pajamas.

"Brrrr?" she agrees.

I put the car in drive, trying not to think too hard as I head for places unknown.

* * *

We're on the road all night, and well into the morning. The gas gauge seems stuck at full, but my stomach is on empty. Glancing at Pajamas, I'm fairly certain she could use a can of tuna, too, and maybe a dirt patch to do her business.

Driving slowly, I search both sides of the street until I find a little café with a promising parking lot where I could open shop. Nervous butterflies swarm in my empty belly. What if this works? What if people actually buy my books?

I head into the café and order a coffee, a yogurt, and a can of tuna. The girl looks at me strangely, but accommodates my requests.

I glance outside to see Pajamas waiting patiently for me at the café door, apparently done with her duties.

"Just a moment," I promise her.

"Shhh!"

I turn to find a guy at one of the tables glaring at me through his thick-framed square glasses, hunched over a computer next to three empty coffee cups.

"Oh sorry, I thought this was…"

"Aaaand it's gone again," he mutters, slamming his laptop shut and kicking the chair across from him. "Thanks a lot."

"Um, you're welcome?" I eye the toppled chair, wondering if I should set it right.

"Amelia!" the barista calls, saving me from this disgruntled guy. I grab my items and rush out of the cafe, Pajamas at my heels.

At the bus, I give the cat her food on a paper plate, accompanied by a bowl of water. Even though I'm hungry, I set up shop. I pull out tables, then open the shelves. I find an A-frame sign among the books, along with a black Sharpie. I think for a moment, then scrawl out "Amelia's Magic Traveling Bookshop," because this surely feels magic.

Once I'm set up, I settle onto a park bench next to the van and enjoy my breakfast. When that same guy storms out of the café, I brace myself and put on my friendliest smile.

"Can I help you?" I ask, standing as he approaches me.

"Likely no." He ducks his head and lets out a loud breath as his shoulders slouch. "I'm Jacob. And I'm sorry for that back there. I'm on deadline, and unfortunately suffering from the worst case of writer's block. I seem to have forgotten how to write anything. Everything ends up a word salad of adverbs and cliches. I just..." He looks at the sky. "I think I've run out of things to say."

"Now hold on a second." I take his arm and lead him to the side of the bus. "My mother used to tell me there is nothing in the world a good book can't solve. And I happen to have a whole bus of them. What if you take a look and see if something spurs a little inspiration?"

Jacob hesitates, but then shrugs and enters the bus.

I have no idea what's in there. I could be wasting both of our time on this venture. But like this guy, I have nothing to lose. If he leaves without finding a book, I'm no worse off than I was before.

"Wow, I've been looking for this everywhere," he says, holding up a book on method writing. "Oh, and this one! Wow, first edition!"

Jacob keeps finding books he wants. I try to hide my grin, but I'm elated. When he's done, he has a stack of twelve books, and he keeps looking back at the shelves.

"You didn't tell me these books were for writers," he says as I ring him up.

I deflate a little at this. They are? That's such a limited inventory. What if someone wants a romance book? Or a mystery? Or one that tells about the stars?

We part ways, and I hang around town for a few more hours, hoping for another sale. A few curious people look in my direction, but no one stops. So, while the sun is still high, I pack it in and head to the next town.

I don't get far. The bus sputters and coughs on the coastal highway, then whines to a stop at a long turnoff overlooking the ocean. I turn the key, but the engine only utters a death rattle.

"I think I know why the bus was for sale," I tell Pajamas. Never mind that it was free. Now I'm stuck in the middle of nowhere with a bunch of books and a useless vehicle.

I get out and open the trunk, revealing an engine I know nothing about. I fiddle with a few things, coming away with grease on my hands and no solution. I'm about ready to kick the tires, but that's when I notice a girl at the cliffside, a canvas in front of her and a frustrated look on her face. Then she winds up and throws one of her paintbrushes over the cliff. I watch in horror as it drops out of sight.

"What are you doing?" I run toward her.

"Quitting!" She winds up again. I snatch the brush from her hand before she can throw it.

"You can't quit!" I look at her painting, noting her version of the ocean gracing the canvas. "You're quite talented."

"I'm not, though. See there? My proportions are all wrong. The colors are muddy. The shadows aren't consistent." She goes on, pointing out things invisible to my eye.

"I never would have noticed," I say honestly.

"*I* notice. I have an art show coming up next week, and nothing is turning out right. I don't know what to do." She sighs. "The great Hannah Alistair. Wait till they find out I'm a fraud."

I look at the painting, which still looks pretty good to me. Then I look at the van.

"Hannah, is it? Well, Hannah, maybe I can help. I have a whole bus of books over there. Most are on writing, but I might have something that will help you see things in a different light. If anything, a break could help. Would you like to take a look?"

"I guess." She places her brushes on the easel and follows me to the bus. I slide open the door, and her eyes widen. "Wow, you weren't kidding!" She steps in and gasps at the first book she picks up. "This one on Monet! I saw it once in a bookstore in France and haven't been able to find it since. But you have it!" She continues perusing the shelves, eliciting breathy exclamations as she finds one book after another.

"I'll take all of these." She thrusts a stack of twenty books at me. I ring them up, realizing that I've sold more today than I have in the last week at the store.

I tidy the van when she's done, looking at the shelves as I do. They are all books about art—some picture books, others on technique, and all wildly fascinating. But when I take a second look, all I see are dusty old tomes with uninteresting titles. Nothing about art. Nothing about writing.

I get back into the driver's seat, and just for kicks, start the bus again. This time it springs to life, purring just like Pajamas in the passenger seat.

Careful, it's magic, that guy had told me.

I think I'm starting to understand.

I honk my goodbye as I leave the turnout, but Hannah is engrossed in her painting—a book in one hand and a paintbrush in the other.

* * *

I spend years on the road, traveling town to town. At every stop, I put books in the hands of people who need them. A mother with her colicky baby. A shy young man looking for courage. A future soccer star. A hobbyist ready to start a business.

Pajamas has been at my side the whole while, witnessing transformations that started with a good book. Now she's getting old and gray, and I'm starting to wonder what it's like to stay in one place.

The air conditioning quits as I approach a small town in California. I've driven this darling long enough to understand and take the next exit. The bus sputters to a stop in front of a small pastry shop, surrounded by empty tables despite the warm morning sunshine.

I get out, thinking I might find something to eat, but then I notice the sign on the window: "Closing. Last day Friday."

That's today. And not one customer appears to have shown up.

"What do you say, Pajamas?" I scoop her up and head inside. The bells jingle when I open the door, but the two people at the counter don't even look my way.

"We can get jobs," the young man says, consoling the crying girl. "Maybe move in with your parents."

I clear my throat.

"Oh, sorry." The woman looks up, brushing away tears. "You've just caught us. I'm Alice, and this is Peter, and today is … . Well, it's our last day. Can I get you anything? It's all half off."

"Your bathroom," I say. "Can my cat hang out?"

"It's not like the health inspector will shut us down," Peter jokes, but his laugh sounds like choking.

I leave Pajamas in the cafe and use their facilities. When I return, the place is empty. Pajamas sits alone on the concrete floor.

"Brrr?" she chirps.

"Outside, you say?" I peer toward the van, biting back a smile as I watch the couple circling the red and white vehicle. Pajamas crawls back into my arms, and I join them outside.

"You have an oven in your van?" Alice exclaims. The side door is wide open even though I had left it shut. Sure enough, there's an oven and counter space where the bookshelves used to be, and a pantry full of jars and containers with labels like sugar, flour, and salt.

"I suppose I do." A "For Sale" sign rests on the van's window.

"How much?" Peter asks.

"We can't afford it," Alice whispers loudly, swatting him on the arm.

"Well, why don't you take it for a test ride?" I hand Peter the keys. "When you get back, we can work out a price." I lean close. "Careful, it's magic."

The two of them hop in, chattering excitedly.

I imagine when they look up, they will wonder where I went.

The Talk
John J. Lesjack

"I'm not afraid of death. I just don't want to be there when it happens."
—Woody Allen

"Jenette?"

On our drive to Pacific Grove, the landscape morphs into sand dunes prior to our Del Monte Boulevard turn off. Jenette works a crossword puzzle beside me. She lifts her head and says, "Yes, Jean-Pierre?"

"What if … I go first?" I say, expecting her to say she'll miss me.

She says, "Don't say that."

"Why not?"

Jenette responds, "Be … because I'll be going first," and leans back in her seat.

* * *

We met at a church singles event over a decade ago. Petite and slender and, by her own admission, weighed a hundred and seven pounds. A glass of chardonnay in hand, she asked how I transitioned into single life, after fifteen years of married life.

Sandwich in hand, I said, "Easily. First, because I no longer looked under my bed or in my closet before going to sleep in my new place, I got eight hours of rest every night. Second, while she was in Acapulco, my children and I bonded in our new address close to school. How about you?"

"After thirty years of marriage," Jenette said, "My spouse took his romantic interests out on his catamaran. That left me enough alone time with our joint checking account to learn that half of our rental property income, savings, and equity had me financially set for life. Plus, instead of driving a used car, I could drive a brand-new hybrid of my choice. My children were grown, so I joined spiritual groups that gave me the emotional support I needed."

During our first date somewhere between dinner and a movie, I confessed, "Jenette, I'm not looking to get married or live together."

Jenette said, "Neither am I. How do you feel about traveling together?"

I responded, "Dutch treat?"

We visited Maine and Vermont that fall, where leaves were changing colors. I didn't think I would, but I appreciated Picasso's exhibit in Seattle's Art Museum. During our New Year's Eve dinner in New Orleans in Emeril's Fish House, Jenette toasted our good times with, "Joie de vivre." Our families were happy that we were happy.

We shared expenses and traveled well together through fifteen states and several years. Then Jenette experienced a minor stroke while driving home. Alone as she recovered, she got scammed out of a hundred thousand dollars, so her daughter took control of Jenette's income. Next, Jenette's car accident and lawsuit led her family to sell her house and enroll her in assisted living. Invited to Jenette's seventy-fifth birthday luncheon in Sunset Manor's main dining room, I was the only person to show up with a wrapped gift—a book on butterflies.

* * *

Jenette looks at El Estero Lake as I glance at her and ask, "What's new at Sunset Manor?"

"Nothing," she says, but suddenly turns to me, tears in her eyes, and adds, "I joined a stroke survivor's support group. Survival time for women my age is six years. My stroke happened five years ago."

I rub away an itch under my nose bandage and say, "You've got longevity genes in your DNA. Your mother lived to be ninety-three."

Jenette says, "Ninety-four."

I say, "You've been correcting me for ten years."

Jenette says, "Closer to eleven."

We enter Monterey's Tunnel and enjoy a curving road with a view of sailboats on Monterey Bay. On other excursions, we've been farther south and seen Pismo State Beach Monarch Grove. We've visited the Natural Bridges Monarch Trail an hour north in Santa Cruz, but Jenette likes the Monarch Grove Sanctuary. Neatly trimmed cypress trees wave gently as we cruise down Lighthouse Avenue where gabled Victorian buildings are as familiar to us as family.

* * *

It is April and we are strolling through the Sanctuary when Jenette says, "This place is like a cathedral without the acoustics."

"Friends of the Monarchs" and Boy Scouts are planting eucalyptus trees. Monarch Activist, Bob Pacelli, stands on a memorial bench. He begins his lecture with, "Butterflies overwinter here between October and March. They taste with their feet and smell with their antenna. They transition from eggs into caterpillars and then go through a massive transformation, crawl out of their skin and become beautiful black and orange critters who fly south."

* * *

Checking into the 1887 Gosby House Mansion situates us in downtown Pacific Grove, and within walking distance of three good restaurants: Fandango, the Red House Café, and The Passionfish.

Jenette calls them the "Bermuda Triangle of desserts."

I choose the Red House Café for dinner—I'm buying—and order a cheesy stuffed portabella mushroom with vegetables. Jenette orders a brownie topped with chocolate sauce.

I object with, "You can't have dessert until you eat everything on your plate."

Jenette comes back with, "That's what Republicans tell their children. Democrats eat dessert whenever they want."

Our server looks at my nose-bandage and says, "Looks like Mohs surgery." She points to her eyebrow and says, "Can you see my scar?"

I look at her eyebrow and say, "No. Are you sure you had surgery?"

As the sun sets, we linger on the café's narrow wooden porch. I'm conscious of how her stroke and weight gain affect her balance. When her daughter took her to the police station to file a complaint about being scammed, Jenette fell. Two police officers gently lifted Jenette back onto her feet.

Knowing she likes poetry and beaches, I say, "We're only a walking poem away from Lover's Point Beach."

Jenette hasn't smiled much since her stroke, but she smiles as I open my car's trunk and take out a king-size blanket my mother knitted years ago. Mom sent it to me when I was first married. Her Canadian relatives, a century ago, covered themselves with similar "lap robes" during winter carriage rides.

"Jenette," I say, respectful of her balance issues, "How do you feel about walking by streetlight?"

"Confident," she says. "I'll just look ahead to where my feet are going."

I button my jacket. She wraps a scarf around her neck.

"A tippet?" I ask.

English major Jenette says, "Only to Emily Dickinson. To me, it's just a long, warm scarf."

Jenette takes my arm. We walk carefully—we know no reason to hurry—down, down, down Nineteenth Street, past one old cottage whose roof is barely visible under lighted streetlamps. We cross Jewel Avenue, pass the Beach House restaurant, and follow our feet down gritty steps leading to Lover's Point Beach, where moonlit Monterey Bay has tiny waves caressing its shore.

I say, "Because I could not stop for death." Jenette finishes with, "He kindly stopped for me." It's one of our favorite poems.

With our blanket spread out on cool sand behind an old fire pit, Jenette and I sit side by side. I pull my big old covering over our heads and enjoy a private view of Monterey Bay.

I stare at water as smooth as winter ice and become mesmerized by the memory of my mother's experience as a farmer's daughter. Bundled up in her lap robe, Mom often traveled over a snow-packed trail in a horse-drawn sleigh on her way to a one-room schoolhouse in old Quebec.

Stars above bless us with a clear night sky.

I talk about how my vision of reciting poetry with her on this beach helped me endure three rounds of Mohs surgery. "Every time the nurse covered my face and chest with a heavy blanket and left only my nose vulnerable, I braced myself because I knew a needle was approaching, closed my eyes, and silently repeated, "The carriage held but just ourselves" and I waited for you to finish with, "And immortality."

Jenette responds, "Did you bring me down here just to tell me you are cancer-free?"

"Not exactly," I say. "Hopefully, our conversation will transition to our final plans."

Jenette says, "We used my lawyer to create our wills and trusts. We know your children get your stuff, my children get mine. What's left to talk about?"

Chilled, I wrap our blanket around my legs and say, "The horses' heads," and Jenette replies, "Are pointed toward eternity."

"The horse's head is a guide to the afterlife," I say. "My final plans call for cremation and spreading of my ashes on a sunny hillside. No funeral. No memorial. I've also written my obituary."

Jenette laughs and says, "You correct the spelling on your grocery list, too. You write and rewrite everything. That's just you. My will has no directions as to a funeral, memorial service or cremation because I'm not ready to face eternity. My daughter will decide all that."

I say, "The carriage held but just ourselves," which elicits no response. I mention how we've been one couple under two roofs for a long time, about how one of us will be home alone someday knowing that person will never hear from the other person again because someone has made their transition from this world into another. The survivor then transitions into single life again, and must learn if a new partner likes butterflies, Dickenson poetry, and eats dessert like a Republican or a Democrat.

Jenette says, "My mom left plans that included flower arrangements and lyrics from that song she liked ... 'I see the stars; I hear the rolling thunder' ... and she lived to be ninety-three."

I remind her gently, "Just before we entered the tunnel, you said your mum was ninety-four."

Jenette says, "Well, that's what she was!"

Which makes me appreciate our separate rooms where she can work on her crossword puzzles book late into the night. I change the subject with, "Maybe I'll join a travel group and go to Europe."

Jenette stiffens and yells, "I begged you to go to France and all you did was take me to that stupid Wood Allen movie, *Midnight in Paris!*"

I say, "You liked when Gertrude Stein said, 'We all fear death and question our place in the universe.'"

Jenette says, "I'm cold," and leans into me. I look into her glistening blue eyes as she says, "I can't tell you my final plans, Honey, but I can tell you this: I give thanks every day for our time in Butterfly Town."

She kisses me which ends our talk while wrapped in a blanket older than our relationship, a blanket resting on sand older than time, under stars my ancestor saw in Canada, her relatives saw in Utah—the same stars our grandchildren and great grandchildren will see wherever they live on this planet.

I collect Mom's blanket, take Jenette's hand, and look ahead to where our feet will land. Knowing no haste, we walk up, up, up Nineteenth Street, not falling once.

Standing on the Gosby House porch, we look beyond Lighthouse Avenue toward stars and heavenly bodies. We clink our wine glasses. It seems like centuries since we surmised the transitions in which our lives point.

I look toward Polaris and say, "I'll miss this place."

Jenette lowers her glass and asks, "The Gosby House Mansion?"

I hold her hand and say, "No, Honey … Earth!"

The Angler's Arms
Beth Lewis

"Don't stay out too late!"

Father's voice followed Mani as he rushed out the door of their shack. Mani knew his parents didn't like him spending too much time with humans, but he needed other people and as far as he knew the only other Person of Talent alive outside of his family was the mute boy the Guardians kept in the compound this village served. The king had slaughtered them all and would do the same to every member of his family, including all four of his younger siblings, if discovered.

He wandered the streets until he came across a young woman sitting on a bench outside an inn, watching the river carry away the filth of the inhabitants. He could feel her need for comfort and sat down beside her.

"I lived near a beautiful river before I was brought here," she said.

"I'm sure this one used to be beautiful. You could close your eyes and try to imagine it."

"That was before there were Guardians, before I was thrown out here with the rest of the refuse."

"You could imagine you're at the river near where you used to live," Mani said, allowing his legs to settle apart enough that his thigh made contact with hers. She immediately relaxed. He knew he shouldn't have used his talent to comfort her without permission, but he was tired of the headaches he got when he didn't help others, even though he never knew if he was risking his life by possibly revealing his talent.

The young woman looked over at him and smiled. "I'm Kishana. I know a creek near here that's as clear as glass. Would you like me to show you?"

Mani returned her warm smile when he answered, "Very much so."

She took his hand and led him past the huts and hovels that made up the outskirts of the village and into the surrounding forest.

They walked for the better part of an hour. By the time they reached the creek, the sunset was glowing on its ripples.

"Stunning!" Mani exclaimed.

"Mmm," she responded, leaning into him.

Mani was not unaccustomed to the affection of working girls. He'd spent time with humans his physical age, including the Leftovers, the children thrown out after they reached maturity and were no longer useful to the Guardians.

He wrapped an arm around Kishana's waist and held her against him while they watched the last light of day fade from the trickling water.

She turned to him, resting her head on his chest. "I wasn't going to work tonight. Then you came along."

"You don't have to work. I'll walk you home."

"No, I … I want you to stay with me. I want to pretend you want me. Now that the Guardians have finished with me, no one wants me."

"Surely you have family who want you."

She shook her head. "I'm dead to them. When I went home, they wouldn't even look at me," she continued. "I was only twelve when the Guardians threw me out. I came back here because I thought maybe I could keep working for them somehow. But no one wants me."

"You could go somewhere no one knows you. You could tell them you're a widow. There are a lot of jobs you could do in a city."

"There's only one I'm good at."

"What did you do for the Guardians?"

"I was a maid."

"You could work as a maid in a city."

"You don't understand. I didn't learn how to be a maid. That's what the Guardians call the girls who … ."

As she said this, she turned away and looked at the ground. Mani was beginning to feel the weakening effects of the extensive amount of comfort he was doling out. He took her hand and led her to sit on a nearby stone.

"You can learn a trade. You have to try."

"I suppose I could go to a city and do the same thing I do here," she said as her melancholy faded and her attraction to Mani returned. She ran a hand up and down his leg. He pulled his knees together and shifted on the stone.

"You don't want me?"

"It's not that," he said. "You're very pretty. It's just that…"

"I won't ask for compensation if that's what you're worried about."

"No, I … I don't want you to do anything you'll regret later."

"I won't regret it. I want to thank you for making me feel better."

Mani felt a moment of panic before he decided she wasn't aware of the true nature of her improved mood. She looked into his eyes. Overcome by an irresistible force of nature, he kissed her lips. She responded with overwhelming enthusiasm.

* * *

When he got home in the wee hours of the night, his parents were waiting for him.

"Your mother and I have been very worried. She mindcalled you and you closed her out."

Mani blushed when he remembered hearing his mother's call at a very inopportune moment. "I don't know why you worry. I'm old enough to take care of myself."

"You seem to forget that our lives are forever in danger. How could we be sure you weren't captured or even killed? This is a very dangerous village for our people."

"I still don't see what the problem is. I wouldn't reveal myself. I've had plenty of practice at it. I'm well past the time of indiscretion. I can control my talent perfectly well now."

Mother gave her husband a knowing look. "I had a couple of friends who thought that, only to find themselves very young parents. Just wait until you have your own. Then you'll understand the fear we feel."

"And when exactly will that be? I don't see very many eligible girls of my race in this village. In fact, I haven't seen one since the king murdered them all. So I can never have children."

Mani stormed out. He spent the night wandering the dusty streets, feeling lonelier than ever and entirely too sorry for himself. When the night faded into a warm glow, he headed home.

Before he arrived, he could smell breakfast. Although she didn't have a cooking talent, Mani's mother had a strong talent for growing children that spilled over into her cooking abilities. Mani's mouth watered.

"I'm sorry," he said, kissing her cheek.

"I'm sorry too," she answered. "I forget sometimes how difficult it must be for you. I don't know what I'd do if I didn't have your father. I just have to believe that someday we might find another family like ours."

Mani shook his head. "I can't. I have to believe that what we have now is the way it will always be; that I will be alone in the end."

"Not alone, Mani. You have us. Your brothers and sisters will be there when we're gone."

Mani shrugged and sat down to eat.

* * *

The next morning, Mani got up early and helped his father build furniture. He didn't have a building talent, but he was extremely helpful.

"Why don't you take a break and go find some friends to keep you company," his father suggested. Even though he didn't like it, he knew there was something about his son that created his restless need to be with people.

Mani thanked his father and headed towards the river. Kishana wasn't on the bench, not that he expected her to be there, but it wasn't long before she joined him.

"I figured you were still asleep," Mani said.

"I had to work this morning."

He gave her a sideways look. "You work in the morning?"

"Yes, well, sometimes, if I'm finishing up from the night before."

"Oh."

"I'm free now. Do you want to go for a walk?"

"Sure, I mean, you're not too tired, are you?"

"I got plenty of sleep. This morning wasn't very difficult." She giggled. "He was in a hurry to get home before his wife woke up."

Mani started to comment but stopped himself. "Let's go to the market square. I want to get something for my little brother's birthday."

As they strolled through the market, Mani fingered the few coins in his pocket. He wasn't sure if he could afford much in the way of a gift and as the morning wore on he became more and more disillusioned.

"I wish I could have worked a little more before his birthday," he said. "I don't have a lot to spend."

"There aren't many jobs around here. What can you do?"

"Just about anything that everyone else can do, and read and write besides."

"You can read!" Kishana shrieked.

"Shhh!" Mani scolded. "Yes, I went to school when I was younger," he said, looking around to make sure no one was listening. Most teachers in the kingdom had been People of Talent and he wasn't sure if letting on he could read might give him away.

"If you teach me, I'll buy you whatever you want," she said. "I'll even pay you to teach me."

"You don't have to do that. Teaching is free."

"Then how do teachers live?"

"People they teach give them food."

"I don't have any food with me right now. I could buy you some, but wouldn't you rather have the currency?"

Mani chuckled at her logic. "All right, but it may take a while to teach you. I mean more than one day."

"I don't mind. Can you start now?"

"I suppose so. Where can we work?"

"At the inn. Everyone there's asleep."

"I'll go get one of my little brother's books. I'm sure he won't mind."

"I'll go ahead and straighten up," she said, blushing.

When Mani arrived at the inn, Kishana was waiting outside, pacing back and forth.

"What's the matter?"

"The innkeeper thinks I'm working. He wants his share."

"Tell him he can watch if he wants."

Kishana laughed. "I'll do that." She took Mani's hand and led him to the kitchen where the innkeeper was supervising the preparation of the midday meal. "Mani says you're welcome to watch."

He scowled at them and turned back to his work. Mani and Kishana hurried away, laughing.

* * *

For the next several weeks, Mani spent the mornings teaching Kishana how to read. She was a fast learner and soon could read all of Ili's books. When she finished the last one, she slapped it closed and hugged Mani, then kissed him hard on the mouth. While he was catching his breath, she grabbed her shawl and pulled him along behind her.

"I wanted to thank you," she said over her shoulder, "and I have some exciting news."

Mani picked up his pace.

* * *

As they lay in each other's arms, Kishana snuggled up to him. "We'd better go. I have to get to work soon."

"What if I hire you for the night?" he asked.

"You get me for free. Why would you pay?" she asked, tossing him his trousers and buttoning her blouse.

"It's more comfortable in your bed," he answered.

She grinned and poked him in the ribs. "The innkeeper would want me to pay him for all those other times you came."

"Tell him no."

"He'll throw me out. Although I did a pretty good business for him. It doesn't matter, anyway."

"What do you mean?" Mani asked.

"That's my news," she grinned. "Now that I can read and write, I have a job as a tutor! I'm leaving in three days."

"I'm so happy for you! I knew you could do it. I'll pay tonight so you have traveling money and if the innkeeper says he wants you to pay him for the other days, you can tell him no."

She looked at him askance. "Hmm, all right. We can go to my room, but you can't pay me. You're my friend."

"But you paid me to teach you."

"I only paid the first time."

Mani laughed. "I got my first time for free."

Kishana laughed along with him as they headed back to town. When they got to Kishana's room, they fell onto the bed laughing, prompting the innkeeper to pound on the door, demanding his share.

Shortly afterwards, Mani's mother mindcalled him. There was nothing he could do. She was almost bowled over by the intensity of the activity she had interrupted. She didn't say anything but left him to finish and explain himself later.

Mani tried to sneak in the next morning, but didn't quite make it past his sleeping parents in the front room of the shack. His little brother Ili lay sandwiched between them and he knew Ili must have awakened in the night and wanted him. The moment he saw Mani sneak in, he hollered.

"Mani, where were you? I had a scary dream."

"I've told you that dreams aren't real," he said, lifting the little one into his arms.

"Mother said she had a friend who had dreams that came true."

Mani opened his mouth to say something, then remembered that he probably wasn't in any position to be angry with her. He took his little brother into the other room to get him dressed and went to his father's workshop.

"You can't let yourself get attached to anyone," Father scolded.

"We're just friends."

"Human friends don't touch like our people do. They see it as much more intimate. You could be giving her the wrong impression. She might think you want a more permanent arrangement."

Mani grinned to himself as he carried a newly made table over to the corner of the workshop. "I don't think so."

"How do you know? Maybe she has a father or a big brother who'll decide you've sullied her honor in some way. Humans are highly volatile. You never know what they might do."

Mani sat on the edge of the table. "No, Father, that won't happen. She doesn't have any family anymore. They disowned her when the Guardians defiled her. She works at the Angler's Arms now."

"As a barmaid?"

Mani shook his head. "She has her own room."

Father looked away. "I see."

Mani picked at the dirt under his fingernails.

"You're telling me that you're simply a customer," Father continued.

"No, nothing like that. I've been teaching her to read. Now she can leave this village and get a respectable job."

Father looked up and met the eyes of his eldest child and was overwhelmed by pride. Then he asked, "And what exactly were you reading when your mother mindcalled you last night?"

Mani blushed. "Kishana was thanking me."

Father nodded, turning away to hide his grin. "If you do any more favors for your friend, try to get home earlier so your mother doesn't mindcall you during a display of gratitude."

"Yes, Father," Mani chuckled.

Damocles
Roger Lubeck

I am surprised to find Bert's All-Night Diner and Bar empty. New Orleans never sleeps. At three in the morning, the bar stools and booths are normally filled with hookers, sleeping drunks, and drug addicts. Originally, Bert's was a shotgun house built a century ago for Black workers employed by a now-abandoned factory. The bar runs half the length of the building with a kitchen behind the bar. There is a window booth at the front and five booths across from the bar. At the back, past the two restrooms, is a curtained-off room with a small stage and dance floor. Bert's has music on Friday and Saturday. This is Sunday.

Bert is behind the bar reading the daily racing sheet. He and I go way back.

"Mr. D," he says. "What will it be?"

"Coffee with room for cream and extra sugar," I say.

"Not hungry?"

"Any donuts?"

"Not until four."

"Just coffee," I say.

Good news. Donuts mean cops. Cops and I don't mix.

Coffee in hand, I check out the bathrooms and peek through the curtains. Satisfied that I am alone, I sit at the last booth before the rest rooms and sip my coffee, waiting for the caffeine and other drugs to kick in. Tracking is never easy. The older I get, the more I question the sensibility of it all. The need for it.

A college crowd, two boys and a girl, stagger in from a bar down the street. The girl is an overly made-up blonde with large half-exposed breasts. She collapses into the window booth at the front, laying her head against the window.

A small skinny boy takes the seat across from the blonde. The other boy is large, with broad shoulders and a beer belly. He orders a burger and fries from Bert and then sits beside the blonde, putting his arm around her shoulders. Alone, the blonde might be a good choice for a hunter, but her large boyfriend would make the play more difficult.

A second girl stands at the diner door, scanning the room. She is pale, with short jet-black hair, green eyes, and a wide mouth. Her lower lip has crimson-colored lipstick. Her upper lip is painted black like blood. Her eyebrows have been penciled into a V-shape, giving her an exotic look.

She turns and glances my way. The blood coursing through her jugular makes the skin on her throat glow pink. Her green eyes dart back and forth. Tasting the air, I sense something hiding beneath her cool, dark demeanor. She might be a first-time hunter going through the change.

Taking a dollar from my pocket, I select E-17 on the mini-jukebox in the booth. "I Feel Love," by Donna Summer. The electronic beat sets the mood. Donna and disco made hunting easy in the 1980s.

I stand and slow-walk toward the front booth. My eyes focus on the green-eyed girl. I stop and wait for Donna to begin. "Ooh, it's so good, it's so good, it's so good," she sings.

I approach the girl.

"Would you like to dance?" I ask.

She gives me an appraising look. Wetting her lips, I see sharp teeth.

"Fuck off, old man," says the fat boy.

"I'm not talking to you. I'm talking to the young lady." I give him a hard look.

"Tommy, call the manager," says the blonde to the fat boy. "He looks dangerous."

"I don't know about dangerous, but he certainly stinks," says the other boy, trying hard to sound both brave and clever. His eyes betray his fear.

"I mean no harm, and I smell as nature intended."

I stare at the girl. The connection is there. I lean down. "Donna Summer," I tell her softly, "stirs old memories in me, and I feel the need to dance. To dance with a pretty girl."

"Where can we dance?" the girl asks.

"There is a small dance floor at the back of the diner."

I take her hand.

"Violet, stay where you are. Freddie, get the owner," says the blonde to the skinny boy.

"Violet, beautiful like your eyes. Dance with me. I think you are ready. Ready for the dance."

She looks deep into my eyes.

"I am ready," she says, walking ahead of me toward the curtains.

Sensing a threat, I turn as Tommy reaches for my shoulder. I grab his hand and twist his arm backwards, driving him hard to his knees. Freddie is hiding under the table.

"Violet will be fine. You should go."

"I'm not afraid of an old man like you."

"I am not the threat. Violet is going through a change. I want to help her, but I can't if you are here. Go before it is too late."

Tommy looks at the other boy. Confusion and fear. They want to leave.

"There isn't time to explain," I say. "If she comes back out, none of us may survive. Take your friends and go."

I lift Tommy to his feet and push him toward the door.

"Run," I shout.

The three flee the diner. Bert, holding a tray of food, gives me a sour look.

"Bag it up," I tell him. "I'll take it home after my dance."

I walk to the back of the diner and part the curtains. The stage is dark. A single spotlight illuminates the dance floor. Violet sways to the music. She has her eyes closed, dreaming of some long-forgotten place.

"Are they gone?"

"Yes."

I move close to her, and I put my arm around her waist. Her body is on fire. She is electric.

"Are you a hunter?" she asks.

"When I was younger, I hunted. Now I am more like a tracker. I help new hunters."

I take her in my arms. We move as one, letting the music guide us.

"What about the owner? Is he one of us?"

"Bert only knows burgers and the ponies."

She looks back through the curtains. Bert is sitting at a booth eating a plate of fries. Her green eyes sparkle. She wets her lips; the hunger in her is clear.

"We need to get out of here," I say.

"I don't know if I can. The transition has started."

"I live close by. I can help you."

* * *

We walk the three blocks to my house in silence. It isn't much; a colorful shotgun in a block of similar homes. The inside is neat and orderly, like its owner. I show Violet around, pointing out the bathroom and the guest bedroom. While she is using the bathroom, I set out cheese and crackers, pour glasses of wine, turn on Miles Davis' "Kind of Blue," and sit in one of the two easy chairs by a fireplace.

"Is this your first?" I ask when she is seated across from me.

"My first was an infant. A neighbor's little boy. The change happened in the summer before I entered college. My parents helped me. It was awful. After, I felt ashamed, but I also felt alive for the first time. My father says human sacrifice is necessary for us to live as true Gians. We must feed or die."

"Feeding during a change keeps the cycle alive," I say. "In my experience, if you can keep from hunting and feeding on humans, you don't die, you just return to normal."

"For how long?" Violet asks.

"That's up to you. If you are willing, I can show you another way."

"Isn't it too late?"

"When I was in high school, I only needed one hunt to sustain me for a year. When I was thirty, I was hunting all the time. Consuming more than I needed."

"Why?"

"I loved the hunt. In college, I used sex to capture my prey. I found in the act of sex, as the woman climaxes, she is most vulnerable. In consuming her life, for an instant I saw a vision of Gia, before the great death. Back then, even sated on human life, I hunted and fed, if only for that brief vision."

"I've had that vision. How did you stop?"

"The newsfeeds talked about the police hunting for a serial killer."

"I suppose in their eyes, that's what we are, serial killers," says Violet.

"On Gia, hunting was a way of life. We are hunters. From birth, we learn to track and trap our prey. One day I caught a young woman, very much like you. Her name was Faith. Beautiful and clever. In hindsight, I didn't trap her … she trapped me."

"How?"

"We were hiking on a trail along the coast. The area was remote and isolated. At some point, I stopped and tried to kiss her. She pushed back, saying she wasn't ready for sex."

"Did that matter?"

"It did for me. I didn't rape my victims. I never used violence. Their lives ended in a moment of shared ecstasy. She took my hand. 'Look around,' she said, 'what does this remind you of?'"

"The windswept coast, untouched in its beauty, made me feel like I was back on Gia and my hunger was gone. 'I'm on another world,' I said. 'Gia,' she said. Only then did I realize she was Gian."

"Finish your story."

"Off the trail, Faith took me to a meadow of flowers. We lay together and I slept. When I awoke, Faith was kissing my chest. Soon we were naked, and the urgency of our lovemaking overwhelmed me. Nothing in my experience prepared me for the magic when we came together. My sense of being one with another person—not two—not human and alien. Gian and Gian. One being in a moment of ecstasy. To my surprise, when I lay back exhausted, Faith continued to climax; wave after wave of pleasure washed over her and onto me. When she finished, I realized my need to feed was gone. All I wanted was to make love again. Lying on the flowers with the sound of the waves, I wanted nothing more in life. I slept for a time and when I awoke, Faith was dressed and I was bound with my zip-tied hands behind my back."

"'Are you with the police?' I asked her."

"'No, I'm a healer,' she said."

"Healer?" Violet says.

"Healers find Gians. They are like anglers who love to fish, but they release the fish once caught. Faith was like that. She tracked Gians and when caught, she helped them overcome the need to hunt and kill. Like a fisherman who catches and releases his prey."

"Is that possible?"

"Faith's parents didn't believe in hunting. They taught her a different way. She told me her role in life was to help hunters like me become human. 'I don't want to be human,' I told her. 'To be human is to die inside.'"

Violet is staring at me intensely.

"Faith asked me if I had ever wondered why it is we look like humans; why we can breathe their air and eat their food. Why we can have sex."

"I've wondered the same thing," says Violet.

"According to Faith, the human's idea of a supreme being may not be that far off. It was her belief that billions of years ago, a race of aliens visited our two worlds and planted the seeds for life. Similar worlds with the same seeds and after millions of years of evolution, we are cousins."

"Where's the proof?" Violet asks

"There isn't any. That is why she called herself Faith. She had faith that Gians can live with humans without hunting. Faith is the reason I became a tracker."

"You mean healer," says Violet.

"No, I'm a tracker. On Earth, trackers find the prey for the hunters. They don't hunt and kill. They track and find. What happens then is up to the hunter. I found you. What happens now is up to you."

"I don't know your name."

"I'm called Damocles."

"Like the story of the sword?"

"There is a sword hanging over your head. Life or death. Determined by your actions."

"How long will it take?" Violet asks.

"Tonight may be the worst. I'm putting you in my spare bedroom. If your hunger is too strong, wake me and I will keep you safe until your need to hunt is over."

It is hours later when I feel her slip under the sheets, her sweating body naked. The first rays of sun have turned the sky dark blue. In the Quarter, they call this time of morning *l'heure bleue*. The blue hour.

Our lovemaking is violent at first and then tender and sweet. As we climax, I expose my throat, giving her the option to change; to complete her hunt. Instead, she writhes on top of me, allowing me to share in her ecstasy. In that moment, I take her life, as I had Faith's all those years ago, and I am back on Gia. A prime hunter. The lord of a dying world. The joy of being on Gia doesn't last. It never does, but it is enough. I am a true Gian again. Tracking and hunting my own kind. Faith wanted to heal Gians of their need to hunt humans. On Earth, we only hunt humans because they are so plentiful. For me, predator and prey are two sides of the same tarnished coin.

Life Review
Nancy Martin

"Ohhh Mommy, look how cute. I want that one. Please, oh please!" Six-year-old Cathy begged as she swooned over one of the blond pups. She lay on the floor while the puppy bounced all over her and licked her face. Above the two stood Cathy's parents. Next to them, the owners of the dogs looked on proudly.

"These are prize-winning AKC-pedigreed toy poodles, as advertised. Both parents are champion show dogs. While the pups you see here won't be in the show ring, any one of them will make an excellent pet and companion dog for your child."

Following some discussion between her parents and the breeders, Cathy chose her pup and they left for home with a new family member.

"Geez, I can't believe we paid that much for a *dog*," her dad said once they were safely ensconced inside their shiny red Tesla.

Mom had brought along a pink satin-lined puppy bed. Cathy watched a video of last year's Westminster Kennel Club Dog Show on the overhead screen in the back seat while her new puppy snoozed in its lavish little bed.

"Can we call her Honey? She's almost the color of honey," asked Cathy.

"Sure, sweetie," her mom replied. "That's a cute name. But we'll have to come up with a fancy name for her registration papers. Now you watch her closely, Cath. Make sure she doesn't fall out of her bed."

"Oh Mom, I would *never* let anything happen to Honey. She'll be the number one most pampered dog in the whole world."

Honey whined. *"Who are these people? Why did they take me away from my brothers and sisters? I want my mom."*

Cathy immediately picked up her new puppy and snuggled her against her cheek. "Don't worry little one, you're going to love your new home."

As time went on, it was clear that Honey ruled the roost. Nothing was too good for the little golden poodle. She was Cathy's most cherished possession, companion, and family member. Honey had a huge, manicured back yard with a swimming pool as her domain. She went regularly to a pricey pet groomer in town and slept with Cathy in her bed.

"Everyone knows that I am a queen. Only the best for me," were Honey's ever-present thoughts while snubbing the neighbor's mutt or contentedly snacking on a piece of rare steak. Humility was not her strong suit.

Twelve years went by in a flash. Cathy, now eighteen, was heartbroken that her cherished life-companion was so ill and took Honey to the vet.

"How could you leave me here in this dreadful, smelly place in a cage, surrounded by the motley vulgus of the dog world?" Stuck with needles and force-fed medicine that caused her to vomit, Honey felt herself slipping away.

* * *

The first thing he remembered was waking up in a cramped cage on a filthy blanket with his mom and many siblings—all different colors. He had dreams of people petting him and feeding him tasty food. The men came twice a day to feed mom and toss the pups around, often inflicting pain on them.

"Look at these ratty little bastards. They'll bring plenty in the fight ring," one man said.

"We gotta make 'em mean from the get-go," a second man said, kicking the pup they called Bruno.

Bruno was ninety pounds of pure muscle and bone. He hated the men. He had long since been separated from his canine family and placed in a small, foul cage. Every day, one of the men either mercilessly beat him or threw him in with another dog to fight over food, often leaving him wounded. After one year, when he had reached full weight capacity and knew nothing but how to fight for his life, the night arrived when they took him in a truck with other dogs to an unfamiliar place. *"This won't be good,"* the dogs told each other. *"Some of us won't come back."*

The room was thick with smoke and the sounds of snarling dogs. Coarse, angry men shouted out bets and curses. Bruno was chained to the side of a large fight ring at a safe distance from the other dogs. He had a pretty good idea what would happen next. Soon enough, he heard a man on the loudspeaker say his name. His handler roughly dragged him into the ring where another man on the other side was doing the same with his dog. When a bell rang, the handlers released their dogs, who rushed at each other, snapping and snarling.

It was kill or be killed. Bruno felt his hide being ripped apart. Tasting blood from his attack on the opposing dog only heightened his hatred and will to live. Just soon enough, the dogs were separated before one of them died in the ring. Bruno was stitched up in several places and medicated into a deep sleep. Always hungry and in pain, this became the pattern of his life until one of his opponents finally conquered him. But throughout his pitiful life, he kept the dream of a pampered life.

* * *

It was a typical day at the animal shelter. The air was filled with the sounds of eager cats and dogs. When James and Martha entered the building, friendly volunteers greeted them and completed their adoption application. Then, another volunteer in the dog section escorted them down the hallway lined with cages. Everything was spotless. Some dogs cringed as they approached, fearfully pasting themselves to the backs of their cages. The volunteer explained that many of the rescued dogs had been mistreated and abused, leaving them wary and shy. Others barked uproariously and angrily lunged at the cage doors. Some looked very sad, while others were listlessly eating or sleeping.

One dog, a medium-sized black and brown mixed breed with silky ears, quietly approached the front of his cage and seemed to smile at them. James asked the volunteer, "What's the story with this dog?"

"This is Quigley. He's a good old boy, just looking for his forever home. Somebody picked him up on the street and brought him here, but nobody has ever come looking for him. He's been here for about six months and never given us a bit of trouble."

James and Martha took Quigley to a quiet room in the animal shelter where they could observe him. He lay right down next to James, resting his jaw on James' left sneaker, gazing up at him adoringly with soulful brown eyes. Well, that pretty-well clinched the deal and they left with the dog. They re-named him Buddy. When Martha came home from work each day, Buddy would be over-the-moon with joy. Her classic comment was, "Dogs are so nonjudgmental, they just want you to love them."

James took Buddy for walks or to jog with him in the evenings. Folks passing by often stopped to offer Buddy a pat on the head or a scratch behind the ears and often quipped, "That is one happy dog. He is actually smiling!"

Most dogs dream, but Buddy had howling dogmares. When he wasn't dreaming about living the life of Honey, he would have unbearable visions of beatings and pain. First James would feel his dog tremble, hear the high-pitched whining begin, and then notice snapping and growling. Buddy's legs would kick and run uncontrollably in a frenzy.

But always, through the fog and confusion of his dream, he would hear James' voice cutting through the mental trauma: "Hey Bud, you're dreaming. Come back." And Buddy would.

Blood
E. J. McBride

"Your father had a heart attack."

Mom's voice from across the continent without even a friendly *hello* first. I hold the phone for a few seconds, calculating the time, the distance, my own heavy schedule, the responsibilities of a son to his father. What are the responsibilities of a son to his father? How do you calculate that? On what formula is it based?

Most father/son relationships are complicated, and ours was no exception. As a kid, my father had "learning disabilities." He left school at sixteen, barely able to read and write. He never read a book in his life. He told me that once, but he didn't need to. I was there. My wife, Donna, who wasn't there, who is herself the daughter of a prominent lawyer, never understood that. She continued over the years to give him books for Christmas: books on Irish history, Irish fables, Irish poetry. Books that made him smile when he got them, but which he never read.

He worked as a porter, carrying boxes, loading trucks, cleaning, sweeping. A life behind a broom. I never wanted to be like him. Even as a child, I felt I was higher class, with my straight A average from strict Catholic school, with my reading and writing years above grade level, with my ability to add, subtract, multiply, and divide faster and more accurately than anybody else, child or adult, I had ever encountered.

In high school, one of the city's best prep schools where I attended alongside the sons of bankers and doctors, architects and judges, I never mentioned my father or what he did for a living. I sometimes wondered what my mother saw in him.

"He's sleeping now," Mom says, pulling me back to the crisis. She's on a pay phone in the hospital lobby. She hasn't gotten used to her cell yet. Still thinks of it as a toy I'd bought her for Christmas rather than an essential communication device. "They want to do some tests tomorrow."

"What kind of tests?"

"I don't know. I didn't really understand…"

"Okay," I say gently. "Let's see how he is tomorrow. If it looks serious, I'll come right in."

Unlike me, with mixed genes, my father is an Irishman fully and completely, fifth of ten children, born just after his parents' arrival in New York. The first language to hit his ears was Gaelic. To look at him, the pale blue eyes, fair, freckled skin, you could hardly mistake him for anything else. Sober, he is a shy, quiet man. Though he's lived there all his life, he seems out of place in New York. Out of place among the hustlers, the raw ambition, the awesome energy of the big, pulsating city. A man who would have been a better fit on a farm in cool, rocky Donegal, feeding his animals, going about his daily chores, season after season, like his ancestors had done for generations before him.

He had no lofty desires, no goals I'd ever heard expressed, except regarding his funeral. He wanted a big funeral. A traditional Irish wake. He'd told me this at Christmas, after a few cold beers.

In the teenage years, we emphasize the negatives. I hated that he smoked, leaving the ugly smell hanging in the air, polluting our little apartment. And that he drank, coming home a different person, talking to himself, laughing, tripping on the stairs. As a child, it scared me. There were nights that went on too long, nights of raised voices, nights of listening to my mother's nervous tone, cajoling, trying to keep things under control. There were occasional nights that ended with mom's tears. Those were the worst nights.

When I was in college, his drinking seemed more foolish than frightening. In those years, we saw things from opposite camps. We never talked about Vietnam, but I knew he was part of Nixon's "silent majority," while I was on the streets protesting. He hated long hair on men, while I wore it rebelliously. He had no use for the civil rights movement, while I had friends and lovers of every race and creed. He had no religious education, no training in complicated doctrine, but he never missed his Sunday mass.

* * *

The next morning, when the phone rings, I am reluctant to pick it up. He is only sixty-eight, but he never stopped smoking, never took up an exercise program, never changed his diet. He hasn't looked good lately. We all noticed that, noted it individually, but he wasn't a complainer. No squeaky wheel, he never got the grease.

"He's awake today, but he's not good. He's calling people crazy names. He called Danny Dominick. I never knew any Dominick."

"What about his heart?"

"They said there's damage. The nurse said he was stable. I don't know what that means."

Stable? He has always been that. One wife for forty-seven years. Two jobs in a lifetime. Church every Sunday in the same blue suit, if weather permitted. He hasn't missed a day of work in as long as I can remember. He was in church when his heart stopped. Though there were people all around him, he didn't ask for help. He was blue when the paramedics arrived. He was born blue; what they called in those days a blue baby. As a twin, he hadn't gotten enough oxygen in his mother's womb. If the paramedics had been a few minutes later, he would have died the way he was born: blue, unable to breathe, surrounded by people.

As a kid, I was crazy about sports. But never once did he throw me a baseball or a football. In high school, I became a track star, won a scholarship to a prestigious university where I competed against, and sometimes beat, Olympians. But my father never saw me run a race. Athletics were frivolous to him. My own son, who isn't very athletic, sees me standing on the sidelines for any event he tries. I want to be a better parent. I want to be … closer.

What are the responsibilities of a son to his father? What columns do you add or subtract? Does it depend on what kind of father he has been? Does it depend on wealth or power, how affectionate he is or how much he has taught? What are the responsibilities of a father to his son, and of a son to his father?

After lunch, while I am trying to decide what to do, Donna calls me at the office. "I talked to the hospital in Brooklyn." She sounds nervous, upset. "I wanted to send flowers. They told me he's in intensive care. Did you know he's in critical condition?"

"No," I say. "I didn't know that."

Death is close. Closer than we think.

I moved to the West Coast in my mid-twenties. At thirty, I got married. By thirty you see things in a larger context. Life is messy. It isn't pretty when we come in, or any prettier when we go out. In between, we spend our time trying to control the mess. For a depression-era child whose own father was unemployed more often than employed, whose own father moved out when he could no longer cope, the struggle was just to survive.

When my father was nine, he and his older brother built a shoeshine stand. They invested a nickel for the subway, went into Manhattan, and spent their days shining shoes from morning to night. They gave the money they made, every cent of it, to their mother. In the summers, they went to the beach, not to swim—my father never learned how to swim— but to sift through the sand for lost change.

"They need to operate," my mother says when I get her on the phone. "He's gonna die if they don't operate. They asked me for permission. They said it was urgent."

I book a flight on the red-eye, the soonest flight I can make. I take an envelope of old pictures with me, for mom, and spend time on the plane looking through them. There is a family picture, taken on a summer day in the 1930s: my father's family standing together on the roof of their Brooklyn tenement. It's a flat roof, without plants or fence or any kind of safety railings. In the picture, the only picture I have ever seen of my father as a child, he is dressed absurdly in baggy pants and a shirt obviously passed down from his older brothers and doesn't come close to fitting. But among the pack of ten rugged looking, poorly dressed kids, he is the only one smiling.

On the plane, looking through photos of their early life, I can see that he was a handsome man, with the looks and features of a young Patrick Swayze. But that isn't something a child notices. Not something a son cares about.

I used to be surprised when people liked him. Liked his odd way of saying things, his directness, his simplicity, but liked him, I thought, in the way one likes a Forrest Gump. For a long time, I was afraid to introduce him to Donna. I was afraid of what he might say to her, or how he might say it. We didn't have a big wedding. We got married alone, just the two of us, without the warmth or burden of family. But eventually, inevitably, they met. He had a few drinks, told her how pretty she was, and called her by the wrong name: the name of one of my ex-girlfriends. But she liked him. Later, they became friends, talked on the phone, exchanged holiday cards and letters. In later years, he began writing regularly: short, funny things on weird scraps of paper, written in large, crooked, child-like printing, half the words misspelled. He used to tell us about celebrities who died, as if we didn't get that news all the way out in California.

"It's me. I'm at the airport."

I can tell from the cracking of her voice that it is bad. "He has … cancer. They said it's everywhere. That's why his heart stopped. They won't even let me see him."

My father hated hospitals. He believed that once they got their hands on you, you never got out alive. Yet, when John Kelly, his oldest childhood friend, was dying of cancer, he went to see him every afternoon in the hospital. Every day for weeks, he sat alongside his friend's hospital bed even after Kelly had gone into a coma and no longer knew he was there.

He was willing to talk about that. Death. Dying. But never about life, about what made him happy, what he lived for. He seemed incapable of pursuing a pleasure, a desire, a thrill. He never went to a movie. I never saw him dance. I never saw him exercise for its own sake. His personality was formed in his early years and his childhood did not allow for anything beyond necessity. As an adult, he got his pleasures through my mother. Watching her swim. Or dance. Or laugh. And that seemed enough for him. When they came to visit me in California, every year in the last years of his life, they followed her agendas, pursued her desires. Though he never liked the beach, he walked with her there every day and sat on a bench, fully dressed, while she swam or did yoga or soaked up the sun.

What kind of father had he been?

One who was there. One who never went away.

The only one I had.

At the hospital, I go to the front desk and ask about the ICU. "Fourth floor," I'm told. "But visiting hours don't start until ten o'clock."

"Thank you," I say, and walk past her to the elevator. On the fourth floor, I summon my most authoritative look as I walk through the double metal doors, daring anyone to stop me. There are several old men in the room, hooked to machines, barely alive. The men are all gaunt, with little hair on their heads and lots of white hair on chin and cheeks. I have to look closely at each face to find him.

He has tubes up his nose, down his throat. He can't speak. But when I call to him, his eyes open, still intense blue, and he nods in recognition.

I talk to him for a while, about his heart attack, his operation, my wife and son in California. His lips move, he shakes and struggles, but no words come out. "I'm sorry," I say. "I don't understand."

I go to the nurse, ask if they can remove the tubes, at least temporarily. "He's trying to tell me something," I say. It seems important, that he has something to tell me, or ask me, now, this close to the end.

The nurse shakes her head, gives me a stern look. "He can't breathe without those tubes. That's what's keeping him alive. You're not even supposed to be in there," she adds like a nun scolding me.

I ignore her and go back to him. His lips continue to move. I come closer, put my ear near his mouth, but here, now, verbal communication is impossible. "Relax," I say. "When you get a little stronger, they'll take the tubes out and you'll be able to talk."

I am lying, of course. Those tubes will never come out, not for the rest of his life.

I touch his shoulder, his arm. When I reach his hand, he grabs mine and squeezes. His grip is surprisingly strong. For a long time, I stay there, holding his hand. He was never loose with physical affection. If I'd ever held his hand before, it was beyond the reaches of my memory.

When he calms down and dozes off, I walk back into the hallway and start to cry. I cry hard, beyond control, a flood of tears I didn't think I was capable of. Finally, a tall doctor comes out of another room and hands me some tissues. "Are you a relative of Mr. McDermott?" he asks.

I take a deep breath to calm myself. "I'm his son." I wipe my eyes with a tissue. "Yes," I say more clearly now, defiantly. "Mr. McDermott is my father."

We hold the funeral at McMannus & Sons on Flatbush Avenue. When we lived in Crown Heights, Flatbush was the neighborhood we aspired to but could never afford. Now, we fill the fancy room with flowers and people for the traditional Irish wake he wanted. It seems to me like everyone he ever knew is there.

Lost and Found: A Dog's Way
Sherry Morton-Mollo

I am a writer who hates to write. Writing torments and harasses me. I feel compelled to write, but I must (metaphorically) jump through psychological hoops to put words on virtual paper. And continuing the next day, and the next, and the next … well that's a conundrum. Each day is another hoop day, each writing is a torture, each day that I write is a triumph of will.

Today, however, I sit in a breast center waiting room in Southern California awaiting a postponed mammogram. With its high ceilings, pastel walls, and brightly colored decorator-approved furniture, the room seems to be trying too hard to belie its real purpose: determining my future as a breast cancer patient—or not. I don't much believe in mammograms anymore because of the current controversy about them. But I submit to my doctor's orders.

The wait for the mammogram seems eternal. I sit in an uncomfortable, glaring blue armchair, silently musing over my life and where it is going. *I need a transition. I need a transition from wanting to write to writing. And, I need another transition—changing my life so that I feel that I'm living it.* I remind myself of a generic definition of a transition: the process of changing from one state to another. *Well, I'm not moving to Nevada.* I allow myself a silent chuckle. When I look at my body, I see little opportunity for remolding that structure. I imagine a caterpillar-like condition transitioning to full-blown splendiferous butterfly. But my academic acquaintances remind me that process is really a metamorphosis. Look at Gregor Samsa to cockroach or Jesus Christ to man. What I need is a simple transition—a renewal of selfhood, eminently more achievable than metamorphosis.

I'm really not fearful about breast cancer, just impatient. A tall, perfectly Nordstrom-groomed woman takes the chair next to me and, with jangling bracelets and stiletto heels, begins an unwelcome monologue about cancer rates, national death percentages, nutritional approaches, and strangely termed treatments for breast cancer. (What in the world is "angiogenesis?" What are "mycological" supplements?) I shrug. I'm sure none of it applies to me.

I close her out and continue my internal monologue. *I need a transition from no purpose to purpose. I need a way to bridge my old life as university professor to retired older female without a job, without a husband, with adult progeny. (Sigh).*

I truly have no regrets: I have thoroughly enjoyed teaching hopeful faces the ins and outs of European literature before they faced the slapping wind of the real world. I believe in the importance and efficacy of my chosen profession. *I had value, meaning then.* But now, I wonder what to do with myself after the years of lectures, critical analyses, and literary awards. How do I make meaning once again in my life? How do I write about it?

Today my body will be pinched and squeezed and scrutinized by a monolithic steel contraption and monitored by a myopic radio-technician. Fear rises in my throat when I consider the possible outcome, but I tamp it down with the reminder that no one in my family has ever had a bout with cancer (fingers crossed) but there is always room for an outlier like me.

As I wait, another lady enters the waiting room—energetic, warm, interested in life, waving her hands like flags in the air—and deposits her buxom body in the chair across from me. She seems uninterested in cancer, breast or otherwise, and begins discussing her dogs—two Great Danes she rescued and with which she is now completely enamored. I smile because I also love dogs but have not found the time to deal with walks, vaccinations, doggie dental cleanings, and hound training, not to mention the myriad volumes of internet advice about canine food and grooming.

"I've always wanted a dog, but just couldn't find the space or time for one," I interject.

She smiles indulgently at me. "You don't really need to worry about that. Once you have a dog, they become your space and time."

"Yes, I suppose that is true," I respond. But what she is getting at becomes transparently clear in the next sentence.

"Do you know anyone who wants a dog? Needs a dog?"

Needs? I think to myself. No one *needs* a dog.

She rifles through her purse and finds her phone. "Here is a picture. She's a puppy, maybe six weeks old. Someone threw her in a dumpster. My daughter heard her crying."

I murmur an indignant expletive in an appropriately shocked tone. The photo on the phone shows a white and tan pixie-faced Jack Russell and Chihuahua mix. Endearing. Subtly sad. The bottomless brown eyes are full of both yearning and promise.

"We can't keep her—our dogs would eat her alive or, well, trample her to death."

I hesitate for a moment and then explain. "I don't really know anyone and I can't … I don't have time for a dog."

Or do I? I shake off the thought with my usual excuses. I need to write, I need to find *myself* again.

"Oh, yes, all right," she nods.

After my exam, in which my breasts are flattened between two cold and insulting metal plates, I get dressed and return to the waiting room. The lady is still there. I start to walk out, but something makes me look over at her to at least wave goodbye.

What do I want to do with my time? What would fill the vacuum of an ended career and an empty nest? Would a furry, smelly, begging, cuddle bug fill the void that now, paradoxically, takes up space in my life?

My feet propel me to her side and I sit down so close to her I can see the shimmer of her eyes. "Show me the photo again."

That is the point of no return. I arrange to meet her the next day to see the dog. The dog with eyes sad with promise.

In the morning, as I drive over to the home of the dog's savior, I feel both determination and consternation. *Me, a dog owner? Me, on a new learning curve? Me, time and space now restricted by an animal?* But I am determined to move forward to a new adventure, a new me.

I am in T-R-A-N-S-I-T-I-O-N, I think to myself, smiling.

The lady of the house ushers me into a rather dark living room with heavy Spanish-style furniture. Two Great Danes are confined in the backyard, barking relentlessly at the sliding glass door. The lady, who I now know as Nora, brings out a cardboard packing box. Huddled in the corner is a tiny white bundle of a dog with tan patches on her back and doggie derriere. She is so small that I hesitate to pick her up; when I do, she barely covers my cupped hands. She shudders softly as I hold her, and I am overcome by the vulnerability of this petite creature. Her eyes open and close as she maneuvers herself in my hands and I feel her furry softness warm my palms. *Will she trust me? Is she afraid? Is she comfortable?*

The enormity of the responsibility for this minuscule, helpless being overwhelms me. *Will she want to be* my *dog?*

Nora watches me closely. "Well?"

I look up from where my hands cradle the dog. "Of course."

As I move to place her back in the box amid blankets and tipped water bowl, she opens her enormous saucer-shaped eyes and stares into my own. Instantly, I feel connected to her.

I have been found by a rescued dog.

Sadie is the beginning of my transition from tired, retired university professor to full-fledged dog lover. Some might call it a transformation, even a metamorphosis. Outwardly I look the same—maybe a bit more harried, a bit more hurried. My days are filled now. I plunge into dog ownership as if it is my last breath of fresh air, my last chance to transition into a meaningful existence. I become a dog walker, a reader of dog signals, a specialist in dog poop consistencies, a dog food nutritional expert, a fetch ball thrower. Sadie is a born "circus dog," as I christen her antics, high jumps, and squirrel detection skills. She has her own car seat, neon harnesses, and monogrammed dog bowls.

And, I am writing. I am writing dog rescue stories and tales of foster doggie parents. I am researching dog shelters and rescues (there's a big difference!) I am beginning to look at my computer screen with relish—not fear or hopelessness.

Who have I become? Well, a person not so obsessed with myself. A person who has found recesses of love within her unknown before. I write with purpose. I foster dogs. I contemplate daily a ranch in Colorado where I can bring a myriad of dogs for security and safety. I have transitioned from academic loner to group leader of dog walkers. People call me for advice and dog sitting. I am no queen of dragons, but more than one person has termed me "Mother of Dogs." Writing is no longer a bugaboo and a chore, but a release and an inspiration. There are thousands of books and articles about dogs. But there is room for one more.

I am writing one now—four foster dogs later.

And, by the way, my mammogram was negative.

Reality Of Carbohydrates
Rod Morgan

"You need to finish eating your turnips. They're full of the carbohydrates you need to grow up big and strong," Mom said in her I-mean-business voice.

I didn't know what carbohydrates were and I didn't care; I was already one of the biggest and strongest kids in my class. I couldn't see the little buggers and I wasn't about to eat any! I figured since there were so many in turnips, they must be responsible for the awful taste. I mashed those turnips to reduce the wee beasties into mush. It was a childish attempt at revenge, and the mess only succeeded in raising my mom's dander. I got so carried away in my youthful exuberance that squashed turnip pulp flew all over the table and Mom's apron. That's when the little voice in my left ear talked me into refusing her direct order to eat. Now I *really* hated carbohydrates. Not only did they ruin the taste of turnips, they were getting me into trouble. Mom had that look, and I knew a lecture was forthcoming.

"Listen up, son, I'm telling you, carbohydrates are your friends. I'll bet you'd want to eat them if you knew how good they were for you."

Gee, that wasn't so bad. Then she dropped the bomb.

"Maybe you should do a little research on the subject and give me a report before dinner. That will be your punishment."

"Please, not research," I pleaded. *I really hate doing research.* Oh boy, Mom sure knew how to make a guy feel sorry. Luckily, the little voice in my right ear convinced me to stifle any rebellious replies. Besides, maybe, just maybe, she was right. After all, she had been right about Aunt Mary's au gratin potatoes. With a weird name like that, I had assumed a similar odd and unappealing taste.

My first stop was the downstairs den and my dad's medical dictionary. I settled in the big leather chair and opened the book. There it was, between carbohydrases and carbohydraturia. It was even worse than I thought. The evil little creatures had mutant relatives that I couldn't even pronounce. Fearing the worst, I read the definition:

Al-de-hy-dic or ke-ton-ic derivative of poly-hy-dric alcohols. Most common examples of such compounds have formulas that can be written Cx(H2O)y.

"What the heck?" I was quite baffled that the truth about the demonic little beasties hid in a maze of cryptic gibberish.

The group includes compounds with relatively small molecules, such as those mentioned, as well as mac-ro-mo-lec-ular substances such as starches, gly-co-gen, and cellulose. The carbohydrate most typical of the class contain carbon, hydrogen, and oxygen only, mu-co-poly-sacc-ha-rides contain nitrogen and often sulfur.

Now it was even worse than ever. Those big words made my head go numb. I decided to change gears and consult a less perplexing source of information. My next stop was the friendly confines of the family room. I curled up on the couch to see what the encyclopedia had to reveal about the accursed carbo clan. As I read about them, I couldn't believe my luck. But there it was, in black and white. My perfect excuse.

Food allergies are real and can sometimes be caused by carbohydrates.

I just knew I must be allergic to carbohydrates. I bound up the stairs with the volume in hand. Mom was loading the dishwasher as I delivered my passionate statement: "Here's the thing Mom, I hate carbohydrates because I'm allergic, it says it right here!"

I knew I had failed when she turned, smiled, and giggled. "If that were true, you would have been sick long ago. You're not done yet. Now, back downstairs and hit the books again."

This time, I hoped to dig up some real dirt about my invisible little adversaries. I could hardly believe my eyes as I continued to read through the text.

Excessive carbohydrate intake can cause obesity and dental caries.

Golly, those encyclopedia guys were smart and it just might deliver me from my fate. I raced upstairs to deliver my task-ending triumphant speech. There was no way Mom would want me to turn into an obese, diabetic tweener with a mouth full of cavities. I knew there was nothing she hated more than tooth decay; she taught me to brush after every single meal.

"Guess what Mom, the encyclopedia says too many carbs can cause obesity and cavities. You don't want that, do you?"

Mom stopped wiping the Formica counter and looked me right in the eye.

"You need to dive a little deeper, young man. Carbohydrates provide a lot more benefits to a healthy growing body than there are negatives. You have two more hours."

Back down the stairs and to my research, determined to find something even more incriminating. But, alas, that was not to be. The article continued:

The carbohydrate cellulose is indigestible by man, but is of great importance in providing dietary fiber (roughage), which is important to good health.

I didn't care to hear that, because good health was important to me. I'd rather eat a few icky carbohydrates than die from bad health like Uncle Joe. I read on.

Glucose provides the essential fuel for the body's activities.

I really didn't like the sound of that. The word "essential" made carbohydrates sound kind of important. I skipped the rest of that paragraph and went on to the next. It didn't get any better.

Carbohydrates provide our main source of energy for immediate use.

I got the creepy feeling that, once again, Mom knew more than I did. The next line sealed my fate.

Carbohydrates play a vital role in the proper function of the internal organs and the central nervous system, and in heart and muscle contraction.

Oh my, I didn't want my internal organs to malfunction. I was smart enough to realize that heart and muscle contraction were critically important to a living body. It annoyed me to think those pesky little critters should be so important. How did they work? What made them so necessary? I wasn't quite ready to admit having learned my lesson. I kept reading.

Energy is locked into a carbohydrate molecule such as glucose in the form of chemical bonds between atoms. If one of these bonds is broken—say, a bond holding together a carbon and a hydrogen atom—a bit of pent-up energy is released. Just as in a stalemated tug-of-war, if the rope suddenly breaks, both sides would go hurling off a few feet in opposite directions. This is precisely the effect of respiration within a cell. The cell 'breaks the rope' that holds the carbohydrate molecule together. The result is the release of energy—either in the form of body heat or to power other activities in the cell.

The vision of those plump little imps falling on their butts each time their rope snapped made me chuckle. I felt better about chomping down on carbohydrates. Just knowing that they faced such a droll twist of fate would make them easier to swallow. I kept reading, hoping to be further amused.

The liver receives the basic building blocks of proteins and carbohydrates, amino acids and sugars, and with them builds up molecules and cells that can be utilized by the human body.

What a glorious revelation. Sugar and carbohydrates were one and the same. Maybe I *had* been a little hasty in forming my hostile opinion about them. It wasn't too late to salvage the situation. In fact, there was a good chance of a reward for all my trouble and suffering. I sat in quiet contemplation and devised a plan.

Confident the plan would work, I climbed those stairs once again. Mom hung a frying pan on the overhead rack as I approached her and unloaded my newly acquired knowledge about carbohydrates.

"You were right, Mom. You always seem to have wisdom and foresight in such matters. I respectfully admit that carbohydrates are indeed my friends. I now realize why they are an essential part of my diet."

She turned to face me and smiled. "Nicely done, son. I'm glad you finally came to that understanding."

"Yeah, and I volunteer to eat a bunch right away."

And then, bold as you please, I walked over to the cookie jar on the counter, seized a peanut butter cookie in each hand, and high-tailed it out the back door before she could call my bluff.

The Limits of Revenge
Paul Moser

Beth was fifty-five when she made up her mind to cheat on her husband. She had chosen a partner carefully: he was well-off, a world traveler, someone busy enough that she could easily avoid seeing him again. The experience would be new to her, and likely awkward since she had never enjoyed sex very much. In her mind, it would be an act of liberation, a blow to Jack's dominance. Over thirty-plus years of marriage, she had felt manipulated and powerless in the face of his steely control, and most especially his financial muscle, which had given her and the three children whatever material comforts they could have wanted. The price tag for all this largesse, it was understood, was unquestioning acquiescence.

It was an old story, one she knew had played out many millions of times in the human record book, with minor variations. It was pretty depressing, really, but that didn't weaken her resolve. She had collected humiliations enough to power her through this rebellion and a thousand more.

In 1947, just one year into their marriage, Jack had begun criticizing her, chipping away at her self-confidence.

"You need to relax more when we're doing it, babe. You're always so tense. Kinda takes the fun out of it," he would say.

Was he right? That was the hell of it, having to constantly question herself. Am I good enough? Am I a good wife? A good lover?

Two years later, when Jack was staying late at work, not coming home until eight or nine, she finally realized he was screwing his secretary, probably right there in his office. It wasn't hard to figure out; traces of her perfume and a mix of rank body smells were all over him. He didn't even try to hide it. Because she stewed over it, weighing the costs of confrontation and never speaking up, he assumed she had accepted the arrangement. In that, he was wrong.

One hot summer day a few months later, hefting grocery bags out of the back of the station wagon, she boiled over. What the hell was she doing? Being a paid slave while the master services his harem? She left the groceries on the floor of the kitchen and drove to Jack's office. She burst into the building, red-faced and puffing. Jack's secretary, sitting behind her desk, smiled lazily at first, her bright red lipstick sharp against her smooth white skin, the scoop of her satin blouse suggesting easy access.

"Beth! Hi! Jack's on the phone right now, but…"

Beth stormed past her, grimly enjoying the shock on her face. She threw the door open and charged right at him. She reached across the desk, ripped the phone from his hand, and slammed it into its cradle.

His eyes were wide. "Beth, what the … what do you think…"

She didn't let him finish. "You son of a bitch! You think I don't know what's going on with you and your little piece of ass out there?" She slammed him repeatedly with her purse, emphasizing each word she shouted. "And you're the BIG—CATHOLIC—FAMILY MAN, right? You make me sick!" Tears were coming now, her chest heaving.

Jack came around the desk, expecting to hug her. She wound up and gave him a powerful slap in the face. "Get away from me, you shit! You know what you're going to do? You're going to fire that bitch right now! Get rid of her! Or don't bother coming home!"

Back at the house, throwing out the frozen food that had left puddles on the kitchen floor as it defrosted, her self-doubts came back with a vengeance. She could hear Jack's voice from months before, trying to be gentle and persuasive as he handed her a couple of paperbacks about "sexual surrender" and tips on how a woman could learn to experience orgasm.

Maybe I really am a terrible lover. Maybe I just can't let go, she thought. Her temper flared again. So that's the excuse he wants me to buy into so he can screw anybody he wants? Fuck that! He can take his books and his sex toys and shove them. Was it always going to be about her shortcomings?

She cried as she put the celery and carrots and wilted lettuce into the fridge, thinking back on her childhood. Born to a party-girl mother who separated from her father when she was three, one of her earliest memories was being shunted off at age five, from San Francisco to her grandmother's place in small-town Utah. It was a lonely life, feeding the chickens and helping clean the house. She had no playmates because the Mormon parents in town found out she was from a divorced family and wouldn't allow their kids to play with her. Her grandmother was a stoical pioneer type who refused even to let Beth sit in her lap. She said many times she was not a believer in "all that huggy stuff."

It was worse when she returned to San Francisco in 1934, at age nine, after her grandmother's frailty forced her to move to a convalescent home. Beth felt like unwanted baggage. Her mother's wild drinking and carrousel of sex partners only served to frighten and isolate Beth even more. She spent many nights lying in bed, shivering with fear, hearing every kind of thumping and howling imaginable. Was it physical violence? Was it sex? Maybe both?

Right out of high school, she got a good job at radio station KGO and was soon running the desk in the traffic division. Her slim figure, easy smile, and bright brown eyes, coupled with job mastery, made her as popular with her bosses as with her peers. Jack was a young reporter there, gutsy, sarcastic, and brash. He'd gotten Beth's attention the night there was a prison break at Alcatraz. He told her he was going to commandeer a boat to search the bay and eventually land on the island to interview officials.

"You can't do that!" she said. "No one is supposed to go out there!"

He gave her his cocky grin. "You just watch me, sweetheart."

* * *

They married in 1946, with a child already on the way. Co-workers were a little surprised at the announcement, since he was no great physical specimen and she was considered a catch with a devoted platoon of suitors.

If she chose Jack as a promising provider for a family, it was the right move. In just a few years, Jack was a successful screenwriter in the heyday of television, and they moved to a large house in Los Angeles. It was a dream for her. He took her to the Polo Lounge at the Beverly Hills Hotel for drinks, and to exclusive restaurants like Chasen's and the Brown Derby. When she walked into Chasen's the first time, taking in the sheer luxury of the main dining room, she exclaimed, "Do they do this *every night?*"

Then there were the seesaw decades that followed: more success for Jack, more drinking and carousing, more flashy vacations. Was there much less intimacy over those years, or had there not been much to begin with? His insistence that she convert to the Catholic religion when they married seemed comforting at the time, giving her a sense of belonging, but only made her bitter as the years passed. Jack seemed interested in religion only when at church on Sunday, or when there was an interesting theological discussion with guests at the weekend dinner table, the only time he ate dinner with his wife and children.

There were his increasingly blatant sexual dalliances and—in some ways worse—loud, drunken rants that inevitably included a fusillade of stinging insults aimed at her. These scenes were followed by lavish guilt gifts: a diamond and pearl bracelet, a mink coat, a Mercedes sports car. She finally realized that these gifts were not signaling remorse and a change of heart in him, but more a clearing of accounts that allowed him to do more of the same.

Their home conspired against her, too. The kitchen seemed miles away from the den, with its bar and congenial sofas, where guests inevitably congregated. Jack had a home intercom installed, so he could ask her for more hors d'oeuvres or more glassware without leaving a lively conversation. She could hear the laughter, the animated voices of the guests, but could not, of course, participate. At the end of these evenings, she often complained, but, just as often, he shrugged in response. "You can join us if you like, though I doubt you'd enjoy it much."

They went to posh parties in Brentwood and Beverly Hills, where Beth was usually left on her own. Jack would stand in a group of partygoers, drink in hand, laughing in the peculiarly manic way drunk people often do.

At one party, held at the Bel Air estate of a TV network executive, she wandered out into a manicured garden with a koi pond at its center, dramatically lit. The noise, the cigarette smoke, the shrieks of laughter all felt like an attack, and she needed to retreat. As she stood looking at the play of light on the surface of the pond, a man approached from behind, startling her. She recognized him as a character actor, one who had had many guest slots in various TV series. He was short, with a chunky build and curly dark hair. She couldn't recall his name. He smiled faintly. She could tell he was pretty drunk.

"Do you fuck?" he said. His tone was straightforward, as if he had asked her for the time.

She stared straight ahead. "Not very well," she said ruefully. He turned and walked back to the house.

* * *

Once she turned fifty and the kids were long gone, Beth's world changed. Jack had nearly killed himself with his drinking and had quit only two years before. He'd spent a month in an aversion-therapy clinic at the insistence of his doctor. He hadn't worked since then, his industry connections in tatters. Somebody in the house needed to earn money, she told herself, and just because she had only a high-school diploma didn't mean she couldn't find work.

She saw it as a great opportunity that they had left the San Fernando Valley and now lived in Malibu, where the real estate market was astronomically expensive—and booming. She talked with a few local agents, women with whom she had played tennis in the past, and was assured that she could join the agency. Within a year of getting her license and a nameplate on her desk, she began to make money. Just rental commissions at first, but after a few years, she had a good client list that included wealthy film industry women who took a shine to her. In rapid succession, she sold two pricey estates that together netted her more than $250,000.

She was now calling the shots at home.

Jack spent his time working on his hillside garden or listening to classical music after he smoked a pipe of marijuana. When Beth got home in the evening, he had done the shopping for dinner and had a drink ready for her—usually vodka and tonic. The change in dynamics between them was subtle, mostly because she didn't lord anything over him; still, she felt great satisfaction in occupying center stage with Jack as an audience of one.

* * *

On the day of her planned assignation, morning routines were observed. Jack was up early, sitting at the table eating a Danish, drinking his mug of

Yuban instant coffee and watching the waves through the gauzy morning mist. Beth appeared just before nine, making herself some tea and eating a small container of yogurt while standing at the sink. She observed Jack and the ocean waves through the pass-through that connected the kitchen to the dining area.

He stood up and faced her, looking reflective and grave. "Looks like it won't be too hot today," he said. "Got a big schedule?"

Beth ate a spoonful of yogurt before she answered. "Pretty much. A showing this morning in Temescal Canyon, two others this afternoon." She looked up at him. She saw a hunched-over old man in his buff-colored Wranglers and denim work shirt, holding his yellow coffee mug. He looked tired. His glance carried regret, a sadness as deep as a seafloor canyon. Was this look always in his eyes? How had she missed it?

"Let me know what you want from the store," he said.

She looked down at her yogurt, scraping the inside edges of the container with her spoon. "We've got plenty of left-over pasta, don't we?"

"I guess so."

She put the container in the sink and turned on the tap. "Just leave that!" he said with sudden force. "I'll take care of it."

She walked back to the bathroom to brush her teeth and put on lipstick. When she returned, he was rinsing dishes and loading the dishwasher.

"I'm off," she said. He turned to look at her, smiling ruefully, holding his dripping-wet mug. Beth was expressionless.

"Beth?" he said. "Why have you stayed with me all these years, anyway?"

She paused, then raised her eyebrows, looking as if she herself were just discovering the answer to the question. "Financial considerations," she said. "See you later."

In the musty dimness of the garage, she stood still for a moment, looking straight ahead at nothing. She got into her Mercedes and drove to the Temescal Canyon property. The look in Jack's eyes kept coming back to her. She spent a listless hour with a young couple who seemed almost as distracted as she was. She drove to the office and called her prospective lover. She used one of the conference room phones so she would not be overheard. She called off their tryst. "I'm sorry to be so erratic, Jerry. I just realized this was not a good idea for me. I wish I had something more to offer you as an explanation." She fended off his objections and hung up.

She felt relief. Not only would revenge sex have been meaningless at this stage of her life with Jack, but she saw again just how little she would enjoy it. The phony passion, the weird electric jolt of repeated friction. It would have been awful, even with the cold satisfaction of richly-earned infidelity. It seemed sadder than Jack's eyes. An emotional nothing. The look in his eyes was so clear to her now. The terrible burden he was carrying. The truth was: the dagger plunge of her desire for revenge had created self-inflicted wounds.

It was an old story.

She drove to the local market, where she picked up a beautiful tray of sushi, her favorite. She brought it back to the office and savored lunch at her desk.

The Moms' Group
Jennifer Murphy

In the morning darkness of the tiny studio apartment, Jenni was jostled out of her slumber by the addition of thirty-five exuberant pounds bouncing onto her bed as Rogue climbed onto the top bunk and pulled back her covers.

"It's snowing!" he said, his dark eyes glowing with wonder. He pulled the curtain back to provide proof of his declaration.

Jenni reached out and touched her hand to the window. Unlike in the previous weeks, there was no frost on the inside of the glass.

"It's perfect snowman weather!" Jenni answered, suppressing a yawn and smiling at her son. "I'll make us scrambled eggs and juice." And coffee for me, she thought.

With the promise of gentler weather, they rushed through breakfast, which they ate sitting on the floor in the small room, put on winter layers, and walked to the playground. There were several little kids, all around Rogue's age, bundled against the cold and playing in the snow. He ran to join them, and Jenni waved at their moms. Today, she was happy to see them.

Delicate snowflakes floated down, blanketing the playground in puffy white. Jenni stood back, cold hands dug deep into the pockets of her secondhand parka, watching the kids play in the snow and, as she knew they would, the women approached her. They dressed in designer ski resort wear, with their winter hats alone costing more than Jenni made in a week as an Uber driver.

It had been early fall of the previous year when Jenni met the moms. They were part of a group of about twelve women, who were so strikingly similar in appearance that she utterly could not tell them apart. Her initial thought was that they were sisters and cousins because they bore a strong resemblance to each other. As time passed Jenni learned they were simply related by their love of plastic surgery: Botox, lip filler, foxy eye lift, and heavily highlighted hair. In their mid-thirties, stay-at-home moms in an upper middle class income bracket, they were an organized networking machine, and got together a few times a week for play dates, coffee, nights out, and exercise. The exercise frequently took place in this downtown playground, in a gentrified section of the city, and consisted of yoga, stretching, or some sort of thing that involved the bossiest of the group directing the rest of the women to put out mats and move in a specifically choreographed manner.

The playground was an oval consisting of a basketball court, a sandbox, and an open area which was situated over rubber flooring and festooned with bright yellow and blue towers, bridges, walls, and slides made of recycled materials, with no sharp edges or excessive heights. Jenni used Rogue's park time to run laps around the perimeter. She could get in three miles while he played. She completed her workout by doing planks, chin-ups, and push-ups in the playground.

The moms laid claim to the large blacktop area located under a basketball hoop because it was situated directly next to the play area, where they could be a few feet from their children. Anyone who thought they would shoot hoops during the time the women planned to meet soon found they were sadly mistaken. The moms were as aggressive as any street gang when faced with the loss of their territory. No one wanted to give up her free time and be forced to sit on the benches near the playground for the sole purpose of actually watching her own children. They came there for "me" time and fully intended to get it. Jenni enjoyed watching them chase off all manner of young men, whose experience with the moms was likely excellent birth control.

The women immediately took notice of Jenni on that beautiful fall day, and they passed out their business cards. She stared at the stack in her hand and was speechless. The cards were expensive-looking 16-pt. cardstock, very similar in verbiage but varied in color and font and lovely to behold. On the front of the card was each woman's name printed boldly in her chosen script. Written underneath was "Mommy of…", and the last line of the front of the card was the woman's phone number. On the back was the job description of the stay-at-home mommy, to include doctor, administrator, chef, chauffeur, teacher, scholar, writer, wife, and lover.

The grandeur of the cards and the confidence the women exhibited overwhelmed and intimidated Jenni. She didn't have a card to trade, so she handed the stack back to the most aggressive of the moms, whom Jenni assumed was the leader, and said she didn't think she would have use for any of their services. The women were offended and horrified. From that point on, the tone was set, and every encounter filled with questions and judgment.

A couple of days later, several of the group approached Jenni after she finished her run. They wore matching uniforms of designer leggings pulled tight over skinny hips, tank tops barely able to contain firm perfect breasts, bleached hair pulled into ponytails, covered by baseball hats, and on their fingers, enormous diamond rings. The women encircled Jenni, her old high school track uniform drenched with sweat, as she stretched her calves on the rim of the sandbox.

"You can't leave your son unattended while you run," one of them informed her. "Anything could happen to him, and we aren't going to be responsible."

Jenni was shocked. She truly believed Rogue was safe and happy while she ran. She only had her back to him during a small portion of the run and he delighted in keeping track of her laps while he played with his trucks in the sandbox. But these women were furious, and Jenni considered the possibility they might be right. She would never do anything to hurt Rogue. Humiliated, she dipped her head and thanked them.

At this point, the other women gathered closely around Jenni.

"You're welcome to work out with us. Clair has created an excellent program that targets problem areas. It could transform your ass." Sophie lowered her eyes, focusing on Jenni's ample behind.

"Oh please, Soph, her husband—or some man, anyway—paid a fortune for that ass. I don't think she could do anything to change it, even if she wanted to. Surgery is permanent," Clair responded. Clair was extremely thin and very fit. No breast implants or Brazilian Butt Lift for her. She was natural, except for her hair color, lip filler, and some Botox, but it was all very tastefully done.

Jenni didn't attempt to explain the maternal DNA that resulted in her ample behind. She was focused on Rogue and worried that she had once again proven to have woefully inadequate parenting skills. She said goodbye, helped Rogue pack up his toys, and left.

That day, Jenni took Rogue to the store and, using most of her limited funds, bought a jogging stroller. It was transformative. It allowed them to expand their wanderings; Jenni got more exercise, and Rogue could join in. After each run, she took him to the park so he could play, often joining him on the play equipment or digging in the sandbox. Shortly after acquiring the stroller, several of the moms approached Jenni, hands on their skinny hips, ponytails bobbing under caps, leggings tastefully stretched over tiny firm butts, breasts straining, diamonds glistening in the sun.

Their words tumbled over one another. "Isn't he four?"

"That's too old for a jogger."

"He should be riding a bike by now."

"He isn't getting any exercise."

"You're really holding him back."

"Thank you, but we're fine." Jenni's honey laden southern accent infuriated the Chicago born women. She turned away, worried they might be right.

One beautiful late fall day, Jenni made the mistake of wearing her long hair loose and flowing. The sun's rays caught the glistening curls and threw back a prism of mahogany, copper, coffee, and gold, which gleamed as she pushed Rogue in the forbidden stroller past the moms stretching on the blacktop. They stopped and stared at her. At twenty-three, Jenni was the epitome of sexuality, her hourglass figure showcased in only shorts and a tee shirt.

A cacophony of voices spilled over one another. "Who does your hair?"

"Is it Charles? He's impossible to get an appointment with."

"Will you call him for me?"

"Is it a balayage?"

"Do you get a perm, or do you curl it every day?"

"Is it a weave?"

Against her better judgment, Jenni stopped running and answered. "My hair? I just wash it."

Mirroring the lionesses whose exceptional teamwork and strategic approach to hunting is essential for the pride's survival, several of the moms rose together and sprinted towards Jenni, flanking and ambushing her with diamonds glistening like jeweled claws in the sun. They tugged on her hair, separating colors and holding curls out and apart from the mass. Knowledgeable fingers separated the hair on her scalp to find anchoring points for hair extensions. By the time Jenni managed to pull away, they had determined that her hair was indeed hers, likely natural, and not containing any product.

"Who cuts it?" Their demand was almost in unison.

"I just do it myself when it starts bugging me." Jenni tried to twist her hair into a bun to diminish their fixation and allow an escape. Unfortunately, this had the effect of allowing tendrils of cascading curls to fall, gently framing her beautiful, youthful face, further enraging them.

"No way is that natural," one of the women declared.

The rest of the moms, who had now joined them, agreed and expressed their deep disappointment with Jenni's refusal to come clean.

Clair crossed her thin, toned arms and confronted Jenni. "Why don't you join the group today, Jenni?" It was more of an accusation than an invitation.

"No, thank you. We have to get going," Jenni called out as she sprinted away.

Jenni was embarrassed because of her lack of education and intimidated by the wealthy and successful moms. She invented a rich fantasy life, complete with a stay-at-home lifestyle, and a wealthy, devoted husband, in order to hide the reality of her truly humble circumstances. Jenni worked seven nights a week as an Uber driver while Rogue slept at a neighbor's house. Her mama had died years before and Jenni had no close friends or support system in their new town.

Jenni told the moms that she and her husband were very private. She was certain this would end the barrage of questions, but only resulted in Linda, who seemed to be one of the leaders, insisting Jenni provide her phone number. Jenni did not want this woman or any of the moms calling her, so she gave an incorrect number.

Using one short, rounded, immaculately polished fingernail, Linda dialed the number right in front of Jenni. A tone came over the phone and a mechanical voice announced, "The number you have dialed is not in service."

Jenni assumed this would discourage them from pursuing the issue, but it had just the opposite effect.

With one hand on her skinny hip, Linda held up her phone and sarcastically announced, "Jenni, it seems your phone is out of order."

Jenni was not about to turn her phone number over to these women. "Oh, sorry, that's old. I had to get a new one because I was getting so many unwanted calls. The entire process of changing my number and memorizing the new one irritated my husband, so he doesn't want me to share it anymore."

"Oh, well, maybe he just doesn't want you to hand it out to other men. Is that what you were caught doing?" The women looked knowingly at Jenni.

When the winter came with its winds and frigid air, snow and ice filled the streets, it became harder to push the stroller. On the upside, the moms moved their workouts to an indoor gym. Their absence motivated Jenni to come to the park as often as possible.

But standing here on this mild winter day, as the dainty snowflakes drifted lazily down on the children, whose laughter drowned out some of the city noise, Jenni was actually happy to see the moms.

"I am so glad to see y'all." Jenni was careful not to smile widely, which would reveal her crooked teeth. "I'm looking at preschool for Rogue, just a couple days a week. Do you know any good ones?"

"He's too old for preschool."

"He should be in prekindergarten."

"You better get him enrolled soon."

"Have you been homeschooling him?"

"You should have gotten on the lists when he was born."

"You aren't going to get him anywhere decent now."

Jenni felt defeated. She had let Rogue down again, but then Sarah spoke up. "John and I have decided to give our son the gift of time. We just want him to enjoy his childhood. He's Rogue's age and is just starting preschool. Jenni, I'm certain you can get him into public preschool."

An overwhelming feeling of warmth and joy flooded over Jenni as she happily expressed her thanks. She realized she was no longer intimidated by the moms and was likely a much better mother because of them. She wasn't sure why their opinions on motherhood were so important to her. Maybe it was because they were educated, professional women and they had happy, healthy kids. Jenni thought about her own mama, who loved her children unconditionally. She had been a perfect mama. Her way of mothering had been nothing like these women. It occurred to Jenni that there was no perfect way to raise a child. She wasn't ever going to be as wonderful as her own mama, or as perfect and professional as the moms in the group, but maybe she could be good enough.

The next day, Jenni and an overjoyed Rogue entered the office of the local elementary school.

Hamerton
Excerpt from the novel *Hamer*
Gary Nelson

It was just before 10:00 a.m. when Rodney Stoner pulled out of the Heathrow car rental and into his first thrilling roundabout. Forty minutes later, he stopped at a crossroads some twelve kilometers northwest of Cambridge. A small sign read "HAMERTON—5 km."

The town, if it could be called a town, consisted of a scattering of eight quaint houses overlooked by an old stone church bordered by a graveyard. The houses were well kept, some with thatched roofs, some with gardens of vegetables and flowers neatly laid out beside them. There was a woman tending the garden along the last in the line of the thatched houses.

"Hello," said Rodney, stopping and getting out of his car. "Is this Hamerton?"

"It is. You're American, are you?" asked the woman, turning her attention away from her task.

"Yes. I'm from California. I'm a Hamerton, or rather my grandmother is a Hamerton. I promised her I would visit the town."

"Not much to see, I'm afraid," said the woman. "Except for the church, of course. It goes back forever, built by William the Conqueror."

The woman stood. She was short, maybe five-one under a loose shirt and work pants. A crown of pure white hair framed a pleasant face with intelligent, inquiring eyes. Rodney guessed her age to be in the seventies. The gardening clothes made her look older, while the twinkle in her eye and the smile lines at the corners of her mouth suggested younger.

"Is it open? Is there a chance I might see it?" asked Rodney, gesturing to the church that stood above them on the crest of the hill. Rodney wasn't one to put much store in the past, let alone ancestry, but he had a free day and he promised his grandmother.

"Wait here, please." Rodney watched the woman until she went into her house, passing through a door on the other side of the small kitchen. She returned with a large brass ring that held three keys. "These will open the door. You'll need all three. Please return them when you're through." The old lady smiled as she held out the ring to Rodney, holding on to it while she studied him. Just before he became uncomfortable, she released the ring with a nod and closed the door.

As Rodney walked down the path through the garden, he caught a slight movement at the window. He turned and glimpsed a younger woman peering from behind the curtain, which had been pulled aside.

* * *

The main door to the church took a little more than just inserting and turning the keys to open it. Finally, after Rodney had become frustrated going through the sequences, trying each lock in combination with the others, the door swung open.

Inside, the church showed the same stone construction that made up its exterior. To the right of the door, rows of wooden pews stretched to the altar. Rodney moved into the small open area behind the pews. Against the far wall there was a glass-faced case, a small lock protecting the item inside from touch.

Instinctively, Rodney moved toward the case and the single, two-foot-long document it contained. At first, he was not sure what he was looking at; then realized he was viewing the church's charter—if not the original document, then an excellent copy. Below a text in Latin was a long line of signatures, each followed by a date.

About a third of the way down the list, Rodney recognized, written in bold script and larger than the signatures preceding it, the signature of Henry VIII. With a journalist's eye, he looked back over each signature. For the most part, they were undecipherable. He had only recognized Henry's because he had seen it before. After several minutes, Rodney moved away from the document, passing through shadows as he walked up the aisle to the pulpit.

Rodney had never been particularly religious in the classical sense, but he felt strongly that there was a higher power here. Alone in a stone church that was over nine hundred years old, he felt in awe of his emotional connection to the place and the power of the structure to elicit it. To the right of the altar was a squattish pulpit, elevated only eighteen inches above the church floor. The pews to the left terminated against the stone outer wall, but there was a small walkway that provided access along the wall on the right.

Rodney studied the way the stones were set without mortar, buttressed with more of their own to withstand the centuries in a land where few castles had been as fortunate. Finished with the altar, he moved down the right-hand aisle. At the fourth pew from the front, just above ground level and set into the wall, was a rose-colored square of marble, six feet long and fourteen inches high.

Rodney knelt, his fingers running lightly over the marble and the inscription carved into the monument in Old English block lettering:

KNIGHT OF HAMERTON
1268

A line of carving just above the inscription had been defaced, chiseled into an uneven, ragged gouge, making the name that had once been there unreadable. Rodney stood, backing away for a better perspective on the stone. Bumping into a pew, he turned to steady himself and saw he was not alone.

In the back of the church, standing near the charter, was a young woman. She was watching him, hands clasped in front of her in a relaxed attitude that spoke of her having been there for some time.

Instead of apologizing for startling him, the young lady took a step forward, speaking to him. "Church documents tell us that Richard du Hamerton secured that for his final resting place in the reign of Henry II." Smiling, she walked slowly toward Rodney. "That is what most people believe, anyway. We believe it is his father, Alfred, Knight and Lord of Hamerton, whom Richard had buried there."

As the woman continued toward him in the poor light afforded by the small stained-glass windows of the church, Rodney—a man who wrote speeches for Senator Kent Beck, putting words into the mouth of a presidential candidate—found himself speechless. She was blond, her hair pulled back from her face. He could not tell if it was fixed in a bun or a braid, but the effect was to accentuate her forehead and her long, delicate nose. Her cheekbones were high, but neither diminished the size of the clear blue eyes nor overly hollowed the cheeks below.

She continued moving toward him, her strides long and purposeful, until she was standing next to him, looking down at the inscription. A faint scent of flowers, barely noticeable, nevertheless imprinted on his memory.

"My name is Katherine. I am a docent for the church. The woman who keeps the keys tells me you are a Hamerton?"

"My grandmother is a Hamerton," said Rodney, still taken aback at the sudden appearance of the woman. Recovering somewhat, he offered her his hand. "My name is Rodney Hamerton Stoner."

"Please pardon me for being so nosy, Mr. Stoner, but the Hamerton family is very important to this village," Katherine said with a smile that hinted at an apology for interrupting Rodney's study of the stone's inscription. "Was your grandmother married to Alistair Stoner?"

"Yes. He was my grandfather," answered Rodney, wondering at the woman's knowledge of his family. "He died when I was in high school."

A sigh, followed immediately by a smile radiant even in the diffused light, came across Katherine's face. "Nice to meet you, Mr. Stoner. We don't get many visitors here. You are the first American of the Hamerton line to return, at least to our knowledge."

She spent the next hour walking through the church and graveyard with Rodney, sometimes answering questions, sometimes relating the history of the church and town.

"I'm afraid I've kept you long past lunch. Could I offer you a spot of tea and a sandwich?" she asked, her voice shifting from the authoritative tone she had used to impart the history of the church and grounds to the lyrical accent that Rodney suspected was her normal speaking voice.

"That would be nice. I would also like to understand how you knew about my grandfather."

"I'll meet you at the house where you picked up the keys after you lock up. Margaret can help with that." She turned and walked quickly down a footpath toward the thatched-roof cottage. Her perfume lingered, but only for a moment, leaving a fading trail of spring flowers. He took another walk around the church's interior, stopping in front of the stone that was inscribed in his family's name, then locked the church.

By the time he had reached the thatched roof cottage and entered the garden, Rodney found Katherine had set up a small table among the roses with a white linen tablecloth and three settings.

"It's a little informal, but the roses are beautiful when they're in bloom and the weather obliges." She motioned him to a seat facing a magnificent hedge rose of the deepest red.

From behind him, he heard the door to the house open. He turned to see the woman who had given him the key coming down the path with a teapot and covered china plate.

"This is Margaret Radcliff. She watches over things when she is here at Hamerton. Margaret, I believe you've already met Mr. Rodney Stoner."

"Yes, briefly," said the old woman, taking the remaining chair before offering her hand to Rodney.

Rodney saw she had changed from the loose shirt and pants she had been wearing earlier into a flowered dress. She still had the twinkle in her eye, but now it was accompanied by a genuine smile. He had no idea how she had brewed a pot of tea and made whatever was below the porcelain cover in the time it had taken him to get down the hill.

"Katherine tells me that you are Bette Hamerton's grandson."

"Yes. I wondered how you knew."

"The Hamerton line is kind of a hobby of this village. It is my duty to try to keep up with the family. Bette's grandfather was William Charles Hamerton. As a young man in 1847, William left England for Nova Scotia, but in the fall of 1862, he moved again to San Francisco, where Alfred, your grandmother's father, was born. He had three daughters and no sons." As the old woman spoke, she uncovered the tray of six neatly arranged half sandwiches.

"Would you pour, dear?" she asked Katherine, while she arranged the sandwiches on the plate along with some white grapes.

"Margaret is an expert on the genealogy of the Hamertons," explained the younger woman.

"Yes, well, it's not like there are a lot of people to keep track of, are there? At least not in England. You see, Adam du Hamerton lived during the reign of Henry III. He allowed none of his subjects to take the name of the town. Your father was an only child, as I remember. I lost track of him after the divorce. I was in rather a bad patch concerning my own father's health. It took almost all my time, and I'm afraid that I neglected the American branch shamefully. Is your grandmother still alive? I lost track of her as well."

"Yes, very much so."

"And your father? He was in training to become a physician."

"He graduated from Stanford and did his residency specialty training there as well. He does chromosome research into cures for hereditary diseases."

"I see," said the older woman. "Perhaps you should know that at present, you and your father are the only males left in the Hamerton line."

"That can't be true. The only males?"

"Unless you have brothers or a son," said Margaret, looking directly at Rodney.

"No, I have no brothers, and I'm not married." Rodney hoped he was correct in noting a slight turn of Katherine's head at the mention of his marital status.

"Enough of our curiosity," said Margaret with a laugh. "We get so serious over Hamerton minutiae."

"What brings you to Hamerton?" asked Katherine, changing the subject while smiling over her untouched sandwich. The light reflected off the roses and tinted her blond hair with streaks of red. Rodney was struck again by her ethereal beauty.

Rodney told them about his job as a speechwriter, and how he had accompanied Senator Beck to England. He had promised his grandmother he would visit the town of Hamerton. Now he wondered if his grandmother had known what was waiting for him here. He was the last male in a line that went back to the thirteenth century, and these two women knew more about his family than he did.

"I'm supposed to be doing research so I can place appropriate references to English history into some speeches the senator might need to make after the monetary conference."

A sudden thought came to Rodney, and with it, a smile to his face. "I have to work tomorrow manning Senator Beck's desk, but Saturday evening there's an official function I'm obliged to attend with the senator and his wife. It's at the U.S. embassy. Usually, these evenings are a boring obligation, but this one could be fun. Would you like to go with me?" he looked at Katherine.

She glanced at the older woman quickly before answering. If she received a signal of approval, Rodney couldn't detect it. "I'd love to go with you, Mr. Stoner."

"Great," said Rodney. "I'm afraid it's formal."

"I'll see what I can do," said the young woman with a laugh that reminded Rodney of the tinkling of silver bells.

In the next five minutes it was decided, because of the uncertainty over what, exactly, Rodney's official responsibilities would be before the reception, that Katherine would meet him at the Mayfair Hotel.

"As long as you're working tomorrow," said Katherine, as she walked Rodney to his car. "I'll bring some historical information for you. My office isn't far from the Mayfair, and it might give you an idea or two for your speech."

"Great," said Rodney, meaning it, but not because of the historical data. "I'll be in room 840 from 9:00 a.m. until after 6:00 in the evening. I believe the reception starts at 7:30."

It felt like his entire reason for being in England had changed since asking for the keys to the church. Certainly, his reason for attending the ambassador's reception changed from obligation to desirable, linked to a warm feeling in his chest when he thought of Katherine. Rodney drove back to Heathrow with a great feeling of anticipation to see Katherine again and a sense of wonderment at his newly found heritage.

Champion of the Swine
Pamela Pan

My grandma always said one could be a champion in every line of work, but at eighteen, I had never considered swine herding a line of work.

On a chilly November morning in 1969, in Beidahuang, the northernmost wilderness of China, I waited in line to board a truck headed towards the construction site where our military farm was building a new road. Captain Zhang pulled me aside. "Sergeant Wang's assistant took a leave because his mother was ill. We need your help with the fifty pigs until he returns."

"But I know nothing about pigs."

"Sergeant Wang will teach you. Pack your things and head to the farm."

I trudged back to the men's dorm, slowly packed my necessities, and walked twenty minutes to the pig farm. Coming to Beidahuang to develop China's borderland was already a significant detour from my dream of going to college and majoring in electronics in my home city of Shanghai. Now, being assigned to deal with smelly, stubborn pigs all day felt like another crushing blow. Was there anything worse than being a swineherd?

Entering the gate, I was surprised to find that, instead of a chaotic mob of pigs running amok and wallowing in stinking manure, the yard was clean, the fence well maintained.

Nobody greeted me as I stepped into the one-story mud-walled building. The air carried the smells of food, straw, and a faint earthiness. The building's southern side had six pig stalls, the kitchen, and three furnished rooms. I settled my belongings in one of them. Four-foot-tall wooden fences enclosed the stalls. The backside bordered a seven-foot-high exterior wall, with a small pathway in between. About ten pigs milled within each, their snouts grazing the straw-covered ground. The sixth stall housed a single sleeping pig. Why just one? The rooms on the north side contained supplies for raising livestock. The building was well ventilated and warm.

I went outside. Nearby fields rested under the azure sky. The forest stood in the distance, verdant treetops glistening. Hoofbeats echoed and grew louder—a fast-moving carriage pulled by a brown mare. A man cupped his mouth and bellowed, "Da-shan, I'm Sergeant Wang. Welcome to the farm!"

The horse pulled to a stop. Sergeant Wang, a stout man with stubble on his chin, who appeared to be in his mid-forties, handed me a heavy bag and heaved another on his own shoulder before descending. We carried the bags to a supply room. The pigs pressed against the wooden planks, squealing, snorting.

Sergeant Wang laughed. "Your food is coming."

He strode to the kitchen and emerged a few minutes later, each hand carrying a bucket.

"What's in these?" I guessed this would soon be my job.

"Dried grass, corn, wheat, and water. I've found that if I cook it, the pigs like their feed better and are less prone to digestive problems."

He poured the mixture into the large trough of the first stall. The pigs dipped their snouts into it, slurping. After doing the same with the other five stalls, he said, "Now, let's see to Mama Pig."

"Mama pig? Is she in the stall with only one pig?"

The sergeant grinned. "No, eleven pigs. She gave birth to ten piglets last night. I covered the newborns with straw to keep them warm."

Ten piglets. That sounded exciting. "How do we feed them?"

"They suckle milk from their mother. Some bags we brought in today contain fresh soybeans, especially for her and the piglets. Instead of three meals a day, we'll give her five."

Mama Pig devoured her meal, grunting with delight. Then she lay down, letting the piglets latch onto her.

I noticed something pink in a corner among the pale-yellow wheat straw. "Is that a piglet, too? Why isn't it eating like the others?"

Sergeant Wang picked up the little creature and handed it to me. "This was the last one born. She's too weak to suckle."

I sat on a chair in the corridor, cradling the piglet. She was all pink except for a prominent gray patch shaped like a dragonfly on her back. Her skin felt smooth and warm. She was so small she fit into my palm. Her eyes were closed. Something stirred in me as I gazed at her. My initial reluctance gave way to a sense of purpose—to ensure this tiny runt lived and to shield her from any harm. I had never cared for a pet before, but this fragile being ignited in me a spark of awe that flared into fierce protectiveness.

She opened her mouth, turning her little snout to the left and right.

"What does she want?" I asked.

"Food." Sergeant Wang fetched a bowl of soy milk, pulled a chair opposite me, and fed the piglet spoon by spoon.

After she gulped the milk down, she stretched in my cupped hands, emitting contented snorts.

"I thought of a name for her," I said. "How about Dragonfly?"

Sergeant Wang chuckled. "I've raised pigs all my life. Never heard of giving them names."

I blushed. "Just an idea."

His eyes sparkled. "As you wish, Dragonfly she'll be. Since you like her so much, I'll entrust her to you. Four to six meals during the day, and one feeding in the middle of the night."

Feeding Dragonfly became my favorite chore. I had always thought of pigs as stupid. Dragonfly proved me wrong. She knew my scent and sound. Long before I approached the stall, she would wobble over to the door, her snout nudging at the hinges.

One day, after eating, she looked up at me and smiled. I touched her little toes and tickled them. She let out a squeal.

I laughed. "You're a silly one!"

I ran my fingers along her back and belly. She stretched out further and purred. I had never imagined that piglets could purr, yet there it was —a series of low-pitched, throaty, almost melodic notes that filled me with wonder and tenderness.

Weeks went by. Dragonfly became my little companion. As I fed her, I told her about my days, my homesickness, and she listened as if she understood, offering a quiet empathy that consoled me. Watching her drift off to sleep on my arm brought a sense of peace I hadn't imagined possible, her gentle weight anchoring me in this remote and lonely place far from home.

I also took care of the other piglets, giving them extra soy milk at least once a day to supplement their mother's milk. One barked when he finished eating, so I named him "Bark." Another danced when we took them out in the yard for fresh air. I called him "Dancer." Sergeant Wang laughed every time I called them by name, but he used the names as well.

The piglets grew fast. By early December, most of them reached up to my ankle. The weather grew colder. Snow blanketed the entire area.

One early morning, as I lay in my bed, reluctant to leave my warm quilts, Sergeant Wang barged into my room. "Bark is missing."

"What?"

We checked the doors—they remained locked. We combed through the yard. No sign of Bark anywhere. The fence was intact.

Sergeant Wang reported the incident. Captain Zhang ordered a search of the company properties. No Bark, alive or dead.

The next morning, before I even opened my eyes, Sergeant Wang pushed the door open. "Dancer is missing."

My stomach tightened. Could Dragonfly be next? She had become my little companion. I had double checked all the doors before going to bed. Who could this mysterious thief be? I dressed and grabbed my flashlight. If the culprit didn't enter from the ground, could he have descended from above? I shone the light on the ceiling.

Sergeant Wang shook his head. "The piglets are too heavy for a human or bird to carry up that high wall. Plus, how could they get through the roof?"

"Wait." I stepped inside the sixth stall and focused my light on the rafters. Sergeant Wang had said that when constructing this building, he and the workers had woven straw into thick, tight blankets and tied them to the beams. These roof-coverings kept the building cool in summer and warm in winter. But now I felt a cold draft.

Sergeant Wang brought in a ladder. I climbed up, located the source of the draft on the roof, and pushed. The sheets lifted, letting in a blast of icy wind. The robber had severed several thick ropes that bound the sheets to the rafters. Instead of clean cuts, the ends of the ropes appeared frayed. What tool had the robber used?

Placing my hands on two thick beams, I squeezed through the space between the rafters and hoisted myself onto the roof. No tracks were visible—perhaps the snow had covered them. I could see the forest. Could the thief be hiding among the trees? I had never heard of fugitives in these areas, and the weather was too cold to survive in the open.

Sergeant Wang made several short ropes. I used them to tie the wheat-stalk sheets firmly back to the rafters.

That night, I made a temporary bed near the sixth stall, wrapped in everything except my jacket, which was too thick to lie in comfortably. Something woke me. I turned my light straight up to the ceiling. A pair of eyes gleamed in the darkness, staring back at me from the exact spot where I had reattached the sheets. Heart pounding, I bolted upright. Scuffling sounds filled the night air, and the eyes disappeared.

I slipped on my jacket and dashed outside. Under the moonlight, a shadow climbed over the fence and darted towards the forest. Unable to jump over the fence, I dashed to the gate, opened it, and chased the shadow. By then, it was only a small dot in the distance, moving faster than I could. It soon disappeared.

Sergeant Wang met me outside the gate as I trudged back.

"We need horses," he said after I reported what I saw. "We have the mare. I'll ask the company to lend us another one."

Captain Zhang gave us a chestnut stallion.

The next night, Sergeant Wang brought a table from his room and rested on it. I slept with my jacket on and kept a spear I had brought in from the tool shed by my side. I woke with a start. My flashlight revealed a hairy figure perched on the stall fence near the wall, its front paws gripping two beams overhead. It climbed to the ceiling and gazed back at me: a dark muzzle, brown eyes, and raised furry ears. The light illuminated the shape of a dragonfly on the back of something grasped by the creature's mouth. My dragonfly!

I shook Sergeant Wang's shoulder. "Wake up! A wolf has stolen Dragonfly."

Sergeant Wang sat up. "A wolf? Where?"

"Over the roof. Let's go!"

I grabbed the spear.

"Get on the horse!" Sergeant Wang picked up a cleaver.

I rushed to the barn and jumped on the mare—I had saddled both horses before going to bed. Behind me, Sergeant Wang mounted the stallion. We burst through the gate, our breath forming frosty clouds in the cold air. The wolf had gained a significant lead. We spurred our horses forward and closed in the distance.

The wind sliced into my face. The moonlight reflected off the snow, illuminating the landscape with an eerie brightness. The dark silhouette of the forest loomed. Once the wolf reached the forest, all would be lost. The wolf would be in familiar terrain, but the horses would have a hard time navigating through densely grown trees.

Only a short distance remained between the wolf and the forest. Sergeant Wang hurled the cleaver towards our adversary, but the wolf swerved to the side and dodged it.

He shouted, "Da-shan, throw your spear!"

I glanced at my spear.

"Hurry!" he yelled.

I spurred my horse onward and came closer to the wolf. I wanted to pierce its head, but feared it might hurt Dragonfly, who hung limp between the beast's fangs. I aimed at the wolf's mid body and unleashed the spear with all my might.

Whoosh! The spear hurtled toward its target. The wolf lurched forward, emitting an ear-piercing howl. The hair on my head stood on end. I had never heard anything so blood-curdling.

"I think you got it!" Sergeant Wang leaped forward with his horse.

Before I could follow him, my mare gave out a long squeal, likely startled by the wolf's howl. She reared up. My mouth opened in terror. I had barely learned to ride a few months ago. In no way did I know how to handle a rearing horse. If I lost my grip, I would be dragged across the fields. *I could die.*

"Sergeant!" I shrieked.

Sergeant Wang turned and raced toward me. "Lean forward and pull the reins toward her ear!"

I followed his instructions, my heart thudding.

"Kick the hindquarters and make her go forward."

My legs felt as soft as the mush I fed the pigs, but I kicked the mare's flanks. To my immeasurable relief, her head lowered, and she trotted.

The wolf had collapsed only a few feet from the forest. Dragonfly lay near its body, motionless, covered in blood.

I knelt beside her, feeling as if a large stone had lodged in my chest. "Is she dead?"

Sergeant Wang placed his hand on her neck. A grin brightened his weather-beaten face. "The wolf might've banged her head against the wall or the fence. She's unconscious, but alive."

We washed off the blood from Dragonfly with snow and rode back. She hung draped in front of my saddle, wrapped in my jacket.

A crowd had gathered at the pig farm. Captain Zhang stood in the front.

We dismounted. I took Dragonfly inside and cleaned her wound. The wolf's fangs had punctured the back of her neck. She flinched but didn't open her eyes as I poured salt solution on the broken skin. I bandaged her with a clean cloth and ran my hand along her back. Eyes still closed, she gave a slight grunt and offered me the same lopsided grin as when I fed her soymilk with a spoon.

I smiled down at her, wiping away the sting in my eyes, and stroked her head. She gave a contented purr and fell asleep.

When I came out, Sergeant Wang was telling Captain Zhang, "We'll nail wooden planks on top of the wheat-stalk sheets to prevent future incidents like this."

Upon seeing me, he patted my shoulder. "Now, Captain, allow me to present our Champion of the Swine! Da-shan is smart and courageous. Without him, we could've lost all our piglets, and perhaps the pigs, too."

And that was how I earned the medal and the title "Champion of the Swine."

Grandma was right, after all.

A Mother Brachiosaurus Glimpses the New World
John Patterson

"Babe, that's it, you're reaching just fine. I'm not eating the lower ones. They're for you."

Brachi adored her six-year-old daughter, Iso.

The little girl learned to hold her neck upright when she was only two weeks old and stood a couple of days later. Mom's cooing bursts were loud enough for young Iso to hear them and lean towards her. Mom gathered some leaves, chewed them, and spit them up, making sure they were soaked, slimy, and munched to a pulp. Iso could drink her mom's smoothies a few times a day just by sucking, the same way she would drink water for the rest of her life.

Brachi's group lived in a beautiful canyon, with pleasant warm days. Water draining through the warm canyon misted the land, ensuring the abundant growth of all rooted things. A rainbow of green colors, shades, and tints, streaked by stems of purple, red, yellow, or orange, filled the valley. The plants and trees came in hundreds of shapes and sizes.

As her young daughter grew, Mom shared her communal knowledge. Their family had been walking the same trail for generations. Every spring, their group headed north. Then, when the twelve-foot grasses fell over and turned brown, they started south again. Brachi didn't know unhappiness, only life. For forty years she had been taking in the misty air and walking the pleasant land that yielded under her huge feet. At sixty feet tall, weighing over forty tons, she was in the prime of her life.

Days after Iso started walking, she began cooing with Brachi. Slowly, over days spent eating leaves and drinking water, Brachi shared some basic information about their traveling commune. Iso lived and traveled amongst some twenty-eight adults. The tribe was evenly split amongst males and females, with eleven young brachos aged three weeks to four months.

Iso, the youngest, wanted to keep up, so she learned to chew quickly. Brachi had to push her away from the rivers because she would easily fill up on water. It was much easier for the little ones to drink than eat leaves because their necks tired so quickly. It took a few months for the brachos to get strong enough to hold their necks up so they could eat. The adults knew the kids had to overcome the lazy factor of just wanting to drink. They consulted each other in low coos, keeping track of how long the young had been at the water. If an adult decided a child had drunk enough, they would bump it away from the water. The rest of the group hummed their approval when this happened.

The last few mornings, the adults got up a little faster. Little Iso wondered about this. She'd never noticed it before. Arising quietly, the adults formed a large, protective circle around the young, and looked and listened. No leaves were rustled, pulled, or chewed. No water gurgled. Then, after first softly cooing to each other, they would start their morning routines.

On today's walk, Brachi called out to Arv, the group's sage leader. He passed the coo along and the long-necked group gathered.

Brachi started. Short, no-nonsense coos. "I found turtle eggshells back there at the edge of the river." A long pause. "And half a turtle shell."

The group fell silent.

This was the third sighting of a plundered nest by someone in the group. No large birds had been seen or heard. Their commune wasn't close to the great saltwater basin where most of the large birds lived. They'd heard about the saltwater basin from elder Brachiosaurus stories. The surface there was endless, constantly changing size and shape. It would spread out in front of them before collapsing, like a fierce bird showing how big it could be. These communes wanted nothing to do with such a strange place.

So, it wasn't a bird. Something new had arrived, and it ate eggs and meat. A carnivore. They'd seen the eggshells recently, but the meat? None of the Brachiosauruses could contemplate this new information. No place existed in their collective memory for the possibility of meat eating.

Faced with this strange sight, the group froze. There was no movement, no coos. The kids clung to the legs of the adults, frightened.

Brachi broke the silence.

She told the group these eggshells were like the ones they'd seen destroyed before, and not by the birds. She suspected veloTors—smaller dinosaurs with short front arms and a vicious attitude. These four-to-six-foot-high creatures had been popping up for the last couple of years. Most communes tried to hunt them down and stomp them out.

Brachi knew this bit of information would be disturbing, but important to share with the troop. She cooed sharply for attention. "There were some marks around the half shell. Three long prongs with long pointed ends and one similar type of prong pointed in the opposite direction. A foot. Well, I assume it was a foot."

All eyes turned towards her. "There were a few of these feet printed in the mud," she continued. "Each footprint left a deep impression."

They looked around, and then Saurius, one of the youngest adults, took a bite of some leaves, making noise and reminding everyone they had to keep eating.

The adults continued their daily routines, and the others followed. Hardly any cooing occurred.

Iso nudged Brachi and asked quietly, "Mommy, how long have we been here?"

Brachi answered. "About sixty eM."

"What's an eM?"

"An eM is about the sun," the mother replied. "We circle the sun a million times for every eM. So, we've been here about sixty million years."

"Gosh, Mommy!" Iso exclaimed as she continued to munch on her leaves. "How old are you?"

"About forty."

"So not an eM?"

Cooing adult laughter interrupted their conversation.

"No, Iso, I'll probably chew leaves until I'm sixty to eighty years old."

They both ripped into more leaves.

"That's why our legends are so important," Brachi continued. "They help us understand the world. We saw the turtles start after our first communes. They were such different creatures. So unusual. All the communes thought they were so clever and different. We enjoyed seeing that new species. Telling stories about them."

They continued chewing until dusk, then drank and slept.

In the early morning, a sound split their peaceful valley.

"RRRRRRRRRROOOOOOAAARRRRRRRRRR!!!!!!!!!!"

None of them had ever heard anything like it. The sound permeated every living thing. It made the ground tremble or vibrate. They all looked skywards, thinking about the elder's descriptions of volcanos.

Two more roars came, louder, quicker together, growing closer. The group moved to a new grove, gliding silently through the foliage. The young brachos were quiet and knew to stay behind the grown-ups. The adults peeked through the trees.

There. Confirmation. Fear. Change. None of them doubted they were entering a new world. From down below, they heard another longer, louder roar. And then they saw him. Tyrannus Rex, they called him. A little more than half their height, but a hundred times more belligerent. He weighed less than they did, but his movements were quick. He looked angry. He swished his tail, knocking over trees, and snorting his frustration at not being able to find their group.

He seemed silly to them. The Tyrannus had a rough hide. He wasn't sleek and beautiful, like the commune members. And he was mean. His talk consisted of different types of roaring and demanding. The commune couldn't help but softly laugh coos at him. He had the silliest thing on his head, an orange poof, that looked like it wouldn't move if pushed. They'd never seen or heard anything like this Tyrannus before.

Saurius whispered, "Doesn't he see himself in the water when he drinks?"

But their laughter faded when they all recalled the turtle eaten off the shell. The commune, seeing the matching footprints, knew this beast was a carnivore. Their carnivore. A creature that could tear through flesh would forever change the way they lived.

The way things had been done and discussed by legends didn't matter anymore.

Arv cooed up to everyone. "I'm going out there. I'm the tallest, way taller than him. I'll explain we're living here, but he's free to roam through our land."

The commune cooed in agreement. Sorette added her sensitive, adolescent voice. "Tyrannus is a new species. He might be defensive."

Arv, after consulting the others, circled away from the commune so as not to give away their position. He broke out into a clearing and stood in front of Tyrannus. Looking down at him, Arv knew he had to succeed, that they couldn't be rid of this intruder just by stomping.

Tyrannus instantly started walking towards him. Arv was obviously larger, so no one was concerned. Then Tyrannus lunged at Arv. Tyrannus pivoted on his left front leg, bringing his body around sharply and lashing his tail into Arv's front leg.

Arv let out a coo no one had ever heard and looked up at the sky, gasping as his bone snapped. Tyrannus bit into the back of Arv's other front leg. Tyrannus refused to let go, shaking his jaws up and down. The creature twisted clockwise and counterclockwise, tearing Arv's leg. Arv's lower leg ripped off, leaving it dangling from a thread of white ligament. Arv collapsed onto his front stumps. Tyrannus pivoted left. With expert timing, he whipped his tail around and smacked Arv's fast dropping head. Arv's head bounced off the ground, and the Tyrannus chomped down on his neck.

Arv died in front of his commune.

The slaughter sent the group into a frenzied reaction. Sorette ran out to stop the carnage. She couldn't understand the why of it, the brutality of it. It was completely senseless. Instantly, her world was vacant, and she needed to reconnect.

The others reacted like a mob, not the commune Brachi had grown up with. An adult lost balance and fell on the ground, crushing a baby bracho. Most adults ran from the Tyrannus. Some stayed together, bellowing to their young before fleeing. In their haste, they didn't realize they had left one behind.

Brachi became more solemn as she slowly backed up, more thoughtful. Arv's death shocked her and by the behavior of her commune. This was not the way to respond to a problem. She turned to see Sorette charging the Tyrannus. She wanted to coo out, "Don't Sorette. No! No!" but she knew it was too late. In seconds, Tyrannus killed Sorette just as he had Arv.

Brachi turned away, trying to distance herself from the slaughter. No legend had prepared her for this. *I must train young Iso to think for herself,* Brachi mused. She raced away full bore, concentrating on aligning her neck and gait.

I must find out who can be trusted to think about this new reality and form a new commune. Things have changed with this strange creature. Not everyone will be able to cope. Some will try and fail. We will have to fight him. We're the meat! We're what he's after. Our transition to a new world must start now.

Brachi passed desirable trees and watering holes. She kept galloping. She hadn't caught up with her herd yet. *Funny, we were always the commune and now we're feeling broken.* She crested a small knoll and saw her group down below eating, water off to the left.

She paused to gather her breath.

As she started down the hill, Brachi cooed, not loud enough to be heard, but a goodbye to the world as she knew it.

Who Will Arrive?
Korie Pelka

Three Weeks Out

You arrive in the early afternoon, bathed in the mid-March warmth of the Arizona desert. The sun is so bright you are temporarily blinded as you enter the darkened house. Your brother has closed all the blinds as if to hasten death's approach. The familiar smell of burnt coffee and a cat litter box desperate for a cleaning greets you. The air is thick with musty memories. It is the house you grew up in but never felt like home. Today, it feels like a tomb.

Mom has been slowly, loudly, dramatically dying for over a year. This is the first visit where you believe it. Her decision fifteen months ago to refuse any treatment for early-stage lung cancer has led to this point. The doctors think she's had a mini-stroke. She can no longer get out of bed without help. She's adamant she knows better than the doctors, refusing to adhere to the prescribed medication regimen. It has put her in jeopardy. She is fighting the idea of going to a nursing care facility to allow professionals to evaluate her condition under safe medical supervision. As the eldest and only daughter, it's your role to convince her to go to the facility.

Which you do.

But not until the nasty zingers and snide remarks have been spewed. Since Dad's death eighteen months earlier, Mom has been free to say and do anything she wants. His expectation of kindness had forced her to target her meanness in strategic ways—aiming her barbs and accusations, usually at you, out of earshot, so as not to incur his anger.

Now, the lid he kept on her has been removed. It's been liberating for her. It's been hell for the rest of us.

She emails your sons requesting they not visit her because they haven't been good enough to her. She composes text messages to your brother, making unreasonable demands at 2:00 a.m. Her anger makes you recall a conversation the week after Dad's memorial service.

She phoned to say she's been mad at you for years.

"You didn't let me die."

You were stunned by her ferocity. She barreled on as you searched for a response.

"When I had the heart attack. You should have let me die."

"When you were in the hospital for pancreatitis?"

"Yes," she confirmed, as if you were crazy to question her. "You called the doctor."

"You were having a heart attack in the hospital, and I wasn't supposed to call for a doctor?"

"My life has been miserable ever since, and it's your fault."

She hung up before you could promise to adhere to her wishes next time.

Ironically, she is fighting you now. She does not want death but servitude in her last days.

Later that night, you are alone in the house, watching the gentle play of moonlight reflecting off the pool, listening to the Nat King Cole playlist that Alexa has algorithmically chosen for Mom. A nostalgic playlist that reminds you she was once a spirited young woman who danced at Roseland Ballroom on Saturday nights and wore fashionable outfits to work in New York City. A woman who sailed to London on the *RMS Queen Mary* and stole away to Paris without her parents' permission. A woman with a full life ahead of her.

You sit in the rocking chair, contemplating Mom's well-worn spot on the couch in front of her beloved TV. Over the years, her chronic illnesses forced her to choose a much smaller worldview. It's a perspective you try to hang on to, knowing the coming days will test your resilience and possibly sear your heart.

Mom's decline begins in earnest throughout the week in respite care at the nursing facility. Soon, the expected genial spirits start showing up —ghosts of Dad surrounded by dogs, her sister dressed in an indigo ball gown, and her favorite Aunt Alice offering her a cup of tea. When she isn't fighting so hard, she tells you they have come to visit her. She sees them at the end of her bed and lurking in the corner of the room. But she isn't ready yet, and soon they abandon her.

The nurses tell you the end could be near, or this could continue for quite some time. Every night, you put on the Nat King Cole playlist, hug her, and tell her you love her, thinking, perhaps praying, it could be the last time you see her. Yet every morning, you find her propped up, watching *Judge Judy* and demanding cherry Jell-O.

* * *

Two Weeks Out

Her angry, resentful soul is in full bloom now. She's throwing things at her grandson, who tells you he is glad they were just pillows and soft stuffed animals. She's started saying hateful things at her devoted son, who seeks solace by returning to past patterns of drug and alcohol abuse. They are not used to this side of her. You have honed your coping strategies over a lifetime of co-dependency. You step in, as always, to take care of things.

The week's visitors are sparse. Nurses with kind smiles, deep caring, and displaying more patience than you could ever muster. Paper-pushing administrators bring documents to be signed and a warning that she might need to be discharged soon, given the restrictions on her insurance. Eventually, a doctor shows up to remind you that there is little he can do now. He recommends moving her to the hospice section of the facility.

* * *

One Week Out

A chaplain arrives. They talk politics, not religion. A social worker stops by as part of the contractual hospice arrangement. They talk about the weather and the terrible food. Your cousin drives over from California to visit. They laugh. She drives back. The neighbor next door, a friend for over fifty years, stays twenty minutes before excusing herself. Mom has alienated so many. She is alone, and it is of her own making. This saddens you to your core.

The deathbed vigil begins in earnest.

The hospice nurses let you stay later each night as Mom spends more time in and out of consciousness. For someone who has always touted that she would welcome death gracefully and willingly, Mom is fighting harder than you ever imagined.

Her final days bring two unexpected and unseen visitors—first, her cousin Lois, who died months earlier. Mom rarely talked about her. The only thing you knew about Lois was they spent summers together as young children playing on an island outside of Gananoque, Canada. Now, she is Mom's constant companion, along with an unnamed visitor who clearly frightens her. You have no idea what's happening until one night you hear her cry out, using the childhood nickname for Lois, *"Don't hurt Lo-ey,"* she implores. Her chest rattles, voice whispery soft with deep despair, *"Lo-ey, help me. Don't let him hurt me."*

In the dim light of the hospice room, you flash to a scene three decades earlier.

It was the day Dad had emergency quadruple bypass surgery. The hours ticked by as you waited in the pale green visitors' room while Mom and your brother chain-smoked outside. Once he was in recovery, Mom decided we should go across the street to have lunch at Los Olivos, a favorite Mexican restaurant. It was busy and crowded as we settled into a table in the middle of the room. Mom turned to us after we placed our orders.

"I think you should know I was sexually abused as a child," she said, as if she were commenting on the weather. "I don't remember much other than wearing a yellow sunsuit. And I know it wasn't my father. There's not much else to say, but I thought you should know."

That news landed in the middle of the table alongside the recently delivered chips and salsa.

Stunned, you watched your brother develop a sudden fascination with his guacamole.

"That's terrible," you responded, feeling wholly inadequate. "You don't remember who it was?"

"No, but it wasn't my father," she reiterated.

"Have you sought counseling?"

"No need," she insisted. "I'm fine; I just thought you both should know."

Case closed, just in time for the enchiladas to arrive.

You tried several times in subsequent years to find out more, but were rebuffed each time. Yet, two things became clear after that awkward, uneaten lunch. First, the focus on that day had shifted to Dad, and Mom just couldn't take it. She needed to draw attention back to herself, and that was the card she played. Quite well, you think with a touch of admiration because, boy, nothing got your attention like sexual abuse. The second thing was that she felt she had handled the emotional trauma and was perfectly fine.

Now, as you sit by her bed and watch her curl into a fetal position, you know why she's been fighting so hard. The next life appears to hold the unseen ghost of the man who sexually abused her as a child.

She is too far gone for you to confirm your intuition. You try to talk to your brother about your theory, but he cannot go down that path. He needs to remember her in his own way. You honor his choice.

You know your heart is right, and you are terrified for her.

In the wee hours, you find forgiveness has arrived at your side: forgiveness and small acceptances. You wonder about your life, your runway, which seems much shorter now. You are determined to have a different end.

Mom spends the rest of her days cowering in her bed, calling out to Lois, and desperately, feebly trying to ward off the unseen demon.

You have no tools, no talisman, no list of prayers or mantras to make such a demon leave her in peace. You do the only thing you can in those final hours as she struggles between this world and the next.

You choose to hold her hand … and hold her hand … and hold her hand until she is…

* * *

Gone.

Win A Trip to Mars
Renelaine Pfister

Sara never missed work. She was never late to appointments. She always showed up for friends' birthdays with a thoughtful gift. Yet whenever there was a moment's silence, her only thought was, "I'm so tired. What's the point of living?" She wasn't brave enough to kill herself (it would probably hurt). She was also too *nice* to kill herself. She didn't want her parents to feel guilty about it afterwards, and she didn't want to traumatize whoever found her dead body.

One day, as she made eggs and toast for dinner because that's all the food she had in her apartment, her phone started ringing. A flood of noisy text messages followed.

Puzzled, she picked up her phone. "Hello?"

"I can't believe you won!" Mary, her sister, screamed.

Sara moved the phone away from her ear. "Won what?" She asked.

"The trip to Mars! You didn't even tell me you entered!"

The trip to Mars? Sara thought before she remembered. She'd entered the raffle six months ago. She never thought she'd win. The *entire world* entered, and there were only going to be ten winners.

She was one of them.

She had a golden ticket.

The Trip to Mars raffle winners were briefed and prepared for months, but the only thing Sara could remember about the planet was what she learned in grade school: Mars has one-third the gravity of Earth, is very cold and has two moons.

For the first time, Sara was truly excited about something. All her life she'd felt restless, like she didn't belong. Maybe she was on the wrong planet. Mars seemed like her kind of place: isolated and self-sufficient.

Is going to Mars a homecoming? She wondered.

"You will have ten minutes to walk on the surface of Mars," their instructor informed them. "Then you must return to the ship. You're on a strict timeline. Any delay could jeopardize the rest of your party."

The trip to Mars took nine months, the length of time for a normal pregnancy. In a way, Sara felt reborn. She was going to be a new person … a Martian.

At last, the captain announced, "We are touching down on Mars in five minutes."

Sara looked down at the Red Planet for the first time. She had visited Hawaii once with her family when she was young. They had something there called li hing powder, which tasted sweet and sour and tinged orange. It's what Sara remembered now, peering through the small window of the ship. Looking at the surface of Mars, she saw a barren landscape, a red desert of li hing powder.

Sara finally set foot on Mars, and with limited vision through her helmet, she saw Martian dust swirl beneath her feet. An overwhelming sense of peace washed over her, a sense of rightness. This is where she needed to be: unanchored, weightless, and far away. There was no need to pretend to be alive like she did on Earth.

The captain's voice on her earphones broke the silence. "Attention, visitors. We just noticed some activity kicking up. A dust storm. Please return to the ship immediately."

Sara didn't move. She listened as the others returned to the ship; their names marked off one by one.

"Sara, where are you?!" the captain demanded. "Come back to the ship. Now! We can't waste another second!"

She stared with wonder at the gathering storm, a swirling wall of li hing powder, heading toward her. The sound of the gale drowned out the urgent voices of the captain and the other passengers.

You can't stay here, she heard her fellow passengers protest on her earphones as the ship pulled away from Mars's surface. *You don't have enough air. You don't have food. You can't survive.* Their voices started breaking up until all she could hear was static.

Sara lifted her hand and smiled as she waved goodbye.

A Fresh Start
Excerpt from the novel *There May Not Be Another Day*
Joan Prebilich

Saigon, February, 1963

Friday evening, after surviving a nose-dive landing at Saigon's Tan Son Nhut airport that morning and a wild taxi ride amid a confusion of toxic-fume emitting vehicles to his posh hotel in Saigon, Australian reporter Michael Paxton was ready to meet his mentor for dinner. Despite a long nap after the tumultuous arrival, he still felt fatigued and somewhat disoriented. The reporter he was replacing was tall, red-haired, very British, Tony Hodgeson. He greeted Mike in the lobby with a smile.

"Are you ready for some fine dining, Paxton?"

Mike chuckled and shook Hodgeson's hand. "That was a hard landing. I thought we were going to crash. That, plus the heat. I think I need a day or two to recover."

"Yeah," said Hodgeson with a grin. "The pilots do that to avoid incoming flak from the Viet Cong. You were lucky. Sometimes the planes have to be rerouted to Bangkok. Well, maybe a nice dinner will make up for your rough start."

They took the elevator to the restaurant, already packed with a mixture of Western and Vietnamese diners. A waiter led them to a table and took their orders: steak frites for Mike and Boeuf Bourguignon for Hodgeson. Looking around, Mike thought the elegant Art Déco ambience of the hotel's restaurant would have done justice to the finest bistro in Paris. While they ate, Hodgeson filled him in on what he needed to know at the bureau come Monday.

"The boss will be there to meet you before he goes on to his day's social agenda. So, be there before eight."

Mike nodded. "That's Mr. Drake. I received a 'Welcome aboard' letter from him."

"Yeah," said Hodgeson, mopping up the sauce from his stew with a piece of baguette. "But the de facto boss is Bill Gilmore. He actually runs the show. Right now, we're short-handed, so there's a lot of pressure on the staff to get the best stories out to the world before our competitors do. Did you receive any technical training at headquarters?"

"You mean on using the equipment?"

"Right. We're short on cameramen and soundmen. We need someone to train the Vietnamese staff."

"We spent a couple of days on it, but not enough to make me an expert. I did some reporting in Japan, but that was from the top of a well-equipped truck. I just had to report the action."

"Well, it's more complicated here. So how did you end up in Saigon? Dressed as you are, you look more like a diplomat than a lowly reporter."

Mike chuckled. "Credit that to the suit I bought in London with just that effect in mind. I'll have to write a congratulatory note to the tailor."

Hodgeson laughed. "They send us mostly inexperienced younger men from local stations. Some work out and others have difficulty with the climate, the people, the food and so on. So, I'm curious. Why did you choose Vietnam? This is a war zone, and it is dangerous."

Mike met Hodgeson's gaze. "Headquarters was quite clear about the unsafe conditions here. Let's just say I earned a few black marks in Sydney for supporting the wrong people in a political crisis. You can't accuse one of the wealthiest men in Australia of corruption without expecting some backlash. Especially if he happens to be your ex-father-in-law. There's more to it, but that's the crux of the matter." Mike sighed. *No, he didn't want to go into that now. Maybe some time later when he knew Hodgeson better.*

"So they blackballed you."

"Yes, exonerated after the fact, but nonetheless unemployable in Australia at the moment. I try to report objectively on what I see and know. And that's all." Then Mike added as an afterthought, "I suppose that sounds naïve."

Hodgeson set the bread he was about to put in his mouth on his plate. He gave Mike a serious look.

"I'm going to worry about you, Paxton. That's not how things are done here. You'll get eaten up by all the sharks before you can cry for help."

"Well, then enlighten me."

* * *

After their meal, Hodgeson suggested they continue Mike's education at the hotel bar on the eighth floor. The cozy late-night ambience was right for the information Hodgeson would confide. Mike ordered a beer and Hodgeson had a Japanese whiskey on the rocks.

Hodgeson took a sip of his whiskey before speaking. "Since time's of the essence, I'll get down to it. We call the boss 'Drake the Rake' because he spends most of his time hobnobbing with the military or embassy people and bedding their wives. We can't figure out what the women see in him except for a nice dinner. Then there's Bill Gillmore, a serious reporter, who's moved up the ranks to Assistant Bureau Chief. He's got the weight of the world on his shoulders while his boss, who earns ten times what he does, is out whoring. If Gillmore seems to be in a perpetually foul mood, now you know why."

"So, how do you function in that environment? You don't seem ready to go off the rails."

Hodgeson gave him a lopsided grin. "Well, you have to strategize every mission as to the degree of danger it represents and plan accordingly."

"For example?"

Hodgeson grinned again. "Say I know in advance that the situation is likely to be dangerous, such as bullets flying or Viet Cong coming at me with knives drawn; then I manage to arrive just after the event but early enough to document it. Not heroic, but I will leave intact, which is proof that my strategy works. Drake will give you a month to get settled, and then he'll send you off to more challenging assignments."

"What would those be?"

"Well, hitching a ride out to the country to accompany a military advisor attached to a South Vietnamese army unit checking on Viet Cong infiltration. That's usually done during the day when the Viet Cong are hiding out, so there's not too much danger. It's a different story at night. You don't want to get stuck out anywhere at night. So far, no one on the staff has been injured or killed, but they've had some close calls."

"The advisors would be Americans, right?"

"Mainly, yes. They're CIA or the military. You can bet on it. They're everywhere now. Some are obvious and some are not. My advice is not to trust any of them. The Americans want to replace the French colony with an American one and the Vietnamese aren't having it. Meanwhile, the North and the South are terrorizing each other with the peasant population caught in the middle. And the Americans keep pouring money into this bottomless pit. Common sense tells you they should pack up and leave the settling of accounts to the Vietnamese."

Hodgeson called the waiter for another round of drinks.

"What about containing Communism?" asked Mike. "What about the Domino Theory?

"Would the people be better off with Ho than with Diem? Lies, propaganda, killings and assassinations occur regularly from both sides. The Communists are better organized to fight a guerrilla war. It makes you wonder who'll be left to pick up the pieces. We all know there can be only one winner and I'm hearing it's going to be the North." Hodgeson sighed, drank the last of his whisky, and said, "Anyway, I'm out of here next Friday. My time is up. So you get some rest. That might be the last you'll see once they get you going."

* * *

After Hodgeson went back to his apartment, Mike returned to his air-conditioned room to carry on with his unpacking. Hodgeson had said Monday was going to be busy getting his paperwork in order with the various agencies he'd be working with. Then there was meeting his co-workers and his bosses. Too wound up to sleep, Mike checked his watch. It was a little after the bewitching hour but too early to go to bed after a long afternoon nap and a rich dinner. And he needed time to process the information that Hodgeson had given him. Once he'd familiarized himself with the working of the bureau and was out on his own, he'd be in a better position to come to his own conclusions about where the country was headed. Mike chuckled to himself as Alexander Pope's "Fools rush in where angels fear to tread" popped into his head. Then, a cold beer to top off the evening seemed in order, so he headed back to the bar for a nightcap.

Soft jazz and dimmed lights lent an intimate feel to the bar when Mike passed through its doors. The patrons, hunched at the long counter, mostly foreigners, sipped their drinks quietly, almost introspectively.

There was an absence of the animated conversations he'd heard earlier with Hodgeson. The barman was polishing glassware when Mike approached the counter. The man stopped his cleaning when he saw him.

"Monsieur?" he asked.

Mike nodded. French. He could handle that. "Un Kirin, s'il vous plaît."

The barman brought him the beer and a glass. "Voutré chambre, Monsieur?"

French numbers could be tricky. He had to think for a minute. Room 375. "Trois cents soixante-quinze."

"Merci."

He could have drunk his beer at the counter, but the depressive silence drove him through the doors to the terrace. Tables had been set out for dining during the cooler parts of the day or evening, but now the umbrellas were furled and no one was outside except him. Flashes of red light in the overcast sky and a muffled booming spoke of firefights going on in the outskirts of the city. When earlier Mike had flinched after the first explosion, Hodgeson had said not to worry; it was a nightly show from the Viet Cong and he'd get used to it. Mike knew from his experience as an eighteen-year-old soldier fending off the Japanese invasion of Singapore in 1942 that fear was something you don't get over. You repress those bad memories to keep a normal life going. But this was a different time and a different place and whatever came his way, he would have to deal with it. That attitude had served him in the past, and there was no reason to change it now.

The searing heat of the day had yielded to humidity so warm and heavy it felt like rain. Mike took off his jacket and set it on a chair while he leaned over the parapet to look down on the street below. The plaza was empty except for the traffic circling around the square in what looked like military or police vehicles. The curfew, of course. As he contemplated the view and all the things he'd seen and heard so far, he had a small moment wondering if he'd made the right choice. "Some work out and some don't" is what he remembered Hodgeson saying. He was at the bottom of the corporate ladder, his foot barely on the first rung. Based on the freelance work he'd done for them in Japan, International Productions offered him a year's contract in Saigon. The company liked his style of reporting and the way he got along with the Japanese. They thought he'd be right for Vietnam. Well, there was no going back to the safety of a boring desk job he didn't want. This was his chance to prove he was worth the company's confidence in him. Mike sighed, letting that moment of uncertainty pass as normal for someone starting a new job in a war zone.

"Well," he told himself, "I've made my bed and now it's time to lie in it."

There was nothing more to be learned from staring at an empty street, so Mike drained his glass and headed to his room. He wasn't expected at the office until Monday. Until then, there was time to get a sense of where he would be heading. Mike was determined to arrive at the office looking sharp and confident, ready to tackle any assignment handed to him. After coming home from the war, he remembered his father saying his life had been spared for a reason. Maybe this was it.

Mary Elizabeth
Sarah E. Pruitt

Fourteen-year-old Mary Elizabeth scanned the crowd jammed along the narrow third-class deck. Despite smoke from the smokestack, she found the air fresher than below in steerage.

Mrs. Riley, the woman in the next bunk, stood by the ship's rail, watching her boys play. Mary Elizabeth wove through the other passengers—most speaking in the familiar West Irish dialect.

"How's yer ma this morning?" Mrs. Riley's eyebrows rose in concern.

Mary Elizabeth gripped the rail to keep her balance. "Still vomiting and—" her voice broke, but years of choking back sobs stood her in good stead. "And nothing I give her helps."

"Let's try a little sugar."

Mary Elizabeth followed the older woman down the steps. For a second, the girl's sun-dazzled eyes saw nothing but black. Then the large, windowless room, crammed with narrow bunks and lit by lanterns, came into view.

When they first boarded, Mary Elizabeth heard many of her fellow travelers complaining of no portholes, sour air, and crowded bunks. Not her. Safe with Ma, she had been happy despite the crowding. Happy until Ma's seasickness didn't stop. Clutching beds for balance, Mary Elizabeth hurried to the large tea urn and filled her cup from the spigot.

Mrs. Riley dropped in a lump of raw sugar. "You know, child," she whispered as she stirred the weak brew, "the stewardess warned me. For some, the seasickness never stops."

Mary Elizabeth gasped. *No!*

Mrs. Riley blinked back tears and tried to say something else. Finally, she patted Mary Elizabeth's shoulder and took her sons up the stairs to the deck.

Mary Elizabeth forced herself to smile and walked towards their bunk. The term "coffin ship" made a sudden, terrible sense. *I thought we would be safe escaping Uncle's house.*

For years, Mary Elizabeth felt like the village pariah. The adults scorned her because she was born out of wedlock. Their children yelled "Shame, shame, Finucane" whenever they saw her.

Mary Elizabeth spent years hating her surname. She planned to change it to her father's someday, but her mother refused to name him.

So, Mary Elizabeth only had Ma. They lived with her uncle, a hard-drinking, brutal, and tight-fisted man, who doled out food slowly to Ma and "her brat."

With her mother beside her, Mary Elizabeth felt invincible when they boarded the ship. She was ready to take on anything America offered. *I can't lose her.*

Her mother stirred and opened her eyes. Mary Elizabeth held out a few drops of tea on a spoon.

Her mother took a tiny sip, gagged, and lay still, taking slow, deep breaths. "You need to know about yer da."

"Don't care anymore, Ma. Just get better." Mary Elizabeth's words surprised her in their truth. She felt her shoulders relax, as if she had set down a heavy tray.

Ma smiled. "Your uncle, God rest his soul, filled your head with lies."

Mary Elizabeth's insides tightened, remembering her uncle's disgusting descriptions of her probable conception. She flinched with memories of his belt as he attempted to "drive the devil" out of her!

She knew it was a sin, but almost hoped God would leave him writhing in purgatory for the next ten thousand years. It had been a miracle when the old man died of apoplexy in the middle of a tirade. The money he kept from their wages paid for their tickets.

"Your father was a handsome lad."

Mary Elizabeth jerked her mind back to the present. "It's all right, Ma. Try and rest."

"John Joseph McCarthy. His parents sent him to Dublin to attend Trinity College." Ma whispered through dry, cracked lips.

Mary Elizabeth tried to swallow her fear. *Ma wants to talk, and I need to let her.* "How did you meet?" A quiver of interest grew. She barely noticed the pulse of the motor and the clatter of footsteps on the metal stairs.

Ma's voice fell into the cadence of a bedtime story. "He visited his aunt every Sunday. I assisted the parlor maid in answering the door and serving the tea."

Mary Elizabeth gasped. Parlor maid was one of the best jobs a female servant could attain—only cooks or housekeepers paid better. Being a parlor maid's assistant indicated high skills. Mary Elizabeth worked two years in service herself but as a mere kitchen maid.

"When he thanked me for his tea, I blushed from the part in my hair to the tips of my boots." Ma smiled. "Then I met him outside the house on my afternoon off."

Mary Elizabeth again offered tea, but her mother turned her head away.

"What happened?" Mary Elizabeth set the cup on the deck.

"Well, we were foolish and thought we'd have time for him to finish his schooling, get a job, then marry. But—" Ma's eyes drooped. "One afternoon, I found out he had the typhoid—dead in a month." Her voice faded. "Then I learned you were coming."

"Oh, Ma." Mary Elizabeth leaned in and let her forehead rest on her mother's with the lightest of touches.

"My beautiful, smart daughter," whispered her mother. "Best work of my life when you were born." She slurred the last words, and her eyelids, pale and blue-veined, closed.

Kneeling by the narrow berth, Mary Elizabeth prayed. She fell asleep between one rosary bead and the next.

* * *

Bridget Finucane listened to her exhausted daughter's slow breathing.

She sent up a prayer asking forgiveness for her lie. Johnny McCarthy's angry attack in the dark kitchen had left her bruised, broken, and with child. No need to burden Mary Elizabeth with the truth. Her daughter should arrive in America free of the dreadful man wherever he was.

Bridget prayed for months for a way to tell her daughter about her father. Today, a sweeter story—a reality she'd never known—rolled off her tongue.

More at peace than she'd been in years, Bridgett slept and did not wake up.

* * *

Mary Elizabeth allowed herself an hour to weep and then stood tall in the stiff breeze as she watched her mother's canvas-wrapped body disappear beneath the waves. She bowed her head in prayer, resolving to add an extra decade of the rosary each night before bed. *Perhaps even one for Uncle.*

Two days later, the *Saint Louis* docked in New York City.

Mary Elizabeth stood on the deck with the others and mulled over what name to give the custom agent. She tried Mary Elizabeth McCarthy on for size. It stung as if she'd lost something. Still undecided, she watched the shipmaster hand a book to an American custom agent.

"What's he doing?" asked a nearby child.

"He's giving him the passenger list so the Americans will know who we are," said his father.

Mary Elizabeth shivered, imagining what could have happened to her if she gave the wrong name. *No matter. Once I'm off the ship, I can choose any name I want.*

She followed the Riley family off the boat and into one of the long lines.

"My dear, what are your plans?" Mrs. Riley chivied her sons and luggage ahead of her.

Mary Elizabeth thought of her mother and remembered the elderly parlor maid who worked with her in Ballyheigue. *I helped her set the table, iron the linens, and wash the china. I watched her serve breakfast and afternoon tea.*

A daring idea formed. "I'm hoping to apply for parlor maid."

Mrs. Riley studied her for a long minute and then smiled. "Wear your hair pulled back; it'll make you look older. We'll need to find a good employment agency."

Mary Elizabeth nodded and caught a glimpse of the city—blue skies and tall buildings. Many over five stories!

"What's your name?" asked the custom agent, piercing her reverie.

In that moment, she knew exactly who she was. "Mary Elizabeth Finucane."

Excitement softened her grief. *I've reached America, Ma. I'll make you proud.*

Refuge
N. A. Ratnayake

In those days I had been an old man, having just come from Earth, because they love their old men—or at least, they assume old men are wise. In the form of countless advisors, gurus, swamis, wizards, viziers, pashas, and senators, I strove to pull them back from the brink of destroying their own planet. Over centuries of toil and millions of followers—young, old, men, women, and the range of humanity in between—I failed. I failed to trick them into saving themselves from themselves. And now I was tired.

Whenever I became depleted throughout the long stretches of time I worked on Earth, I found solace and replenishment on a quiet, rocky planet tucked away in a dormant corner of a lonely galaxy. I called it Refuge, because it lurked far from anyone or anything that might disturb it or me.

I named it to make it *mine* in a way, and to use it for my own ends. And in my hubris, I thought I was the only intelligence to sense Refuge, apprehend it, comprehend it, and name it. I knew of no other name by which it might be called, except the one I had given it. And because I found no one else who had named it before me, I assumed there was no intelligence there to do so.

I was wrong.

Refuge is replete with rivers. They start in the many highlands of the rugged mountains, which trap the moisture and hoard the uncountable plummeting snowflakes, which eventually melt and branch from the ridgelines. Trickles merging into rivulets merging into washes merging into streams and then finally mighty rivers, forever searching for the next tiny step downward, potential energy endlessly nosing out the direction of its own annihilation, an in-built craving for the end of gradient road, the inevitable merging with the whole.

The higher altitudes are edenic and lush with diverse scrub and forests. The waters journey through the lowlands downward to the deserts, where they thin and falter. There are no oceans. All rivers end exhausted and ephemeral in baking evaporative ovens of mid-latitude sands, their progeny vapor eventually beginning their descent anew in the snowy peaks.

This is the planet to which I retreated after quitting Earth, still as an old man because I was too tired to change into anything else. In the dry lowlands by a grove of what might on Earth have been called a willow, I sat regenerating on the banks of a thin stream where the living things were forced to cluster against the parch.

I listened to the trickle meandering around rock and root. I felt the presence of scurrying, small life grateful for the life-giving water, little pockets of sentience—able to observe but devoid of the ability to dream of mastering it all.

And isn't that, after all, what we self-styled intelligent beings mean by *intelligence*? The capacity to make the false distinction that there is us and not-us, the propensity to dream and plan to make not-us serve us and our needs better than random chance, and the will and ability to put such manipulation into effect, even to our long-term peril as a species.

It was during these musings that the Beyul first reached out to me, though I did not know its name then or recognize that it had a name it called itself.

At first, I felt only sensations of plant-like being: The smell of gum tree and cedar after the rain, the yearning of a fern to unfurl in the sun, the dark questing of a thousand root tendrils slowly worming over hours into the soft loam, seeking water, water, always more water. I dismissed these sensations as products of my wandering mind. A thought-form, an idea-shape, an artifact of meditation while ruffled—no more.

But the Beyul was persistent against my prejudice.

A thirst grew in me, which I began to recognize as originating outside of me. A simple sensation spreading to dry mouth, cracked lips. Something was wrong. A pain, a yearning, a plea. I understood it then, though we had no language in common.

Now, a being can need help and not be *intelligent*. Does the parched seagrass on Earth, once resplendent in wetland flourish, understand that unseasonal drought erodes its home to nothing? Can each blade comprehend the treason of another species in the web of life borrowing against the future of all and leaving behind the bill? Is the suffering of the seagrass any less because it cannot name itself in a language we *intelligent* creatures understand?

And yet, by degrees, my curiosity led me down paths that parted my prejudice.

I welcomed the Beyul into my mind and followed its life essence where it led me. I saw it was not merely the plants, the river, the rocks. As a being, it was emergent—a result of the connections made by this strand of the river, the particular flow of the water through the roots of a hundred different flora, the passing of their life energy into seeds and flowers and nectar. Its interaction with the world rested in the subtle manipulation—intentional, I at length had to concede—of the small animals which consumed its fruits, and the shaping of the land around itself to better assure its survival.

What is *intention*? Does the cockroach envision its next meal or scheme the best stratagem for gaining entry to the next domicile? Is not "follow this molecular trail wherever you find it, and the universe will provide food" a form of plan? Is a coordinated reaction and directed action toward a pre-defined goal enough to be called *intent*?

I suspected then that the rivers of Refuge were more than a physical life force, but a low-level form of sentience. The flow of these rivers and their life energy from object to object made a system that was, in an emergent sense, alive, and by degrees I could admit … *conscious*.

The waters by which I sat meditating had once been a mighty river, which had over time dried to a creek, and now traversed this soil as a mere stream. Parts of the Beyul now received a mere fraction of what it had grown to want and need. If the trend continued, the life energy of this bounded system would cease its ordered cycles and dissipate into the surrounding environment.

That is to say, the Beyul was dying—and knew it.

My hubris was cracking. I can dissemble, rationalize, and evade blame, like any good intelligent creature. I had been an old man then, remember. Perhaps in my age, I was stuck in my thinking; or as a man then, fell prey to the arrogance of men; or in my then-human form, limited in some fundamental way to the constraints of their primate minds.

But these are excuses only, and I knew it, even then.

It is a hard thing to acknowledge another being as one's equal; because if one acknowledges personhood in another, the natural consequence of such admission is that one's moral sphere must extend to encompass the other. And that can become a complex, tiresome thing. If I had just spent centuries on Earth on the moral compunction of attempting to save its dominant sentient species from itself, should I not intervene here to save this one, this unique new being I had never encountered?

I am ashamed to say that my pride had as much to do with saying yes as my heart did. I had failed on Earth. Perhaps here was a chance at redemption, at saving another being from a changing world. And at least this time, the being I would try to save wasn't actively trying to work against me.

I showed it all I had learned on Earth and countless other places of how to live in changing times, how a water-loving life form can learn to adapt to a drier land, to seek and acquire moisture from other sources, and to conserve carefully what it had. I taught its ground covers to sprawl and shade the soil. I hardened soft skins against the dry winds. I suffused the air with the scent of fruits to entice animals to gather in the water, hoping they would pay for their sustenance with their urine and blood as they decomposed, giving back water and seeding the next species to follow.

It took time, of course. But what is a century or two in the span of things? I had nowhere to be but there. By the end, I'm not sure what the Beyul and I had could be called a friendship. I think our minds are too different for my definition of that word. But we had an understanding, and I felt its gratitude.

It came to me on a whim, what was next to be done. I opened a door, as my kind is able to do, the kind of door that lets us traverse the heavens and avoid the burden of putting up with each other. It was the same door through which I had come to Refuge from Earth, and Earth was still there. Through the door, a hidden valley in the Himalayas opened before me, remote and secret, far from the most concentrated clusters of prying intelligent eyes.

The Beyul twitched, sensing the new planet. It quivered in my mind, awed, hesitant. I knew it knew that this world I had given up on needed help. With a twinge of thanks and farewell, the Beyul willed itself through the door. It shouted its name in the way it knew how, and its name formed as *Beyul* to my mind.

I closed the door.

For the first time in a long time, I was alone on Refuge again, with only my thoughts and my names for things as company. I do not know where I will wander next, or in what form—but I am old and tired of being a tired old man and crave something new. Perhaps it's best I give up helping and begin to learn again. After all, my supposed intelligence nearly missed a being that might yet complete what I started, in ways I cannot imagine. Maybe I have forgotten how to be humble before the vastness of the stars.

I still rue my failure on Earth. But it comforts me to know that, in the mountains at the top of the world on that planet I could not save, there are now humans who know the name Beyul. They speak of hidden valleys that are the last refuges on a dying Earth, of secret wells of being that hold out hope to reseed life and hope, when the moment is right.

It will take time, of course.

Start Small
Donna Rawlins

Colin chatted away at the bar while Mike tallied up the till. It was a nightly routine between the two men. The pub's combination safe was in the upstairs apartment where Mike and his wife Kate had lived for two decades until she died last March. Colin's voice trailed off until the unusual silence caught Mike's attention.

"Are you OK there, Colin? I don't think I've ever heard you not talking before."

The two men locked eyes.

"Well, ya know, I've been thinking, Mike. Ya can't go on like this forever. I know ya get lonely; you're always here taking care of the pub by yourself, and hardly ever go outside the village. Ya don't even have a dog anymore. So, I was wondering if you're planning anything? Are ya keeping in touch with Kate's family? Maybe ya should take some time off. Go visit her sister and the kids."

Mike's shoulders sank as he blew out a deep breath and shook his head. The lighthearted smile he wore a few moments ago straightened into a thin line.

"Now you know that just isn't possible. Nobody but me and Kate ever knew how to run this place—well, except George. Great barkeeper, but you can't trust him with the money or the booze. Plus, I don't feel like doin' nothing."

"Well, it's not like you'd be leaving forever, for Christ sakes. Take yourself ten days or so. And I can keep an eye on George. Think about it, Mike."

Mike stuffed the cash in the bank bag and poured himself and Colin one last nightcap of Redbreast.

"Here's to your well-intentioned idea, Colin." They raised their shot glasses with a knowing nod and tossed back the comforting Irish whiskey.

"Maybe later … when the weather warms up. Flying from Vermont to Dublin is too complicated with bad weather causing so many damn flight cancellations. You never know when you'll end up sleeping in airports and getting where you're going two or three days later than planned. No thanks."

They walked across the well-worn oak floors to the front door and exchanged their usual slap-on-the-back goodbyes. Mike locked up the old brick pub as Colin pulled his jacket up over his ears and trotted through the empty parking lot toward his house a block and a half away.

As Mike listened for that final click of the deadbolt and rattled the door handle to make absolutely sure he had locked it, a disturbing sensation overcame him. It felt like someone was watching. He patted the left side of his corduroy blazer, feeling for the bank bag he habitually placed in the inside pocket. His mind raced with disjointed questions about who stayed late at the pub, searching for faces he didn't know. Braced and as ready as he could be with no source of protection except his fists, he slowly turned his gaze away from the door in front of him and looked all the way to the right, then to the left, but saw nothing except large snowflakes falling under the beam of the security light.

Attempting to resist the nefarious scenarios that flashed through his mind, he backed away from the door. Cautiously, he surveyed the parking lot, but again, saw nothing unusual. He scurried toward the stairs leading to his apartment but as he approached, stopped dead in his tracks. There, on the edge of a shadow between the slats of the first and second steps, was a small kitten. Mostly black except for the white fur around her neck. She crouched down low and fixed her intense golden eyes on him.

Releasing the breath he didn't realize he was holding, he said, "Oh, for Christ sakes. You scared me half to death. Go on! Scat! Go on home, you scrawny little bird-killing beast."

Mike couldn't tell if she was scared stiff or just too cold to move, but not even a whisker twitched.

"Oh, good God. Now what the hell do I do? If only Kate was here, she'd deal with it." Mike ran his fingers through what was left of his once-thick red hair and took a slow step forward. The kitten still didn't flinch. But when Mike took one more step toward her—bam! She bolted like lightning into the blackness under the landing and Mike stomped up the stairs, mumbling to himself as he went.

"Thank the heavens that ordeal is over."

* * *

Before opening the pub, Mike always enjoyed a pick-me-up to get him through until it was an acceptable time to start drinking. He poured enough cream into a cup of deeply steeped, black tea to turn it white and held the mug with both hands to warm and coax his arthritic fingers into another day of work. It was always a day of work for him, except for official holidays—the very days he wanted to be at work so he wouldn't think about his life without Kate on Christmas or Easter or Thanksgiving.

Predictably, Colin appeared at the pub about five o'clock for a nip of whiskey and a bit of conversation with his friend before dinner.

"You'll never believe what happened last night on my way upstairs." Mike was excited to have a story to tell; he kicked off their chat with an enhanced version of the tale of a potential thief turning out to be a small tuxedo kitten, and how proud he felt about scaring off the wayward creature.

"Ya didn't take the poor thing in? Mike! What's gotten into ya? Have ya no sense of decency? She might have died from the cold last night, and you'd have her innocent blood on your hands, my friend."

"What in God's name would I do with a cat, much less a kitten? I might be allergic, and then I'd be the one waking up dead in the morning. What about that? Besides, I don't know the first thing about taking care of a cat. Plus, they scratch your couch and smell up the house."

"But they're great hunters! The best mousers, they are. Seriously, ya can't leave that little bugger out in the cold one more night."

"But it probably belongs to someone and they're out looking for it," Mike said.

"Well then, let's get busy making some posters and put them around. Meanwhile, you can keep the kitten warm in the house tonight and feed her some cream. I know you have that on hand at least. And ya won't have to worry that she became dinner for a coyote either. As a matter of fact, I'm gonna look for her right now. If she'll come to me, I know where your key is, so I'll just let her in for ya. In the morning, we'll put out the posters and you'll be the hero of the neighborhood."

* * *

Colin successfully lured the petite feline into the upstairs flat in plenty of time to join Mike as he tallied up the money for the night.

"So, you know what to do when ya get to your place, right? Be real, real quiet, open the door softly, and close it quickly—but not too fast cause she might be waiting there ready to run out and ya don't want her to get caught in the door."

"Oh, dear God. What have I gotten myself into, letting you talk me into this? Can't you just take her home?"

"Are you kidding me? My two old gals wouldn't be havin' it for a moment. That poor little kitten would get scratched, bitten, and chased like a cat toy all over the house. Mine are fifteen-year-old litter mates and have not one ounce of tolerance for other cats."

Mike shoved the cash into the bank bag, catching a few bills in the zipper as Colin watched.

"Stop fretting, will ya? We'll go upstairs together and get ya safe inside," Colin said. "And don't be mad. It's just for a night or two. I'll help you get it sorted out."

Mike groaned as the two men headed up the stairs to the apartment.

Colin cracked the door open about two inches, scanning as much as he could see, then widened the opening until convinced it was safe to enter. Without taking his eyes off the doorway or saying a word, he signaled for Mike to follow him. Inside, they quietly scoured the apartment but couldn't see or hear the kitten.

"Alright then, I'll be going." Colin said. "But keep in mind you might not see her tonight, or even tomorrow, for that matter. Cats are masterful at finding hiding places, especially if they're scared, so keep an eye out. It's impossible to know where she might be."

Mike shook his head. "Great. Well, that's just grand. And what am I to do if I do see her?"

"Nothing really. They take care of themselves if ya leave out a little milk and a litter box. And don't worry, I took care of that for ya. I got some supplies from home, even brought over a little kibble. Oh, and by the way, the litter box is in the loo."

"What? Go home, Colin. I've had enough of this. I'm going to bed. If she shows up and it's daylight, I'm pitching her out the door. You can find another halfway house for the damn thing for all I care."

"Oh Mike, get a hold of yourself."

222

"Get a hold of myself?"

Colin felt a cold silence fill the room as Mike stared at him.

"After burying the love of my life and our twelve-year-old pup before her, I can't take it. I just can't take it."

With heavy steps, Mike stumbled toward the bedroom. Colin saw himself to the door, and without a goodbye, headed home.

* * *

Mike awoke at three o'clock to squeaking sounds coming from Kate's old makeup vanity.

"What the—" The whiskey hadn't quite burned out of his blood yet, so he got up from the bed slowly, tempering his anger about getting talked into this preposterous scheme. As he approached the small, mirrored dresser, the high-pitched sounds suddenly stopped.

"Mother of God. Where the hell is she?" He sat down on the bench-seat of the vanity, gazed into the mirror, and pondered his weary reflection. "So, this is it?"

"Meeeeooow." Her resounding call for attention interrupted his questionable resignation, but at least it revealed her hiding place.

Mike felt odd opening drawers he'd never thought to look in when Kate was alive. "I guess it's time I cleaned out this thing, anyway."

There was the kitten, curled up amidst lovely, soft lingerie. She had pawed them into a messy pile, quite different from how Kate would have left them. But the little thing seemed curious and didn't recoil from Mike's touch when he reached inside the drawer. That surprised him.

"Well, it looks like you've made yourself comfortable."

The kitten stared up at him as if her mission was complete. Mike rubbed her tiny chin with his index finger and she softly purred.

"I guess you may as well stay the night. But I can't figure out how the hell you got into that drawer."

Perhaps because he had not opened the drawer in many months, he could still smell the haunting scent of his wife. He held one of her thin nightgowns up to his nose and inhaled until he wept.

"I'm sorry we didn't do all those things you dreamed of, Kate. I really am."

As he laid the nightgown back in the drawer, he felt paper underneath the ruffled pile. He pulled out an envelope and read the letter addressed to him in Kate's hand.

My dear Michael,

I want to thank you for encouraging me to go home to Dublin to see my sister and cousins before I get too sick to travel. I know you'll be working extra hard at the pub while I'm away, which is why I'm going to wait till I get back to give you this letter. I don't want to add to your burdens while I'm away, but there's a few things I need to tell you before I'm not able to explain.

I know you feel bad we didn't travel to all the crazy places I had my heart set on seeing, but I want you to know it's OK with me. We had each other, and being able to make that dream of ours, to have a real pub here, across the sea in this little Vermont village, come true is what life is all about. Sharing dreams and building them into real things. Together. I know we worked harder than maybe we should have, but we did, and I would not trade that for anything, including visiting places I can see in a book. You ... are not in a book.

I say this because I know you feel you let me down, but it's not true. And I love you even more as I write this. As hard as I know it will be for you to manage without me, I know you can do it. But don't you be afraid to love again. I mean that. You have so much in your heart to share with someone. And if you have to, start small. Just keep your heart open.

With all my love,

Kate

Mike folded the letter and placed it back into the envelope. He looked in the drawer where the kitten lay licking her paw, settling in for the remainder of the night. She stopped and looked up at him as if nothing had changed. But for Mike, it was a whole new world.

Welcome Aboard
Cheryl Ray

This year's visit with Dr. Jenkins, the cardiologist, sends shudders and goosebumps down Jack's spine. It's the doctor's voice of doom, the finality. "Jack, all your tests show that you're facing a coronary event sooner rather than later. You're only fifty-eight, but you aren't going to make it much longer if you don't learn to relax and change your lifestyle."

"My ticker is getting sicker. The doc really scared me," Jack later says to Jill, his wife. "I've always dreamed of buying a boat and sailing to a tropical paradise with you. But I thought it was just a fantasy. Now I really want to live that dream while I'm still alive."

"It's about time you got some sense into that concrete crown of yours," Jill says. She is a type B, always easygoing. "Do you mean it, Jack?" This isn't the first time she's mentioned retirement. Ever since he took on the management job at the Gators plant, he'd been short on temper and long in hours, coming home well after dinner every night. There was just so much to do. "I hear those weird, bright-colored plastic clogs are going out of style anyway," she continues.

She's wrong, Jack thinks. Gators' sales motto, "Snap 'em up," is all over television. It's been part of their sales plan to expand their market with new additions. It's also contributed to Jack's heart palpitations and nervous anxiety. Gators made a marketing decision to put doodads on their shoes like charms on a bracelet: bears, fairies, mermaids, shells, and boats. The bigwigs said they'd sell like hotcakes.

Just the thought of it, plus Doc Jenkins' prognosis, and Jack realizes Jill is right.

"I can't cope," Jack says. "I've always wanted a boat, but never had time for it. King Neptune has spoken to me through Doc Jenkins. I'm writing my resignation letter tomorrow, then I'm off to shop for a sailboat. Do you want to come help me decide?"

"Any boat you like, I'll like," Jill replies. "You're the expert and know all about boats. I don't. But I do like to look inside the cabins. Sure, I'll go with you."

It took them six months to find *Jumping Jack*, a forty-five-foot Gulfstar Ketch. Both attended two weeks of boating school and spent a month of ocean sailing with an experienced sea captain. Soon they were ready to live the dream, sailing under the Golden Gate Bridge with confidence, determination, and excitement. They headed south with plans to anchor and travel the countries along the Pacific Coast, no specific destination in mind. Their adventure would lead the way.

A year after setting sail, *Jumping Jack's* anchor drops into the water of a Panamanian cove surrounded on three sides by a white sandy beach and tall palm-fronded coconut trees.

"This is paradise," Jack says. "But, hey, look what I see," he adds, pointing his index finger. "Here comes another sailboat." They watch the fellow at the helm drive the boat into position, and a woman drop the anchor. On the boat's blue hull, its name is stenciled in gold letters: *Shore Loser*.

"Let's dinghy over and meet our new neighbors," Jill says.

Jack, more than happy to see other sailors with whom he can hash over cruiser scuttlebutt, puts down his binoculars. He throws life jackets into their small boat and starts its engine.

As they putter their dinghy the short distance, Jack notices the couple come to the side of their boat's deck to welcome them. The tall, tan, and slim bikini-clad woman stands next to a muscular man who sports an untrimmed gray beard and a short ponytail the same color. He wears black boxer undies and a red tee. "Welcome, neighbors, give me your line," he says as he reaches out to tie their dinghy to *Shore Loser's* hull. "I'm Noah, and this here is Jinx."

The newcomers had also sailed from San Francisco. They, too, are escaping the pressures of the daily grind. They are sailing enthusiasts with years more boating experience than Jack and Jill. The two couples chat and laugh about their similar sea adventures along the Pacific Coast, then snorkel a reef together later that afternoon.

During the following week, the foursome explore the island and enjoy happy hour together. They decide to buddy-boat up the nearby San Pedro River, and Jack offers to organize the trip. He studies the navigation charts, tide tables, and currents. He will lead them through the shallow water channel that opens into the deeper river. The friends agree to follow Jack to their next Shangri-La. The two boats depart the cove in the early morning on a rising tide.

The voyage goes exactly as Jack calculated, except for one tiny mistake—the narrow and shallow waterway turns on a bend. As *Jumping Jack* approaches the curve, an enormous pelican lands on the bow and distracts Jack when it fires off the railing like a flare. The distraction causes Jack to motor into the shallow water close to the channel's inside edge. With that, the boat lurches to a stop as the keel thuds into the sandy bottom. Jill falls to her hands and knees but then stands up, calm as ever.

"It's no big deal, Jack," she says, then goes below into the cabin to get ice for the lump on her knee, already turning different hues of blue.

I should know better than to get flustered. That damn bird. Lordy, lordy, lordy, how embarrassing. Of course, Noah would know to stay in the curve's deeper outside edge. No good deed goes unpunished. Jack looks back and observes Jinx bend down to drop their boat's anchor into the deeper water.

An hour later, the rising tide floats *Jumping Jack* off the sandy bottom. The two boats motor-sail the rest of the way up the channel and enter the wide Rio San Pedro. They anchor a quarter-mile apart.

The next day, the sun rises on what promises to be an exceptional day. "Happy Birthday, Jack," says Jill, kissing him on the cheek. "Let's have a party."

Jack is thrilled with his adventurous life. His heart never felt better, and yesterday's humiliation of running aground will not ruin his sixtieth birthday. Jill wants to celebrate with dinner. Jack calls his friends on the marine radio and invites them over. He will run his small boat upstream at 5:00 p.m. to pick them up. "No need to put your dinghy in the water. I have mine in."

Always on time, Jack arrives at the exact hour. Jinx hands down the birthday cake she baked, and Noah delivers two bottles of fruit-flavored wine. Both climb into the dinghy, and Noah unties it from *Shore Loser*. The wind blows in their faces, and the water forms short, choppy waves. Jinx holds a plate with the double-layered chocolate cake on her knees, hoping it won't slide off the dish as the dinghy bounces all the way to *Jumping Jack*.

The three arrive at the boat, and Jack ties the dinghy to the stern. They all sit outside in the cockpit to enjoy the sunset. The birthday boy serves ice-filled glasses of citrus-flavored sangria. Jack adds soda water to

Jinx's drink, which causes her hearty sneezes. Inside the cabin, the aroma of Jill's zesty cheese-crusted lasagna floats like a cloud over the threesome. Jack overhears the rumble of hunger in Noah's stomach.

"Let's eat," Jill says.

After dinner, Jack blows out the number sixty candle on the lopsided layered chocolate cake that survived the dinghy trip. The friendly group plays the dominos game of Mexican Train. They tell boating stories, gossip about other cruisers' mishaps, and laugh at each other's jokes. Eventually, the nautical clock chimes four bells for 10:00 p.m. The birthday merrymaking is over, and Jack is ready to return Noah and Jinx to their boat.

"Stay inside, keep warm, and enjoy yourselves," Jack says. "I'll let you know when everything is ready for your ride back."

He goes outside to fetch the dinghy from the stern and bring it alongside. The wind direction has swerved 180 degrees since the threesome's earlier arrival. The bow now faces upriver, into the wind, and the stern down. Jack unties the small boat's fifteen-foot line that tugs hard behind *Jumping Jack*. He pulls hand over hand against the river's spirited outgoing current. Finally, the dinghy next to the hull, Jack bends down on the deck to retie it. He stands up, and a brisk gust nips at his face in the pitch-dark, moonless night. He presses his hips against the safety line and bends over it to shine his flashlight on the dinghy. The lifeline, his safeguard, gives way. In a tick-tock of a second, Jack tumbles overboard.

In the dark murky Rio San Pedro, he pushes off the muddy bottom as if bounding from a trampoline. His head pops out of the water, and fear races through his body as he tries to remember what happened. He reaches out to grab the boarding ladder. *Oh my god, I forgot to drop the ladder.* After returning to *Jumping Jack* with Jinx and Noah, he had pulled the ladder aboard. *I'm an idiot! The ladder!*

With his left hand, he grasps the taut-tied dingy line that pulls alongside *Jumping Jack's* hull. He looks at his right hand, surprised he is still holding the flashlight. His body faces down the river, the outgoing current pushing hard on his back. *Can I climb into the dinghy? No, high sides. Exhausting. Hang on. Why doesn't someone come out?*

River water slaps his head and face, dripping from his hair to his chin. He kicks his bare feet, his Gators now lost in the river's undercurrent. The moving water's hunger tries to consume him. "Help!" he screams. The screeching wind swallows his voice. He pounds on the hull with the flashlight, to no avail. Inside, Jill and their friends must think the noise is ordinary river debris clunking past the boat. Outside, no one from the distant shore can see him in the dark. Heart hammering, he yells, "Hell, is this the way it will end? It's my birthday!"

The warm tropical water turns cold on his skin. He pants, and his body shudders, *I don't want to die. I love life. Water will finish me. Better than hospital. Beeping heart monitor. Sailing, dream life. Grand prize Jill. Okay, desperado death. Old-salt memorial.* "Adios amigos," he sputters.

In a flash, Noah jumps into the water beside Jack.

Hey, what the hell is this? Jack senses a firm grip under his armpits and around his chest from behind.

"Let go of the dinghy line!" Noah shouts.

He turns Jack toward the boat's ladder, lifts and pushes him up. Jill bends down and pulls on his arms. Jinx holds tight to Jill to prevent her from tumbling after Jack.

On the deck, stretched out and exhausted, Jack's body quivers. Jill covers him with a thermal blanket. Jack's water-logged mind slowly comprehends Noah telling him how the three climbed from the cabin onto the deck. As their eyes adjusted to the darkness, they grasped Jack was nowhere to be seen and the boarding ladder up. To their horror, they knew Jack had fallen overboard.

His thoughts rush like the current. *The Gators' factory didn't get me. My heart didn't get me. The water didn't get me.* He pushes away the cover with purpose. Without a signal to the others, he bounds up. "I'm ready. Let's go."

"You ought to change into dry clothes first. You'll get hypothermia," Noah says.

"No way." Jack shakes his head.

Cold and dripping wet, Noah picks up the thermal blanket and drapes it over himself. The three stare at Jack, shocked.

"I wanna take you to your boat right now."

Let's get this night over. I bet Jinx and Noah think I'm a stupid swabby.

On the dinghy ride upstream, the three don't say a word. The only voice is the howling wind.

When they arrive at *Shore Loser*, Noah hands Jack the thermal blanket. "Thanks for the party invite, and happy birthday," he says.

"Yeah, Jack, and many more. See you tomorrow," Jinx says.

The wind blows at his back on the return ride and smooths the water ahead. The small boat coasts. Jack shivers in his wet clothes. He picks up the thermal blanket and wraps it around his shoulders. Now within sight, *Jumping Jack's* glowing lights shine out their call of warmth from inside the cabin. His head clears, and waves of gratitude move through his body. He yells into the darkness. "I'm alive!"

Assembling the Pieces
Darlene Stern Robson

I'm so absorbed in my funeral fantasy that I almost take the freeway exit for my former condo instead of my new home, my childhood home. My abrupt swerve out of the exit lane draws honks from the man behind me, and I look into my rearview mirror and wave apologetically. He honks in return—more of an *eff you, lady* than a *no problem*, I think—and I move into the middle lane and back to my reverie.

There will be no crying, no screaming, from the cheap seats up front at my funeral. That day, I'll be the main attraction, wearing that black silk dress from my last New Year's with Sean, my beautiful, professionally done (hopefully, Mom will remember that part) face looking serene and at peace.

If only Mom could leave Kyle home, not drag him and Michael along with her as if he won't make a scene and ruin the day for everyone else who will attend to talk about what a wonderful daughter and big sister I was. Tall, weird thirty-two-year-old twins who can't get their act together in public don't need to show up. I won't be hurt if they skip it. I'll live.

Hah.

Hey, don't forget that wife part in the eulogy about how wonderful I was. It's not like Sean will do it.

Who am I kidding? I'll write the eulogy to make sure it gets done.

Sure, let's add Sean showing up, eyes red, barely keeping it together, no new wife Chelsea in sight. She stays home. He'll hover over the casket, begging my forgiveness. I'm dead, but I'm up there somewhere, enjoying the groveling.

I snort out loud in the car. That image takes this escape fantasy too far.

I'm brought back to reality as a call comes in. Mom. Nope, not going to answer. No grocery runs.

I sigh. "Hi, Mom."

"Hi, sweetie. We're all out of milk."

"Okay. Anything else? I'm tired, though, no stocking up."

She proceeds to add ten items, and I make a mental note of the ones I know she really needs. The rest can wait. I'll put in an Instacart order after my next paycheck.

I forgot to ask if she made dinner. She usually does, unless Kyle's had a really bad day and she couldn't get to it. Just in case, I pick up a frozen pizza. I get the milk and bread and peanut butter, then head home.

As I pull into the driveway of Mom's house, I hear Kyle's screams through the single-pane glass windows. The neighbors never bother calling the police anymore, so if burglars or murderers ever break in, we're on our own. *There was always screaming over there, Mrs. Landry tells the Dateline reporter. No, we didn't suspect a thing was wrong that night.*

I take the one grocery bag and go inside. No cooking smells emanate from the kitchen. Kyle is pacing around the room, screaming, howling, while Mom sits at the table, where they have set up a jigsaw puzzle. He sees me, keeps going. I try to hug him, but he backs off, so I show him the pizza as Mom preheats the oven.

"Your favorite," I tell him. "Thick crust, Supreme."

He quiets for a moment as he studies the pizza, then begins again. He throws the empty pizza box at me and hurries down the hall to his bedroom. The door slams.

Kyle resents we removed the lock he put on the door. His screams subside to grunts as he shoves his dresser against the door. When he eventually comes out, we'll find clothes all over the floor, his attempt to lighten the weight of the dresser. Despite my telling Mom to leave the clothes there, she always puts them back. He wears the same two shirts, the same two pants, on a rotating basis, but she keeps the drawers filled in an unyielding hope that one day his old friends might call, make plans for dinner, a movie, a party.

Kyle's pill bottles are on the kitchen counter. Today's dosage set out as a reminder, untouched. Mom can't force them down his throat.

"Sorry, sweetie," she says, smiling ruefully. "He's been like this for hours. Something on TV set him off."

"Something? You need to keep an eye on what he's watching."

"I had the Food Channel on. You know he likes that. But I was taking a shower, and he changed the channel. Found some terrible horror movie. I don't know why they show those movies on TV."

"You need to hide the remote, Mom," I remind her.

"Did you buy ice cream?" she asks. "We're all out."

Uh oh. Ice cream is the one food he'll eat when nothing else interests him. We never run out.

"I forgot," I say. "I'll put in an order for delivery."

She chatters as she follows me into the hall bathroom and perches on the tub to watch me remove my makeup. Since I moved back here, I take my time at this routine, giving myself some breathing room before I head out into the melee. No point tonight.

I never craved solitude during evenings with Sean. Now, I just want to be alone. Mom follows me around like a toddler clinging to my leg, her cane tapping against the floor as she moves. She's trapped here with Kyle. Of course, she's eager for some other company, needs to talk to someone and have a real conversation.

I can't blame her. "I'm sorry it's been such a bad day," I say, hugging her before settling at the round table in the kitchen with my laptop to keep her company. I carefully move aside the puzzle pieces they've assembled and pick up the ones I find on the floor to return to the box. I see a corner piece and place it on top of the pile for Kyle to find. Corners are his favorites. He loves assembling the pieces, finds it calming to create a whole picture from so many fragments, but tosses pieces away if he can't make them fit anywhere.

Mom makes a salad as I check my email. Confirmation of bill payments going through my account, offers to upgrade my phone, internet, TV, because I am so valued that I deserve more. My favorite foreign prince asking for money. I am very popular.

Kyle's banging now, throwing whatever against the wall. "Should we see if he'll come out for pizza?" I ask.

"He didn't sleep well last night. He was agitated today. I'm hoping he'll fall asleep soon. I'll save him some."

"Did he eat today?"

"Just ice cream. That's why we ran out."

I didn't forget. I just worry about him eating so much fattening food; he's gained weight on the meds. I know Mom tries to cook for him. But ice cream makes him happy, helps her out when he's happy.

We eat in front of the TV. Mom loves *Jeopardy* and *Wheel*, so I make occasional comments to be supportive while scrolling through Instagram and Facebook. The noises have stopped, but Kyle's loud snoring travels down the hall.

My Instagram page is dormant. I used to share pictures of Sean and Goldie, our Lab. I posted my dinner creations, pictures of the condo we bought and decorated, photos of our weekend trips, Sean's open mic singing nights. I liked my friends' news, sent everyone hugs and birthday greetings. All happy, happy over here with the happily marrieds.

I visited Mom and my brothers—Michael was still living at home then—but never posted their pictures. Sean came with me sometimes, but Kyle never warmed up to him. I finally just came over on my own, tried to carve out time for them. Sean always said family was important, that he knew they needed me, that he understood.

I thought he did.

I rarely post anymore. Not much to say. I don't get together with old friends these days, but I see them here online, having babies, taking trips, buying homes, new jobs. Living.

My share of the beautiful furniture Sean and I picked out together is crammed into Michael's old bedroom.

I never go in there. I stick to my childhood bedroom. My soccer trophies are still on the bookshelves. Boxes of childhood mementoes are stashed on the closet shelves.

"I knew she'd beat him!" Mom says gleefully, as the new *Jeopardy* winner is declared. I look up, smile at her. She feels the ousted winner has been too smug.

I see Jenna is pregnant. How great, I'm so glad for her, they've been trying for a long time. She's four months along, looking beautiful, she and Dean beaming at the camera, holding up the ultrasound picture.

It's been months since we've talked, since I've responded to her texts, her calls. I just wanted to be left alone. It all hurt too much. She finally stopped reaching out.

She was my best friend, my maid of honor. She wanted to be there for me, just as I was there for her through all her miscarriages.

I never imagined that I wouldn't be sharing this happiness with her.

I post. **Congratulations, fantastic news! I'm so happy for you both!**

I am, I really am.

That's enough. No checking on Sean and Chelsea tonight. No. *No.*

"See you tomorrow, Mom." I kiss her cheek. "I'm going to read for a while. Get some things done."

"Good night, sweetie." She turns back to *Wheel*.

I read for an hour, then check Dad's bank account, make sure everything looks okay, sign off on his caregiver's invoice. Dad can't hear well enough to use the phone and is too stubborn to wear his hearing aids, so I write him a short letter to let him know that the twins and I are doing great and getting good grades in school. *I won the spelling bee*, I add, because he always asks how I did in the fifth-grade spelling bee.

The house is blissfully quiet as I brush my teeth. I'm getting into bed when a text pops up from Michael.

not working tomrrw can I come over OK 2 sleep over?

I've told him to ask first, not just show up. Sometimes, he has nightmares and likes to sleep here. Sometimes, he has nowhere else to sleep. He and Kyle don't do well together. Kyle doesn't always recognize Michael, gets scared at seeing someone with his own face. Michael resents that, wants their closeness back. They were inseparable as kids until Kyle's illness began consuming him as a teenager. Michael felt abandoned then, at loose ends. All these years later, he still can't seem to get it together on his own.

Not best time, I text back. **Bad day today. Going to bed. Why no work?**

Quit? Fired? Just taking another day off? He has to show up. He can't keep quitting, losing these jobs.

Long pause. Too long.

told me not to come back

Didn't he just start this job a few weeks ago? He told me how much they liked him, might make him a supervisor. What happened?

No, he shouldn't come over. He's thirty-two, made it through college. Kyle can't live on his own, but Michael can and should. I've told Mom this. I've told Michael. No, I'm not moving my furniture out of his old room. I help with the mortgage, the utilities. I'm keeping two rooms.

no rent money can't stay need to sleep there pls
coming over

I drop the phone and stare at the ceiling. Mom will cry and tell me he can stay until he finds a new job. She'll move my things around, find room for him. She'll give him money. I'll do tough love, and she'll just go with love.

I pull the covers over my head to shut out the light.

"They drive me crazy," I told Sean the last time I saw him, before he finally decided that *he* was better than *we*. Before Chelsea. The two of us were stuffing ourselves with Chinese food in his tiny studio apartment that he didn't have to share with anyone, that he chose not to share with me. I didn't cry, not in front of him, just pitifully grateful to spend the occasional evening with him and, yes, the occasional night.

"You want everyone happy all the time," he said, not for the first time. "That's not real life. They're who they are. You can't fix them, make them be who you want them to be."

"I don't want that," I countered. "I want them to be happy. My mom is trapped. Her life is going nowhere."

"And where was our life going?" he said, Goldie sitting on his lap, a shield against me. "How were we supposed to add kids to all this? I tried, Becca, but you expect too much."

It's what I know, what I do, taking on what needs to be done.

If *not* me, who will do it? Who keeps it all from falling apart, makes sure everything functions when nothing is functioning?

In the land of crazy, the sane one gets that job.

I look around my room, stare at the soccer trophies. A lavender desk tray and matching pencil cup and stapler sit on top of the white corner desk. The white bookcase still has my high school yearbooks with pictures of my teenage triumphs sprinkled throughout all four volumes.

I needed some time before moving on with my life, but instead, I've gone backward. Not exactly a sane move.

If I talked to Jenna, told her about the trophies and the yearbooks, that's what she'd tell me. I can just hear her laugh, lecturing me to get off my butt and out of this bedroom. God, I miss that laugh.

If I moved out, took my condo furniture with me, Michael could have his old room back. He could help around here, try to work things out with Kyle. I could stop by on weekends, check in on them.

I'd have breathing room, work on tying up my own loose ends.

If, if.

I call up Michael's last text: **coming over**

He'll be at least a half hour. No matter how desperate he sounds, he'll meander, forget a few things, stop to smoke.

I stare at his Contacts photo, his beguiling grin, his dark hair swept across his forehead, his bright eyes. I've always loved this picture, love how radiant he looks here after a day at the beach. Not a care in the world.

I need you to bring ice cream, I text.

OK.

An Instagram notification pops up. There's a heart emoji on my comment to Jenna.

I message her. **Can I take you to lunch to celebrate?**

Of course!!!!! When? Can't wait to see u!!!

I smile. She's still there.

ASAP! It's been way too long.

The Slight Chip
Charity Romstad

She reaches for a coffee mug, notices a slight chip in the lip, and slides it over for the one behind it. Sheila only keeps the chipped one because it is part of the set. The mug she chooses still has a smooth rim; she fills it with coffee and finds her way to the couch, her only new household purchase in years. She thinks about the chipped mug and looks at the empty mismatched chair recently pulled out of her mother's storage: it smells musty, but it is functional.

Will she replace these things if she gets a raise? Or continue being frugal? Sheila's eyes close and she imagines new things in her home, but in the vision she sees herself: a chip and a long crack appear on her hand; when she lifts it closer to look, a stale smell emanates from her skin, almost like the chair. She opens her eyes quickly and takes a sip of coffee, breathing in deeply so the smell of coffee overtakes the thought. It's not things she needs to replace—but something inside herself.

She feels the weight of her life and the clutter of memories handed to her. "Take this," someone always seems to say to her as they divest their traumas. She loved to hear the stories, to collect them into her experience. But they are piling up next to her own. Just like the hand-me-down furniture and dishes.

Sheila pulls her feet up off the floor and curls her legs onto the new couch and wraps her fingers around the warm, smooth mug. She sips her coffee with her eyes open.

* * *

The next morning she wakes, startled by a dream in which the musty chair and the fresh couch danced around her living room, the smell of dust swirling with the scent of new fabric. She jumps up and starts the coffee pot, anxious for the aroma to fill the house. She sprays the clean counter with lavender-scented disinfectant, grabs the small vacuum off its charger and sucks up the bunnies under the couch.

Again she sits on the couch and stares at the chair. It is burnt orange, like an overripe persimmon. She goes to the closet, pulls out a sheet, and spreads it over the chair, tucking it into the crevices around the cushion. At the beep of the coffeemaker, she wastes no time in pouring herself a cup, hesitating only to choose among the remaining favorites. Today, a blue ceramic mug handmade by someone her aunt knew, probably an artist or old hippie. It had been her aunt's favorite, the perfect bulbous shape for morning coffee or tea on a rainy day. Drinking her morning brew from it makes Sheila remember her aunt's stories of protests and efforts to improve the world.

Sheila swims in the memory through half the cup, then turns her attention to the chair sitting empty across from her. She imagines her aunt sitting there. Aunt Nellie would surely like its style: "They don't make furniture like they used to! What cute carved wooden feet it has!" Sheila can hear Nellie's resolute voice. "Besides, consumerism is a waste of your hard earned money. Not everything needs to be bought new."

So true, thinks Sheila. Of course, she was raised to appreciate older things and to reuse items whenever possible. That's why, on the corner table sits a lamp that is not pretty, nor is it ugly; it is simply useful. She reaches to turn it on and hears the voice of its previous owner: "What are you wearing?" It was a snide comment directed at her by a long-gone former roommate whose words frequently fill Sheila's head when she wears one of the criticized outfits or reaches to turn on the lamp. Sometimes she thinks of getting rid of these things in order to stop the hurtful memories, but that hardly seemed fair to the lamp or the outfits. Frugality is her culture.

Sheila places the empty coffee cup in the sink and turns the water on; in the moments it takes for the water to warm, she notices the crystal cake plate on the drying rack. Yesterday, it held a bundt cake she had made for a colleague's retirement party. Crystal is not her style, but again, it is functional. She had bought it at an estate sale for a young neighbor down the street. After wandering through the woman's small home and perusing her belongings, Sheila had found the cake plate. "It was a wedding gift, but I'm divorced now," explained the young mother who had three days to dispose of her household. She had suitcases packed, but the rest had to go. Sheila remembered scanning the house for items she might need. While she wanted to help the young woman, she certainly didn't need another dining room table or china cabinet. She could carry the crystal cake plate home and, occasionally, she made cakes.

At the retirement party for her colleague Louise, she had set the glistening glass plate holding the cake on the table after carefully transporting it in a firm cardboard box. When the last piece was served, Sheila had wiped it clean of crumbs and placed it in her bag, wrapped in a small towel to protect it. Without a cake to transport, the hefty glass plate was easier to maneuver.

Louise had handed her a "#1 Pencil Pusher" mug that had held pencils on her desk for longer than Sheila had worked there. Sheila was not sure about this supposed rise in status. Was this like a bouquet thrown at a wedding? The subtext surely was "You're next!" She shoved the mug in her bag with the cake plate.

Standing at the sink, Sheila looks around for the mug. It must be still in her bag. The bottom of it is full of pencil and pen marks and accumulated dust. She studies it while she rinses it. How long had it sat on Louise's desk? Is she now obligated to keep this item on her desk at work for years to come? It will be at least ten years before she can retire. Then she remembers her finances and the pension requirements. No, it will be more like fifteen years and by then, she'll be older than Louise is now.

Tomorrow, Louise is off to Vegas and in three months, Niagara Falls. She has plans that don't involve paperwork and taking notations. But her husband has a good pension, so combined, they are set for years of enjoyment, free of work.

Sheila holds the cake plate up to the morning sun shining through her kitchen window. The cuts in the crystal sparkle. She carries it into the front room and sets it on the end table with the lamp. The 60-watt light bounces off the glass but does not glimmer like sunlight.

Sheila leans back on the couch and talks to the musty chair that sits empty across from her. "I understand you were once a very nice chair, and I'm sure your bones are as strong as ever. Your wood spine will never be a breakable pencil, but the outfit must go. I'm sorry, but I cannot let you sit here in my front room as if you owned the place."

Jumping up, Sheila pulls off the sheet she had tucked around the chair, letting the fabric drop on the floor, and pushes the chair out the front door and into the driveway. She tips it on its side. Her tool choices are limited. With a screwdriver, she pries upholstery staples from the underside and tugs with all her might until the chair is naked. The aged stuffing exposed, she pecks at it as if the screwdriver were a pickax. It takes her nearly three hours to get the chair down to its wood bones and wire muscles.

The sun is out, and she is hot. She decides to let the midmorning sun bake the chair, to clean it the way only the sun can. She heads into the house for a shower. Refreshed, she returns to the kitchen and makes eggs on toast. Just as she eats the last bite, the doorbell rings. She is surprised to see the young mother who sold her the cake plate.

"I'm sorry to bother you," the woman says, placing her hand on her chest in a posture of sincerity, "but when I resettled back in Tennessee, my mother noticed I didn't have the cake plate. I hadn't realized it was a family heirloom; I just thought it was a wedding gift. I need it back or my mother will never forgive me."

Sheila nods. "Of course. Come in." The woman steps inside. Sheila lifts the crystal plate from under the lamp. "I just used it yesterday. It is quite lovely."

"Yes, I suppose so." The woman sighs. "More useful than the husband I married."

Sheila considers the strength of crystal and the weakness of a man who left his wife on their second anniversary, just after the birth of their child.

"I hope things are good for you back in Tennessee with your mother." Sheila hands the woman the cake plate.

"Yes, I have a job in a pencil factory!" The woman smiles. "My mother babysits while I am at work."

Sheila can't hide the startled look on her face. A pencil factory?

The woman misunderstands Sheila's expression. "Really, I like it! I know it isn't an exciting career, but I like my colleagues, and it isn't much of a commute."

"Oh, the job sounds fine. It's just that I have the perfect cup for you!" Sheila springs into the kitchen and retrieves the recently washed "#1 Pencil Pusher" mug.

When the woman sees it, her eyes widen. "Oh, my! It's perfect!"

The two laugh, and the woman tells Sheila of her baby's first steps and the trees in Tennessee, compared to California, before rummaging in her purse. "I mustn't forget, I owe you for the plate. You bought it from me, but I used all the cash for moving expenses, and I'm only back in town to sign the divorce papers and retrieve the cake plate. But I have something valuable to offer as trade—I need to get rid of it, anyway."

The woman opens her palm to reveal a gold necklace. Not a beautiful dainty one like she herself would wear, but a chunky masculine one that a rough and tumble louse of a husband might wear.

"I'm not one for blingy jewelry." Sheila shakes her head. "It's okay, you don't need to pay me back; I was glad to help."

"No, really, it's solid gold. You can take it to the pawnshop or something." The woman smiles meekly. "It was his, and I don't want it. It just reminds me of him and if I sold it, the money would be tainted. Whatever I bought with it, the object would always remind me of him. But the cake plate was my grandmother's, so it holds good memories."

Sheila nods. "Yes, I understand completely." She takes the gold necklace and slides it into her pocket.

That afternoon, Sheila stops by the library to pick up a book she had on hold. On a display table is a book about the Japanese art of Kintsugi, the practice of repairing broken pottery with gold. She thumbs through the book for a few moments and decides to check this one out, too.

On her way home, she stops by the craft and fabric store. She fills a cart with foam cushions and fluffy stuffing, then finds textured yellow upholstery and matching ribbing. As she heads to the checkout counter, she passes the crafting section. On the end of an aisle sits one large box containing a small furnace specifically for melting gold. Imagine that. Sheila notes that even the sale price is out of her budget, but so is the upholstery fabric. She flags down a sales clerk to help her put it in the cart; sometimes it pays to be frugal so later you can splurge.

"A while back we had a workshop on Kintsugi," the clerk says, "but not everyone wanted to melt gold themselves after the workshop. I suppose they didn't have much gold lying around waiting to be melted into something else, or maybe they just didn't think they could do it."

"I'm willing to try." Sheila smiles as she pushes her cart toward the door.

On Monday, she calls in sick, heads to her mother's storage unit, and pulls out the Juki sewing machine. She finds the custodian to help her load it into the back of her hatchback. Under the carport, she plugs in the Juki. She lays out the musty rust-colored fabric and traces the pattern onto the new yellow upholstery. The process of piecing it together and sewing is exhausting and tedious. By the time the sun goes down, she has only part of it completed. She begins to think this idea is crazy, but it's too late now. She is neck deep into the project.

She calls in sick again, her spirits only partially improved. By the end of the second day, she has cut the foam pieces and fitted them into place, and then she pulls on the chair's new outfit.

When she is finally done, she pours herself a cup of tea in Aunt Nellie's bulbous mug and sits in the newly dressed chair, still in the carport. She takes the rest of the evening to read the book on how to melt gold and pour it into chips and tiny cracks.

On her third day off work, she turns on the furnace and melts the gold necklace. She practices painting the gold first on a leftover brick from last year's yard renovation. The gold liquid brushed onto the broken corner of the brick makes it look like a jagged piece of elegance. Once an old broken brick, now a beautiful bookend.

Her hand now steady with some experience, she fills the slight chip in the cup with gold. When she is done, she places it in the cabinet next to the rest of the set. She centers it in the front. The once banished cup now leads the charge.

The next morning, the gold-mended cup is ready, as is her newly dressed chair now sitting proudly across from the couch. She sinks into the chair, pulls up her feet, and breathes in the smell of coffee. Closing her eyes, Sheila bravely sniffs her hand. She smells fresh and feels the warmth of good change.

Something old, something new, something reborn.

The Watermelon Patch
Janice Rowley

Tomorrow marks fifteen years since Emma's death.

Little has changed since the summer of 1963. Narrow gravel roads and trees sparse until one's eyes stretch past the potato and cornfields. The air smells of dust, pollen, and machinery as the heat exaggerates and blisters all it touches. No one lives in the house now; it is a place to store seasonal farm tools and an escape from the spring rain and the summer sun for those working the fields. Kate's memory cast ghosts of unhusked cotton bolls piled high on the wrap-around porch where kids burrowed in their games of hide-and-seek, leaving behind specks of blood from the husk scratches.

Summers Kate had spent at least two weeks, some years a month, in the Mississippi Delta with her grandparents. Momo and Papa Tucker lived miles of winding dirt roads out from Houston, a place of wonder for an eight-year-old.

Ten-year-old Emma, the only Tucker child still living at home, was Kate's daddy's youngest sister. And there was Sarah, the cousin five months older than Kate, who always arrived first. Always. And spent the whole summer.

***

"Kate, come on. You gotta see Sarah's new stuff," Emma called as she led the way down the long hall. Sarah's mother owned a girls' dress shop in Jackson, so whatever Sarah brought with her for the summer generated curiosity and envy.

Fashion show concluded, savory smells of supper drifted through the hall and into the shared bedroom. Fried pork chops from pigs raised and slaughtered on the farm, boiled potatoes dug that day, greens Emma and Sarah picked the day before, and hot cornbread with freshly churned butter.

It rained most of that first week. The girls explored the musty attic and cut out paper dolls from the Sears catalog. Once the rain stopped, they had outdoor chores: hang out the wash, gather eggs, pick vegetables from the garden. One morning of that second week—Wednesday, Kate remembers, because they went to church that night—came bright and hot. Sounds of life crowded through the open windows as the girls jumped out of bed in a race to be first to the outhouse. Mid-afternoon, chores done, they snuck out to the watermelon patch. The melons grew beyond Momo's garden, out past the cornfield where the dense forest began. The pond where the cows and bull drank lay within the fenced pasture to the right.

Papa Tucker had warned them not to go to these parts of the farm alone. Every adult had a scary story about wild boars, mountain lions, and snakes. That afternoon, the trio ignored the warnings, and with Emma in the lead, arrived out of breath and pleased with themselves.

Emma gave lessons, as she did every year. "First," she began, "pick a dark, dark green one, tilt it back and look for a golden tummy, then thump it hard with your thumb and middle finger right in the center and listen for a deep, hollow echo."

The girls' feet carefully moved between the rows, avoiding the creeping vines, checking the melons against Emma's list. When a watermelon passed the test, they called the other two over for The Drop. Once the melon dropped to the ground—from knee level—it would crack. If they had chosen wisely, the heart of the melon would be almost seedless, its taste cool, crisp, and sweet.

The trio squatted over Sarah's successful pick and dug in with bare hands; the chunks held away from their clothes; the juices cascading over the vines and soaking into the dirt to fatten up the worms and bring other small critters to the muddy nectar.

They didn't count the watermelons they left cracked and heartless on the ground. Full and exhausted, the sun low in the sky suggested suppertime. All three walked off the watermelon patch, but as soon as they were submerged in cornstalks, Emma and Sarah took off running, leaving Kate behind with their giggles ringing in her ears.

Kate, fifteen years later, still carries remnants of her fear at being lost and alone. She traces her map addiction to that day. Abandoned, with no sense of direction, she hadn't known which way to run; nothing but cornstalks in any direction. After a frantic race, first one way and then another, she threw herself down between the rows and sobbed.

When she heard Emma call her name, Kate's fear turned to anger. As the two reached her, she yelled, snuffling back tears: "Why did you run away and leave me? Did you want that ol' boar to eat me? Why don't you like me?"

Sarah made some remark about being a scaredy cat, after which Kate made a fist and pummeled her cousin in the stomach, knocking her to the ground.

And that's when Papa Tucker showed up.

"What are you chillens doing out here? And what's all this cryin' and hollerin'?" He was a tall, angular man with dark eyes that absorbed everything. They knew he would brook no nonsense.

Sarah doubled over. "Kate hit me in my middle."

"They ran away and left me to die," Kate cried.

He turned to Emma. "You gonna tell me what brought all this on?"

"We thought she was behind us," Emma told her daddy with a shrug of her shoulders.

"Well, get on back to the house and help your mama with supper. We'll talk later, mind you."

As soon as they hit the backyard, and Papa was out of earshot, Emma shook her finger in Kate's face and in a stern, no-nonsense Aunt voice said, "You better not tell him we were in the watermelon patch."

Momo came out the back door wiping her hands on her apron and told the three to go wash up and come set the table. Emma and Sarah got to the washbasin first. When finished, they ran to the kitchen, leaving Kate behind again.

* * *

It could all have happened yesterday, given the strength of Kate's memory. She shook her head as if to clear the image, found a long branch to use as a walking stick and prod, if needed, and started down the dirt path across the rough fields toward the tree line. Danny, the uncle still living on the property, had told her the old watermelon patch had sat fallow for some years now. The distance from the house to her destination looks a lot shorter today than fifteen years ago.

The three girls had helped each other decide what to wear to church that night and giggled a lot. Yet, the young Kate still inside the adult

Kate can feel the distance which had been inserted between herself and them. She had found it hard to sing the hymns with her usual gusto. Kate shivers as she remembers how upset she had been when she woke that next morning and found her bedmates had left without waking her. That feeling of abandonment could still cause her to clench her teeth and grab for the ache in her stomach.

There had been no sign of them; they had even put away their bedclothes. She had believed they had pushed her aside again and wondered if this was the way it would be from now on. She had shed her first tears of the day.

The hallway smelled of fried ham and biscuits, so Kate expected to see Emma and Sarah eating breakfast, but found Momo Tucker alone in the kitchen. When asked about the other girls, Kate said she didn't know, they were gone when she woke up. Momo's eyes took on a worried look.

"They're prob'ly in the barn. You go on and eat your egg, and I'll check on 'em." She pulled the apron strings over her head and hung it on the hook next to the hutch.

Just then, the screen door burst open and Sarah fell forward onto the kitchen floor, her skirt torn, face and hands streaked with dirt. She took loud gulps of air in a struggle to get her breath.

"Emma," Sarah gasped. "Hurt. Emma's hurt."

Momo grabbed an arm and pulled her to a sitting position, shook her, and demanded, "Where's she? Where's Emma?"

"Watermelon," Sarah's breaths came heavy, but Momo's strength seemed to calm her, "patch. Bleeding."

Momo shot out the kitchen door, yelling for Papa. Sarah gained her feet and followed, with Kate close behind.

They all reached the near boundary of the watermelon patch about the same time. Sarah continued to race toward the forest, followed closely by Momo. Papa Tucker slowed down to check that Kate was still close.

Momo's scream pierced the air.

Kate jerked to a stop, sunk to her knees, hands over her ears, and head in the skirt of her dress. She did not see what they saw. She did not hear what they cried. She barely felt the arms as they later lifted and carried her away.

* * *

Kate can almost see the watermelon patch as it looked back then. Her steps falter and she stops, as fixed in place as at the edge of the watermelon patch that morning. Something has triggered a memory—a vulture's screak, a smell on the breeze, the rustle of a tree branch? The scene before her reverts. She is back in the house, in bed, the covers shifting. Emma tells her to get up and get dressed, they have to go back to the watermelon patch and get rid of the broken melons. Sarah nudges her, urges her to hurry and to be quiet. Kate doesn't move, but falls back to sleep as the two leave.

But that was a dream. That wasn't real.

Kate kneels and the tears come as she realizes this memory, repressed for fifteen years, is real, not a dream. She cries for the conflicted emotions of that child, torn between relief that it was not she who had met tragedy, and concern for her aunt and friend.

Kate had done nothing. She had felt Sarah's blame for having done nothing, but not understood the reason. Even though she had repressed the guilt and shame, they had taken up residence in her that long-ago morning. This morning she needs to let it go.

She has always known there was *something*. She knows she cannot see what Momo, Papa, and Sarah saw that day. She has only pieced together a picture from the words and images allowed to surface. She can now place that restored memory in its proper setting, allow herself to grieve, and to the best of her ability, determine her role in what happened. She stands and moves forward to the edge of ground between melon field and forest, the spot where they found Emma.

* * *

Papa Tucker had called Kate's daddy after he and Momo returned from the clinic in Vardaman. Her parents had immediately driven from New Orleans to the farm, arriving after eight o'clock. Momo had been in bed, unable to speak with anyone. Papa took it real hard, too, and paced around the house, banged his fist into his palm and muttered under his breath. Sarah's parents had come earlier from Jackson and heard the story while at the clinic and were the ones to pass on the details to Kate's folks while Kate hid in her mom's arms.

An old, rusty plow blade.

Emma must have tripped on it and fell. She lay face down. Papa grabbed Emma and turned her over. The blade was buried deep in her chest and stomach, the surrounding earth blood-soaked. A split watermelon lay just beyond her head and outstretched hands.

Sarah fainted. Emma's eyes were open, but she was not breathing.

Uncle Danny and a farmhand arrived with a tractor and trailer after hearing screams and drove Sarah and Kate to the house. Papa and Momo picked their daughter up and carried her back through the cornfield to the house, cradling her body, refusing the ride.

Leaving everyone else behind, they drove their daughter to the hospital in Houston. There had been nothing the doctor could do.

More than a week passed before anyone asked why Emma and Sarah had been out there so early in the morning. After the funeral and burial, everyone gathered at the house. Momo took the girls to the porch and sat between them on the swing.

"Now, I don't mean to upset you girls, but I need to ask why Emma was in the watermelon patch that morning."

Not getting an answer, she turned to Sarah. "Nobody's gonna get in trouble. No. I just need to know so I can put it together in m'mind and then let it rest."

Sarah finally spoke up and told Momo that Emma was scared Papa would find out we had been to the watermelon patch. He had used the razor strop on her before, and she didn't want it to happen again. They had gone back to clean up the field.

Momo asked Sarah, "What were you and Emma gonna do once you got there?"

"Throw those broken melons into the woods and cover where they'd been with vines so nobody would know."

Sarah broke into sobs, which set Kate off.

Momo shushed them, said that would not help anything. She looked at each of the girls. "It was an accident. Nobody's fault."

They all hugged and cried for a while. Momo gave them each a last squeeze, stood, and walked into the house; Sarah followed. This had deepened Kate's feeling of isolation and pushed her further into herself. What Sarah told Momo that afternoon did nothing to lessen Kate's feeling of exclusion.

Even when Kate's family returned for reunions each year, Sarah and Kate did not talk, and Kate never spent time alone with her grandfolks again.

* * *

Had it been because of Kate's decision to pursue a career in psychology and the ensuing coursework that the seal was broken? Or was it the other way around? She had dreams about the three of them, about that day in the watermelon patch, about their abandonment, about hitting Sarah, about waking alone the next morning, about Emma's death.

The closer Kate got to the spot where Emma tripped and died, the clearer her role became. She had not had a role. She had needed to participate to feel the pain, so she had invented the guilt. On an intellectual level, she knew that. It was not until she saw the slender tendril of a watermelon vine stretching out of the forest in search of sun and heat that her understanding no longer strained through the lens of an eight-year-old. Kate knew boundaries were hard when you wanted to be liked and to thrive.

She moved further into the forest and with each step found more watermelon vines; the seeds sown had created a new, quieter, smaller watermelon patch. And, like Kate, they had been stretching toward redemption. At least one of them would make it out of the shadows.

The Evacuation Camp
Christopher Ruttan

April 1942. As the shadows of the Luzon Cordillera mountains settled over the land near dusk, the guerrilla band stopped to make camp. They were armed with a motley collection of firearms, from army bolt action rifles to .22s, pistols, shotguns, even a couple of 19th century .44-caliber Remington rifles. Tomorrow, they hoped to reach the box canyon on the sprawling Mount Bawao, and the next day ascend to the mountain shoulder, the site planned for a secret base.

The men launched into the brush, looking for suitable material to make shelters for the night. When completed, the lean-tos consisted of two forked branches pounded into the soil, supporting a long, reasonably straight sapling trunk horizontally between them. They laid angled sticks upon the trellis and then covered the structures with large, palm-like leaves from the small samak trees, creating water-resistant enclosures.

"Look, Maria, our honeymoon suite, rainproof—provided it doesn't rain too hard," James Novak said. James was an out-of-work gold mining engineer, now a fugitive trapped in Japanese-occupied Philippines, accompanied by a squad of Filipino resistance fighters and his new wife Maria. George Butler, his supervisor at the Itogon mine, had said, "Look, I'll let her come with us, but consider marrying her first. You don't want these men to think she's just a camp follower, or she'll be up for grabs."

James drove as far as he could before the road ended; then the party set out on foot on the final leg of the trip. They faced a long trek into the remote backcountry of Northern Luzon, into the boondocks, surrounded by the fetid smells of rotting vegetation.

He had first met Maria, the former office clerk, while working for the Itogon Goldmine. As the welcoming face at the mine head office in Baguio, Maria had exuded a delightful smile on initial meeting. Taken at first sight by her dark liquid eyes and comely figure, James had struggled to refrain from staring, awkwardly glancing away or past her. Maria's fine-boned face accentuated her eyes and sensual lips.

The one complication when they first met was his fiancé back home in Minnesota, who had refused to join him in the Philippines.

Maria later told him she had found his attempts at deference amusing, and his dark hair, deep eyes, and straight jaw pleasing. Before long, she looked forward to his visits to the office and added that he impressed her as a gentleman in a profession known for rough men.

When she asked him the meaning of his last name, Novak, he replied, "It's Croatian for a stranger in a new place." She told him that Baguio was as different from the hot coastal plains of her hometown as it was to James from his starting point in the northern Minnesota iron range. "So I am a Novak, too," she said.

The day he sat in his office, reading the Dear John letter, he thought about Maria. It was just as well, he realized, and that evening they had their first date.

When the U.S. military ordered the mine decommissioned, he had watched as Butler twisted the handle on the detonator and yelled, "Everybody ready to see your jobs blown to hell? Leave nothing for the bastards!" The explosions ripped through the mine, throwing dirt, wooden planks, shredded metal roofing, and siding into the air that rained down through the smoke. Butler replaced the two wires with two more and engaged the detonator again. As the headframe towers folded and crashed to the ground, explosions reverberated from the tram shaft below ground, as if amplified in an echo chamber.

When the smoke cleared, James peered through the dissipating dust, his ears ringing. He spied a shattered partial drum hoist and shaft trailing cable—leading edge mining equipment—from the array of Koepe hoists that he had so painstakingly installed. It lay there, a smoldering omen that life as he knew it was over.

Now in the camp, as the newlyweds wearily stared at their slapped together shelter, James said, "Sorry it ain't the Baguio Pines Hotel, honey." Before the outbreak of war, he had booked a room for a night at the Pines Hotel, a celebration with Maria of nothing more complicated than a growing awareness that their relationship had entered a deeper stage of commitment for both of them.

The Pines Hotel ranked as one of the finest examples of boomtown gold mining wealth in the growing Baguio city. The huge gold strikes in the Philippines in the 1930s, coupled with the end of the U.S. gold standard in 1933, drew James to the islands. He enjoyed his carefree, expatriate life as a young man with money to spend in a land where the

American dollar went far. He had time and money to spend on booze and women and no responsibilities other than his job.

On weekend nights, the Pines Hotel had been the place where the who's who of Baguio gathered; the nightlife flourished ostentatiously in full swing. Maria's eyes radiated in awe as a uniformed doorman ushered them inside. The usual crowd included the upper echelons of the mining industry, vacationing bureaucrats of the Philippine protectorate, and businesspeople, the ambitious sorts found throughout the Orient.

Also ever-present were the men and women of the American Army Officer Corps, General MacArthur's command, who lodged nearby and had money and time to burn. The guests drifted between the crowded bar, the dance floor, and the large crackling fireplace in the main lobby that was so inviting after entering from the cool mountain air. Narra wood panels finished the walls and ceilings, and the music of tango and jitterbug floated in from the Crystal Room dance hall. The restaurant boasted an extensive menu and wine list, steak from Australia, and seafood from the coast. A pine scent permeated the air from the forests that thrived in the temperate mountain climate around the city.

Maria had been mortified at the thought that the desk clerk would suspect they were not married. "I do not wear a wedding ring," she whispered. "He will know."

"Nothing I can do about that now," he had told her, winking. James knew the desk clerk had seen it all—adulterous couples, high-end escorts, and charlatans—so a registration by a young couple, one American and one Filipina, meant nothing to him. An advanced reservation was the important criterion.

Maria watched as James signed the register, "Mr. and Mrs. James Novak." He smiled as the look of relief came over her face.

Maria had been awestruck by the elegant décor in the room. She delighted at the French oil paintings above the large bed, cream-colored drapes, and extravagant flower arrangements. She luxuriated in a long bath with the perfumed salts before presenting herself to him. She had chosen a pink dress with a flared skirt, which allowed for the flurry of jitterbug and the long dance strides of the tango.

"You look beautiful," he said, and she laughed.

On the dance floor that night, James and Maria danced under dimmed chandeliers. While some dances were new to Maria, she learned quickly. The orchestra struck up Glenn Miller's "In the Mood."

"My favorite!" she exclaimed, swaying her hips gracefully to the pulsating music. The tune made popular round the world, James thought. Probably even the Japanese knew it.

James directed her through the five-step tango. "Quick right foot back, quick step left, slow forward, slow forward, pivot right and around we go for another five steps." He gave her a mock bow. "Very good! You'll be ready to learn the Argentine eight-step next, if I can remember how it's done."

Maria laughed as James leaned her back, supporting her with his arm as her right leg spontaneously lifted off the floor. Her dress slid up her leg, delighting James with a flaunting glimpse of her shapely thigh.

For their last dance, they swayed in self-absorbed slow rhythm and full body embrace to Glenn Miller's "Moonlight Serenade." The spell had been cast—soft breath against his cheek, the scent of her perfume, the invitation in her almond eyes. It was the perfect song on which to retire to their room.

Maria met his eyes and demurely turned her gaze toward the exit. With her hand in his, James led the way down the hallway to their room. Once alone together, they embraced in the foyer, exchanging kisses. "Your eyes are like stars, brightly beaming," James crooned, staring deeply into her dark eyes.

"Bravo, my darling! We Filipinas love a good moonlight serenade." Her eyes probed his, her lips pursed invitingly.

"What a shameless mimic I am," James said, then kissed her deeply. Uninhibited from all constraints, she responded eagerly to his lead, clothes discarded at her feet. James freed himself of his own clothes, encumbrances he couldn't rid himself of fast enough. Embracing, they fell together onto the bed. They returned passion with deep kisses and probing caresses, consummating in joyous lovemaking, and cuddled in contented sleep.

The next morning, James and Maria enjoyed breakfast in bathrobes on their private balcony with a view of the morning sun in all its warm hues rising over the east-facing mountains. The lush potted plants offered a secluded haven. Checkout time was approaching all too soon.

"I love you," Maria murmured. "Nothing can ever change that."

Falling in love in Baguio, he remembered nostalgically, had been easy, the perfect escape from the disturbing thoughts of war sweeping the world—Hitler's Nazi aggression across Europe and Japan's imperialist conquests in Asia. In the mountains of Luzon, the horrors of the outside world could be confined to news bulletins on a shortwave radio, newspaper headlines, and cinema newsreels.

Now, lying on his back in their makeshift honeymoon suite in one of the most remote areas of Luzon, Maria sleeping by his side, James looked up at the fan leaf cover of the lean-to and took stock of their ominous reality. Water droplets from the night drizzle seeped between the fan leaves. In the morning, they would eat cold rice for breakfast, not tropical fruit cocktail. The Japanese aerial bombings had changed everything in an instant, upending their complacent lives like a nightmare from which there was no awakening. Their new reality amounted to survival, hiding in the forests of northeast Abra province on the slopes of a mountain that the native Tinguian tribe called Bawao.

The day after the scouting party reached the foot of the mountain, they began the ascent to the clearing they had spotted high up the slopes. To reach the campsite, the guerrillas had to traverse a main trail along switchbacks that reached up the box canyon between the extending ridges. Up close, they noted the natural defensive features of the mountain. Observing the mountain sprawl, Lieutenant Ruiz pointed out, "We can spy any approaching enemy well in advance. It will make a fine evacuation camp."

Scanning the ridges, James envisioned the defensive advantages of terrain provided by the steep slopes of the canyon. "A properly armed machine gun nest guarding the last stretch of the trail would make a bloody mess of any enemy choosing that route," Ruiz observed. "But since we don't have the damned guns, we'll have to make sure our camp is well hidden."

They all felt the dread of a world suddenly turned dangerous. General MacArthur's promise of "I shall return" was the flame of hope intended to keep them going, but they wanted his return to happen before they would have to test the defenses of their mountain citadel. None doubted the Japanese would eventually find them. All it would take is the capture and torture of one of the supply cargadores or guerrilla fighters for the enemy to learn the secret camp location on Mount Bawao.

James watched Maria staring at the mountainscape and could see her apprehension. This responsibility was new to him. He had persuaded her to join him on this dangerous mission, and he needed to make sure she was safe.

He had it in him to do this.

They embraced. "Today we are safe," Maria said. "Tomorrow? I don't dare think that far ahead."

"Whatever happens tomorrow, I will be right here with you," James said, with his arm wrapped around her shoulder. "Nothing can ever change that."

Fairy Tale
Florentia Scott

"Damn! These hospitals are noisy," someone says.

Sylvia turns her head, carefully, towards the voice. Who is there? And where is she? She can't move without tugging on a tube or wire. She is aware of pale blue, the color of the curtains that divide one bed from another. There are voices and buzzing sounds. A high-pitched voice wants Dr. Barry something to go somewhere.

Her left nipple itches. She wonders if she can displace enough tubes and wires to scratch. Then remembers she doesn't have a left nipple. Or a right one.

Charlie used to lick them. How long ago? She can't remember. She tries to summon the sensations, the secluded pool, the scents of the Yucatan on their honeymoon. His touch burned beneath the water.

All she feels now is pain rising behind her eyes. It was cold in the tent that last camping trip with their grown son and his fiancée. Charlie walked slowly up the mountain trails he used to run. They didn't make love on that trip. And later that year, months after his surgery, weeks after the chemo ended, she took Charlie to the hospital and stood by his bed. He seemed to have trouble seeing her, hearing her. He kept saying that he was thirsty. She brought him a glass of water. He pushed it away and repeated that he was thirsty. She'd been up all night. Nurses came in, told her to go home, get some rest, have a meal, then return. And when she did, his skin was cold, his eyes rolled back into his head so only the whites showed. The doctors pleaded with her to let them disconnect the wires and tubes. They were waiting only for her consent, because he told them she would make the decision.

She thought she could never stop wailing.

In time, the color of life faded from black to pale gray. She went to work, fitness classes and book clubs. Then lumps came and needles drew out poison and her breasts disappeared. First one, then a few years later, the other. The tests were clear in between and after, but then they weren't. It was in her blood this time.

She had stayed by Charlie's bed, but there was no one beside her now.

"Charlie!" she screams. "Charlie, come back, please come back. I need you."

Sylvia can't see much without her glasses so shapes have ceased to exist, only vague masses of faint colors. A sage-colored form comes through the foggy blue curtain. Kind brown eyes in a freckled forehead, framed with curly blond hair, come into focus.

"Who's Charlie, hon? Someone I can call for you?" the nurse says.

"I'm thirsty. I want my husband." Sylvia moans. She feels a straw scraping at her lips.

"Here's some water, dear."

Sylvia takes one sip and holds it in her mouth, then turns her head away from the scratchy straw.

Sylvia whimpers and feels a gentle hand stroke her forehead. She thinks of Charlie's strong hands and the scent of the roses he brought her. This hand smells like disinfectant.

"How's your pain, dear?" the nurse says. The heart monitor beeps louder and louder, and seems to tap out a pattern that somehow seems familiar.

"What's that song?" Sylvia says.

"What song, hon?"

"A song I know from long ago. Who is singing? Where is it coming from?"

"I don't hear anything, Sylvia."

Another fuzzy figure appears at the foot of the bed. A deep voice says, "She's hallucinating."

"OK," the nurse says, "I'll back it off a bit. Sylvia, I'm just going to turn down the morphine drip, but if your pain increases, let me know." She pats Sylvia's hand.

When she was in the hospital to have Stevie so many years ago, Charlie stood by the bed, held her hand and stroked her hair.

"You have such fine, soft hair," Charlie said. "Pale brown, just like our little Stevie's."

Such a tiny perfect being. So sweet to feel his little mouth latch on to her huge dark nipple.

Steve would try to come; he was under a lot of pressure at work. They were sending him to Milan. Melanie was after him to finish tiling the downstairs bathroom. And little Stella was sick again.

She sees him as a little boy, running towards her in the red, white and blue sweater she knit for him.

Someone beats a tambourine; bells tinkle. Sylvia thinks of Lily of the Valley grown out of control into the lawn. The blossoms smelled so sweet. And the Pieris by the crumbling walkway, with clusters of pink bells that cascaded like a thousand little waterfalls for the fairy people.

There is a needle inserted into the vein of her right hand, taped down. The tape tickles, like someone is dancing on her hand.

She blinks. Someone *is* dancing on the taped-down needle. Against the blurred background of the hospital curtains and the attendants' amorphous, fading presence, Sylvia clearly sees a tiny black woman draped in bright orange silk with long black hair that brushes her ankles as she leaps and twirls. Soft, silky black hair swirls around her. She wears gold bangles on her ankles and wrists, bells on delicate toes that twitch as she gyrates. Scents of orange flowers, ginger and sandalwood float around her.

Sylvia knows this woman, has seen her before, but where?

There were office parties and bridge parties. There were golf games and promotions. And meetings, so many meetings. Late at night, early in the morning, over lunch, dinner. You had to be on call twenty-four seven in case someone needed to get information or give an order. Because someone's opinion was critically important. She forgets what all those meetings were about, forgets whose expectations had to be exceeded at all costs. All of that, like the colors and forms in the hospital room, was blurring and fading.

But the tiny people, she sees more of them now, so clear and distinct against the disappearing shapes and voices of the past.

There is the white princess astride her white-winged horse. Her skin and hair gleam like sunlight on snow, her clothing clings to high pointed breasts and her long white cape billows behind her.

Now come the rainbow queens: green, orange, red and violet. Barefoot, with rings on their toes and jewels that match their skin and bright waist-length hair. Each leads an army of naked multi-colored warriors on horseback. The soldiers hover as the queens alight on the bed rails, bring golden trumpets to their lips, to play a song that Sylvia knows.

She remembers now where she first saw them, when she was a little girl peering into clumps of moss, marveling at the tree-like plants only half as long as her finger.

As she gazed, she saw she was looking into a forest, and saw houses, paths, roads, and people going about their business: walking, gardening, skipping rope, flying. Some lived higher up, in lady slippers and Lily of the Valley blossoms. Up and down the big trees, highways teemed with traffic. The scenic routes were built along the ridges of bark. And sheltered tunnels down in the bark valleys because some fairies prefer darkness. The light blinds them, the wind blows them screaming into the void, they fear the birds who pluck them off the ridges and whose sharp beaks probe the valleys for plump fairy babies to eat. Because there is terror, even among fairies. Oh yes.

So many beautiful and varied fairies, so many worlds to explore, one at a time. There were fairies at the top of the tallest trees and mountains, fairies in the air and sky. Oh, how bright and shining and clear they were…

"There she is, looking more beautiful than ever." The voice is loud. A large being hovers over her bed, holding a smaller one in its arms.

"Say hi to grandma, Stella," the voice says. She knows that voice. She remembers the first time she heard it: a wordless cry, in a hospital long ago. The voice came first, then someone called out the gender, and presented a tiny wrinkled body.

"Stevie," she remembers saying. "His name is Stevie."

Now a little girl is being held close to Sylvia's face. A little girl with enormous blue eyes, wispy light brown hair and a runny nose. The child stares balefully at Sylvia and starts to cry.

"Come on, Stella, be nice to grandma, please!" Stevie's voice is higher than usual, with just a hint of whine.

"Hello, Stella," Sylvia says. The little girl quickly jerks her head away.

"Look, Stella: fairies," Sylvia says. The child turns back, smiles, and giggles.

"Mama," Stella says and laughs at the little black woman dancing on grandma's hand.

She points and squeals as the fairy waves, beating the tambourine and singing in a high, sweet voice. "Stella, Stella, little star, do you wonder what you are?"

The violet army flies around Stella's head. The queen has landed on the baby's outstretched index finger. "Oooh," Stella croons, matching the fairy queen's tune, and gently, lightly, kisses the queen's violet hair.

The child's eyes turn slowly towards Sylvia; she sees into her granddaughter's eyes, so huge and blue like the fairy oceans...

"Mom!" Steve's loud, frightened voice echoes down an ever-lengthening corridor. Stella's happy giggle seems to follow Sylvia as she recedes away from the sounds, shapes and experiences of a long life that now seems to have lasted only an instant.

Then little Stella, the blue curtains, the long, long hall, Stevie ... fade into soft white light, and all she sees are the fairies, who surround her, lead her out of the long tunnel into the lush green forest, where a young man waits, smiling, arms outstretched in welcome by a cottage door.

All she hears is their triumphant music, and Charlie's gentle voice saying, "Here you are, darling, at last."

The Persimmon Constellation
Brian Shea

"Absolutely not. I didn't even know her," her brother Joe said, and so Liliana drove by herself to clear out Grandma's little house after the death. Liliana's back now showed the same hunch Grandma had, back in those summers long ago when Joe stayed in the valley plucking cabbages and plums with a crew he wasn't big enough to be a part of, and Liliana's parents sent her to stay with Grandma in the cottage in the foothills.

As she pulled into the narrow driveway, sun frolicked down the sloped orchard, spilling its glare between bare branches locked in spasms, like arthritic fingers that couldn't capture the light. Yet inside the cottage, darkness prevailed, a mood Liliana didn't recall from her visits. Only the scrolled base of a brass floor lamp glinted, fragile and tentative like the radio signals Grandma dialed in when she prepared food. The enameled hard candy tray beckoned like it used to, though it now offered only dust.

Liliana sank into the worn rocking chair, where Grandma would plant herself to tell humorous stories. Reflecting on summers with Grandma, Liliana sensed a presence behind her, hovering and watching like a dragonfly.

She turned to the small kitchen at the back of the cottage. No dragonfly, though that's where her imagination was nurtured. Using short paring knives in that tiny space, Grandma whittled carrots, nicked cucumbers and molded rice, deftly transforming them into characters. Food was family. Food was life and joy. Food was history, as well as the future.

The kitchen was joined by a pantry, no larger than a closet, that led to a skinny back door, and then down steps into the orchard. During summers in the cottage in the foothills, Liliana loved making believe and playing in that tight space behind the kitchen. She'd close her eyes and turn in little circles with delicate ballerina steps, and imagine herself flying among flocks of shriveled Imo and Fuyu persimmons suspended by impossibly thin threads. Each fruit from her grandparents' orchard was the same, yet different, the way people were.

Because the little room was built unfinished, Grandma thumb-tacked colorful fruit crate labels to the walls and ceiling. Many said Penryn, from the fruit trading company down at the next junction of Rock Springs Road. The improvised wallpaper was taunted by gravity, but Grandma had been stronger, applying tacks that still bit into the wood.

Standing there now, a lifetime later, Liliana remained enchanted by the bright colors and the dynamic renderings of trains, Indians, beefy block letters, a sunny Golden Gate Bridge and maidens in wispy robes cradling fruit baskets like babies.

The earlier labels were obscured, allowing only a few letters to squint out—so "ears" was all that represented Pioneer Mountain Pears, and "Blue Goo" stood for Blue Goose Lake County Bartletts.

Mixed in among the layers, though mostly covered over, were a dozen or so handbills on rough paper, printed in Army green ink. While mostly in English, they also featured Japanese characters. Dress Nicely for All. Be Like-Minded. Work Hardest at Home. Watchful Neighbors Make Good Neighbors.

People Liliana grew up with didn't talk like that. When she was at school, her friends had dressed in ripped jeans and sported green or pink spiky hair. They voiced opinions. They were boisterous, even defiant.

When Liliana asked about the phrases on the posters, Grandma would remove herself, like she had to get away from something in that little room. Then, from the rocking chair, she'd hold out the candy tray to entice Liliana to come sit with her. "Come, my green-eyed avocado girl."

And her hard eyes would soften as she told an amusing story that might start with Grandpa climbing a ladder in the dark to check the orchard trees at first frost, or one of her own adventures with the dog she bought after she came back from the camp in the desert and had to live alone. Grandma talked a lot about the dog, but never why she lived alone.

On this visit to the cottage, Liliana realized the little back room had meant something special to Grandma. In the way she wanted everything just so in there, in the way it was so close and personal, and in the way she sometimes needed to leave that space so suddenly. Liliana fretted. As a young girl, she'd danced and swung her arms with abandon through the hanging fruits to make them sway and swing. However, the little space wasn't a stage for puppets and play. Perhaps she'd disrespected her grandma?

Liliana offered a quick blessing and turned to retreat to the old chair, just like Grandma used to do—and froze. She spied a handled case tucked under the table and opened it a crack. A portable Royal typewriter. Finger oil blushed across the A, Y and K keys. A crinkly sheet of translucent paper curled around the roller, as if ready to listen.

Liliana imagined her grandma, sitting in the tiny room alone, perhaps cold and unhappy, or maybe smiling, hiding from the heat at the end of a summer day. What had Grandma typed in the small room, stringing words and sentences together on the English keys under persimmon constellations? If so, where were those pages?

The room had only a chair, a small table, and several hooks for dishtowels. And now the typewriter. A bump. The toe of Liliana's shoe caught, and she noticed a floorboard that curved up at one end. When she bent down, the plank almost jumped into her hands, as if never intended to lie flat, and it revealed a herringbone pattern below. Liliana drew in a breath and held it. Hoping not to disturb any black widows, she plunged her arm down into the unknown space and pulled out a small suitcase.

Liliana made a pot of hot water and found a canister of sencha leaves. Then she brought the suitcase out to the shallow porch. She sat in the sunlight, and read, leafing through the onionskins and absorbing the story of a life that Grandma kept close and secret, stories she hadn't voiced from her rocking chair.

Joe's hard life made his personality hard, and Liliana's connection to him was frayed. Maybe he wouldn't be interested to hear what Grandma wrote about, but others would.

The starch coating on the paper itched, but that wasn't what caused Liliana's fingers to tingle. As a literary agent, and more important as a granddaughter, she vowed to the little room in the cottage to spread the stories of Grandma's life.

Fat Tuesday
Lisa Shulman

The day before her 40th birthday, Myra woke up craving a black leather miniskirt, an ankle bracelet, and long silver earrings that dangled to her shoulders.

She could hear Frances and Jeanie bickering in their room over whose Barbie got to wear the firecracker-red high heels. Myra added Barbie's stilettos to her ensemble and tossed around the idea of a tattoo to go with it.

The sky outside the window was a miserable gray, the tired color of her worn flannel nightgown. Myra closed her eyes again. Just the thought of that Portland sky made her long for a fast car and a snaking highway that would pull her out of the stale skin of her life into something fresh and tight fitting, damp with newness.

The sudden jangle of her phone sent a spangling of gold and purple and green behind her closed lids. It was her sister Addie calling from New Orleans.

"Hey! Y'all're awake now, aren't you?"

"With two kids under five, I'm always awake at dawn," Myra yawned. "What's up?"

"Why, it's Mardi Gras, baby! Mardi Gras *and* your birthday!" Myra thought she could hear the bright, brassy sounds of Dixieland jazz coming over the line.

"My birthday's tomorrow," she said, pressing her ear to the phone. Yes, she was sure she heard music.

"Tomorrow? Shit!" Addie giggled. "Oh well, *cher*, Mardi Gras' today!"

Myra thought she could smell the bourbon on Addie's breath and see her bright red lipsticked mouth stretched wide in a smile. She clutched the phone as if she were drowning, and only her sister could save her.

"What are you wearing?" she asked. Her need to know, to see it, to feel it all was so strong, Myra felt feverish.

"Well, sugar, I had this yellow tutu and a cowboy hat, and see? I wanted to wear them both, but couldn't figure out how they'd go together until my friend Suzy ... you remember Suzy?"

"I've never been there. How could I remember Suzy?"

"Oh, well, Suzy says to me, 'Addie, why you could be the Yellow Rose of Texas,' and so you know, that's what I am this year. "

The Yellow Rose of Texas. Myra sighed and relaxed her grip on the phone. Now she could see it: Addie's long tan legs emerging from the yellow tulle, her feet in thrift store cowboy boots, a ten-gallon hat pushed back on her curly black hair, and strands and strands of Mardi Gras beads, gold and purple and green, clicking around her neck.

A blast of music burst from the other end of the line, and Myra heard the low rumble of a man's voice, like a bee's sweet buzz. Then Addie's laugh rang bell-like from that far-off city of sun and music and color.

"Hey, I gotta run, baby. Happy early birthday. I don't know what I'm giving up for Lent this year, but whatever it is, you'll be happier not hearing from me tomorrow."

All through her morning routine, Myra thought of Addie. Her sister's costume superimposed itself over her own reflection in the bathroom mirror, as if she were an old-fashioned paper doll, posed, waiting for the next coordinated outfit. Myra could almost see the paper tabs at her shoulders and waist.

* * *

Myra sopped up pools of sticky apple juice and soggy Cheerios. She slapped together PB&J sandwiches. She peeled her daughters' clingy little fingers off her skirt as she handed over the wailing girls to the preschool teacher. Now here she sat in bumper-to-bumper traffic, forcing cold, burned toast down her throat while trying to steer away from the self-pity which lapped at her ankles.

"You made your bed," she could hear her mother telling her, forever disapproving of Myra's divorcing Jack two years ago. Yes, she had made her bed, and now she could lie in it as she chose. It might be lonely at times, but in Myra's book, loneliness was preferable to Jack's constant complaining and bickering that had made her feel as if she had another child instead of a husband.

During the crawling commute into downtown, Myra turned on the radio, and the golden tones of jazz poured into the car like fine wine. A ray of weak sunshine glinted off the bumper of the car in front of her, and suddenly she was squinting in the hot New Orleans sun. Sweat beaded on her forehead as she flowed along the street in a river of thousands of other revelers, the feel of satin, tulle and feathers brushing against her skin. The mask she wore narrowed her vision, broke the world into bright slivers of color and movement, making her feel drunk.

She craned her neck to see the float making its way up the street, led by a trio of wizened trumpet players. All around her, people cheered and hollered, the waves of music seeming to lift them above the littered sidewalk in a wild dancing frenzy.

The float drew near, and hands waved and clapped over heads as the krewe tossed the shining bead throws into the crowd.

"Throw me somethin', mister!" screamed a woman riding on the shoulders of a masked and grinning man who stood sweating next to Myra. The woman wore tight gold satin shorts and a halter top of rainbow sequins; a mask of peacock feathers and red glass beads rose above her tangled dark hair like a wild crown. "Throw me somethin', mister!" she screamed again, and pulled down on her halter so her breasts bobbed free.

Her skin was the color of good whiskey, and she shimmied her shoulders, pointing her nipples at the krewe like a dare.

"Show it to me, baby!" a man in a red satin cape shouted from the float, tossing her a long shimmering strand of purple beads which she caught above her head.

The man on whom she rode grinned wider, a white-hot smile below the mask, and gripped her smooth knees more tightly. The woman draped the beads about her neck, then leaned over so the necklace and her breasts danced before his face.

"Check it out, honey," she said. "The first of many."

"Oh, yeah," he said as she straightened up, pulling her halter back into place. "Oh, yeah."

The angry honking of the driver behind her jerked Myra back to the drizzling Portland present. She pulled into a parking space and sat for a few moments in the idling car, trying to get her bearings. Even as she turned off the motor and stepped into the damp chill of early Oregon spring, Myra felt herself split in two places at once.

The feeling stayed with her all morning. She looked at her clients not as a social worker would, but as fellow participants in a masquerade. When DeeDee strutted into her office, manic and off her meds, Myra looked at her with secret admiration and a touch of envy.

"Goddamn it, Myra, I'm tired of rain! Tired of this whole moldy city, this mildewed state. Jesus! I can't believe I've stayed here my whole pathetic life, not with all the fine, sunny places I could live. Hey, I hear that down in Mexico they don't even have glass in their windows, or doors either, it's that warm and dry. And you've got bananas and mangoes and pineapples just hanging on branches outside the house. God, it makes me want to just catch a ride south right now!"

It was all Myra could do not to grab her own keys and offer the client a ride. She was glad when DeeDee finally left, leaving the faint scent of papayas and a restlessness behind.

Myra thought again about the miniskirt and ankle bracelet, the dangling silver earrings. She could see herself swinging down the street, high heels clicking and earrings tinkling, her long legs seeming to stretch forever from the shining anklet to the black leather mini. They weren't gold satin shorts and a sequined halter, but they'd do.

Of course, she'd have nowhere to wear such an outfit, since the office, the supermarket, and the girls' preschool were the only places she seemed to go lately. And she couldn't really afford to buy such things, not with the rent due next week, and her credit cards already stretched. But a faint voice that used to be hers a long time ago rose and filled her mouth.

"It's my birthday, goddamn it," she said out loud, the words sounding like DeeDee's as they bounced off the beige walls. Myra slung her purse over her shoulder. She didn't have another appointment for an hour and she knew just the boutique she could go to.

She was halfway out the door when her phone rang. It was Jeanie's teacher with the news that Jeanie had just thrown up and seemed to be running a fever. Myra would have to pick her up right away.

The mini skirt and earrings dissolved in a poof of silver dust, and Myra felt the ankle bracelet tighten into a shackle as she rescheduled the rest of her appointments and assured her supervisor that she would make the time up, and yes, she understood this came out of her personal leave days, and no, she didn't intend on making a habit of this.

* * *

When she arrived at the preschool, both Frances and Jeanie sat slumped on a cot in the office, flushed and glassy-eyed with fever.

Myra brought them home and put them to bed, spent the afternoon bringing them ginger ale and wet cloths for their foreheads, holding their hair away from their damp faces as they retched over the toilet, and singing every Disney song she knew.

When they finally fell asleep at seven o'clock, Myra collapsed on the couch. Sticky breakfast dishes were piled in the small sink, and heaps of wrinkled laundry taunted her from the floor. Myra turned her back on them and clicked on the TV. The insistent beat and twang of zydeco filled the living room as a news segment on Mardi Gras flickered on the screen. Myra leaned forward until her tired face was almost touching the television.

Was that Addie, there in the crowd, cowboy boots kicking and tapping under her yellow tutu? And there—there was the woman in the rainbow halter and peacock feathers, clapping and swaying astride her friend's shoulders.

And next to him, Myra danced, possessed by the mask, the music and the tartness of lime daiquiris on her tongue; she whirled and twisted alongside the float. Her fingers gripping the filmy fabric of her skirt, she swished it above her knees, then dropped it an inch, then flicked it up, dropped it, raised it higher, teasing, laughing as the crowd whooped and roared, and the grinning krewe leered and hollered.

The news program ended abruptly, and Myra stared blankly at a commercial for laundry soap, then snorted in disgust and turned off the TV. She was tired of thinking about clean clothes, tired of cooking, tired of listening to crazy people at work and whining kids at home, tired of being competent, responsible and good.

"I've got to get out," she announced, again hearing that voice that had once been hers. And she saw the girl she had been, wild red brown hair, a tightly wound body, and a brooding look. She paced on long legs within the confines of Myra's soul like a caged tiger, drumming her fingers impatiently, curling her lips into something between a pout and a sneer. *Let me out,* she snarled. *I've got to get out.*

Myra peeled off her sweaty blouse and stained skirt, pulled on jeans, a black sweater, boots. She stuffed some money and her keys into the pocket of her denim jacket and went across the hall to Doreen and Mike's.

Doreen answered the door in orange sweats, a cigarette dangling from her fingers.

"I need a break," Myra said desperately. "The girls are sick, tomorrow's my birthday, and I just—"

"Say no more," Doreen interrupted, raising a palm like a traffic cop, or a priest bestowing benediction.

"Hey, Mike," she yelled over her shoulder. "I'm going over to Myra's for a while to watch the kids."

Awash in gratitude, Myra squeezed her friend's shoulder. "Hey, can I bum a cigarette?"

Doreen's eyebrows shot up like startled birds. "I thought you didn't smoke."

Myra grinned. "I don't."

Doreen grabbed her keys and a pack of cigarettes from the table by the front door. "Happy birthday," she said, handing Myra the cigarettes and a lighter. "Knock yourself out."

"Thanks," Myra turned towards the stairs. "I won't be too late."

"Take your time!" Doreen called after her. "Live it up!"

Out on the sidewalk, Myra put a cigarette between her lips and, cupping her hands around it, flicked the lighter. The flame flared, and looking into it, Myra was momentarily blinded, as if she had gazed into the noonday sun. Then she closed the lighter, and the darkness covered her again like a mask.

She strode down the sidewalk, her boots tapping out a lonely rhythm on the pavement. The night air on her face felt like a cool drink, and she turned towards SE Hawthorne Street, just a few blocks away. It had been forever since she'd been out on her own at night; Myra thought maybe she'd browse the used bookstore and stop at a cafe for a glass of wine.

The neighborhood already seemed settled in for the night; some windows were darkened while others flickered dimly with a television's blue light.

As she neared SE Hawthorne, the faint strains of music drifted towards her in the night. A small bar on the corner blazed yellow light from every window as if it were sunny mid-afternoon inside. Myra drew closer and heard the tangle of voices and sudden bursts of laughter, the hard click of pool balls and the bass thump of rock and roll.

She looked up at the blank windows of the apartments next to the bar and saw, leaning over the wrought iron balustrades, cheering masqueraders decked out in feathers and sequins, daiquiris in one hand and strands of glittering gold, purple and green beads in the other, which they prepared to throw …

Myra took one last drag off the cigarette and flicked it into the street. The music from the bar reached out and grabbed her like a hand around her waist. It wasn't zydeco or jazz, but what the hell, this wasn't New Orleans. In a few hours, she would be forty, and Mardi Gras would be over.

Myra glanced back over her shoulder, past the partiers on the balcony, into the glittering star-sequined sky.

"Throw me somethin', mister!" she called in a voice that was still her own, and danced through the doorway into the bright and cheering throng.

Ninja
Brad Shurmantine

Jack strapped a carton of eggs on the back of his bike. Six for Daniels and six for Oldham. Daniels posted grades that morning. Jack had started doing his homework, a lot of it. He was even doing the worksheets in class, participating, and he was still at 27%, the very bottom of the list. He had only come up ten percentage points. Daniels didn't care. He was all, *You'll pass if you keep turning in work; if you don't, you won't.* Well, he turned in work, and not a fucking thing had happened. *The essays and projects too,* Daniels said. Jack didn't have time for that shit.

As for Oldham, he was a sarcastic asshole; he mocked Jack in class that morning in front of everyone, and Jack was itching to reply.

He hated English, but he'd always limped by until now. This was supposed to be bonehead English. You were supposed to pass this class if you breathed. But Daniels was all, *You have to do the work. You have to come to class.*

Every day he said the same shit. *I take you seriously. I hold you accountable. This is not Romper Room.* What the hell was romper room? What was he talking about? *This work is not hard. You'll learn if you do the work. You'll pass if you do it. Otherwise, you won't pass.* Goddamn. He had done the work and he still wasn't passing.

It was well after midnight as he glided onto the empty campus. There was no watchman. Every building was alarmed, but he had no intention of breaking in.

He would get away with this because he was always joking and pleasant in class. He wasn't some notorious delinquent they would immediately finger. He was tall and gangly with long brown hair he kept tucked behind his ears and hardly ever brushed. It was clean, though. He took a shower every morning. That's the reason he was always late to Daniels's class. It took a while for his hair to dry.

Jack wore dark clothes, including his favorite black hoodie, and he was feeling ninja-like. There was no one around—he could have sung opera if he wanted to—but he was trying to be stealthy. There were plenty of lights on campus but he skirted them. He headed for Oldham's classroom first, in the science building. Outside Oldham's room were all these tall cactuses someone planted a hundred years ago. He had to stand close to the window to throw his eggs, so he wouldn't hit the cactuses, and he made a little speech as he threw each egg. He was sending a message, after all.

"So, you think I'm brilliant? You called me brilliant this morning when I gave my lame answer to your stupid question about photosynthesis. Well, this is for you."

Splat!

"And fuck photosynthesis."

Splat!

"Who the hell cares about photosynthesis? And fuck meiosis and mitosis too, while we're at it. I have no idea what the difference is between those two."

Splat!

He stopped for a minute to think. He had three eggs left for Oldham. He didn't want to waste them.

"Here's for pairing me with Stacy. You think giving me the smartest girl in class as my lab partner is helping me. She thinks I'm stupid and she does our lab reports all by herself. I can't hang with her. She's really into this shit. And here's one for you too, Stacy, for shooting me down when I asked you out.

"I make you laugh. You told me I'm the funniest guy you ever met. So why won't you go out with me? Take that all over your face."

Splat! Splat!

One more egg. What message would he send with this one? He was all talked out for now. Really, Oldham wasn't so bad. Oldham was usually OK. Jack was actually passing his class because of Stacy. Maybe Oldham didn't deserve all six. He probably didn't mean to be insulting.

He stood there in the night, rolling the egg around in his hand. What could he do with this egg? His PE teacher? Yeah, but there was nowhere to throw it—the gym was huge, the message would get entirely lost. His history teacher? Nah, he liked her. Ms. White was friendly. He was failing that class too, barely, but he was confident he could get his grade up by the end of the semester. Ms. White was fair. And history was important. Like Ms. White always said, learning the past helps us understand the present.

Ceramics was fun. No egg for Mr. Simpson. Algebra was easy. He was nearly acing that class.

OK. An extra egg for Daniels. That fucker deserved it.

He snuck over to the English building, remembering how Daniels made a big deal about greeting his students at the door and welcoming them to class. Since Jack was mostly late to class, he didn't get greeted often, but when he did, he didn't like it. *Don't shake my hand and act all pleased to see me. Just pass me.*

Daniels wouldn't talk about himself or his wife or his kids, but he was always getting in your face and asking you if things were OK. He wanted you to believe he was your friend, but when you asked him what he did that weekend, or how he met his wife, he would say, "*You guys are just trying to get us off-track, so we don't do our work.* No, they weren't. They wanted to know how he met his wife. That stuff is interesting. But Daniels was all business.

Soon Jack was standing outside the classroom. There were no obstructions here, so he could stand back and throw the eggs hard and get a good splatter. He was going to get to class on time tomorrow because he wanted to see the look on Daniels's face when he realized what his students thought of him.

"OK. This first egg, Mr. Daniels, is because you're flunking me.

"This second egg is for the same reason.

"This one's because you've got your little grading system that makes it impossible for me to pass.

"And this one's because I have to go to summer school because of you, and I won't be able to make any money. So I'll never be able to afford a car or anything."

Splat! Splat! Splat! Splat!

He had three more eggs; he had to make them count. He thought for a while.

"OK. This egg is because you make us read those goddamn novels. No one likes reading them. We just rent the movie. Those goddamn novels are—Too! Goddamn! Long!

Splat!

"This egg is because you make us do homework. We hate homework. We have lives, OK? We have things to do. Were you ever a kid? Did you like doing homework? Fuck, no.

"Stop! Giving us! Homework!"

Splat!

Last egg. He walked around in a little circle, thinking hard.

"OK. This one is because your life is all set. You're a cool English teacher. You have a wife and kids, though you never tell us a goddamn thing about them. You get a nice paycheck every month. You get the summers off. I'm not getting the summer off. You've got it all, and I've got nothing. You're supposed to help me, and all you do is flunk me. What good are you? You're useless."

Splat!

Jack stood still for a while, breathing hard, admiring his handiwork in the ambient light. Soon he calmed down and walked slowly to where he had hidden his bike.

That had gone pretty well. Success!

* * *

When Gary Daniels arrived at his classroom at 7:00 a.m. and saw the mess, he was infuriated and disgusted. What little cretin would do such a thing? Why? The sun was just breaking over the Vaca Mountains behind him as he unlocked the door. He entered the room and, before turning on the overhead lights, took in the bleary spectacle awaiting his students. The glass, smeared with slime and yolk, scrambled the morning rays that usually brought him such peace. He stared at the classroom door and imagined it suddenly flung open, his students jostling in, shouting and laughing at him.

He took out the folder of worksheets he needed to xerox and headed to the copy room, stopping along the way to notify Ray, the head custodian, of what happened. Gary was almost always the first teacher on campus, so the copy room was empty—no one to confide in or console him. His anger had completely dissipated; he was just sad and confused. What had he done to deserve such treatment? He had never heard of a teacher's classroom being egged before. He felt outed, publicly denounced, branded: a teacher students hated.

Most kids liked him; he was sure of that. He worked on being calm and patient and respectful with students, even kids who couldn't sit still or shut up. He never embarrassed a kid in front of the class; if someone got on his nerves, he asked them to step outside. The only referrals he ever wrote were for tardies, which never did any good, but he felt he had to do something. He joked with the kids at appropriate times and laughed at their jokes and antics with real pleasure. He loved it when teenagers were funny or remarkable, and still respected them when they fucked up, which wasn't all that often. Yet one of them had egged his classroom. Someone hated him.

It was probably Jack. Or maybe not. It could have been anyone. Or not anyone, but plenty of suspects. It had to be a kid who was flunking his class. Unfortunately, there was a bunch of them. He hated flunking kids, but they gave him no choice. They boxed him in, goddamn it. What was he supposed to do? Just pass them? He did everything he could think of to enable kids to pass, even accepted worksheets turned in three months late, anything. They just shrugged, their faces blank. His colleagues thought he was soft. There had to be standards, right?

But the message those kids heard. Not, *Your work's not good enough*, but, *You're a piece of shit. A failure.* He always pulled those kids aside, told them he believed in them, liked them, knew they could do the work if they tried. Some would nod, smile gratefully. Some would smirk. Jack was a smirker. But he still wound up giving too many Fs. A non-negotiable judgment: *You suck.* Why would they like him? Why wouldn't they want to get even?

Part of him was angry at being treated like this, publicly humiliated, when he worked hard and wanted to be good to those kids. And part of him knew he failed them by failing them. He deserved every egg. Cartons of them.

This kid, whoever he was, had invaded his heart and trashed it.

Like he trashed his.

He gathered up the pages warm from the copy machine and headed back to his classroom. To face that kid.

* * *

Jack jumped out of bed as soon as his mother called him. He took a quick shower and walked out the door with his hair still wet. He wasn't going to miss this. He made it to class several minutes before the bell rang. Ray, the custodian, stood on a stepladder with a bucket and squeegee, trying to get the egg off. He rubbed and rubbed at the glass but was having a hell of a time. Broken bits of eggshell and yolk, hardened during the cold night into a shiny shellac, coated the bricks below the window. He'd never get that shit off.

"Wow, Ray," Jack said. "What happened?"

"What do you think happened?" Ray said. "Some little joker egged the classroom."

Mr. Daniels was not standing in the doorway welcoming his students. Wonder why.

He was standing at his podium with his head down. He looked like he wanted to crawl into a hole.

Jack grinned as he waltzed into the room, his usual entrance. He expected to see other students smiling too, at least buzzing about the sick drama he hand-delivered them, but no one was smiling or buzzing. Then Daniels looked up and saw Jack's happy face.

Jack stopped smiling. His teacher looked away, then dropped his eyes back to his podium, as if he was reading something important there. Jack headed for his desk, disoriented by the way his teacher had looked at him and the behavior of the other students. Everyone could see the classroom had been egged, but no one was talking about it. The room was even quieter than it usually was during first period when everyone was half asleep. Jack sat and watched his teacher, waiting for him to come to life, erupt. Everything was more serious, sad, than he thought it would be.

* * *

Gary was miserable, and it was only with great effort that he glanced at the clock and attempted to affect the impatience he usually displayed as the seconds ticked down to the morning bell.

The bell rang, but Mr. Daniels stood quietly at his podium for the longest time, eyes down. Finally, he took a deep breath and raised his head.

"Good morning, everyone. I'm very sorry about all this commotion. I don't know what to say. I guess someone doesn't like me." Then he directed his gaze to Jack. "Good morning, Jack. You're here early for a change. I'm glad to see you." He continued staring at Jack, whose eyes shifted nervously away. His teacher seemed tired and hurt.

Jack suddenly felt Mr. Daniels knew exactly who had egged the room.

"Ray will be cleaning the window for a while—just try to ignore him. We're going to continue reading *Death of a Salesman,* where we left off yesterday. There are quite a few parts—has anyone not had a chance to read?" No one said anything. "Does anyone want to read this morning?" No one spoke. "OK. Scott, you've been doing a wonderful job —would you read Willy? And Barbara, you can read Linda—is that OK? Tom, read Charlie. David, read Bernard. Melanie, you can read Happy. And Jack."

He paused and looked at Jack. Their eyes locked together. Jack felt Mr. Daniels creep right into his heart, and his mouth dropped open.

"Jack. You did such a good job reading Happy. You need the points. Will you read Biff?"

Jack nodded.

"Let's get going, try to have a normal day. Let's hope whoever did this feels better now."

The teacher smiled wanly and set himself yet again to getting this jalopy of a class rolling. He turned the key; the starter churned and churned, caught, and the tired old engine chugged into life.

They Don't All Wear Capes
MP Smith

"Surely she's memorized her shoes by now," Russell said, unable to keep quiet any longer. He'd been pacing a ten-foot path and annoying his coworkers at the Prentiss & Conklin Business Solutions firm for over an hour.

David, who shared a cubicle with Russell, laughed at Russell's comment. He had the same window view of the despondent woman on the park bench across the street. They had watched her as she studied her shoes, flailed her hands as she talked to an imaginary friend, and wiped tears that still flowed.

Russell wrung his hands. "Shouldn't we call somebody?"

"Who?" asked David.

"The police?" *Boy, that sounds lame.* "Or her mother?" *Even lamer!*

David gave him a look. "It's not a crime to cry on a city bench."

"I think we should do something." This attempt at newfound strength was out of character for twenty-five-year-old Russell Bixby. Known as the milquetoast of the office—stoop-shouldered and afraid of his shadow—Russell found it challenging to speak to any woman under the age of eighty.

"Leave the 'we' out of that sentence," said David.

After another ten minutes, Russell couldn't continue watching the pitiful young woman in the blue pant suit crying her eyes out. His imagination ran wild, and he certainly wasn't getting his work done while he paced and worried about the distraught woman. He stole the tissue box off David's desk and headed for the door.

"You're going out there?" asked Lisa from the marketing department who had joined David at the window. "You've never spoken to a woman in your life who wasn't your mother. Or me—and that's because I remind you of your grandmother."

Russell's Adam's apple bobbed as he swallowed hard and took another deep breath. "Then it's about time I did," he said in a not-so-sure voice. His knees shook as he pushed open the heavy glass front door.

Russell felt like a fool once out on the sidewalk. *What am I doing? How can I help her?* He shuddered at the thought of speaking to her. *And what'll I say?* He wanted to spin around and return to the safe cocoon of his cubicle and his desk with the Lego Star Wars characters marching across it, but when he swiveled around, he saw Lisa and David staring back at him. A host of other faces from the accounting department had joined them at the window. Lisa made a little 'go on' motion.

Russell was close enough to see David's smirk. With a new resolve to show his work friends that he *could* speak to women without spontaneously combusting from fear, he strode across the street. As his shadow crossed over the young woman, she peered up at him.

Her red-rimmed eyes trickled tears and her nose leaked, but the brown eyes glanced at him without the usual disappointed look women typically bestowed upon him.

He wondered if she could see him as a man with a solution. Yes, he's not just a rescuer, he's a guy with an answer. He straightened his shoulders and adjusted his gray Harris plaid jacket to fit the part. "A man with a solution," he repeated under his breath. He needed to help this brown-eyed damsel in distress. *Now to figure out what to do.*

"Hi, um, I've noticed you sitting here," he said. *Brilliant opener, Russell. She's sure to tell you her life's story.*

"What?" She stared at him with bloodshot eyes that could double for movie props in a horror film.

"Um, for a long time," he continued.

She stared at him with a blank expression, as if she couldn't place him in the timeline of her young life.

He guessed she must be in her early twenties, a far cry from his matronly woman comfort zone. "Well, the thing is. Um. Are you okay?"

"I'm as okay as I've never been before," she said with a deep sigh, sounding older than she looked.

Well, that is unexpected. It sounded to Russell like she'd been practicing that line for a while. "Yeah, the thing is."

"You said that already."

She apparently is not in the mood to be friendly. He cleared his throat and began again. "Um, I know." He took a deep breath. "Are you alright?" He paused, but she didn't answer. "Do you need help? A ride home?" A bright idea showed up on his face. "Need to borrow my phone? I mean,

I'd like to help you, uh, if you. Need. Help." *Once again, Russell, you're proving you're a man of words.*

As much as Russell wanted to sound strong and super-heroic, her defeated appearance stopped him in his new wingtips.

She twisted her face up to him again from her chipped-paint park bench, gave another long sigh, and said, "My house burned down last night." She nodded, then put the final nail in the predicament. "I lost everything."

Russell choked a bit, not expecting a tragedy of that proportion. He thumped down on the bench, almost missing it and landing on the concrete below it. "Gosh, I'm sorry, I. Gosh."

"But I'm a team player," she said, pulling a few tissues from the box he had thrust toward her. "I went to Target this morning in my nightgown. I bought this outfit and was only fifteen minutes late for work."

"Well, that's—"

"I got fired." She let that sink in. "I guess 'my house burned down' wasn't on the list of acceptable absences, or even fifteen-minute tardy excuses, so they let me go."

Stunned into silence, he couldn't find a single word.

"After the fire, I thought I could hide out in the office. Sleep there, you know, and use their gym showers until my house got sorted out. But pfft," she made a weird noise and raised her hand to mimic a bird flying away. "It's all gone. Even," she choked. "Even my cat is missing."

Her tears returned hot and heavy. Somehow, she was in Russell's arms. His mouth formed the word, "Oh," and he didn't know who was more surprised, him or the folks probably taking bets from his office across the street. He gingerly patted her back, which evolved into a tight, comforting hug. Her hair still smelled of smoke from the fire; it was a pleasant scent, reminding him of campfires and marshmallows. *Russell, focus!*

He held her while she shook with sorrow, and he still hugged her until her cries about her terrible misfortune were mere whimpers. From where they sat, Russell marveled at the juxtaposition of her tears and the happy gurgling from the fountain on the path behind the bench. The fountain, with its lighthearted splashing, seemed determined to drown out her tears.

He held her for so long that David came out to the sidewalk across the street and called, "Everything okay, Russell?"

Russell lied, gave a thumbs up, and waved his friend away.

"Um, is there someone I can call for you?" he whispered into her ear. "And, by the way, I'm Russell."

She pushed off his chest and sat up. "Amanda. Amanda Matson."

He cringed when she extended a wet, smeary hand. As the tissue box was now empty, he handed her a handkerchief. To avoid any awkwardness, he asked again, "So, anyone I can call?"

She wiped her face and shook her head.

Russell never knew mascara could be so picturesque when it smeared. It had spread down each freckled cheek in rivulets resembling a river delta. *Focus, Russell!*

"No. My family's back East. I've been so busy working since I moved here, I haven't made any new friends. Besides, I lost my phone in the fire. I don't have anyone's phone number." She bit her bottom lip and gazed off into the distance.

She chewed on her lip again, then noticed the tear stains on his jacket. "I'm sorry about your suit." She wiped the splotches with his handkerchief.

"That's okay." Something about her touched him. Maybe she reminded him of his mom or a favorite teacher, but her proud manner while she blubbered on a downtown street made him want to help her. It was time to dust off the superhero deep inside. He took the plunge. Braving the risk of rejection, he breathed and asked, "What can we do to help you?"

"We?"

"Well, you said you needed friends. I'm offering." He felt his cheeks redden. "And no strings attached," he added, just in case she thought he was a perv. To prove he meant business, he took out his phone and punched in the number for his employer across the street. "Monica, this is Russell Bixby in accounting." He listened for a minute, said uh huh a few times, and then said, "Monica, I've got a strange request, and please help me out here. Um, do we have any entry-level positions available at the moment? Uh huh. Mail clerk and marketing coordinator?" he said these options aloud for the woman next to him on the park bench, his light brown eyebrows raised in question.

Amanda nudged his elbow. "I have a degree in marketing," she whispered.

Russell caught the first glimpse of life coming back into her features. Into the phone he said, "Yes, she has a degree in marketing. I'll bring her over in a few minutes. Thanks, Monica. What? Yes, I can vouch for her; we're very close." He peeked at the woman sitting a few inches from him and saw a small smile and perhaps a flash of relief cross her face.

"Okay," he said after hanging up the phone. He slapped his thigh as if he'd accomplished something momentous. "One obstacle is looking positive. What about a place to stay?"

She shrugged.

"You're gonna have to do better than that." *Gosh, I* am *a take-charge guy.*

"Um, I have a cousin. She lives nearby. But I've only seen her once since I moved here. I'd hate to call her in dire need when I hadn't—"

"Yeah, but you *are* in dire need. What's her name?"

"Kathleen. Kathleen Matson."

He typed and scrolled on his phone. "Ah ha! Kathleen Matson, over on Admiralty Way?"

"Yes, that's her," she said, eagerness creeping into her voice.

He called the number and handed the phone to Amanda.

She listened to the ringing, then her face lit up in the first real smile of the day. "Kathleen. It's Amanda. Yeah." She listened for a minute. "You did? Oh, that's so nice. Thank you for checking up. No, my phone is gone—along with everything else. Oh, Kathleen." She collapsed in tears again.

Five minutes later, a decidedly happier Amanda Matson handed his phone back. "I can't believe it. Kathleen heard about the fire and has been trying to call me. Wow! She said I could stay with her for a while." She glanced over at Russell. "A lead on a new job and a place to stay. Who are you? Superman?"

"No," he laughed. "Just plain old Russell Bixby."

"Well, Russell Bixby, I sure owe you. I thought my life was over. And then you showed up." She pulled his shoulder to look behind him. "Yep, I thought so."

"What?" he asked in alarm.

"You do have a superhero cape on."

Russell stuttered, flustered at the compliment. "I'm glad to help, Amanda. And, if you get the job, we'll be coworkers."

"That'll be nice." She blushed.

And so did he. Russell sensed the color rush to his face. He stood up. "Let's go talk to the folks in HR—I know they'll like you. And after." He paused as they crossed the street together.

"After you've already helped me find my cousin and may have gotten me a new job?"

"That leaves one more thing to work on," he said.

"One more thing?" she asked, wariness creeping back into her eyes.

"Yes. I know cats. And I believe there's a good chance your cat survived the fire. Let's go over and call for her. We'll steal some cat treats out of Matilda's desk drawer."

Her eyebrows shot up at that remark.

"Don't ask," he said and held the door open.

She laughed. "I hope you're right. Maybe she got out the doggie door." She took a deep breath and walked into the office. "Thank you, Russell. You really are a superhero."

Employees still milled about the lobby, determined not to leave until Russell returned with details of his adventure. No one said a word as he opened the door and Amanda entered with hesitant steps.

He smiled and followed her inside, confidence bolstering his posture, ready to introduce them to the former park bench woman and the new and improved Russell Bixby.

Atlantic City, 1909
Susanna Solomon

"Watch your step, girls," Leonard said.

Standing behind her big sister Hortense on the top step of the railroad car at the train station, Dodo watched her sister's friends, eighteen-year-old Leonard and classmate Harry, hold out their hands for Hortense but she bypassed them, grabbed the side rail and swing herself down to the platform, laughing. Behind her, Dodo struggled with a picnic basket and her older sister's Louis Vuitton bag. It was filled with God-knows-what, but Dodo knew some of what was inside—five outfits, four dresses, three pairs of shoes, two shawls, a blanket, two bottles of wine, and four black bathing costumes. And then there were her two hat boxes.

Dodo sighed. Four years younger and she might as well be invisible. Hortense and her friends were more beautiful than she was, had more fun than she did, and even though she didn't like being called Dodo instead of her Christian name, Dorothy, she had grown used to it. Most days she felt like a dodo bird, too stupid to run, too stupid to fly, too stupid to complain, and too young to have her real name. She struggled to carry her sister's bags to the top of the steps where they were whisked away.

Her own carpet bag, worn from use with broken leather handles and half the size of Hortense's, was hard to maneuver around a very fat gray-haired grandma who was now blocking the vestibule of the train with her caged cockatoo, three bags, and a steamer trunk. Beside her, a five-year-old boy squeezed his way around and quickly jumped off the train.

"Stop him!" Grandma cried.

Leonard caught him and held fast. The boy kicked and screamed and tried to run away while Harry helped Grandmother with her trunk.

Still holding the cockatoo in a cage, Grandma put her bags down on the train platform, dug into her handbag for a few dimes, slipped the money into Leonard's palm, and closed her hand around the boy's arm. "Come with me, Jonas, and quit your whining."

Harry, a big galoot of a guy, waited in vain for his tip.

Leonard thanked Grandma and winked at the boy while Jonas, his face red, tried to pull away from Grandma as she dragged him down the platform.

A moment later, Hortense, Dodo, and the boys were alone on the platform. As usual, whenever they arrived at the shore for their months' vacation, they looked at the sky before leaving the station.

"It's perfect," Dodo said to no one in particular. No one heard a word she said.

The little party walked down the platform—Leonard and his friend Harry carrying the bags, and Hortense, with her enormous hat, tucked arm in arm between the two of them, giggling. Dodo, following along behind, struggled with her carpet bag and her sister's hatboxes.

Twenty minutes later, they dropped their bags in their rooms and changed into their bathing costumes—black fabric from ankles to wrists, skirts and oversized blouses for the women, long black shorts to the knees, and sleeveless black tops for the men.

Five minutes later, they were on the beach, same as always. Dodo grumbled as she set their picnic basket on a blanket on the beach. She pulled out her worn *Baltimore Sun* newspaper and read more about Peary's adventures. At least someone was doing something different. She picked at her hair and reached for another piece of coconut cake as she wondered what life would be like at the North Pole. Should she say something to anyone that he made it? No, they didn't care. About her or Peary. At this rate, no one would ever pay her any mind. At fourteen, she was already overweight and didn't care. She was a dodo indeed.

"Pass me the picnic basket, please," Hortense asked, as she took off her high-flying black hat with the feather that reached the sky. "And Dodo, quit eating all the cake."

Dodo stuffed another big bite into her mouth and grinned.

Hortense gave her a funny look, then dug into the picnic basket for cheese and crackers. With Leonard and Harry around, she had other things on her mind.

If Dodo were to run away, no one would ever know.

And no one was going to follow her.

"I'm going to get some ice cream," she said.

"Order a kiddie cone, Dodo, no more," her sister said. She gave her a quarter and waved her off.

Dodo wandered past the concession stands that lined the beach. There was a long pier just before the "Rat Maze" and the "Big Dipper," but she didn't want to go that far. The pier was best—long, far, far away from the beach and so way out in the ocean, walking to the end always made her heart race. Maybe this time she'd see sharks or rays or boys. Boys her age. Boys who liked her.

The wind was gusty, making the red ribbons on her straw-hat flitter, her favorite hat with the enormous brim that seemed to take up the whole sky. She tucked it under her arm and took to the pier. Wooden boards creaked and wobbled under her feet.

Out at sea, waves rose and crashed beneath the long pier. Posts and a railing protected pedestrians over the beach, but once the pier was out over the water only the posts remained. Dodo kept to the center. She never liked heights. She could feel the pier rocking under her sandals as the sea below churned, twisted, and raged against the supports below.

Fishermen in overalls dangled their feet over the side as they whispered to the fish.

"Take a seat, darling," one of the fishermen said. He was leaning against one of the posts wearing a plaid red flannel shirt and overalls, patting the boards beside him. "No one out here but us and the fish, and the fish aren't talking."

He nudged his buddy, a redhead baiting his hook. "Want some company, Thomas?"

"You like smelt? Anchovies? Tuna?" Thomas asked Dodo, smiling, showing a gap between his front teeth.

Neither of them looked washed. Dodo shook her head and walked on.

The sky had taken somewhat of a somber turn; clouds collected overhead and grew gray. And dark.

The end of the pier was still a ways off. Dodo thought she could walk to China, but no, that was the wrong hemisphere. She tucked her voluminous skirt around her and still had a good grip on her hat. She'd have to turn around soon enough, but still, the rising wind and the break of the waves surrounding her made her feel invigorated. No puny picnic for her. She was a great explorer, like Peary, and he had endured a lot stronger winds than this.

She kept to the middle of the pier and heard seagulls crying, diving, and soaring around her, protecting their nests. She wondered for a moment what kind of birds Peary saw and whether he was ever afraid, until she heard a small cry, not a bird cry at all. Wind buffeted the waves and her clothes. Maybe she was mistaken.

No, there was the cry again, and it wasn't far. Feeling nervous, she became very quiet. Gently and slowly, she headed to the edge of the pier. Hugging one of the posts, she looked down. Nothing but waves, white now, crashing beneath her. She straightened. That sound again, that strange cry. Now, close to the end of the half-mile long pier, close to where wildness took over and the ancient explorers found adventures and solace, ate seal and fish, played cards in the damp cabins that swung and swayed in the waves, no one would care if she was missing. She could just jump off and get in one of those ships, find the North Pole like Peary did, and come back alive.

That sound again. What was that? Hair on the back of her neck stood up.

She scanned the pier, saw ropes that had been left for boats and cleats for tying up. But no ships in sight, just a small pink thing, caught in one of the ropes. One of those slimy sea slugs she had learned about in biology class?

What the hell?

She stepped closer. No, it was a hand, a pink hand, caught up in the ropes and the cry was unmistakable. And human. Alive? Dodo's stomach took a turn.

Being careful not to fall, she bent down on her knees to see what the thing was.

"Don't come any closer," a voice said from behind a post.

"You seem to be crying," Dodo said, doing her best to mask her fear.

"It's the wind," the voice said. "Go away."

"You're right," Dodo said. What would Peary do?

"Leave me alone."

"Ah." Dodo sat back on her heels. Peary would stay calm. She studied the waves. "Not a pleasant place to be on Saturday afternoon."

"The air's fresh. I like it."

"Looking for fish?" Dodo asked, trying to stay calm. Trying to peer underneath the pier. "You have a line?"

It was that boy, that boy from the train, Jonas, standing on a rung of a metal ladder mounted to the side of the pier. He was clinging to a rope.

"I'm fine."

"I'm scared. You too? No? You're a brave kid."

"Go away."

"You're kind of small to be out here all on your own. Waiting for a boat?"

"I'm waiting for my mother, she said she was coming."

In the distance, Dodo saw nothing, no line of a ship, no rigging, just heard waves crashing underneath them.

"She's coming? Here?" she asked. Oh, dear Jesus.

Behind her, the wind caught, tugged at her skirt.

"That's what she said. 'Jonas, I'll be back in ten minutes,' and then she was gone," the boy said.

"And that was?" Dodo asked.

"A month ago," the boy sobbed. "So I'm going to find her myself."

"But there's no boat here," Dodo said, trying not to sound alarmed.

"I'm a good swimmer."

"I don't think it's so smart for either one of us to be out here," she said. A gust of wind from nowhere blasted the end of the pier. The boards shuddered and squeaked and swung wildly to and fro, creaking and swaying as Dodo thought Peary's ship would be until she was falling, falling to the ocean below.

She came to a stop a few feet above the water, her feet tangled in rope, almost upside down, facing a wave that came crashing in. She closed her mouth, saw a post of the pier not more than two feet away, and swung for it. Missed. Feeling panic rise, she swung for the post again. Her long skirt tangled in the sharp nails sticking out from broken boards, keeping her from getting out far enough. Her hat floated up and down ten feet away, the red ribbons tailing off.

A large roller was backing away from the beach. She swung again, this time holding her skirts and black bodice away from the supports that held her down, and went for the post. She pulled herself up, hovering two feet above the crashing wave. Then, keeping an eye on the next roller, she grabbed the post with everything she had as the freezing water lashed at her body. She held on, her hands bloody from splinters and nails, her heavy clothes threatening to pull her under.

"Help!" she shouted, two feet under the pier. A bit of rope was hanging over the side.

No one was at this end of the pier, she'd made sure of it.

The wind screamed in her ears.

Where was the boy? "Jonas!" she cried. "Where are you?"

She scanned what she could see. No sign of him underneath the broken pier.

"Jonas!"

A bare foot tangled in the ropes below her feet. She reached down, tried to pull him close, as close as she could, but he was heavy, and the ropes were slick with moss. Continual waves buffeted her face and pulled at her clothes. The taunts of her classmates ran through her ears. *You're too fat to play with us, Dodo. You're too weak, Dodo. You're useless, Dodo. You will never be strong enough.*

But Peary could do it. Peary could do anything.

Peary would not hesitate to save his men.

Jonas' face came out of the water, his mouth open, one hand searching for hers.

"Help me!"

Dodo reached down, grabbed that hand. "Tighten your hand around the rope, grab me and hold on with everything you've got!" she cried. His little body swung into hers as a wave broke over both of them, but he was with her, tangled in the ropes, in her clothes, their heads above the water. The iron ladder swung awkwardly nearby. "Grab the ladder!" she cried. "Make sure it's fast before you climb!"

A moment later, his left foot was on the swaying ladder, and then he was up.

Now it was her turn. Each rung twisted and turned in her hands. She couldn't find a place to put her feet. Thundering waves crashed into her, into the broken pier, but a small voice sounded from above—that boy's voice. Then he was looking down on her.

"Come on!" he said. "You can make it!" Peary could make it, too.

She held on, rung after rung, and, struggling against her wool clothes, barely reached the top of the pier.

She heaved herself up on top.

The pier swung wildly.

"Grab my hand!" she shouted. They walked together for a moment; her damp skirt hung below her knees, making it impossible to move. She tore it off. They heard a crash and turned.

She held him tight as a huge wave came in, holding for everything she ever wanted, love and tightness and warmth and safety, as the pier shuddered and shook beneath them. Peary would have been proud.

Beyond them, the end of the pier broke all the way off and bobbed in the waves.

They ran together all the way toward the shore.

By the time they got to the beach, the fishermen, Hortense, Harry, Leonard, and Grandma came running toward them.

Dodo wasn't ready to relinquish Jonas, not yet. She had her arm around him as he buried his face in what remained of her skirt.

"Dodo! What were you doing out there?" Hortense asked, rushing to hug her sister.

"My name is Dorothy," Dodo said. "Dodo drowned."

The Picnic
Linda Stamps

Endings bring new beginnings ... most of the time. At the end of every Cape Cod summer, the light shifts, and the locals resume their lives without traffic jams. Bright red rosehips signal fall and tourists head home as the dunes shift windward.

Roberto and Remie lay sprawled on a blanket on the beach. They had spent summers together on this shore for decades. Roberto inherited the cottage at the edge of the dunes. This was their cocoon, the place they nestled to shed the hustle of the city and their lives in it. By the end of each stay, they would return to all that striving, reborn.

Remie sat up, surveyed the beach, inhaled the warm, salty air, and announced, "Time for lunch." They unpacked the wicker hamper: raspberries for the champagne, smoked salmon pate, an assortment of olives, and a cheese plate with Roberto's favorite sesame crackers. The gulls gathered nearby, ever hopeful.

"Do you remember the time we spent in the south of France?" Roberto grinned.

"*Mais oui, cher.*" Remie laughed. "Nude beach, sunburned parts!"

They chuckled and continued to reminisce.

"Do you remember the day we met?" asked Roberto.

"Herring Cove Beach at Bobby's July 4th extravaganza," said Remie.

"I was jumping waves when a swell knocked me over," Roberto said. "I couldn't get up. You slogged toward me, bobbing up and down, with your outstretched arms holding back the Atlantic."

"That's when I knew I loved you." Remie smiled and caressed Roberto's cheek.

They recounted a lifetime of journeys together, both mundane and exotic. Other than summers on this shore, their traveling days ended years ago. In their dotage, they preferred revisiting in this way.

Roberto poured them each a second flute of champagne, while Remie served the next course. Fresh lobster rolls piled high with claw meat laced with lemon and mayonnaise. Remie spooned a crunchy Asian slaw dotted with black sesame seeds onto each of their plates. While eating, they spoke of old friends, recalled gatherings both elegant and absurd.

Many of their friends had already died or wished they had. Disease, dementia, and the taunts and torments of aging pushed their minds over the edge. Roberto and Remie promised each other long ago that they would leave this world on their own terms, intact. They would know the right time.

A warm breeze blew from the shore. Roberto and Remie were companionably silent. Remie thought about their lives together, how much like the endless waves of the sea they had become, sometimes gently rolling, other times powerfully raging. Yet, they always navigated the tides and erosion of so many years of living, loving, and letting go.

Roberto broke the silence with musings about why they'd done this or not that over the years. Neither of them spent much time philosophizing and reflecting. But lately, they had become more comfortable looking into the mirror of their lives.

Remie brushed the sand off Roberto's shoulder, leaned over, and kissed him tenderly on a small scar just above his heart. They held each other's gaze. A tear ran down Roberto's cheek.

"You know, I forgave you for that years ago. Let it go, my love, let it go," Remie urged, brushing away the tear.

"It meant nothing then, yet it haunts me now. The pain in your eyes, the months of not speaking—lost to one another." Roberto exhaled and shook his head.

They watched the sun dance on the water as the light anointed each wave.

Roberto gathered up the plates while Remie spooned some lemon ice into two tumblers. "Time to clear the palate, darling." Roberto tasted a sizable portion. His mouth puckered in earnest and in jest. They leaned across the blanket and kissed, holding one another in the moment. More champagne all around.

The tide made its way across the earth's arc, the ocean spilling onto the shores of Iberia. The couple watched two joggers pass by and wave. Roberto asked, "Why are they always running? Where do they want to get to in such a hurry?"

Remie reminded him of his days of training for the marathon he never ran. Roberto smiled, nodded his head, and leaned back on his elbows, his memory a blur. He watched the sun sparkle across the water as the afternoon ebbed and flowed.

"Ready for the last course?" Remie asked.

"Glad we're not counting calories," Roberto replied.

They looked at each other, paused for a moment, and laughed.

Roberto uncorked a fresh bottle of champagne. Remie served them each a slice of the most decadent chocolate cake. They'd found the recipe online for just the right confection to celebrate their 50th anniversary. Ever since, it had been their favorite for special occasions or for any event made special. They baked this one together, adding their own touch to the dark, rich batter.

"Shall we toast?" asked Roberto. Remie raised the champagne glass and gently touched Roberto's arm. The delicate sound of the crystal flutes announced the moment.

"To many lifetimes together."

"To many lifetimes together."

When they finished eating dessert, they laid back down on the blanket and drifted off. The waiting gulls saw their opportunity, pecking at bits of lobster as they grabbed, ran, and squawked. The sun hovered just above the horizon, pouring itself into the sea.

* * *

A seashore ranger patrolling the beach approached the picnic site. She discovered Roberto and Remie's bodies lying peacefully in repose, holding each other's hand. Her radio crackled and hissed as she called for assistance. Once the police arrived, they discovered a letter in the wicker hamper. The communique explained what had transpired, providing all the information they would need to rule this case a matter of lives taken by choice. No foul play. Roberto and Remie had both signed the letter. They added a postscript just below each signature: Cause of Death: KNOWN.

The tide turned as the sandpipers rushed madly back and forth to avoid the crashing waves. A pair of osprey hovered above the dunes and flew into the dusk.

Crossroads
Meta Strauss

The sun beat down on the dirt streets, grassless yards, and paint-peeled houses in Crossroads. The deserted one-room schoolhouse had closed for the summer, leaving countless hours of bored freedom for Logan and Bobby Ray, two fourteen-year-old boys. When in session, the educational funds and number of students didn't warrant teaching anything but basic reading, writing, arithmetic, and the kind of science that omitted evolution.

The town provided no official means of entertainment. The men worked on the desolate prairie, tending the few cattle that survived on sparse pastures until roundup, when they'd take the livestock to feedlots for fattening before slaughter. The women stayed home, cooking, cleaning, and taking care of the kids.

"Look! There's that weird guy," said Bobby Ray, hair and freckles the same color as old rusty farm equipment. He turned to his best buddy as the two sauntered down the sidewalk, bare feet blistering on the hot surface. The smell of scorched dirt permeated the air.

"He's one of them travelin' preachers, the kind without a church." Logan found a shady spot close to the drugstore, motioning his best friend to join him. "I heard he has a direct link to God Almighty."

The two boys squinted, their focus on the man and the gathering taking place around him. "Look there. Even Josie and Margaret are following him, joining up with what looks like all the women in town," said Bobby Ray.

"Dang it! They're the only purty girls around and they're actin' like this kook is a movie picture star." Logan mopped his sweaty face with a dirty bandana and stuck it back in his pocket.

Bobbie Ray led the way around a tree as the pals eavesdropped. "He ain't sayin' nothin'. He's just strollin'."

"He don't look all that special to me." Logan stretched to see. "Why're all the women having a fit over him?"

"Cain't tell about women. My dad was mad as hell when Mom said she was goin' to his meetin' this afternoon." Bobby Ray stooped so Logan could get a better look.

"My dad says he's nothin' but a worthless no-good who wants folks to give him food and money. Says he's stayin' out on government land."

"Just look at his hair. It's like sheep's wool just before shearin' time." Bobby Ray grinned. "Probably has bugs in it."

"I heard he *eats* bugs." Logan chuckled and hiked his worn shorts up over his thin hips.

Bobby Ray nodded. "Probably true. Remember last Sunday mornin' when the preacher warned us to watch out for false witnesses?"

"He had to say that 'cause some of his congregation might decide Baptists don't know it all and choose a different religion. Then he wouldn't have no one to preach to." Logan sat down on the edge of the walkway behind a pickup that hid them from the throng.

Bobby Ray squatted next to his friend. "My aunt says she don't trust this guy a bit. Tries to act like some character right out of the Bible."

"He sure is strange, and that's a fact." Logan moved closer to see the man better. "He don't seem to be a smoker or a drinker and I ain't seen any weapons on him."

"If a travelin' preacher like him gets this kind of attention, that proves there ain't nothin' worthwhile around here. As soon as I find how to move away, that's what I'm gonna do." Bobby Ray stood up and stretched the back of his legs.

"Yeah. That's what you've been sayin' for a year." Logan combed his straw-colored hair with his fingers. "I don't hold out no hope for ever leavin'. Startin' next month I'll be nothin' but a ranch hand. I'll work like every other man around and you'll be stayin' home helpin' your mom can peaches."

"That's what I'm sayin'. There ain't nothin' but dead ends here. We have to get away from this place." Bobby Ray socked his friend's arm. "Maybe we can go somewhere and get rich and famous."

"Face it. We're gonna be poor nobodies," Logan said. "Why are we watchin' this joker anyway? I say let's get some ice cream like we started out to do." Logan led the way back to the drugstore.

A half-hour later, the boys sat on a dilapidated bench under the town's one oak tree finishing their Fudgsicles. "I think we're the only livin' things left in downtown Crossroads, except for those two old dogs on the church steps." Logan wiped his mouth on his shirt. "I say let's go down to the creek. It's too hot to do anything else."

Bobby Ray frowned. "My mama said I cain't go there no more. Might be snakes."

"Holy cow, you wimp. You ain't afraid of some little ol' snakes, are you?" Logan ran his hand up his pal's arm and laughed. "The water'll feel good. You know the place. Back in the hollow."

Twenty minutes later, Bobby Ray and Logan piled their clothes under the limbs of a giant cottonwood tree. In complete peace, the friends floated around in the cool water.

"Logan, what would you do if you did leave Crossroads?"

"I ain't given it any thought, 'cause it ain't gonna happen."

"When I think about it, I think of seein' some of the sights in our geography book." Bobby Ray's eyes closed as he talked. "Like some mountains or an ocean or maybe a big city with skyscrapers."

"You're some kinda dreamer, Bobby Ray. All I see is more of this damned dried-up prairie, my daddy gettin' drunk, and more visits to my mama's grave."

Crunching and crackling of dried vegetation near where they'd entered the creek interrupted their reverie. Bobby Ray screamed and paddled away from the sound. "Snakes! Snakes!"

"It ain't snakes, Bobby Ray, or at least not the kind you're thinkin' about." Logan leaped out of the shallow water to recover their wad of clothes, Bobby Ray right behind him.

There on the bank was the man looming over them. He wore a long robe, tied with a wide black belt, and tattered leather sandals. His almost-black eyes stared at the boys, expression impossible to read. Their shorts and shirts hung suspended from his large hands. "You boys missing something?"

"Yeah, mister. Those are ours," said Logan, hands covering his privates.

Bobby Ray hid behind a bush, staring wide-eyed at the stranger.

"You can just toss 'em over here," said Logan.

The preacher gazed skyward. "Since it doesn't look like either of you have much going on this beautiful God-given day, I'll make a deal with you."

"What d'ya mean? What kind of deal?" Logan, hands still in place, frowned at the intruder.

The man's eyes traveled back to the boys. "I'll return your clothes if you come to my meeting. I've been watching you two lost souls all day as you followed me around town. I think you might benefit from what's going to be said."

"Thanks just the same. We're not much for church goin' except when our mamas make us."

"Aren't you man enough to make your own decisions?"

Gaining courage, Logan stood straighter. "Those are our clothes and you've no right to them. They're private property."

"Right now they're mine because I found them. Who says I have to give them back?

"If you're a preacher, you cain't steal. The good book says so." Logan looked the man right in his eyes.

"You'll look real cute going through town in your birthday suits with all the sweet little gals seeing what you ain't got." The man turned and started walking away.

Bobby Ray poked his sunburned face around the bush. "I'll come to your meetin', Mister. Please. Just toss me my clothes. Logan'll come, too. Won't you, Logan?"

Logan thought for a moment, then nodded in agreement, one hand reaching for his clothes.

"Okay, boys. The meeting will be down that trail, at the creek." The stranger studied each boy from head to toe before pointing the way. "I'll be expecting you."

The boys struggled back into their clothes, heartbeats fast and breath short, the memory of the afternoon's peaceful swim disappearing like rippling water.

"Let's get back to town fast." Logan started to run.

"He said we got to go to the meetin'!" Bobby Ray yelled to his friend.

Logan stopped and turned around. "Okay, you big sissy. I'll go with you, but you're a real chicken."

The two friends followed the trail where a congregation of women, some children, and a few old men gathered, some singing gospels while others raised their hands in celebration. Despite the sweltering temperature, most had chosen to wear their Sunday best.

"See, Logan, whatever is happenin' here is better than being bored to the bone back in town," Bobby Ray said.

The two watched the assembly from a cluster of brush several yards back from the water. A breeze slipped by, so slight it was noticed only because of the swaying of willow branches.

"Hey, Logan. You wanna git closer?"

"Nope. I don't see him anyway."

"You think he's not gonna show up?" Bobby Ray whispered.

The sun hung just past the top part of the sky and beamed down with nothing but a line of trees along the creek blocking the rays. Flies as big as bees swarmed around the crowd, their buzzing punctuated by swatting sounds.

In the distance, heat waves bounced across the dried-up trail. Like a mirage, the man they'd waited for appeared, his image undulating as he walked, long robe waving around his legs. There was a slow, steady orderliness in his steps, as if he was keeping time with an inaudible beat. He shook the reaching hands that ushered him into the midst of the group.

"Welcome friends. How good of you to join me to hear The Word." His voice was deep and mesmerizing. "God knows each of your souls."

As an offering basket was passed, the preacher continued reciting scripture, and telling about the promised return of their Savior in the end times. "For thus says the Lord, 'I will visit you, and fulfill my promise and bring you to a good place. For I know the plans for you are for welfare and not for evil, to give you a future and a hope. Call upon me. Come and pray to me, and I will hear you.'

"I'm here as a messenger. I'm not the great diviner you've been praying would visit Crossroads to relieve your pain and suffering, but He will come soon to speak the truth to all of us. Meanwhile, I vow to cleanse each of you in this creek."

As he spoke, the boys inched closer to the man, Logan leading. "He sees your sinful nature but offers you change. Whatever sins you've committed will be taken from you and will flow away in the moving water. Gone forever. All you have to do is give your heart to Jesus; to ask to be led in God's service."

The preacher waded belly deep into the creek with the two boys following, quiet and slow, just two more members of the assembly. The man pressed body after body under the water. "You are cleansed from sin. Ready to begin your life anew." Over and over again, he spoke the same words.

He dunked Bobby Ray, who came up sputtering and moved on like those in front of him. The preacher smiled, repeating his hypnotic mantra, while his piercing eyes focused on Logan. "Son, you are cleansed from all sin. Blessed. Washed clean."

The man's arms held Logan as he immersed the boy's entire body in the water. Logan had never experienced such complete security as he surrendered. He arrived at a place, another dimension he had felt only in his dreams. He saw himself in a flowered garden with birds singing. A picnic table overflowed with fried chicken, potato salad, and cakes. His mom appeared in a cloud and smiled, motioning for him to sit with her and eat all he wanted.

"You are ready to begin your life anew," the preacher said as he helped Logan out of the water.

The group had reassembled on the creek bank while the preacher stood in the water and raised his arms skyward.

Bobby Ray whispered to Logan. "He's actin' like he's some kind of real Bible disciple, but I don't feel anything special."

"Shhhh. Listen and you might learn somethin'." Logan followed the man's gaze with a dreamy stare when a sudden flash of light interrupted his reverie.

Like magic, another man materialized on the opposite bank of the creek. He wore jeans and a pristine white shirt. Dark wavy hair covered his shoulders. The preacher opened his arms to the newcomer. "Cousin, I've been waiting for you."

After a greeting of hugs and pats on backs, the new man spoke loud enough for the crowd to hear. "I'm here to be cleansed."

As he had with the others, the preacher placed his hands on his cousin's shoulders and pushed him under water. He repeated the same words. "You are cleansed from all sin. Blessed. Washed clean, ready to begin your life anew."

The man stood, water dripping off his body. A huge flock of crows rose from a thorny mesquite tree at the side of the creek, obscuring the intense sunlight for a couple of minutes, turning the day to dusk. Then the brightest rays of the day landed on the head of the newcomer.

The preacher raised his hands in the air, as if embracing the throng. In a melodious voice, he declared, "I pray for peace and love to surround all of you." He looked at Logan, then brought his hands into the prayer position and turned to the man he called cousin. He bowed and walked out of the creek, into the clearing, put the cash collection in his pockets, and disappeared into heat waves the same as when he arrived.

The new man followed, but turned to Logan and looked into his eyes with a startling intensity and whispered. "You are a chosen one. Follow us on our journey. We'll be downtown tomorrow morning at 5:00 a.m. sharp when the Greyhound arrives." Then he followed the preacher.

The crowd gradually dissolved as the two boys watched.

"Bobby Ray, you wanna to do it?"

"What?"

"Leave Crossroads tomorrow! Like you always said you'd do."

"With this preacher? You lost your mind? We cain't leave Crossroads. It's home."

Logan patted his friend's back. "Bobby Ray, this our chance to leave this hellhole. Don't you feel God calling us?"

At 5:00 a.m. sharp, only one boy boarded the Greyhound with the men, a sack of clothes thrown over his back. "I'll write," he mouthed. Logan stared and waved out the bus's back window to his best friend until the town disappeared. Then he turned, squinted at the rising sun, took a deep breath, and smiled.

The Hush That Comes After
Karen Sundback

Jorge, being the newest rookie on the force, keeps his mouth shut and his eyes and ears open as he sits with the two other cops at the table.

"I ever tell you I was stationed at Edwards?" Mike surveys the restaurant.

Kevin says, "My dad was a contractor for the Air Force, so we lived close by in Lancaster. The sonic booms drove all of us nuts. But still, it was nice there."

Mike chuckles. "Oh yeah? Same with the wife. Barbara hated that noise, but liked the life there on the whole. I was no good in the Air Force. My size worked against me. You know, everyone's small in that branch of the military." He takes a sip of coffee.

Kevin smiles with the perfect dentist-made incisors of a former wrestler-turned-boxer. "Well, Mike, there's enough of you that everyone else is diminutive in comparison."

Mike responds, "So you guys are diminutive?"

The guffaws of Jorge and the others would raise the rafters if Ruby's restaurant had rafters.

Mike continues, "But those sonic booms were something, weren't they? They shake your house, your car, the ground you stand on. And afterward, dogs go bananas with the barking. And then, the hush. Came as sudden as the boom. Everything's calm. Like it's the only way a person can get peace in this world." Mike looks into his coffee as though reminiscing about good times.

Jorge and Kevin exchange an uncertain glance. For Jorge, the idea of sonic booms bringing peace on Earth escapes him, but Mike's a good cop and one of them, so he nods in agreement. "Sure, Mike."

Their food comes. Plates clunk. Flatware rattles.

Later in the restaurant's men's room, Jorge's radio crackles, "9L30, carjacking." He groans—*Is there no peace anywhere?*—and hurries as fast as he can.

In the dining area, the two others have cleared out. Outside, their squad cars are gone. When he slams his door shut, another voice comes on, "Child in stolen Malibu. License plate 9-Zulu-Oscar-Yankee-7-0-0." *Kevin's voice?*

Jorge hits the siren and lights.

"Main and Central." *Is Mike there too?*

Jorge guns his car and heads to the location of the carjacking. On Main, he spots the stolen Malibu driving the other way towards the outskirts of Salinas. The driver has slowed to a crawl to survey the inventory at Five Stars Dealership. As Jorge drives past, the perp's gaze doesn't waver from the rich possibilities at the car dealership. Turning off his siren and lights, Jorge makes a U-turn on Main and catches up with the perp. He calls it in, "9J30 following carjacked Malibu heading east on Main and 22nd. License 9-Zulu-Oscar-Yankee-7-0-0."

Keeping one car between, he follows. Jorge patiently watches the dawdling perpetrator bobbing his head back and forth as he cruises in the slow lane.

Jorge's parents have a small grocery store. While he was in Afghanistan, it was hit so often they came close to selling it. Now that he's back, his parents and their store will be safe. He'll make sure of that.

Three blocks ahead on Main Street, just after the freeway on-ramp, is a roadblock—an organized confusion of flashing blue and red lights. Jorge understands the tactic: divert the suspect onto the freeway, away from the city's population. He eases his car closer to the Malibu. The perp slams on his brakes. Does he see the roadblock? Jorge hits his siren and lights to jar the driver to his only open option: the freeway, then breathes a sigh of relief as the Malibu roars away towards Highway 101.

* * *

Up ahead, on either side of the on-ramp, cops wait with traffic spikes. Jorge waits until the spikes are thrown and cleared from the road. His patrol car blocks the on-ramp, keeping bystanders out of harm's way. He glances into the rearview mirror. A line of cars queues up behind him. When he was a kid, cops were heroes. Now, with the Defunding Police movement and the attacks on officers, he maintains his guard at all times. Just like in Afghanistan. His eyes pivot between the action in front and possible problems in back.

With its tires punctured by the spike strips, the Malibu slows, but continues on. As soon as the on-ramp is clear of the traffic spikes, Jorge follows, keeping his distance. Even though there are no roadside bombs along Highway 101 in California, no Taliban snipers with their sights set on Americans, the U.S. citizenry is well armed, so Jorge stays back beyond bullet range.

The spike strips have taken full effect. As the Malibu's engine growls, the tires flap and tear apart until the car runs on rims—their sparks light up the night. Crumpled and bent, they finally stop. Jorge anticipates the thief bailing, so he speeds up until he's close enough to catch him.

Jorge calms himself for the takedown. But for an instant, his world tilts. Blurs. Into Afghanistan forgettery. Stationed in an upstairs window. His spotter, Jackson, watched a Taliban operative … clutching a cell phone … watching an American installation. Jackson set up the scope, Jorge pulled the trigger. His first kill.

Jorge shakes his head to clear it and vows that the combat zone violence won't follow him home. He had his fill of killing in Afghanistan. His job here is to keep his family safe—without bloodshed.

The Malibu stops. The perp leaps out, but slows mid-air. A gun barrel rotates slowly towards Jorge. The windshield explodes. The man lurches backward. The night blurs as Jorge stares through his broken windshield.

The night is hushed, but for a baby's wail.

A breath. Two. Five more. Rubs his wedding ring to settle himself. And his world rights itself. Before him, his windshield is a messed-up starburst—a jagged hole surrounded by broken spirals—but no glass inside. His own shot must have broken it. Outside, he examines the man: no pulse. A 357 Magnum still clutched in his hand. No bullet casings. No traffic on the freeway. Opens the Malibu's backdoor. The unhurt baby gapes expectantly at Jorge. He sighs. Unless he picks up the kid pronto, it'll be screaming like the tires of a get-away car. Luckily, the car seat buckles are unfastened. Unluckily, the parent must have been shoved aside before the child could be untangled from the seat. Jorge picks up the infant. Finds an empty spot on his shoulder among his clutter of equipment and holds it close—soft and warm on a chilly night. Jorge walks the child away from the scene of horror to the back of his vehicle. Together they wait.

The comfort of pliable baby fat and the smell of innocence: Jorge knew them well. They were part of his childhood: waking to brilliant mornings; hot afternoons fishing with his ankles in the piss-warm waters of the Salinas River while his parents' store was closed for their afternoon siesta; and playing soccer with his friends in the cool evenings until it was too dark to see.

The absence of kid smells meant graduation from high school, the Marines, training, drills, Afghanistan, packing equipment, unpacking equipment, patrols, and no news from home—writing's not his parents' thing. He'd volunteered for sniper duty. A good job. Jackson and he spent their days holed up in buildings—Jackson, at the scope, Jorge cleaning his rifle and chewing on grit. Sand was everywhere. When Jackson found a target, Jorge took the shot. As soon as Jackson confirmed the kill, they got the hell outta there. At the beginning of the tour, Jorge felt blessed, protected by the righteous hand of justice and hidden in buildings from the watchful eye of the Taliban; he felt he was doing right, guarding America from extremists. He felt removed from Death. Jackson ordered it and confirmed it; Jorge only did what he was told. But then the dream came to invade his sleep. His victims' clothes littered the dusty streets. Furies filled the Afghan garments. They flew at him, covered him like sweat, and picked at him. Things were different after the dream. The war didn't seem as righteous. He didn't volunteer for a second tour.

Jorge rubs his wedding band to push away Afghanistan. The baby fusses, disturbed by an approaching cavalcade of flashing lights and wailing sirens. When the procession stops, men form a barricade in preparation of further firefights. He should tell them the gunfight is over, the perp is dead, but doesn't.

Khaki uniforms with assault weapons flow towards him like a muddy river, like what's welling up inside him. He turns away and focuses on comforting the child. As long as it doesn't cry, he can block everything out and hold it together. Kevin stands in front of him and shouts, "You okay?" After studying him, Kevin sighs. "Stay here. I'll get someone." He disappears into the turbulent darkness. Jorge is alone with the baby.

The infant … Jorge is ashamed he used a stranger's kid to enter his own forgettery, to explore his own humanity, to find a sanctuary. He blinks. They're here. Mike brings the parents. He blinks again. They're gone. He's alone.

Kevin returns, takes Jorge's gun, and says, "Come on. The commander wants to talk with you." Jorge follows. Commander Roberto Hernandez waits in the driver's seat of his clean, PD-issued vehicle.

"Get in, son."

Jorge sits in the passenger seat. While they drive, Hernandez asks, "You served in Afghanistan?"

Jorge nods, "Yes, sir."

"Desert Storm for me. Second one." As Jorge sits in the passenger seat, the commander speaks of sergeants and privates, and of the few good times of combat that seem sweeter and funnier now than they were then. Every time he turns right, he watches Jorge closely.

At the station, Jorge is led to the interrogation room, where two men wait for him. They both introduce themselves. Jorge has seen around the one with the notepad and pen but doesn't remember his name. The one with the briefcase is Jorge's lawyer.

The one with the pen says, "Mr. Jorge Garcia, I need to ask you some questions and get your statement. Mind if I record this session?"

When Jorge is done talking, they sit in silence. Jorge asks to see his statement. He scans it quickly, then reads it again, his finger following every word on the page. In his mind's eye, he compares it to reports written for him in Afghanistan that kept his record clean. When he's satisfied, he nods.

His lawyer gives him a grim smile.

Kevin drives him home. Jorge glances at his watch: 2:04 a.m. Neither of them spoke.

"Here you go." Kevin stops his car and scrutinizes Jorge. "You going to be okay? There's people you can talk to. You know, you should consider…"

"Yeah. Got my guys at the VA. This episode will give us a ton of fresh material to rake over. I'll tell 'em 'bout it, then we talk sports. Sports always saves the day."

Kevin blows out a laugh. "Sounds like it's under control, bro. Take care."

"Yeah. Thanks for the ride." Waves to Kevin.

Jorge slips between the sheets into a bed already warmed by Carla's body. Her pliant body cannot draw him deeply into his childhood like the babies could. But does he want that now? As far as he's concerned, she's enough.

Her voice is husky with sleep. "You're late. Everything okay?" She's calm because she hasn't heard the gunshot; her life is intact. The sheets rustle and she sits up. "What is it?" When he still doesn't answer, fear creeps into her voice. "Jorge! Tell me."

"I killed a man."

"No." She inhales deeply. "I'd hoped this day would never come." Her hand touches his face and neck. "What do we do?" Her fingers clutch his shoulder as though squeezing out the answers. "Your parents would know. Isn't your cousin Alfonso a lawyer?" Her words wash over him; his breath deepens; his shoulders relax. "We'll get the family together. I'll make tamales with the women. You play soccer with your cousins. We'll talk. Someone will know what to do."

Play soccer after I killed a man? He scoffs at the idea.

Her voice, scratchy with sleep. "We'll get enough people together until … we'll do the right thing … keep you safe and near us."

Carla's voice fades into the background as Jorge burrows into his place of safety, a protected partition in his mind where he can examine the repercussions of the killing. Could he end up in prison? Not likely, but who knows? Getting buried under mountains of bureaucracy is more likely. Keeping Afghanistan out of his head. He didn't recognize the deceased man, but he could still have family in town. How would he deal with them? He had dedicated his life to his country and keeping his family safe. What more could he have done?

The idea of playing soccer is ludicrous.

As laughable as a sonic boom bringing peace. Or a stranger's child bringing comfort. Or a woman's murmur pushing away Afghanistan.

A rising moon lights her face. She has fallen asleep. His eyes follow the curve of her honeyed cheek down to her rose-kissed lips. His worries exhaust him. He lets them go and wonders,

What's wrong with playing soccer?

Bread
Tice Swackhamer

"You must not repeat to anyone what I am about to tell you," my mother said. "You understand?" I sipped a pinot grigio in her kitchen as she chopped carrots for soup. "Your father had a phobia about bread."

"Bread?!"

"You don't remember?" She expertly rocked a chef's knife, making quick business of five carrots, then scraped them with the spine of the knife into a boiling pot of soup. "He would pitch a fit if he found the bread upside down in the breadbox."

I added an ice cube to my wine, assuming my mother wouldn't object since it was a twist top. "You know, I do remember an over-the-top moment with him over bread once. I had just made peanut butter toast. He spotted the loaf upside down next to me and yelled something about me being reckless, or careless, or something."

"That's nothing." She turned the burner down and started on the celery. "It was far worse than that."

I leaned over to sniff the pot. My mother put her hand on my chest. "No sniffing. No one wants your nose droppings in their soup."

I grabbed a saltine cracker to tide me over and leaned on the kitchen island. Of course, I should have known better than to come within three feet of her cooking.

"At first," she went on, "he would turn the bread right side up, but then that wasn't good enough anymore." The heat from the stove curled her bangs, a strand of which dangled above her right eye. Her floral apron had a tiny split seam on the pocket.

I pulled some brie from the refrigerator.

My mother shot me a disapproving look.

"I know, better with red, but I'm hungry."

"Pfft." She snorted. "Suit yourself."

I cut a few slices of baguette, stuffing the brie inside the small soft centers of the bread. Just as I was about to take my first bite, I shrunk under her stare. "What!"

"Your father." She sighed, adding the celery to the pot, then held up the serrated knife I had just been using. "He'd find the bread upside down and shred it in the garbage disposal. But first, he'd slice—no—hack at it. Like he was trying to kill it." She stabbed at the air to demonstrate.

"That's a bit dramatic."

"You think I'm exaggerating?" She folded the cheese into its wrapper and returned it to the fridge, a signal that I was done eating bread and brie.

"Aren't you?"

She shook her head. "You don't remember the incident then."

I suppressed a smile, because she now sounded quite serious.

"A freshly baked loaf had accidentally rolled off the counter onto the floor and landed upside down." She checked the soup, adjusting the flame to a simmer. "Your father stared at that bread like it was a demon. His hands gripped the counter." She grabbed the edge of the tile for effect. "He brought the loaf to the cutting board, contemplating his next move."

She placed two forks and chilled salads on the island, pulled up a stool, but stayed standing. "This time, instead of destroying it, your father waved his hands over the bread several times. He didn't know I was watching; I saw his mouth moving, as if he were casting a spell."

I served myself some Pinot Noir from an open bottle, because of course the white wine did not pair well with the cheese. My mother smirked, a tell-all, *I told you so* grin.

"It was the time our neighbor, Mr. Miller, was found dead in his home." I held a forkful of salad in mid-air, gaping at her. "The same night your father brought him that bread."

"What!" I nearly choked. "You're telling me that dad gifted him voodoo bread and the man died?!"

"That's right." She ate tiny little mouthfuls, pecking at her salad like a bird foraging.

"That's not possible." A cherry tomato nearly squirted out of my mouth. I pushed it back with a bare finger, struggling to remember that night, the sirens blaring so close to our house, the lights of the ambulance flashing. "I was ten, right?"

"Yes."

"And Mr. Miller had a wife and a boy about my age."

"That's right."

"So why didn't *they* die?"

She held up one finger to finish chewing. "Because he cursed the bread only for the father."

I stabbed at my salad. "And why would he do that, even if he could?"

"Because Mr. Miller poisoned Kayid."

"The wolf dog?"

"He was a German Shepard ... with *maybe* some wolf. Your father loved that dog. He took one look at him as a puppy and named him Kayid, 'the cunning one'."

"Everyone in the neighborhood was afraid of that dog. I was afraid of that dog." I noticed my pinot was already running low but knew it was too soon to pour more. "Kayid was poisoned?"

She got up to stir the soup, adding a pinch more Mrs. Dash, then sat back down. "When we were on vacation. Aunt Margaret was taking care of him and found him dead in the backyard. His dog dish had been laced with—something."

The salad dressing had accumulated at the bottom of my bowl. I wanted to slurp it up like I would at home but had lost my appetite. I picked up my dish and brought it to the sink. "Did anyone ever prove this?"

"Mr. Miller was a pharmacist."

"That doesn't mean he killed Kayid!"

"He knew how." She set her half-eaten salad to the side. "Who else would do that? He hated Kayid."

"This still doesn't explain how dad managed to kill one person when everyone must have eaten the same bread."

"Your father confessed it to me. He cursed the bread to harm only the person who had harmed Kayid. That night, when Mr. Miller died, he got his answer." She checked the soup again, this time turning it off and moving it to a cool burner.

"You believe this? This ... story." She didn't answer, instead ladling out the soup and placing a tray of saltines between us. "What was the official cause of death, anyway?"

"Heart attack. But it was no heart attack. No sir. Mrs. Miller said he was in perfect health. The man was forty-nine years old!"

It seemed pointless to mention that heart disease was the number one killer in America, and as I recall, Mr. Miller had a bit of a gut. This story reminded me of one of those tabloid headlines my mother liked to pick up at the checkout stand: "Man Gives Birth to Twins" or "100-year-old Grandmother Breaks Marathon Record." Besides, if anyone in the family had psychic powers, it was my mother, not Dad.

"I always thought you were the one with the—" I showed her my jazz hands. "—magic powers."

She snapped a saltine in half. "Why would you say that?"

"You know. The horse races—the way you'd always dream the night before and pick the winner." She stayed silent. "Come on. Don't pretend you don't know what I'm talking about."

"That?" She sipped her soup without making a sound. "That was nothing. A joke, really." Her mouth tightened. "If I had such skills, don't you think I would have bet more?"

It wasn't in my mother's nature to get defensive, so I decided to drop it.

"Have you told anyone else this 'Man Kills Neighbor with Bread' story?"

She dabbed her lips with a cloth napkin. "You mock me?"

"No. Absolutely not." I dropped a saltine cracker into my soup and waited for it to soften.

"I told you. No. I haven't told anyone this. And no one must ever know!" She studied me between spoonfuls of soup. "Why would you bring up the horse races?"

"No reason." I loved the flavor saltines added to soup, particularly since my mother moved away from salt to seasoning substitutes. Mrs. Dash, the senior citizen version of flavor, once all your tastebuds ceased to exist.

"The soup isn't salty enough for you?"

"See!" I laughed. "That's what I mean. I was just thinking—"

"I know."

I hated the way she could unnerve me like this. It wasn't powers. She just knew food—and me.

"You know, this isn't one of those tabloid stories you read about in *The Star*," she said. "I have better things to do." She cleared our bowls and started doing the dishes. "I wanted you to know because of how your father died."

"He ate his own bread?" I joked, but instantly regretted the comment. My father's death was no laughing matter.

"He was racked with guilt over what he did to Mr. Miller, to the family. That poor boy had to grow up without a father. It was disproportionate to what he had done to Kayid. Your father realized this, and it tormented him."

I grabbed a dishtowel and started drying. "Mom. You don't really believe that dad was able to kill a man with cursed bread?"

Her body stiffened. "It doesn't matter whether I believe it or not." She handed me a plate. "It's what your father believed. Bread became intolerable to him. He'd imagine homes with bread turned upside down, the careless way people brought about bad luck on themselves." She stopped washing, letting the warm water run over her hands. "He was going mad," she whispered, staring at the empty porcelain sink. "I had to help him. He—"

"Mom?" I shut the water off. "What do you mean you had to help him? The night he died—it was a heart attack—right?"

She reached into the cabinet for a large glass bowl and proceeded to transfer the soup into it. "Yes. Yes, of course it was a heart attack." She scraped the sides. "Just this one pot to clean and we're done."

"Why did you say that you wanted me to know because of how dad died?"

"You know they looked at me," she said. "The investigators. They thought I might have something to do with it."

My legs felt numb, but I kept standing. "I know. But that's common when a spouse dies. Especially how he was found with his head all bloodied."

"He hit the edge of the tub when he fell!"

The steam from the sink clouded the air.

"I know. I know." I pulled a fresh towel from the drawer to dry the pot. "That's what it said in the police report. They cleared you." I eyed her carefully. "Has something come up?"

"No."

My mother sponged off the countertops, coming across the bread and breadboard we had not yet put away. The bread was halfway on its side but had not rolled upside down. She recoiled, unwilling to touch it.

"I can put that away."

She grabbed my arm. "Don't touch it!"

"Mom, it's just bread."

"Stop! This is what I didn't want. For it to infect you, too. It's poison. A poison that gets in you, disturbs the cells."

"Mom, I'm fine. It's—"

She lunged at the bread, tore a piece off, then another and another. Sweat ran in thin lines down her cheeks, smearing her makeup. She approached the sink, shoving the broken pieces down the disposal, letting the water and grinder take care of the rest.

"There," she said to herself when the deed was done, breathing heavily. "There. That's good. That should take care of it." She gripped the counter, then started what looked like an incantation.

"Mom?"

"It's fine. Be quiet. Just be quiet."

She chanted with her eyes closed, "Repellum Omni Malus Spiritus." She waved a hand, motioning in circles three times over an empty sink.

I had never heard my mother utter a word in Latin outside of church. Her eyes seemed momentarily locked before returning to me. She gave me a shaky smile, then walked over to brush off the cutting board and slide it back into a corner.

"You know, I don't bake. But I do have ice cream," she offered as she headed for the freezer.

"Mom. What the—"

"It's fine." She returned her apron to a hook on the wall. "It's nothing. You're safe." She smiled, tilting her head to the side. "It's over."

No Walk in the Park
Charlotte Tressler

Patrice leaned forward, arms pumping, thighs burning, as she approached the summit of the first hill heading into Spring Lake Park. She had enough time to make it all the way around the lake and maybe grab a snack before picking up the twins. Then three whole hours before Mike got home, churning the atmosphere in the trailer into a storm with his nightly diatribe describing everything he'd suffered at the hands of passengers, motorists, or bureaucrats. Anyone who crossed his path was fair game.

"Patty? Patty, is that you?" called a voice from behind her.

Patrice cringed at the dreaded nickname. She turned and saw two women pushing strollers up the wide paved path, each with an Aussiedoodle alongside, hurrying to catch up.

"It's Patrice," she said automatically.

"See, I told you it was her!" the blonde said to the redhead triumphantly. Turning back to Patrice, she continued. "We saw you in the parking lot. Sandra thought you moved away after junior year, but I said, 'No, that's Patty! I'd know her anywhere!'"

"I've been right here in Santa Rosa." Patrice wondered how Kristen had recognized her. She'd worn a size seven in her teens; now she was lucky if she could squeeze into a twelve. And the highlighted hair she had painstakingly straightened every morning before school was now an unruly mass of mousy brown curls. They had gone to high school together, at least as long as Patrice had attended. While these two had been prepping for the senior year Winter Formal, Patrice had been in labor.

Kristen and Sandra stopped beside her, pulled Starbuck's iced coffees from their strollers' drink holders, and took long, noisy slurps. Patrice held her freebie water bottle, emblazoned with the logo for Merck's latest prescription flea and tick medicine, behind her.

"Come on," Kristen said. "I wanna keep my heart rate up. We can catch up while we walk."

Patrice had wanted to spend this morning alone, to walk and weigh her options, figure out what to tell Mike, but peer pressure compelled her to fall into step between the strollers, each occupied by a pink, sleeping infant. One for each of the pink lines on the test strip she'd buried in the bathroom trash this morning.

"How old are your babies?" she asked, grasping for something to say.

"They're both six months," Sandra replied. "Kristen and I were in labor at the same time. She had Natalie five hours before I had Austin. Do you have any kids?"

"Yeah, I have two … twins. Mark and Marie."

"Wow, twins!" Kristen gushed. "How old are they?"

"Fourteen."

"Wow," Kristen said again, huffing and puffing as she pushed her stroller up the hill.

They paused at the summit overlooking Spring Lake. Kayaks and paddleboats dotted the water, the shallows on the far side filled with small children wearing floaties, everyone drawn out by the warm spring day. The dogs sat, tongues lolling out the sides of their grinning mouths. Patrice reached down to pet them. One rolled over for a belly rub.

"Do you have any pets?" Sandra asked.

"My husband's allergic."

"How long have you been married?"

"Fourteen years."

"Oh … and what does he do?" Kristen asked.

"He's a CityBus driver."

"What about you? Do you work?"

"Yeah, at a veterinary clinic." Patrice didn't elaborate. She'd rather have them picture her as a technician or receptionist than the cage cleaning, floor mopping kennel person she'd been for years.

"Oh, that must be so fun, all the puppies and kittens!" Kristen gave the typical response of someone who's never worked in a veterinary practice.

"What about you, Kristen?" Patrice asked. "Do you have a job?"

"Obviously not." Kristen gestured toward her baby like a game show hostess displaying a prize showcase. "I mean, I could if I wanted to.

I finished my law degree, passed the bar exam. But David made partner at his firm, so there's really no need."

"What about you?" Patrice pinned Sandra with a stare.

"Me? Uh, no. I stay home with Austin."

"Did you get to go to college?" Patrice asked, tension rising in her throat.

"I studied Sociology at Stanford. That's where I met my husband. His name is Dallas."

"Dallas," Patrice repeated flatly. "What does he do?"

"He's a pediatrician."

"Uh-huh." Patrice rose from petting the designer dog, looking from one of her old friends to the other, eyes settling on Kristen. "Where do you live?"

"In a rental in Skyhawk right now," Kristen said. "We just bought a Victorian in the McDonald District, having it remodeled. The historical preservation people are making us jump through all sorts of hoops." She rolled her eyes. "I mean, it's my house. Shouldn't I be able to paint it any color I want? Hey, didn't you live on McDonald Drive? Are your folks still there?"

"As far as I know. I haven't seen them in almost ten years."

"Why so long?" Kristen's eyes widened.

"We had a falling out."

"Must've been a doozy. You know, I was always a little scared of your dad."

"So was I," Patrice muttered under her breath. "More than a little."

Kristen started down the path that circled the lake, tugging her dog's leash with a little more force than necessary. Sandra followed, looking back over her shoulder at Patrice. She smiled apologetically and made a beckoning motion with her hand. Patrice took too big a drink of water from her bottle, choking as half of it tried to go down her trachea. Water spewed out her mouth and nose, followed by most of the meager breakfast she'd choked down before driving the twins to school.

Kristen and Sandra hurried back up the slope and set the brakes on their strollers. They fluttered around her like a pair of startled hens, one second patting her on the back, the next offering her a baby wipe to clean up with. One of the dogs rushed in to gobble up the remains of Patrice's

Cinnamon Toast Crunch. Kristen dragged him to a nearby bench and tethered him there.

"Bring her over here, Sandra. She needs to sit down."

Patrice sat sandwiched between them and their pampered dogs. She considered the expensive strollers and all the other things Sandra and Kristen could provide for those babies. All the things her children had never had. Because she'd been stupid enough to be lured into a relationship with a thirty-two-year-old man when she was sixteen. She'd felt so grown-up. Now, with her daughter fast approaching the same age, she finally realized how young and gullible she had been.

She felt another wave of nausea coming on and pushed herself off the bench. She reached the far side of the path just in time to part ways with the rest of her cereal.

"Patrice," Sandra said hesitantly. "Are you pregnant?"

"I can't do it," Patrice whimpered.

One of the babies started crying, and Kristen rushed to its aid. Patrice stayed where she was, bent at the hips, hands braced on her knees.

"Can't do what?" Sandra kneeled beside her.

"I've been waiting so long to leave … looking for a decent job, waiting for the twins to graduate … and now, if I have another baby, I'll be right back where this whole mess started. I'll never get out!" She looked up at Kristen, bouncing fat little red-haired Natalie, and tasted a bitterness far stronger than the bile coating her mouth. "I should be walking around the lake with my first baby, like you. *After* college, *after* marriage, not the other way around. But no, I had to get knocked up by some bus driver twice my age and have twins—goddamn twins—when I was seventeen. Now I live in a double-wide trailer on the wrong side of town, drive a car that's older than I am, and I'm pregnant again! I'm so stupid!"

"Oh, honey. Let's sit down." Sandra put her arm around Patrice's shoulders and tried to steer her back to the bench.

"No, I need to keep moving." Patrice set off down the path. Sandra and Kristen scurried after her, Kristen steering her stroller one-handed with Natalie balanced on her hip.

"Wait up, Patrice." Sandra caught up with her. "What can we do to help?"

"Why would you want to?"

"Why wouldn't I? We were close friends. I still care about you. That hasn't changed."

"Nothing will ever change for me. Not if I don't do something."

"Wait," Kristen said, pulling up alongside Patrice. "You're not saying what I think you're saying, are you?"

"What if I am?"

"Look at this baby." Kristen held Natalie up for display. "She's a gift from God. They all are. How can you possibly think about getting an abortion?" She whispered the word the way some people whisper "cancer." She returned Natalie to her stroller with a bottle.

"Oh, get off your soapbox, Kristen," Sandra snapped. "You have no idea what she's going through." She turned to Patrice. "Ignore her. She's been influenced by her Southern Baptist in-laws."

"My father grew up Southern Baptist," Patrice said. "He kicked me out when I got pregnant."

"Was that your big falling out?"

"First of many. The last was when I asked him to help me leave Mike. The twins were just toddlers. Dad said he wasn't running a charity. His last words to me were, 'You made your bed, now lay in it.'"

"*Lie* in it," Kristen said.

"Don't you think I know that?" Patrice spat. "It was a direct quote."

"You always were good at English," Sandra said, squeezing Patrice's arm. "I guess you haven't told your husband about this new development?"

"Ha, no. He sides with my father and Kristen on this issue."

They walked by the boat dock, through a gaggle of belligerent geese that drove the dogs wild, and past a stand of cattails in the shallows, each stem occupied by a twitterpated redwing blackbird. Sandra slowed as they neared the path leading back to the parking lot.

"Listen, I want to help you if I can. You want to get a coffee?"

"I don't know…"

"I'm not going," Kristen said. "I won't be a part of murder."

"Then, yes," Patrice told Sandra. "I'll go."

They finished the walk in an uncomfortable silence broken only by the occasional "on your left" of a passing cyclist. Back at the parking lot,

Sandra handed her leash off to Kristen with a dismissive "see you around." Kristen stalked off with both.

"That's not your dog?" Patrice asked.

"No, I just take one off her hands when we're out walking."

"Good. I can't stand doodles. Two-thousand dollar mutts."

"Exactly," Sandra said. "Listen, don't worry about Kristen. We bumped into each other at a mommy-and-me playgroup and she just glommed onto me, started calling me all the time. We hadn't seen each other since high school, either; not until three months ago."

Sandra led the way to the café across the street. After they placed their orders, she got right down to business. "Now, what can I do to help you?"

"I feel weird talking about this in front of your baby." Patrice glanced uncomfortably at Austin, propped up in a highchair, shaking a rattle at her in judgment.

"Don't worry about him. He won't tell anybody."

Patrice let out a laugh and a long breath, releasing some of the tension she'd been carrying in her chest. As much as she'd wanted to be alone today, Sandra made her realize how isolated she'd been. The other moms at school were too much older. She worked behind the scenes at the clinic, with little interaction with clients or other staff members. Her husband treated her as if she were the oldest of his three children instead of the mother of their two, except in the bedroom, where he treated her like a tramp.

"Seriously, Patrice, what can I do? I can give you a ride to and from your appointment, if that's what you decide to do."

"But what do I do after that? If I do that? What if I can't go through with it?" Patrice sipped her ginger ale. She considered the hills across the street, the grass bleached out by the noonday sun. "I should've left a long time ago, but I had no place to go."

"Dallas and I can help you find a place, no matter what you decide."

"I'll lose my health insurance if I get a divorce."

"Don't let that stop you. There are lots of resources out there: healthcare subsidies, food stamps, WIC, rental assistance. You could even get grants for college classes."

"I'd have to get my GED first."

"Then you'll do that first." Sandra made it sound so easy.

Austin dropped his rattle. He looked at Patrice, lower lip quivering, and raised his arms.

"Go ahead," Sandra said. "He likes you."

Patrice stood and lifted him from the highchair. He nestled his cheek against her collarbone. She breathed in his baby scent, absorbed the warmth of his soft body, and felt a visceral tug deep inside her.

She couldn't bring another child into that crushing double-wide squalor. It wouldn't be fair to either of them. She wanted a better future for the children she had now, not to mention herself. But here, now, overwhelmed by indecision and doubt, she did not know what to do. No matter what she decided, she'd be making a sacrifice. No matter which path she chose, she'd be dogged by a shadow of regret.

Patrice nuzzled Austin's downy hair and inhaled. He had grown drowsy, and rested a hand on her shoulder, breathed his warm, milky breath against her neck. Without realizing it, she had instinctively been jiggling and swaying since she picked him up, just as she had with the twins when they were babies, and lulled him to sleep.

Perhaps she was seeing this from too narrow a perspective. Maybe there was a gray area between the black of staying with Mike and having this baby and the white of getting an abortion and leaving him. If what Sandra said was true, she and the twins could move out before they graduated. She felt foolish for not having looked into it before.

"Tell me more about those resources," she said, looking down at Sandra. "Maybe I can do this."

Dust Country
M. Golda Turner

A dot in the distance represented the home of their nearest neighbor in Stephens County. Bertha gazed at it out the window over the kitchen basin. Her hands steadied baby Verona, who kicked and hit at the bathwater, while a gentle wind blew in the sweetness of button bush flowers. Since late spring, she'd taken to sprinkling water on them to keep them alive after Sam left to work the fields in the morning.

A glance at straight rows of crops on the land gave her a shiver, even in the afternoon heat. Like the yields going seven years back to the summer of 1930, the wheat blended too much with the parched ground. All around the county the drought, like the Great War of her childhood and the ongoing Depression, clouded conversations of farmers and city folk alike. It seemed like everyone, especially politicians, scrambled for agrarian solutions, resorting to prayer when none came. Just the same, people on the radio kept calling Oklahoma a Dust Bowl. Bertha paid close attention to all of this, though many believed these problems weren't the concerns of women.

Their older daughter Peggy played off to the side in the parlor. At two, she often pattered down the hall and into the bedrooms of the small house, exploring every cubbyhole and corner. Other times, like now, she entertained herself quite well in one place while Bertha did household chores.

A warmth spread through her, grateful for their strong, healthy children, especially during these times. It would help if they ever had to move to California like so many farmers. Having resided nearabout the city of Duncan every bit of her twenty-six years, she sometimes daydreamed over the possibility of relocating there and exploring its beaches and national parks. Though some of those who'd left had written it was not the promised land they'd expected.

One day she'd brought up the subject with Sam. "If the crops fail again this year, Edith and her husband are leaving Oklahoma. In fact, it wouldn't surprise me if half my family up and left. They've all been struggling like us and sayin' there's lots of field work in California's Central Valley."

"What about those people you told me about that are livin' in cars or tents over there?" he'd asked.

"I'm sure it's only temporary. At least they've got work and food. I don't want to start over either, but——"

"You ain't never left this state, but I did, when I was sixteen. I jumped the railcars with the hobos all the way to Mississippi and worked there for two years. It was fine for me to rough it, but I tell you what, it's a whole 'nother story to take little ones half way across the country. Don't forget, your sister's kids are older than ours."

Bertha had quieted. Edith's youngest would start first grade soon and already knew how to wash dishes on her own, whereas Peggy and Verona had to be watched constantly. Besides that, within her extended family, some young ones had already been lost to fires, childbirth, disease, and accident. A move to California might involve even more risk. But she still wondered whether it would be worse if they stayed in Oklahoma and lost their home and livelihood.

Despite Sam's resistance, she had continued to sprinkle him with updates about the drought she'd heard from other watchful women, shortwave radio broadcasts, and *The Duncan Banner* newspaper. Her husband knew what was going on, but he remained of a mind to stay in Oklahoma and keep trying. To her, moving at some point seemed inevitable, each year worse than the last. Their opinions differed, but Sam encouraged her reports, so she kept it up. He'd give her a glance when menfolk recounted facts that she'd already given him.

It occurred to her that Peggy had become as quiet as a bunny hopping through a cornfield. Bertha turned her head and saw Peggy's hand-sewn rag doll and blocks strewn around the floor, but no child. *That girl must have wandered down the hall again,* she thought.

"Peggy," she called out while taking a washrag to the baby's shoulders and neck.

But there were no tapping footsteps or babble of words in response, sounds that brought smiles to Bertha on the stillest of days. Only splashing bathwater echoed empty through the room. She lifted Verona from the sink and wrapped her in a towel. Cradling the baby against her chest, she walked the entire house, checking each room, behind and underneath the beds and chairs. A sudden sharp wind belted through the kid's bedroom window. She turned her back toward it to shield Verona from any incoming grit. Peggy on her mind, she didn't think to close it and walked away.

Back in the sitting room, she didn't know where to look next. She paced the floor, bouncing and shushing the baby, even though Verona wasn't fussy. The hum of blustering air engulfed them and vibrated in Bertha's ears.

The front door was propped open with its screen shut. With a bang, a gust of wind hit the screen door against its frame. It hadn't occurred to her the latch might not be secured, that Peggy might have wandered outside. Bertha shook her head. *I forgot to hook the dang thing when I brought in the eggs this morning.* She swiftly set bundled-up Verona on her back on the floor, so the infant wouldn't roll off anything, and closed the kitchen window to keep the dust out. There was no time to worry about a mess in the bedrooms with Peggy outside and a windstorm on the rise.

She pulled the front door shut, let the screen close behind her, and squinted at the road, desolate and far from the house. There was no sign of Peggy's bright blue shirt amid the swirling dirt. When she stepped off the porch, the wind flapped the hem of her dress and gusted through her wavy red hair. Circling the yard, she scanned the surrounding wheat fields, hands cupped around her eyes to protect them from flying soil. The barn and chicken coops remained closed off. There was no sign of her daughter.

"Peggy! Peggy!" Bertha's hollering seemed hushed by the harsh gales.

Then a horrible thought crossed her mind. She ran over to a small opening into the crawl space under the house. Peggy's giggles, like a sharp roll of thunder, startled her to the ground. On hands and knees, Bertha ignored the arid dirt that burned her skin as she peered inside. Crawl marks bordered by torn cobwebs forged a path into the dark underbelly. They had to be Peggy's. Snakes and spiders holed up in the shadows during the day to keep cool, and her daughter was in there with them. A sloughed snake skin rolled by, making her shudder.

The wind suddenly died down to a light breeze, surprising Bertha and settling the dust. But that provided little relief. More laughter erupted, not filtered by the wind this time.

Frightened, she blurted out, "Peggy Jo, you come out of there. You hear me?"

The giggles stopped.

Lord, help me. Bertha drew in a deep breath and slowly let it out. She knew she mustn't scare her daughter. "Crawl back to the light, honey. You need to come here to Mama."

Silence. Her Peggy had a stubborn streak. Minutes passed while beads of sweat and silt crept into her eyes, making her blink. She used her dress to blot them away. *What can I do?* There was no way Bertha could fit through the passageway. If Sam were home, he'd probably tear the boards off, which would likely agitate every creature down there. But still, she wished he were there to help. Her only hope was that the child would somehow come to her.

Bertha's narrowed eyes softened. Peggy loved hard-boiled eggs. She raced inside and gathered a fresh one from the wood-paneled icebox, almost dropping it in the hurry. *Uncooked will have to do.* A side glance revealed a bare-naked Verona, scooching on her tummy toward her sister's toys. Bertha threw a hand to her forehead. She rushed to Verona, rolled her over, and tucked her inside the towel again.

Outside, she dashed back to the cursed gap and crouched down, placing the egg next to it. "Peggy, I brought you an egg. It's right over here."

Time dragged on as slowly and intensely as labor pains while she stared at the hole, ready to pounce. It seemed like forever before a little hand whipped out and grabbed the bait. She latched onto Peggy's arm just as quick and dragged her from the gritty tomb.

Peggy screeched in her little girl voice, "No, Mama," and squirmed in protest while being brushed off and checked for bites. The egg broke during the tussle and landed in the dirt. Peggy stared at it with pouted lips and burst into tears.

Back in the house amid Peggy's whimpers, Bertha wiped the yolky mess from her hand and Peggy's leg at the sink. She picked up Verona too, and soothed her daughters in the rocking chair until Peggy settled down. She put sleepy Verona down for a nap, closed the open windows, and started a couple of eggs to boil. She would sweep and dust later. Once Peggy was bathed and dressed in her other set of play clothes,

Bertha gave her a long hug, a peck on the cheek, and a hard-boiled egg with a pinch of salt.

Peggy used both hands to hold the egg high and then yanked it back to her chest, eyeing her mom. "My egg, Mama."

Bertha turned away to hide her smile. Her daughter was still upset that the other one had been taken from her earlier. That's how it was when someone lost something they loved.

She closed her eyes. What she saw in Peggy was what had nudged at her all these years. Bertha was as rooted to Oklahoma as her button bush to its bed of soil. Maybe she and Sam were closer in their views on leaving than she'd wanted to admit.

Their front door remained closed until Sam came home from working in a neighbor's field. Bertha stopped sweeping, met him on the porch, and told him about Peggy's adventure. They smiled and laughed about it before Sam, still wearing his dusty overalls and sweat-grazed shirt, lumbered off to get a board, a hammer, and some nails.

Bertha stayed and leaned against the house for a few minutes. Her eyes moistened as she gazed across their wasting homeland. Then she stood straight, took a long breath, and lifted her face west, toward California.

The Thing with Feathers
Bill VanPatten

I drum my fingers on the arm of the chair as the psychologist stares at me. He always does this—asks a question, then waits for me to say something. I stare back. His eyes aren't sexy. They're the color of fudge— or shit, if I think about it—and I wish they were blue. Blue like the ocean, blue like a sapphire, blue like Jake's eyes. I used to get lost in those eyes. *Those* were sexy eyes.

In the background, a clock ticks softly. The psychologist keeps one of those old-fashioned ones on his desk. Big hand and little hand slowly sweeping around to remind us we have an hour together—an hour for him to ask questions and for me not to answer them. On occasion, I throw him a bone. Like the time he asked me if I missed Jake.

"What do you think?" I said. "Of course I do."

"You do?"

I twisted in the oversized leather chair. "I loved him."

"What was it like, loving him?"

A pervy question. I narrowed my eyes as I wondered what he really wanted to know. What the sex was like? What I felt in my heart? In my gut? Or was he a pervert, just interested in teenagers getting it on, so he could jack off later when he was alone?

"Don't you think that's a bit personal?" I asked.

"You don't like talking about such things?"

That was enough. I wasn't going to give him anything else.

This is our fourth session. I'm not crazy. I don't need a shrink. I just need to be left alone. I know about grief. I got the lecture from the doctor in the hospital. The five stages, blah, blah, blah, how people need to work through them, blah, blah, blah. I don't want to move on. If I let go of how I feel, I'll let go of Jake.

I look past the psychologist, pretending to study the array of books on the wall-to-wall wood shelf behind his desk. I think he has all those volumes on display to show people how smart he is, how much he's read, how much he knows. But my focus isn't on any title. I'm conjuring Jake, thinking about the time we met. He'd walked into Mr. Hanson's English

3 class five minutes late, carrying a note. Mr. Hanson read it, then addressed the class.

"Everyone, this is Jake Manners. He's transferring to our school." He motioned for Jake to take a seat. There was an empty desk next to mine, and my heart rate ticked up when he slid into the chair. He looked at me and smiled, flashing those gem-like eyes, his face framed by blond hair that curled around his ears and swept across his forehead. I smiled back, sure that I was blushing at the same time.

"Jake," Mr. Hanson said, walking toward him, "we're reading Emily Dickinson this week." He handed him a copy of our textbook, opened to the poem for the day.

"'Hope is the thing with feathers,'" Mr. Hanson said as he returned to the front of the class, "'that perches in the soul.' What do you think Dickinson is saying in this poem?"

There was a moment of silence. Then Jake raised his hand.

"Yes?" Mr. Hanson said.

All eyes turned toward the new kid. How daring! To be new and to answer a question right away when you weren't even called on.

Jake cleared his throat. "It's a metaphor."

"Go on."

"Hope doesn't really have feathers. And it's not really a bird. It's this thing that lives inside us, like we're the cage and we won't let it go." He paused, then looked up at the ceiling. It was clear to me he had more to say. Maybe he was thinking of the right words. "It flutters around, always with us. It never leaves. Without hope, what are we?"

"Very interesting, Jake." Mr. Hanson surveyed the room. "What do you all think about what Jake just said?"

All I could do was turn and look at him. He turned at the same time, his gaze meeting mine. I wanted to dive into those eyes, become part of him, swim forever in his soul.

* * *

"Aaron."

Pause.

"Aaron."

I blink several times, then focus my attention on the psychologist.

"Where is your mind right now?" he asks.

I shrug.

"Were you thinking about him?"

"Maybe."

The psychologist tilts his head. "You can't stay locked up forever."

I want to say *Fuck you*, but instead I say, "Hope is the thing with feathers."

"Excuse me?"

I pull one side of my mouth up, creating something between a smile and a smirk. "Emily Dickinson."

The psychologist clasps his hands. "I know. I've read that poem. I'm wondering why you quoted the first line."

I shrug again. He continues to study me. Then he says, "Does that poem have something to do with Jake?"

"Stop prying!"

I immediately regret the outburst. I know he'll seize on it, want to ask me why I'm angry. Am I angry? Shit yeah. The second stage of grief, right? I look down at my wrist. At the hospital, they said the scar would be permanent. I was angry then, that night. I was so pissed off I grabbed a kitchen knife on impulse. It wasn't particularly sharp, and it hurt like hell.

"A souvenir?"

"Huh?" I say, directing my attention to the psychologist.

He juts with his chin toward my wrist. *Oh*, I think, *yeah. One fucking hell of a souvenir.* What a stupid thing to call the scar. I nod to let him know I registered what he said. I pull the sleeve of my shirt down over my wrist. Out of sight, out of mind. He jots something down in his notebook, then he looks up at me.

"Hope is the thing with feathers," he says.

I nod again.

"Why is that significant?"

I remain silent. The office dissolves, replaced by an image of Jake and me in his bedroom. We'd just kissed for the first time. His tongue was hot on mine. Our arms were wrapped around each other, me gripping as tight as I could, not wanting to let go, wanting to meld with him. I wanted there to be no more me and no more him, just us. One entity. I felt a stirring in my groin. I was sixteen and no stranger to erections. But that heat, that electric pulse, was new—like an explosion was welling up inside and traveling to my dick. He pulled back, probably for a breath. As he held me, he said, "You are the thing with feathers."

"What?"

He rested his forehead on mine and smiled slightly. "You. You are hope. The thing with feathers."

"I'm hope?"

He smiled and nodded. "You give me hope."

"I do?"

"Yeah," he said. "I didn't think I'd ever meet anyone like me. And my parents…"

I furrowed my brow. "What about them?"

"I can't talk to them. Can't tell them … about me … about us."

This was small-town Central California, not San Francisco, not Los Angeles. I understood. Jake was the younger of two boys—his brother a macho football player in college. On his front lawn was a large wooden crucifix. He had to hold it inside. He would be a disappointment, a sinner that needed saving—the subject of whispered voices.

I wanted to cry. Instead, I grabbed his face and pulled him in again for a kiss as I pressed my body against him. We fell onto the bed, legs intertwined. I emptied my mind of thoughts, purged the sorrow from my heart. I was pure, raw elation. I was the thing with feathers.

* * *

"Aaron, you keep drifting."

The psychologist is studying me again. Tick. Tick. Tick. I glance at the clock. How slow the one hand moves, like it doesn't really want to mark the passage of time, forced to do some job when it wishes it were elsewhere.

"So what? You have somewhere else to go?" It's a smart-ass remark, but I don't care.

"I'm hoping you'll tell me more about Jake."

I can tell by his voice and his look he means well. But he gets paid to act that way—speak in a soothing tone, not show what he's thinking, show concern from time to time. I'm not giving in, though. I need to hold on, not let anyone take my feelings away.

One day, me and Jake were at Pablo's, a local place. Kind of a hole in the wall. We were sharing a plate of nachos on their outside patio. I laughed at the string of cheese hanging from his lip. He wiped, then grinned.

"Is it gone?"

I smiled. "Yeah. But I bet you'll do it again."

He reached over and punched me in the shoulder. I chuckled, then before I could stop myself, the words tumbled out.

"I love you."

He looked at me, those blue eyes wide, sparkling like two gems.

"I love you, too," he finally said.

We were kids. Yet, we knew what love was. We felt it, deep within us. Who says teenagers can't know real love? It coursed through my veins, mixed with my blood, fed my heart. I felt my eyes moisten and saw that Jake, too, was tearing up. He pulled the back of his hand across his eyes, then offered a slight smile.

From that day on, we spent our afternoons together. He told his parents I was his study partner. They accepted that story with a simple, "That's great, honey. Nice to meet you, Aaron." My own parents didn't suspect, didn't care. They both worked, enjoyed their cocktails when they got home. They said they were glad I had a friend and was spending less time alone than I normally did. I guess I was less for them to worry about. Occasionally, me and Jake spent the night together—at my house, of course. We learned to love in silence. No girlish giggles, no cries of passion, not even soft moans.

A quiet love. The way he needed it. A secret.

* * *

I look at the clock. Tick, tick, tick. The psychologist must like that sound, helps him measure the time. Maybe he, too, gets fed up with these sessions and can barely wait until the big hand lands on the eleven.

"We only have a few minutes left," he says. He leans forward. "I'm not sure we're getting anywhere."

I pull my mouth into a sneer. "There's nowhere to get to."

He tilts his head. "What do you mean?"

He knows what I mean. Why does he want me to say it? When I don't respond, he sits back, studies me for a minute.

"You tried to kill yourself. Your parents, me, your teachers—everyone wants to keep you around."

"Where was everyone when Jake hanged himself?" The words slither out of my mouth.

"You're angry that no one was there for him."

No, I think. *I'm angry because I wasn't there for him. I'm angry because I was so caught up in being in love I never understood what was really in his head. I was supposed to be his hope, his thing with feathers. But in the end, I wasn't enough. In the end, I was nothing.*

I don't say anything. I just stare at the psychologist. Does he have kids? Any of them my age? Does he get what it's like to be sixteen years old in this town? What would he do if one of his kids was gay? Be a psychologist or be a dad? Maybe both.

The clock chimes. When I look at him, he's been studying me. I say nothing.

"As usual, I need to ask if you're taking your meds," he says.

"Yeah."

"Do you think they're helping?"

"Define help."

I don't tell him it's still hard for me to sleep. That I cry at night alone in my room. That my parents have given up on me and don't even check in on me anymore at bedtime. That's when the crying stops. I lie there staring at the ceiling, the vision of Jake dangling from a rafter in his garage. That's when I dream of sneaking down into the kitchen and grabbing another knife. A really sharp one.

Where is my thing with feathers?

The Fist
Marilyn Wolters

I still can't say his name.

It was a day like every other, or so I thought. The fist that had nearly punched my stomach that morning shadowed my thoughts, haunted my entire day, threatened the edges of workday conversations, hid behind the computer screen that begged my attention. It grew larger as the day went on and, as every other day, during my drive home, it engulfed me with its giant warning.

When I pulled into the driveway, the garage door was open. Cerise was inside, piling books from boxes.

"I know there's one here that's just right for him," she said as I approached.

"Waste of time! You and your self-help books. They've always been useless, just like everything else we've tried."

"You have a better idea?" Her voice was sharp.

"He won't read it."

"You don't understand. He's going through something hard, something he can't talk about. We need to reach his depths—Yes. Here's the book I got from my sister. She said it helped Jerome so much. There's a chapter inside that's perfect." She shoved the book toward me.

I pushed it away. "He's not Jerome."

"No, but he's at the same point in his life as Jerome was before he turned his life around. We only have one son, and we have to keep reminding him how much we're here for him."

She always sounded so earnest, mouthing all the clichés. It didn't help. She thought she was prepared. Neither of us had a clue.

I followed her out of the garage and into the house. How could she always be so perky?

My armchair awaited me in my reading corner. I held up a newspaper to block my view, but it wasn't long before Cerise tugged on the page.

"I read the whole chapter to him! He kept on painting, acting as if he was ignoring me, but you know how he is."

Not really, I thought.

"I know he was listening. It was written for teenagers. Just what he needs. I left it in his room. Maybe he'll glance at it."

He. Him. She hardly ever said his name.

Neither did I. Even then.

"Did you ask him how his day went?"

"No. It's better for us not to hear all the negatives. If there are problems, the school will call. But you should talk to him. And show how much you care. After all, you're his father. And I'm leaving. It's your turn." She tossed her head to shake off anything from our son that may have stuck to her. By then her lips had curved into her false smile. "I'm going to pick up some groceries."

She grabbed her purse and keys and twirled out the door, dancing in liberation, reminding me of the dancing we used to do even after he was born. He didn't frighten babysitters in those days. The fierceness was something that grew like a tumor, starting as a rough spot.

Little things. At first, maybe one meltdown a week. The eggs not cooked right. A missing sock. And then it was more, until it was almost everything that didn't match his ideal.

I heard her start the car. It would be a while. She'd run into somebody and then think of someplace else she had to go. The problem with taking turns is that half the turns were mine.

I ambled into the kitchen and made myself a cup of coffee, convinced that strength meant a pounding heart and a clenched head.

Finally, I was ready. I tiptoed to his door, which I had adjusted so it didn't fit tight. I looked through the sliver of opening. He sat at his easel.

I knocked. There was no response, so I knocked again.

"I know you're there," I said. "I'm coming in to say hello." As always, the caffeine emboldened me. I swung open the door.

"Come in. I have no choice. I'm a prisoner here."

Instead of looking up as I entered, he continued the furied swipes at his canvas. We hoped to give his hands another way to attack the world, so had filled his room with acrylic paint tubes and brushes. He spent the afternoons pushing paint until he was ready to set his latest creation down next to the one from the day before. All of them had the same images—birds caught in funnel clouds and trees tossed on the ground.

But each painting was darker than the last. The one he was working on now was almost all black. I struggled to see any images at all.

"How was school today?" I asked, trying to sound casual.

No answer.

"How's your painting going?" I tried again.

This time a shrug.

When he rose from his easel, I could see the hole in the wall.

"Mom said you might need some work here." Actually, she hadn't said that, but that was the line I used every day to ease into wall repair. I pulled my tape measure, a pencil, and a piece of paper from my pocket.

"Poor walls," I said. "What did they do to deserve this?"

Silence.

I took a deep breath and then said, "Okay. Come on. Tell me. Anybody or anything you're mad about?"

He looked at me as if I had just offered him a drink of sewage.

"Got to go get some things. I'll be back soon." It was a relief to have an easy goal.

I returned a bit later with a patch, a knife, mud, and tape. Cerise and I had had enough foresight to paint the walls of his room sheetrock white.

"You give me purpose and excitement," I said. It was both sarcastic and true. Before he was born, I had felt burdened by a horrible boredom. Each day was as dull as the last and even weekends brought little relief. I missed that boredom terribly.

"You give me a headache," he said.

"How's that?" I asked.

Silence.

"So, how *are* you doing?" I was trying hard to sound as if there wasn't adrenaline rushing through my body.

He had moved to his bed and opened a notebook in which he was writing. His poems frightened me. They were darker than his paintings. His teachers said he was talented, but when I read them, I felt the finger of the fist pointing at me. I had to lighten the mood.

"Homework? Good to see." I spoke as I cut and taped. "I had a hard day at work. A lot of people out today. Had to cover for them."

He continued writing without looking up. I continued talking. Finally, the job was done. He seemed calmer now. Maybe he had left some rage on the pages of his book.

"Where's your desk?" I asked. Getting no response, I searched the corners of the room and found he had disassembled it. The monster had taken me two miserable days to put together, with pieces missing or not fitting as described. Fortunately, it didn't look like he had broken anything. I knew what I would be doing that evening.

I returned the tools to the garage and looked at my watch. Cerise would be gone at least another hour. I longed for a walk. He was sixteen, old enough to be left alone for thirty minutes. Why did we need to watch him so closely? He rarely left his room. He would assume I was still around, reading in my corner or looking for something to eat.

I put on a jacket for the cool evening air and sneaked out through the garage. I would be back before he noticed.

Outside, daylight was fading on a dazzling spring evening. Flowers, grass. I inhaled the whole juicy stew of new life emerging. Just a quick walk around the block, I promised myself. But one block hardly seemed enough, so I added a few more in each direction. The sound of sirens pierced my reverie, and I realized my half-hour walk was turning into something longer. I raced home to be there before Cerise.

When I approached my block, I saw the flames. A fire engine was already there and hoses were pouring water on my house. I saw the stretcher and screamed.

* * *

Days later, Cerise found a page from one of his notebooks lying on the ground. Her voice quivered as she read aloud. "'I have a crack deep in my body that sets off tremors. It's like a fault deep in the earth, part of who I am. The tremors can be sudden or slow. A house that always felt tight and secure can splinter. Or burst into flames.'"

* * *

We rebuilt the damaged part of the house. A lot of the other rooms hadn't fared too badly. The desk had provided plenty of fuel and his art paper had made excellent kindling. We painted the rebuilt room a light tan and gave away everything of his that was left. I gave away my sheetrock tools.

The notebook whose missing page we had found, perhaps the notebook I saw him using that day, lay hidden deep within a shrub. I was with Cerise when she pulled it out. She has since studied every word on every page. It's always in her hand when she visits from her new home about a mile away, but I refuse to read it. I tell her I'm not yet ready.

She says we had bad luck, that we had no control over what came out of the genetic whirlwind, that we did our best, a very weak argument since my best amounted to very little. She says there was a hurtling train and we couldn't stop it. Even if we had stood on the tracks, it would have taken us down too.

When she's ready to leave, she lowers her voice and, with a show of empathy, tells me it's time to move on. I imagine the new stack of self-help books by her bedside.

Once again, every day is dull, but a different kind of dull because I have swallowed the fist. It resides in my stomach and punches me regularly. I am waiting for the fist to crack something inside and for the tremors to start, so meanwhile, I avoid anyone I can. I only go out to work. I've tried taking a walk at dusk, but every house light, every streetlight, reminds me of him. Maybe someday I'll stop thinking about that last day. How sweet the air smelled until I caught the acrid scent of fire. And understood what was burning.

Sandblaster Man
Jaime Zukowski

Tom wanted to toss the damn phone. Every time he picked up, it was a call he didn't need—a creditor, his brother Ned, his mother calling from Florida with her never-ending questions. Still, he couldn't do without it, cut off his link with the outside world. There was always hope a call for a job could change his mood or be some voice he wanted to hear.

Like Gina's? Ha!

More scam. He stood in front of the smudged bathroom mirror and examined his thirty-nine-year-old face. Bloodshot blue eyes, no expression. He rubbed the week-old beard, now getting really scratchy. Why shave? He didn't have to do anything for anybody, least of all his customers, who couldn't care less. Didn't need to hear anybody say he was drinking too much, that he should eat better, *yeah, yeah, yeah*. Whether he was hungry or tired, he never could tell. Just a rodent going round and round in the same old cage. He hardly used the futon and often stayed all night on the pleather La-Z-Boy he dragged in from the street. That was his own choice. Gina took the decent furniture to her new place. "Take it all," he'd told her. "You picked it out."

I live in a pigsty. He walked around the pile of dirty clothes on the floor. Sculpture almost, the way his stuff dried stiff after a power-washing job. *Maybe I like this look.* He turned to the humming refrigerator to get a cold one. "A person's supposed to keep hydrated," his mother reminded every time the national news reported a heat wave up north. Tom put on the TV and didn't look at it.

He shook his head over Ned's "generous" job offer. *Selling appliances again?* He'd done that already with his brother when their uncle ran the shop. No way would he work for somebody else again. He was independent now, a self-made man, no one looking over his shoulder.

Me against the world.

Nothing wrong with what he did to pay the rent. There would always be plenty of independent work in the city. Plus, a guy could see some kind of progress with clean-up—sandblasting, power-washing. He had decent equipment now. You started a job in the morning and had something to show for it at the end of the day. *Pressing buttons on a cash register?*

No, thanks!

Why was his brother butting in on his life again? And did he always have to ask about Gina? *We were together. She left. Life happens.* At least they didn't make the mistake of getting married, go for the "happy family," follow all-the-rules, like good boy Ned.

Yeah, mornings were the worst, but on days there was work, Tom felt better. He knew how to handle any job. Could figure it out. Got paid in cash. Decent work, no government assistance. Why was his mother, even his friggin' brother, lecturing him on how to take care of himself? Nobody was taking care of him. He didn't need any help.

His mom called from Florida the day his father went in the hospital. Said it wasn't critical, he should get better. He was gone three days later. Whenever Tom talked to his mother now, he had to remember getting there too late. How he had stalled making the trip.

She implied there was time. Would it have made any difference *when* he got there?

Dad wouldn't have known me.

But had he really known his dad? After the funeral, Tom had a dream about his father. It was before Gina moved out, but he didn't tell her about it. In the dream, he and Ned were kids. Dad was building a model ship in the basement, wearing a carpenter's apron, his sleeves rolled up. That was the whole crazy dream. As if he was back there in time with the two of them. Their dad, looking like some expert, making something neat and beautiful—he and Ned standing there watching. *That ship in the dream was probably the only thing Dad ever built from scratch with his hands.* He was a salesman, driving around for business all the time.

Tom's dad was a big and loud guy, with an enormous laugh that came out of nowhere.

Tom couldn't even remember what he looked like without a drink and a cigarette in his hand.

First things reached for when he came home, not his wife, his boys. He was a different kind of man in the dream. Patient and careful-like. *Like that time he showed me and Ned how to patch our own bike tires so we didn't have to throw them out.*

Tom once wanted to be like his dad, a man who seemed to take over a room with his commanding voice. But that big, strong father became ornery when they were teenagers, more and more a stranger to the family. No wonder his mother seemed out of it sometimes, two crazy boys and a giant bombed-out husband to deal with.

One time, Gina found an old picture of his dad, what appeared to be his senior portrait. Tom didn't even know he had it in his box of papers—his birth certificate, stuff he couldn't throw away. He couldn't remember why Gina was rooting around in there.

"You're so much like your dad," she said.

That must be Ned, he assumed. But, taking the worn photo from her hand, he saw she was right. There was a familiarity in the eyes, the lock of the jaw. It was the first time he thought he might be like his father. It was a strange feeling.

The very night Tom first met Gina, he was thinking about his dad. Tom already had a few drinks and was loose enough to tell some jokes, stories about the nutty relatives and all.

He had plenty of material there. Tom was in the middle of a room full of people, everybody listening to him, really into it. He was feeling good, in charge that night, the women all smiling, laughing. Especially Gina. He noticed her the minute she walked in. The big eyes, her long dark hair, her softness—approachable.

Taking a break from his too-long anecdotes, Tom went over to get another drink. Gina came up to him. "Those were funny stories, but you don't have to talk so loud," she whispered. Hearing her reproach, his father came to mind. How his voice got louder and louder when he became the center of attention. He could put on a real show. Tom would get anxious, watching him, listening to him. *Who was this man?*

At that moment, even while taking in the beautiful face of the woman standing there before him, the good feelings generated by the crowd left Tom. Why hadn't he kept his big mouth shut?

Still, Gina was the one who came up to him. She didn't stay long that night, but she really looked at him. Like she already knew him. They had almost touched. *It couldn't have been that bad. I got her number.*

Why in hell did he care now about ancient history? Tom got up and turned off the TV. He had a job to do. He'd accepted a clean-up for the storefront of a repurposed market on the edge of downtown.

Sandblasting. He always liked the dry blast best. Holding the gun, pulverizing a surface, seeing something transform in real time. It pleased him. A certain satisfaction every step of the way. He always felt alive, stronger behind the blaster. Results.

Downtown jobs were always a hassle with traffic or pedestrians to contend with, but they paid more. This project's façade was bigger than expected. A couple days' gig. As Tom worked, he saw people come and go out of the buildings. Lots of suit types, secretaries, delivery people, busy, busy, busy. No loiterers here. Well, maybe one. A real pretty girl, with a soft face, long legs like Gina's, standing at the lobby door across the street. She didn't react when she caught Tom looking over at her. Just stood there, waiting a long time, dressed to kill, and smoked one cigarette after another until a fancy car slowed to pick her up.

Did he have to see Gina everywhere?

The following afternoon when he finished up the detail work, he loaded up his equipment and went into the coffee shop to wash his hands. As he came out, he looked across the street to the doorway where the girl had waited the day before. Not there today.

Tom was glad to be done early. He had a headache all morning. He'd drive some slower side streets to head home, keep his windows open to feel the cooling city air.

Blocks off the business district were mostly residential, multi-family apartment houses past their prime. He came to one street where people were working on an empty lot by an old 1920s warehouse. Slowing down, he heard a machine sputter and die. Tom knew that sound. He pulled over to a group of kids clearing junk into contractor bags and metal trash bins. An old guy was trying to get a first-generation blaster going where gang graffiti splashed over a classic masonry wall. Tom parked and walked over.

"I used to have one of those, but I can't find parts anymore," he said. "Would you let me take a look?" The man offered his hand and introduced himself as Roosevelt. Tom realized the guy must have noticed the sandblasting moniker on the truck. It felt good, natural even, for Tom to be offering help without expecting anything in return.

The man's machine had major problems, leaking fuel. Tom brought over his newer one from the truck. Roosevelt knew exactly how to use it. As they worked together, with some of Tom's equipment and the tools on hand, Roosevelt gave two teenagers a lesson on how to sandblast. Tom watched as he patiently showed them how not to over-do, to keep in mind the age and fragility of the brick-and-mortar wall. Roosevelt explained the goal in removing the spray paint was not to destroy other people's workmanship, but to reveal the beauty and character of the old masonry. Tom admired this man's encouragement and his confidence in the boys.

The neighborhood renewal project was fully underway and looked like the volunteers were making a good deal of progress. Other people arrived with wheelbarrows and landscaping tools, bags of soil, and greenery in pots. *This project has a lot more going for it than my get-in, get-out jobs lately.* As the sun was lowering, Tom harnessed his hand tools to eliminate chunks of old paint that had spoiled a nice brick edging. When he finished loading his stuff back on the truck, Roosevelt approached to shake hands.

"You do good work, Tom. Thanks for coming by and stepping in. And these young men want to thank you, too. Now they know how to use machinery," he said as the teenagers sauntered over, looking tired but satisfied. "Job skills," Roosevelt added, smiling.

All of the folks who stayed until the end of the day gathered to say goodbye, even those Tom didn't interact with. The young kids who had played while the adults worked also looked up and waved as he left. The little smiley kid gave a thumbs up.

Tom returned the smiles and waves and drove toward the highway. Nearing home, he stopped at the 7-Eleven where he usually bought his after-work malt liquor. Wandered the booze aisle, but instead grabbed a hero to eat at home. That night, stretched out on the futon, he felt actual comfort in his tiredness.

His mother was his wake-up call in the morning.

"I'm just lonesome, Tom," she confessed. She sounded so old on the phone. He gave her more time than usual, then gathered up his clothes for a long overdue drive to the laundromat. On the return, he realized he was again near downtown.

Heck, why not take a look at yesterday's project? He drove through the business district but didn't even check on the storefront job he'd completed. He headed south toward the neighborhood where he helped out, but found himself on an unfamiliar street. The scattered small businesses there were quiet, empty. No kids were out playing. Where was the lot they'd worked on? The only sign of life was a bunch of teenagers idling on the stoop of an apartment house, eyeing him suspiciously as he drove down the block a third time, hopelessly lost. *Those guys wonder what the hell I'm doing here. Can't blame them. What am I doing?*

Finally, he gave up on finding the right street. Time to head back home, have a beer, get something to eat. When he turned in the direction he thought might lead to the expressway, he saw some grade school kids playing on a patch of dead grass. Tom saw one of the boys wave. He slowed the truck, lowered the window.

"Hey! It's you, Sandblaster Man!" A big grin erupted on the face of the smallest boy. Tom recognized the gap-toothed kid who sat cross-legged and watched him while he blasted graffiti the day before.

"Hey! How do you get to the highway from here?" Tom called. As if they'd practiced it, the whole group pointed straight ahead. Tom laughed and waved his thanks.

"See ya, Sandblaster Man!" shouted the little guy, still waving while Tom drove off.

Back home, Tom flipped on the TV. Sat there a few minutes, not watching, just letting the sound drown the emptiness around him. He stared at the piece of paper on his lap, the green Post-it note Gina had stuck on the refrigerator with her new cell number, "IN CASE ANYONE WANTS TO REACH ME." He dialed, planning on hanging up if he got more than Gina's voice message.

"Hello?" Gina's voice was cool.

"Hey!" he responded, dumb on what to say next.

"Who's this?" Gina asked. As if she didn't know.

"Uh … it's Sandblaster Man!" he blurted, trying out the joke.

"Oh … I like that man." Another pause. "But you know, you don't have to talk so loud."

Tom felt he'd been socked in the chest. He never shared with Gina how he delayed going to see his father, never talked with her about why she moved out. Didn't tell her he really missed his dad. Wished he knew him better as a man, *asked him things*. Most of all, how sad life was without her.

In all their time together, Tom never talked about his family, his dreams. The shame he felt letting everything go until she left him. At that moment, he just wanted to hang up, to get a drink. *It's all too late.*

Then he heard his own voice say quietly, "I miss you, Gina."

"I miss you, too," she whispered.

Authors

Steve Abbott

Steve Abbott has published thirteen articles in national bottle collector magazines about pre-Prohibition Sacramento whiskey and saloon related subjects. Redwood Writers published one of his poems in an annual anthology. Now he is turning his focus to short stories.

Mary Adler

Mary Adler writes the Oliver Wright WWII Mysteries set in Northern California, her home. Her short stories have appeared in several anthologies, most recently in Malice Domestic's *Murder Most Devious*. She creates habitat for pollinators and admits to being in a co-dependent relationship with her rescue dogs from Mexico. maryadlerwrites.com

Joe Affolter

Joe Affolter was born and raised in the San Francisco Bay Area. He studied English Literature at San Francisco State University. In 2023, Joe concluded a 35-year career as an industrial engineer. He now lives in his hometown of Daly City and enjoys writing short fiction.

Kristine Rae Anderson

Kristine Rae Anderson is a Pushcart-nominated poet and author of the chapbook *Field of Everlasting*. Her work has recently appeared in *SALT*, *Literary Mama*, and *Inlandia: A Literary Journey*. She lives with her family and a three-legged rescue dog in southern California, where she volunteers as a literacy tutor.

Judy Baker

Judy Baker's mission is to help authors make real money from their books. 2024 has three books coming out: *The Book to MoneyMaker RoadMap*, her memoir, *Gratitude Gumbo: Recipes and Resilience*, and her nonfiction book, *Cultivate: How To Turn Readers Into Heroes, Raving Fans, and Paying Clients*. bookmarketingmentor.com

Susan Church-Downer

Susan Church-Downer, at 16 years old, was told by a cynical college professor that she had no ability to write and nothing to write about. Accepting his critique, she abandoned her dream until retirement. After 55 years, she's reclaimed her passion - writing memoir, poetry and short stories.

Patrice Deems

Patrice Deems loves to witness and write about the parallel worlds of earth: nature and humanity. She joined Redwood Writers in 2017 and enjoys the comradery of fellow writers in a fiction critique group. She is currently working on a hybrid poetry/fiction genre.

Mike Dwyer

Mike Dwyer is a retired public high school teacher, a long ago journalist, and a new writer of fiction. His work has appeared in the *Thieving Magpie* literary journal.

Arleen Eagling

Arleen Eagling began writing fiction in 2005. Several of her stories have appeared in anthologies, including three which were published by the CWC Tri-Valley Writers branch. Other pieces appeared in the literary magazine *Thema*; in *Written Across the Genres*, edited by Julaina Kleist-Corwin; and in the 2022 *CWC Literary Review*.

Alethea Eason

Alethea Eason is an artist, fiction writer, and poet living in Clearlake, California. Her novels include *Charlotte and the Demons*, *Whispers of the Old Ones*, *Hungry*, and *Starved*.

June Gillam

June Gillam writes the Hillary Broome crime novel series, inspired by her obsession with what makes ordinary people mad enough to kill. A native of the Central Valley, June lives cradled between California's Coastal Range and the Sierra Nevada mountains.

Joan Goodreau

Joan Goodreau's recent books are *Where to Now?*, *Strangers Together: How My Son's Autism Changed My Life*, and *Another Secret Shared*. A Pushcart nominee, Joan was awarded a Hedgebrook Writing Residency to complete her YouTube chapbook, *Covid Silence*. Her short plays have been produced by Off the Page Readers Theater.

Pamela Heck

Pamela Heck is an early education specialist who entertained and instructed children for forty years. Her award-winning picture book, *Amazing Animals: Fun Facts for Kids*, combines her teaching experience with her talent as a writer/illustrator. Pamela also writes memoir, short stories, and poetry. See her artwork at the Cloverdale Arts Alliance Gallery.

John Heide

John Heide's novel, *The Flight of the Pickerings*, was a finalist in the CIPA awards. Two screenplays were finalists in the Nicholls and Page competitions. He has short stories published in *The California Literary Review* and several Redwood Writers annual anthologies. He splits his time between Sun Valley, Sonoma County, and Panama.

Lenore Hirsch

Lenore Hirsch is a retired educator who writes poetry, essays, and fiction. Her books include *My Leash on Life; Leavings; Laugh and Live: Advice for Aging Boomers; Schooled: Confessions of a Rookie Vice Principal*, and *Connection: Stories*. She lives in Napa with her canine buddy, Chewy. See lenorehirsch.com.

Mara Lynn Johnstone

Mara Lynn Johnstone, Vice President of Redwood Writers, grew up in a house on a hill, the top floor of which was built first. With a lifelong interest in fiction, she has published several books and many short stories. She can be found up trees, in bookstores, lost in thought, and at maralynnjohnstone.com.

Rebecca Jones

Rebecca Jones has published a poetry collection, *Beachsight*, a training manual, *Sing Right from the Start*, and performed her one-woman shows. A native Californian, Rebecca's father, born in Wales, gave her the music in her blood and the poetry in her soul.

Denise Kalm

Denise Kalm is a published author; a novel, *Lifestorm*, *Career Savvy-Keeping & Transforming Your Job*, *Tech Grief—Survive and Thrive Through Career Losses* (with Linda Donovan), *First Job Savvy—Find a Job, Start Your Career*, and *Retirement Savvy—Designing Your Next Great Adventure*. Twitter @denisekalm. Blog.

Anne Keck

Anne Keck writes speculative fiction and is published in several Redwood Writers' anthologies. Anne believes in ocean swimming, live music, public libraries, climate action, feminism, inclusivity, and cooking as an expression of love. Originally from Sonoma County, California, she and her husband now call Maui home. Find Anne at annekeck.com.

Joanna H. Kraus

Joanna H. Kraus is an award-winning playwright of 20 produced and published scripts, author of several books for young readers, articles, and reviews. She's a graduate of Sarah Lawrence College, earned an M.A. from UCLA and an Ed.D. from Columbia University. Visit her website at joannakraus.com.

Crissi Langwell

Crissi Langwell, President of Redwood Writers, writes stories from the heart. She's the author of 15 books, with genres that include romance, women's fiction, and magical realism. Find her at crissilangwell.com.

John J. Lesjack

John J. Lesjack (B.A., '65, SF State College) retired grade school teacher, sold eleven stories to the Chicken Soup for the Soul series. Number twelve is "in the mail."

Beth Lewis

Beth Lewis lives in Northern California with a variety of other creatures. She has written poetry and romance, but her favorite work is in epic fantasy. Not only does she love to lose herself in her writing, but then she can visit fantastical places along the way.

Roger C. Lubeck

Roger C. Lubeck, PhD, is president of the California Writers Club and a past president of Redwood Writers. Roger's publications include 11 published novels, 2 business books, short stories and poetry, and two performed short plays. Roger's writing, poetry, art, and photography are on his blog: rogerinblue.com.

Nancy J. Martin

Nancy J. Martin, the author of *From the Summer of Love to the Valley of the Moon*, was born in San Francisco, raised in Marin County and migrated north to the Valley of the Moon, where she has resided since 1976. nancyjmartinauthor.com.

E. J. McBride

E. J. McBride is the author of a popular textbook series for teaching English: *Downtown: English for Work and Life*, available from Cengage/ National Geographic Learning. "Blood" is from *That Thing We Call Love*, an upcoming collection of linked short stories about "love" in its various expressions. His novel *Our Brooklyn* will soon be available on Amazon.

Sherry Morton-Mollo

Sherry Morton-Mollo is a retired teacher and has published numerous academic articles of literary criticism. Her teaching experience resulted in a piece in Chicken Soup for the Soul's "The Power of Forgiveness" edition. She is currently attempting creative fiction (novel in progress) and research projects ("Canine Stories").

Rod Morgan

Rod Morgan has an AAS degree in graphic design with a minor in creative writing and journalism. His choice of genre is tales constructed to amuse, entertain, and mystify; fact and fiction jumbled together in unknown quantities. Short stories, novellas, and poems combine weird equivocations of memories, recollections, and fabrications.

Paul Moser

Paul Moser is a 1971 graduate of Stanford University. He has self-published four books: *The New Revised Catechlysm*, *T-Bull and the Lost Men*, *Inside the Flavor League*, and a memoir, *Seeking*. To escape work on a current manuscript, he blogs at thisunholymess.com. He lives in Napa, California.

Jennifer Murphy

Jennifer Murphy is a retired FBI Special Agent living in Monterey, California. Through her countless interactions with people from different walks of life, Jennifer has developed a genuine empathy for the entire spectrum of human experiences. At the moment, she's immersed in creating a low fantasy crime trilogy.

Gary Nelson

Gary Nelson is a fourth generation San Franciscan. He has been a Merchant Marine Engineer, a Division I college athlete, coach, and athletic director. He has published seven novels. He lives in Marin County with his wife Kellie, and his English Springer Spaniel while keeping their four children close.

Pamela Pan

Pamela Pan is an English professor at San Joaquin Delta College, where she teaches writing and literature. Pamela's work has been published in magazines and anthologies. She writes poems, fiction, and nonfiction. Her current project is a historical fiction based on her grandma's life during WWII, when Japan invaded China.

John Patterson

John Patterson is retired from three different careers: heavy blue collar; law; and public secondary education. He is the host of the Sac CWC Open Reading program. When he's not writing, he enjoys telling stories.

Korie Pelka

Korie Pelka has a background in theater and communications. Now, in her 3rd Act (formerly known as retirement), she spends her time as a certified coach, award-winning writer, and aspiring artist. She chronicles her creative journey through her blog at 3rdactgypsy.com and is busy working on a self-help memoir.

Renelaine Pfister

Renelaine Pfister's stories, essays and poems have been published in her native Philippines and in the U.S. She lives in Oahu, Hawaii.

Joan Prebilich

Joan Prebilich has written assiduously since her retirement from teaching in 2010. Since then, she has written down the stories she'd had to keep in her head during all those working years. Her current novel is about a reporter in 1963 Saigon. She visited Vietnam in 2023 to do research.

Sarah E. Pruitt

Sarah E. Pruitt, author, privately produced several family histories. She has published a short story in *Woven Tales* and contributed articles to *Angels in Disguise* and *What's in a Name? Everything!* She is currently working on a novel about the Civil War and its effect on a poor farm family.

N.A. Ratnayake

Nalin Ratnayake writes fiction as N.A. Ratnayake, primarily in the genres of science fiction and fantasy. His works tend to explore layered identities, connection to the natural world, asymmetric power struggle, colonialism/imperialism, humanism, and veiled optimism. You can find Nalin on the web at naratnayake.com or on Bluesky as @naratnayake.bsky.social.

Donna Rawlins

Donna Rawlins, SAG-AFTRA Voiceover actor, over a three-decade career was the spokesperson of major brands such as United Airlines, Macys, and Tesla. She's the author of *Skinny the Cat* and *The Magic of Kindness*, which received Honorable Mentions at New England and Paris Book Awards. Donna resides in Monterey, California, with her husband.

Cheryl Ray

Cheryl Ray writes creative nonfiction, fiction, and poetry. She has published magazine articles, including *Sail, Latitudes & Attitudes*, and *Writers' Journal*. Her essays were also published in the SF-Peninsula CWC *Fault Zone* anthology, Redwood Writers poetry anthology *Phases*, and a story in Redwood Writers' *One Universe to the Left*.

Darlene Stern Robson

Darlene Stern Robson returned to writing after a long career in the entertainment industry. She has been a copyeditor and edited professional organization newsletters. She writes literary fiction and her work was published in Redwood Writers' *Remember When* anthology. She is completing a domestic suspense novel.

Charity Romstad

Charity Romstad resides in California, yet she has lived on five continents working as a teacher and taking note of humanity. She holds a B.A. in English from Pacific Union College and a Certificate in Creative Writing from UC San Diego Extension. She mostly writes fiction and poetry.

Janice Rowley

Janice Rowley's curiosity has led her many places, from the rural South to the California wine country, from airline to veterinary, from show dogs to rescue dogs, from reading to writing. She has served Redwood Writers as Vice President, Membership Chair, Board Member, and Contest Chair. Jan's prose and poetry are represented in most Redwood Writers' anthologies.

Christopher Ruttan

Christopher Ruttan has worked in auto mechanics, technical writing and grape farming. His work-in-progress derives from living in the Philippines at an impressionable age from 1963 to 1965. Memories of WW2 were still fresh in people's minds. Their stories have been rattling around in his head ever since.

Florentia Scott

Florentia Scott's writing explores connections between perceived reality and imagination. Her work has appeared in various publications, including the 2018, 2019, 2021 and 2022 Redwood Writers' poetry anthologies, the 2020 prose anthology, and *Chicken Soup for the Soul: Listen to Your Dreams*. She was a 2019 Sonoma County Poet of Merit.

Brian Shea

Brian Shea's latest short story appears in the 2024 anthology, *Invasive Species*. Brian once lived in the lower Sierra foothills where, with the help of a fifth-generation rancher, he toiled on a small plot to demonstrate sustainable farming practices. Brian's first novel, set in rural eastern Oklahoma, involves Plains art.

Lisa Shulman

Lisa Shulman is the author of four picture books for children. Her poetry and fiction have appeared in a number of journals and anthologies, and been performed by Off the Page Readers Theater. She's been a Pushcart Prize nominee, and currently teaches poetry with California Poets in the Schools. lisashulman.com.

Brad Shurmantine

Brad Shurmantine lives in Napa, CA., where he writes, reads, naps, and tends three gardens (sand, water, vegetable), seven chickens, two cats, and two beehives. He backpacks in the Sierras, travels when he can, and prefers George Eliot to Charles Dickens, or almost anyone. Website: bradshurmantine.com.

MP Smith

MP Smith served as a technical writer/editor for engineering firms for 35 years and retired 2 years ago to write cozy mysteries. She lives in Northern California near family where she writes mysteries and manages a freelance editing business. She has published two novellas and one short story. mp_smith22@yahoo.com.

Susanna Solomon

Susanna Solomon is the author of three short story collections: *Point Reyes Sheriff's Calls*, *More Point Reyes Sheriff's Calls*, and *Paris Beckons;* and Montana Rhapsody (a novel). She is a long-time resident of Marin County and is a retired electrical engineer.

Linda Stamps

Linda Stamps established careers in law, journalism, and higher education. She worked at the Mendocino Beacon and Fort Bragg Advocate News. She wrote for the Time Warner publication, *Out in All Directions*, an LGBTQ history and almanac. Her work is published in a number of anthologies. She is an award-winning flash fiction writer.

Meta Strauss

Meta Strauss moved to Sonoma from her lifelong home, Houston, Texas, in 2005, began creative writing, and joined Redwood Writers. Her short stories appear in several anthologies, local newspapers, and she reads at various area events. Meta's first novel, *Saving El Chico*, received excellent reviews. A sequel is in process.

Karen Sundback

Karen Sundback has had the honor of winning numerous awards, ranging from CWC SF Peninsula 2019 Writer of the Year, to winner of the 2020 Bay Area Book Festival Writing Contest. In 2022, she had her first short story appear in the statewide *CWC Literary Review*.

Tice Swackhamer

Tice Swackhamer is a writer, editor and photo enthusiast. Her writing has appeared in the literary journal, *Magazine*, the *San Francisco Bay Guardian*, *The Sun* and on KQED public radio. She earned her M.A. in creative writing from San Francisco State University and has worked as an editor in tech, media and finance.

Charlotte Tressler

Charlotte Tressler was born in North Texas to a family of animal-loving English teachers. She worked for many years in the veterinary field before returning to school to pursue a degree in Creative Writing. She is a mother and grandmother, and lives with her husband and two naughty cats.

M. Golda Turner

M. Golda Turner lawyered for years as a public defender in Northern California. Now she lives and writes in San Luis Obispo County. She has a short story published in the book *One Universe to the Left* and a poem published this year in *Vision and Verse*.

Bill VanPatten

Bill VanPatten is an award-winning author of five novels and three collections of short stories. His stories have appeared in various anthologies and online magazines. Because of his background, gay and Latino characters tend to populate his fiction. You can find out more at billvanpatten.net.

Marilyn Wolters

Marilyn Wolters has lived in Northern California for over forty-five years. She spent most of her working years helping college students develop essay-writing skills. Now retired, she can't resist writing regularly. Her poetry, short stories and short plays have been published and performed.

Jaime Zukowski

Jaime Zukowski's prose is published in Redwood Writers' 2022 anthology *On Fire*, and her poems in *Crossroads* 2022 and *Phases* 2023 anthologies. Her work appears in *Moonlight and Reflections*, 2022 and *Sonoma Sonnet*, 2023, Valley of the Moon Press. Jaime presents virtual poetry readings with Sebastopol Center for the Arts.

Editors, Judges, & Proofreaders

John Paul Abbott — Editor

John Paul Abbott is an award-winning writer and editor based in Petaluma, California. His fiction has appeared in *Frisko, Fence*, and the Redwood Writers anthologies. He served as editor of the 2013 Redwood Writers anthology, and is a Redwood Writers contest winner. He has written about his experiences drinking tea with Bedouins in Saudi Arabia, river-boating down the Mississippi, and trading wind surfing tips with King Charles III.

Mary Adler — Proofreader

Mary Adler writes the Oliver Wright WWII Mysteries set in Northern California, her home. Her short stories have appeared in several anthologies, most recently in Malice Domestic's *Murder Most Devious*. She creates habitat for pollinators and admits to being in a co-dependent relationship with her rescue dogs from Mexico. maryadlerwrites.com

Harker Brautighan — Editor & Judge

Harker Brautighan is a California-based poet, essayist, and editor. Her work has appeared in sixteen Outrider Press "black-and-white" anthologies, placing second for prose in 2022, as well as in *Quill and Parchment* and four Redwood Writers anthologies. She also placed second in the 2023 Redwood Writers Club personal essay contest.

Susan Coffin — Judge

Susan Coffin is a paralegal by day and a writer by night. She loves taking "what if" situations and weaving them into stories. She has published both fiction and non-fiction. She lives by a beautiful lake where she is currently working on a paranormal novel. Her website is strokingthepen.com.

Barbara Cottrell — Editor

Barbara Cottrell gave up a career as a professor to write weird fiction. She is the author of *The Shadows Of Miskatonic*, a series of supernatural thrillers. Her debut novel, *Darkness Below*, won a silver medal from Reader's Favorites and a gold medal from The Book Fest. Visit her at barbaracottrell.com.

Marlene Cullen — Editor

Marlene Cullen hosts Writers Forum, Jumpstart Writing Workshops, and The Write Spot Blog. Her workshops and blog provide essential elements for successful writing. The Write Spot anthologies, edited by Marlene, are collections of short stories, poems, and vignettes with prompts to encourage and inspire writing. TheWriteSpot.us

Malena Eljumaily — Judge & Proofreader

Malena Eljumaily is an award-winning writer of short plays, fiction, and memoir. She won the Audience Choice Award at the Redwood Writers 10-Minute Play Festival in 2012. Malena is a Board member of Redwood Writers and the Northern California Chapter of Sisters in Crime. She lives in Santa Rosa.

Cristina Goulart — Editor

Cristina Goulart writes contemporary and historical fiction and poetry. Her work has appeared in Redwood Writers anthologies, the CWC literary review, on stage, and has placed in Redwood Writers contests. She is honored to work with fellow writers as a member of the anthology team. Cristina lives in Santa Rosa.

Susan E. Gunter — Judge

Susan E. Gunter, Ph.D., is a Professor of English Emerita. She has published three academic books on the James family, plus poetry in five different countries. Her poetry reviews have appeared in Crab Creek Review, the Harvard Review, the Los Angeles Review, and other journals.

Osha Hayden — Judge

As a podcast producer and host of *Aspire with Osha: art, nature, humanity*, Osha's goal is to empower and inspire her listeners. Writing credits include stories and poems published in six anthologies. Learn more at oshahayden.com.

Pamela Heck — Editor

Pamela Heck is the author/illustrator of an award winning, non-fiction picture book: *Amazing Animals: Fun Facts for Kids*. Pamela also writes memoir, short story, and poetry. Her work has appeared in numerous Redwood Writers anthologies and the California Writers Club Literary Review. She is a resident artist at the Cloverdale Arts Alliance Gallery.

Mara Lynn Johnstone — Judge & Proofreader

Mara Lynn Johnstone, Vice President of Redwood Writers, grew up in a house on a hill, the top floor of which was built first. With a lifelong interest in fiction, she has published several books and many short stories. She can be found up trees, in bookstores, lost in thought, and at MaraLynnJohnstone.com.

Crissi Langwell — Editor & Judge

Crissi Langwell, President of Redwood Writers, writes stories from the heart. She's the author of 15 books, with genres that include romance, women's fiction, and magical realism. Find her at crissilangwell.com.

Lisa Manterfield — Editor

Lisa Manterfield has published five novels, two works of non-fiction, five non-fiction eBooks, and coached many authors to publishing success. She shares her work through her blog and podcast, creating an online community of 6,000+ members worldwide. Her work has been published in the *Los Angeles Times*, *Psychology Today*, *Huffington Post*, and *The Saturday Evening Post*.

Taylor Metzler — Proofreader

Taylor Metzler lives in Northern California with her family and cats. She's been writing since adolescence and reading more than is healthy for most people. She graduated with a degree in anthropology with an emphasis in museum studies, which she does not use. She enjoys boring hobbies like crocheting and baking things that are too tasty to be safe.

Jan Ögren — Editor

Jan Ögren, MFT, is a developmental editor, international author, public speaker and licensed psychotherapist. She loves helping people rewrite their lives both through therapy and as an editor. She especially enjoys introducing writers to the magical world of developmental editing where creativity multiplies, and readers transform into intimate friends. Jan's magical realism novel, *Dividing Worlds*, was published in Brazil in 2014. Read more at JanOgren.net and JanOgren.Blog.

Darlene Stern Robson — Editor & Judge

Darlene Stern Robson returned to writing after a long career in the entertainment industry. She has been a copyeditor and edited professional organization newsletters. She writes literary fiction and her work was published in Redwood Writers' *Remember When* anthology. She is completing a domestic suspense novel.

Rebecca Smith — Judge

Rebecca Smith made up a story on the fly in second grade. All was well until she turned the paper over. Nuns' glares, the trip to the principal's office, and subsequent explanation to her mother did not dissuade her from continuing with her stories. An upbeat artist, screenwriter, poet, and songwriter—creativity & adventure keep her happy.

Meta Strauss — Judge

Meta Strauss moved to Sonoma from her lifelong home, Houston, Texas, in 2005, began creative writing, and joined Redwood Writers. Her short stories appear in several anthologies, local newspapers, and she reads at various area events. Meta's first novel, *Saving El Chico*, received excellent reviews. A sequel is in process.

Susanna Solomon — Judge

Susanna Solomon is the author of three short story collections: *Point Reyes Sheriff's Calls*, *More Point Reyes Sheriff's Calls*, and *Paris Beckons;* and Montana Rhapsody (a novel). She is a long-time resident of Marin County and is a retired electrical engineer.

Charlotte Tressler — Editor & Judge

Charlotte Tressler was born in North Texas to a family of animal-loving English teachers. She worked for many years in the veterinary field before returning to school to pursue a degree in Creative Writing. She is a mother and grandmother, and lives with her husband and two naughty cats.

Redwood Branch
of the California Writers Club

It was the informal gatherings of a group of writers, including Jack London, poet George Sterling, and Herman Whitaker, that inspired the 1909 formation of the California Writers Club. The early club's honorary members included Jack London, George Sterling, John Muir, Joaquin Miller, and the first California poet laureate, Ina Coolbrith.

In 1975, Redwood Writers was established as the fourth CWC branch, and owes its formation to Helene S. Barnhart of the Berkeley Branch, who had relocated to the North Bay. She and forty-five charter members founded the Redwood Branch of the CWC. Today the club's membership has passed three hundred members.

In 2006, Redwood Writers published its first anthology. This year's volume, *Transitions*, is the twenty-fifth anthology in the series.

Redwood Writers is a non-profit organization whose motto is "writers helping writers." The club's mission is to provide a friendly and inclusive environment in which members may meet and network; to provide professional speakers who will aid in the writing, publishing, and marketing of members' endeavors; and to provide other writing-related opportunities that will further the club members' writing.

Members of Redwood Writers enjoy many benefits with their membership. Monthly meetings are open to members and the public, and feature professional speakers with topics that include writing, marketing, publishing, exploring different genres, and more. Every other year, the club holds a day-long writers conference, offering seminars on all areas of writing that are taught by area professionals. Members are also offered opportunities to share their writing and publications at various venues, in contests, in our monthly newsletter, as well as at our club Salons and Writers' Circle.

For more information about Redwood Writers, visit redwoodwriters.org.

Presidents of Redwood Writers

The Redwood Branch of the California Writers Club is indebted to its founders, charter members, board and club members, and volunteers who make the Redwood Writers a success. The Redwood Branch could not have developed into the professional and successful club it is today had it not been for the leadership of our presidents.

2024	Crissi Langwell
2022-24	Judy Baker
2020-22	Shawn Langwell
2017-20	Roger C. Lubeck
2015-17	Sandy Baker
2013-15	Robbi Sommers Bryant
2012	Elaine Webster/Robbi Sommers Bryant
2009-12	Linda Loveland Reid
2007-09	Karen Batchelor
2005-07	Linda C. McCabe
2004	Charles Brashear
2003	Carol McConkie
2001-02	Gil Mansergh
2000	Carol McConkie
1999	Dorothy Molyneaux
1997-98	Marvin Steinbock
1992-96	Barb Truax
1990-91	Mary Varley
1988-89	Marion McMurtry
1986-87	Mary Priest
1985	Dave Arnold
1984	Margaret Scariano
1983	Waldo Boyd
1982	Mildred Fish
1981	Alla Crone Hayden
1980	Edward Dolan
1979	Herschel Cozine
1978	Inman Whipple
1977	Natlee Kenoyer
1976	Dianne Kurlfinke
1975	Helene (Schellenberg) Barnhart

Helene S. Barnhart Award

Inspired by the first president of the Redwood Writers, the Helene S. Barnhart Award was instituted in 2010 as a way to honor outstanding service to the branch. It is awarded in alternating years of the Jack London Award.

2024	Mara Lynn Johnstone and Les Bernstein
2022	Crissi Langwell
2020	Joelle Burnette
2018	Malena Eljumaily
2016	Robin Moore
2014	Juanita J. Martin
2012	Ana Manwaring
2010	Kate Farrrell

Jack London Award

Every other year, CWC branches may nominate a member to receive the Jack London Award for outstanding service to the branch, sponsored by CWC Central. The following members received the Jack London Award for service.

2023	Crissi Langwell
2021	Roger C. Lubeck
2019	Robbi Sommers Bryant
2017	Sandy Baker
2015	Jeane Slone
2013	Linda Loveland Reid
2011	Linda C. McCabe
2009	Karen Batchelor
2007	Catherine Keegan
2005	Mary Rosenthal
2004	Gil Mansergh
2003	Nadenia Newkirk
1998	Barbara Truax
1997	Mary Varley
1995	Mildred Fish
1993	Alla Crone Hayden
1991	Waldo Boyd
1989	Mary Priest
1987	Margaret Scariano
1985	Ruth Irma Walker
1983	Inman Whipple
1981	Pat Patterson
1979	Peggy Ray
1977	Dianne Kurlfinke
1975	Helene (Schellenberg) Barnhart

Redwood Writers Anthologies

Fiction & Memoir

2024	Transitions
2023	One Universe to the Left
2022	On Fire
2021	Remember When
2020	Sunset Sunrise: A Collection of Endings and Beginnings
2019	Endeavor: Stories of Struggle and Perseverance
2018	Redemption: Stories from the Edge

Poetry

2024	One Day
2023	Phases
2022	Crossroads
2021	Beyond Distance
2020	And Yet
2019	Crow: In the Light of Day, In the Dark of Night
2018	Phoenix: Out of Silence…and Then
2016	Stolen Light
2014	And the Beats Go On

Combined Prose & Poetry

2017	Sonoma: Stories of a Region and its People
2016	Untold Stories: From the Deep Part of the Well
2015	Journeys: On the Road & Off the Map
2014	Water
2013	Beyond Boundaries
2012	Vintage Voices: Call of the Wild
2011	Vintage Voices: The Sound of a Thousand Leaves
2010	Vintage Voices: Words Poured Out
2009	Vintage Voices: Centi'Anni: May You Live 100 Years
2008	Vintage Voices: Four-Part Harmony
2007	Vintage Voices: A Toast to Life
2006	Vintage Voices: A Sonoma County Writers Club Harvest

Editor in Chief

Janice Rowley discovered her love of reading when her mother lulled her to sleep with Mother Goose, and her love of writing when she first held a crayon in her hand. *Transitions* brings these loves together.

Writing played a minor role during Jan's twenty-six-year career with United Airlines (from Mobile to Tampa to Atlanta, to San Francisco, to Seattle, back to San Francisco), showing up as newsletter articles, business plans, employee evaluations, and a final resignation letter. That letter brought her to Sonoma County with her husband of now fifty-four years. The interval between that letter and her retirement from paid employment was spent in sign-making, retail sales, mortgage banking, and veterinary—all allowing some level of writing practice.

In the background of these activities is the ongoing love of dogs, especially the Cavalier King Charles Spaniel. As a past president of Bay Area Cavalier King Charles Spaniel Club (the regional AKC club), regional specialty chair, and six-year newsletter editor, she practiced communicating in print.

And, throughout these years, Jan enrolled in writing class after writing class until, finally, in July 2013, she joined Redwood Writers. Jan has served as both Membership Chair and Vice President, and in 2023 as Chair for the Personal Essay Contest.

Janice Rowley's fiction, memoir, and poetry may be found in *And the Beats Go On* (2014), *Water* (2014), *Stolen Light* (2016), *Untold Stories* (2016), *Sonoma* (2017), *Crow* (2019), *And Yet* (2020), *Sunset Sunrise* (2020), as well as many newsletter contributions. She has served as both judge and editor for several prose anthologies.

Transitions is her most ambitious writing-related activity so far. We wonder what's next.

Made in the USA
Columbia, SC
02 October 2024

42825130R00207